WAGONS WEST ★ VOLUME 24
CELEBRATION!

Also available in Large Print
by Dana Fuller Ross:

TENNESSEE!
ILLINOIS!
KENTUCKY!
ARIZONA!
NEW MEXICO!

WAGONS WEST ★ VOLUME 24
CELEBRATION!
DANA FULLER ROSS

G.K.HALL &CO.
Boston, Massachusetts
1991

Published in Large Print by arrangement with
Book Creations, Inc.

G. K. Hall Large Print Book Series.

Set in 16 pt. Plantin.

Library of Congress Cataloging-in-Publication Data

Ross, Dana Fuller.
    Celebration! / Dana Fuller Ross.
       p.   cm.—(Wagons West ; v. 24) (G.K. Hall large print book
series)
    ISBN 0-8161-4978-X
    1. Large type books. I. Title. II. Series: Ross, Dana Fuller.
Wagons West ; v. 24.
[PS3568.O8428C4 1990]
813'.54—dc20   90-5236

WAGONS WEST ★ VOLUME 24
CELEBRATION!

Henry Blake   Leland Blake
Cindy Holt Kerr Eulalia Holt Blake

Janessa Holt   Toby Holt

Tim Holt   Alexandra Woodling Holt
              (and Michael)

I

The icy sweat of fear on his brow made the wind sweeping across Central Park in New York seem even colder to Cyril Jenkins. It was a dark, raw night in February of 1876 as he walked along a deserted pier with twenty other men. They were silent, tense with apprehension.

Calling themselves the Zeno Bund of New York, they were an anarchist group. Jenkins, in his early twenties, was much younger than most of the men. While he had the benefit of a good education and had worked for several firms as a clerk and an accountant, his slovenly companions were uneducated and had worked only in odd jobs as laborers and stevedores.

When Jenkins had first joined the Zeno Bund, he had been unemployed and believed the organization would help him to establish contacts and create worthwhile changes in society. How wrong he had been!

The Zeno Bund had changed during the past months, ever since Klaus Lukenbill had joined and taken control. Lukenbill now gave each man, once penniless, a weekly stipend. Lukenbill's source of seemingly unlimited funds was a mystery to everyone in the bund and gave him authority over them.

Formerly, the meetings had been a time to argue over plans that never materialized. Now the once ineffective and harmless bund was disciplined and efficient. Lukenbill had required each member to submit a detailed resumé, including all personal contact with anyone outside the Zeno Bund. Following Lukenbill's orders, the men had firebombed public buildings, incited riots, and committed other violent crimes.

The Zeno Bund's most brutal criminals were intimidated by Lukenbill's vicious cruelty. Anyone who disobeyed orders was murdered, and everyone who valued life tried mightily to satisfy the bund's leader.

That night Lukenbill had ordered them to assemble in the park late in the evening, when it was deserted. The time and place for the meeting were unusual, and when Lukenbill did anything out of the ordinary, it meant trouble. The men were silent with anxiety as they walked along the path to the arsenal, where a gaslight burned over the entrance. The men stopped in front of the building. There was no sign of Lukenbill.

Cyril Jenkins, his mouth dry, shivered from more than cold as he tightly clutched his coat collar. He and the others waited under the bare, skeletal limbs of the trees, which swayed and rattled in the wind.

The minutes passed slowly. Lukenbill suddenly stepped out of the dark shadows beside the arsenal, where he had been spying on them. Wearing an expensive, stylish overcoat and derby, Lukenbill was a small man with thin, sharp features. But his size was irrelevant; as he strode toward them, scowling angrily, the most physically powerful men in the bund stiffened. Lukenbill faced them.

"I've been reviewing your personal histories." His soft tone held an ominous undercurrent. "Is yours complete, Jones?" he asked, turning to a hefty, bearded man.

The men, including Jenkins, inched away from Jones.

"I think it is, Mr. Lukenbill," Jones replied cautiously.

"Either it is or it isn't!" Lukenbill barked.

Jones hesitated fearfully. His face was pale in the light of the lantern, and sweat shone on his forehead. "It's complete, sir."

Now Lukenbill asked another man the same question. The man replied that what he had written was complete. Then Lukenbill interrogated another man. After the last man replied, a tense silence enveloped the group. Lukenbill suddenly stabbed a finger at a man named Lubkus. "Tie his hands behind his back!" he ordered.

The men pounced on Lubkus, who cried out in fright. Jenkins felt a twinge of sympathy for the man, but wary of drawing unfavorable attention, Jenkins helped to restrain Lubkus.

Lubkus collapsed to his knees, whimpering,

while Lukenbill drew a knife and examined the tip of the long, keen blade.

"You wrote down that your uncle has one son, Lubkus. Doesn't he have two?"

Lubkus's mouth gaped. "But I never see him."

"Why should I believe that?" Lukenbill demanded. "You could be telling your cousin all about the Zeno Bund. He's a policeman, isn't he?"

"No!" the man cried. "I swear that I don't ever see—!"

He broke off as Lukenbill stepped closer. The knife blade glittered in the dim light as Lukenbill slashed his victim's throat. Lubkus pitched forward, blood pooling under him as his feet kicked convulsively.

Jenkins was stunned, unable to tear his gaze away.

After calmly wiping the knife on Lubkus's coat, Lukenbill put the weapon away. "Let that be a warning to traitors. As for the rest of you, I intend to double your weekly allowances."

The reactions to the announcement proved that money was more important to the men than Lubkus had been.

"I am planning a project," Lukenbill continued, "that will draw worldwide attention to our cause. People will fear and respect us. In the meantime, we will concentrate on smaller tasks. Meet me at the usual place tomorrow, and I will outline your next assignment."

The group dispersed. Some men commented about the additional money, while others ex-

4

pressed satisfaction that Lukenbill had discovered and eliminated a traitor. Jenkins was quiet, still numb with shock.

While he desperately yearned to leave the group, he knew that would be impossible. He would be tracked down regardless of where he went and made to suffer a slow, agonizing death.

The following evening, a winter storm blew across Lake Michigan as Toby Holt rode in a carriage with Dieter Schumann, manager of Toby's business interests in Chicago, and Dieter's pretty, young wife, Abigail. The threesome were on their way to dine with friends at Franklin's Chicago House.

At thirty-four, Toby was a tall, rangy man with ruggedly handsome features. He wore a dark, well-fitted business suit, heavy overcoat, and western boots. A wide-brimmed hat rested on the seat beside him. There was the aura of the outdoors about him: his face was bronzed by the sun and wind of the plains and mountains, and his blue eyes, accustomed to gazing across the vast distances of the land he loved, had small wrinkles around them from spending so much time outdoors.

Toby and Dieter were friends as well as business associates. Some fifteen years older than Toby, Dieter was a big-boned, meaty man. Abigail's and his fashionable, expensive clothing testified to the success of Toby's lumber mill, ironworks, and a large produce outlet, all of which Dieter managed.

5

A question from Abigail about Toby's wife, Alexandra, brought a reflective smile to his face. They had been happily married for over a year now. As a gust of wind caused the carriage to sway on its springs, Toby glanced momentarily out the window before he replied. "She's very well, thank you," he said. "We're expecting our first baby in August."

"That's good news!" Abigail exclaimed jovially. Then concern settled over her features. "But doesn't Alexandra plan to attend the gala centennial celebration in Philadelphia in July? That means she'll be traveling very near the time the baby is due."

Toby smiled ruefully. "Yes, and there's no changing her mind. Dr. Martin has tried, believe me. However, she'll be traveling from Portland with family and friends, including the doctor and my daughter, Janessa. If Alexandra needs medical attention, the doctor and Janessa are capable of providing it."

The Schumanns nodded. Now fifteen years old, Janessa had been trained in herbal medicine from her early childhood by her Indian mother. Since her mother's death five years before, the girl had spent her after-school time assisting Dr. Martin with his patients.

The conversation turned to the events that had brought Toby to Chicago: For two years he had been commissioner of the West, overseeing government activities west of the Mississippi River. He had just returned from Washington, D.C., where he had accepted the great seal and articles of statehood for delivery to Colorado's governor. With several days to spare before he was due in Denver, he had made a side trip to Chicago.

Dieter made a joke about the volume of correspondence that Toby probably had to handle as commissioner.

Toby grinned. "No, my stepfather's administrative staff at Fort Vancouver weeds out the unimportant material and forwards the rest to me. For the most part it's advisory correspondence, to be read and then discarded." Toby's stepfather was General Leland Blake.

"So securing statehood for Colorado didn't involve you in any great amount of written justification," Dieter assumed.

"No, the officials in Denver took care of that," Toby replied. "We had a harder time upgrading the territorial bank in Denver to a federal reserve bank than we did in securing statehood."

"If Denver has a federal reserve bank now," Dieter mused, "they'll need a much larger operating capital."

"That's right," Toby confirmed. "That's being shipped by train to Denver from one of the mints in the East. For security reasons, the arrangements are being kept secret, and the shipment is being escorted by Pinkerton guards."

Dieter snorted. "That shipment must amount to hundreds of thousands of dollars in gold and currency. Very tempting to train robbers."

Toby nodded. "Upwards of half a million in cash is being transported."

As the conversation continued, Toby's daughter was mentioned again. "How is Janessa doing in school?" Abigail asked.

Toby's eyes shone with pride. "For all practical purposes, she's finished school. Her teachers are now tutoring her to take the college placement examinations."

"I'm not surprised," Abigail commented. "She's very mature for her age and extremely intelligent."

"No question about that," Toby agreed. "You'll soon be seeing her. I plan to bring her here in the spring for special placement examinations that evaluate an underage applicant's readiness."

"You'll both stay in our home," Dieter insisted. "And if Janessa decides to attend school in the area, she must stay with us. That would give you peace of mind and be a pleasure for us."

Toby gratefully accepted the offer. It was, after all, a possibility. Luther Bingham, a friend of the Holt family and a recent graduate from Rush Medical College in Chicago, had praised the instructors highly. Although he said nothing, Toby was reminded that Bingham, once a ne'er-do-well, had taken control of his life as a result of Janessa's influence upon him.

A few minutes later, the carriage drew up at Franklin's Chicago House. Inside, the friends they had arranged to meet were already seated: Marjorie White, a professional photographist who had recently returned from a worldwide lecture tour; and Edward Blackstone, co-owner of the M Bar B ranch in the Oklahoma Territory. Edward was in Chicago to exhibit Brahma-longhorn calves, a new disease-resistant breed of cattle developed on the M Bar B, and to make contracts with cattlemen for future deliveries of the crossbreeds.

After a waiter had taken their orders, Marjorie expressed pleasure at their surroundings. "This reminds me of a place where Cindy and I dined in France. Have you heard from her recently, Toby?"

Toby smiled, thinking of his sister, Cindy Holt Kerr, an artist who spent most of her time in Paris. "More than that. I've seen her recently. She's in Portland for the next month or two."

"I'd love to see her," Marjorie said sincerely, "but I can't spare the time. I intend to spend the next few months in Philadelphia, making stereopticon slides of the centennial celebration."

"If you intend to be there until July, you'll get to see her," Toby said. "She's friendly with the sculptor in Paris who's making the Statue of Liberty. The torch will be displayed in Philadelphia on the Fourth of July. Cindy intends to return to France and accompany the party that brings it to the United States."

As the waiter served their dinners, the Schumanns questioned Edward about his experiences.

"It must have been difficult for you to get the

Brahma out of India," Dieter remarked. "Those are holy animals there."

"It was very difficult," Toby confirmed, overriding Edward's modesty. "Our friend here barely got out of India alive." Toby turned to Edward. "How's Edgar Dooley getting on at the M Bar B?"

"He is a bit bored," Edward admitted. "Compared with his work with the East India Company, the ranch is too quiet for him."

"And how are the calves selling?" Toby wanted to know.

Edward took out his wallet and extracted a check, which he folded and handed to Toby. "Our cows will be kept very busy for years to come. It gives me great pleasure to return to you the five thousand dollars you loaned me, together with the cost of the barbed wire for the M Bar B, which you so generously provided."

"I don't want this, Edward," Toby said, trying to hand the check back. "The nation needed a breed of large beef cattle immune to tick fever, and I'd like to think I made some contribution to it."

"You risked five thousand dollars on a very uncertain proposition," Edward pointed out. "We weren't sure the Brahmas would prove immune to tick fever, and whether or not I could get them out of India was even more in question."

Toby shrugged, then pocketed the check. "Well, at least I got him to admit that he had trouble getting those cattle out of India," he quipped.

Edward asked Toby about his business interests in Chicago. Toby replied that a recent incident at the ironworks concerned him: A drive belt on a machine had broken, slightly injuring one of the workers.

"It could have been much worse," Dieter said. "I've given orders for the foreman to inspect all drive belts at the beginning of each shift, and all leather drive belts have been replaced with rubber belts. That will increase our production costs— the rubber belts are very expensive—but they're much more durable than leather."

"Why are they more expensive?" Marjorie asked.

"Rubber is outrageously expensive because Brazil is the only place in the world where rubber trees are found. They keep a tight control on production to keep the price high."

"Someone should steal some of those trees and break that monopoly," Marjorie responded heatedly.

Dieter laughed. "It's been attempted more than once. The Brazilian authorities watch their ports closely and inflict draconian sentences upon anyone who tries to smuggle out rubber trees." He turned to Edward. "But anyone who can spirit Brahma cattle out of India should be able to get rubber trees out of Brazil."

The remark caused general laughter around the table, and Edward joined in. Then he sobered. "I wouldn't want to risk spending years in a Brazilian prison. There should be some way to get rubber trees out of Brazil without being caught."

Toby raised his eyebrows. "It would be a great service to the nation and the world, Edward. I'd underwrite your expenses. I realize, however, that it would be dangerous."

"There would be many problems involved," Dieter pointed out. "And prior arrangements would have to be made to plant them in a tropical climate. They certainly couldn't be brought here."

With the icy winter wind whistling outside, Toby and the others laughed again. Edward remained sober, pondering, before turning to Toby. "I believe I'll give the matter some thought."

"Then think about this," Toby replied, drawing the check out of his pocket and tearing it in half. "A down payment on your expenses. When you need more, contact Dieter, and he'll telegraph the amount to any bank in the world."

"You're making it hard to resist the challenge," Edward said, laughing. "I'll let you know."

The subject turned to newspaper reports about trouble along the Arizona Territory border. The well-informed commissioner of the West explained that a small band of renegade Pima Indians, using Mexico as a refuge, was crossing the border to steal cattle and horses.

"Right now they're only a nuisance," Toby continued, "because they're disorganized and poorly armed. I'm much more concerned about the Sioux in Dakota."

Dieter agreed. "Bands of Sioux are leaving the reservation and threatening settlers. I understand there's a danger that they might be joined by the Cheyenne, and that could lead to full-scale war. What's upset them, Toby?"

"Prospectors in the Black Hills, which are within Sioux territory," Toby answered. "Negotiators from Washington conferred with the Sioux chiefs last autumn, but no agreement could be reached. The negotiators are there again. I intend to meet with them when I'm finished in Denver."

"Perhaps the results will be favorable," Dieter commented. "In any event, the Seventh Cavalry is there, isn't it?"

"Yes. My stepfather's adopted son, Major Henry Blake, is in the Seventh Cavalry, although the last I heard, he was still in Germany, finalizing matters concerning his wife's estate. But if any trouble develops that involves the Seventh Cavalry, Henry will be in the thick of it."

"He's the man who broke his engagement with Cindy, isn't he, Toby?" Marjorie remarked coolly. "I'm surprised you're friendly to him."

"You don't know all the facts, Marjorie," Toby gently reminded her.

"Nor do I need to," she shot back.

Abigail interjected a remark, quickly changing the subject. The broken engagement had caused ill-feelings in the Holt family for years, particularly on the part of Eulalia, Toby's and Cindy's mother.

As the meal continued, Edward remained quiet, thinking. Trying to get rubber trees out of Brazil *would* be challenging, and the venture could produce immense profits. He began to consider this seriously, and he was still thinking about it after he returned to his hotel that evening. Although few private individuals had the resources or connections to establish a plantation in a tropical area, Edward did: His uncle, Major Winslow Cochrane, was the commander of a Bengal rifles battalion in India.

Through Cochrane, Edward had met several officials of the East India Company, which owned large land holdings in Ceylon, Malaya, and India. With the promise of substantial profits, the company would surely be interested in establishing rubber plantations.

Edward took out several letters that had been forwarded to him from the M Bar B. They were from his uncle's ward, Ramedha Cochrane, whose parents had been killed years before by bandits. Ramedha was a compelling personal reason for his returning to India. Two years before, as a young woman of eighteen, she had been attracted to him, and since his return to America, he had received letters from her every week.

The content of her correspondence had become more sophisticated, the hints about his returning to India more insistent. In the meantime, his feelings for her had deepened. In addition to being beautiful and charming, Ramedha was a most fascinating woman, reflecting the best aspects of her English and Indian heritage.

After a knock on the door, Billy Collier, a lanky, tanned ranch hand in well-worn western clothes, stepped in. "I saw the light under your door, Mr. Blackstone. If you're not busy, I'll tell you about the calf sales today."

"I'm not busy, Billy. Come on in."

His spurs jangling, the young man sank into a chair. After rolling a cigarette, he took out his notes and read off the tentative agreements he had made with stock dealers and breeders for the M Bar B crossbreed calves.

"Settle them tomorrow," Edward approved when Billy finished. "You're making very good bargains, and there's no reason you can't approve them yourself." Edward glanced at Ramedha's letters. "I've decided to go abroad for a time, and I'm going to leave you in charge of sales, Billy."

The ranch hand flushed with pleasure. "I'll do my best, you know that. Will you be gone long?"

Thinking about Brazilian prisons and perilous jungles, Edward smiled wryly. "Yes, it could turn out to be for quite a long while, Billy."

II

"Always keep them in fear of you, Lukenbill," Hermann Bluecher advised. "And make them distrust each other, to prevent them from banding together against you."

"Yes, sir, Mr. Bluecher," Lukenbill replied. "You should have seen the look on their faces when I slit Lubkus's throat."

Lukenbill listened closely as Bluecher continued talking. In the large, lavishly furnished study of his luxurious Long Island mansion, Bluecher had, during the past months, guided Lukenbill in transforming the anarchists into a disciplined force.

The men had met over a year before. Bluecher had arrived in the United States and immediately placed advertisements in several newspapers for a general assistant. Of the numerous applicants, Bluecher had decided that Lukenbill was a perfect tool for his purposes.

Furthermore, Bluecher had discovered something in common between them: obsessive hatred for Major Henry Blake, the man responsible for Bluecher's exile from his German homeland. Bluecher had learned that Lukenbill detested Blake for disrupting some petty scheme the man had devised. Bluecher had had Blake's wife murdered, and during recent months, he had kept track of the man by sending Lukenbill to make discreet inquiries at the War Department in Washington. The major was presently out of reach; matters pertaining to his demise were in abeyance.

In the meantime, Bluecher had been concentrating upon a plan with far-reaching possibilities. During the revolution in the German States, Bluecher had seen the power of popular discontent with the established government. He hoped, through the Zeno Bund, to destroy public confidence in Washington, destabilize the government, and position himself to share authority with whatever group seized control of the United States. While he intended to keep his ultimate goal a secret, he would have to tell Lukenbill about actions involving the Zeno Bund.

"The men realize they are training for more important tasks?" he asked.

"Yes, sir."

Bluecher took a drawing from a desk drawer and held it up. "Do you know what this is?"

"Yes, sir. That's the torch of the Statue of Liberty."

"Correct. The torch and hand comprise one huge piece with a door. People can climb to a balcony around the flame of the torch. While it is in Philadelphia, I want a large explosive charge placed in it. When the explosives are detonated, many will be killed or maimed."

"How can we hide enough dynamite to create a substantial explosion? People may notice it. And the detonator wires will be hard to hide."

"Alfred Nobel, a Swedish chemist, has developed another new explosive," Bluecher answered. "Two kilograms has the same explosive force as a ton of dynamite. Also, it can be detonated by percussion, so a simple device with a timer will be a satisfactory detonator." He handed a sheet of paper to his subordinate.

Lukenbill's eyes widened as he read the fact

sheet. "This is *some* explosive, Mr. Bluecher! And a shipment is being sent to Switzerland?"

"Yes, you must send someone there to steal it. Do not send anyone from the Zeno Bund. If he is caught, he could lead the authorities to you."

Lukenbill pondered. "The last time I was in Philadelphia, I met a man, a restaurant owner, who might help us."

"Fine. You'll also need to send someone to Paris to keep us informed about the torch. He should be one of the bund."

"Yes, sir. I have a man named Maritain, a French Canadian. I'll tell him to apply for a job in the place where they're making the statue."

"Very well. In the meantime, Henry Blake could return from Germany, and I want to know as soon as he does. Before you and I meet again, check on his whereabouts."

"All right, Mr. Bluecher. I'll need money to send Maritain to France, and the man I send to Switzerland will want plenty."

"Offer him ten thousand dollars." Bluecher opened another drawer and placed a bag of gold coins on the desk. "That will cover everything. Before we meet again, I want you to check on Henry Blake's whereabouts."

Lukenbill took the bag of coins and left. During his ride to New York City, he thought about Bluecher. Why destroy the torch? What possible benefit could the German derive from killing people in such a dramatic fashion?

A plan of his own occurred to him: One of the

18

largest mints in the nation was in Philadelphia, and when the torch exploded, it would provide a perfect diversion, drawing away all the city police while he himself robbed the mint. Of course, Bluecher must never find out.

Then he put the idea aside to consider later. Now he would concentrate on learning Henry Blake's whereabouts. He savored the thought that sooner or later he would have his revenge and Henry Blake would be dead.

In a cabin on the steam packet that shuttled between San Francisco and Portland, Oregon, Henry Blake knelt in front of his son, helping the boy put on his overcoat. The packet was easing up to its dock at Portland, and Adela Ronsard, Peter's nurse, who was capable of dressing the boy in half the time, smiled fondly as she patiently waited.

At two and a half years of age, Peter Heinrich Koehler Blake was exceptionally tall, and instead of children's clothing, he wore a tiny business suit, complete with white shirt, cravat, and a small, expertly tailored Prince Albert overcoat. His large blue eyes sparkled with precocious intelligence. He had the well-formed features of his Prussian mother, and his father's thick, dark-brown hair.

The amiable, outgoing boy could also be headstrong, so Henry cautioned him to be on his best behavior for his first meeting with his grandparents. Peter nodded, smiling cheerfully. *"Das tut mir aber leid—"* he piped.

"You must speak English here so people will understand you," Henry said, fastening the last tiny button. Smiling, he hugged his son and then stood. "Where's his hat, Adela?"

The woman handed him a small homburg, which he positioned squarely on Peter's head. They turned toward the door. Henry, over six feet tall and muscular, had strong, clean-cut features. His rigid, military bearing was enhanced by his tailored uniform tunic, fitted cavalry trousers, and gleaming knee boots. He wore a wide-brim campaign hat, and a gold tassel on its crown matched the gold-leaf insignia on his epaulettes. He was, at twenty-five, the youngest major in the United States Army.

As Adela took Peter's hand and helped him down the gangplank, people were greeting passengers on all sides. Young women in the crowd glanced at Henry, and Adela drew admiring looks from men. A slender woman in her twenties, her father had been French and her mother Egyptian, so Adela was a dusky, striking beauty.

Across the Columbia River from Portland was Fort Vancouver, where Henry's adoptive father, Major General Leland Blake, had his headquarters. Leland's second wife, Eulalia, was Cindy Holt Kerr's mother. Since the reason for Henry's last visit to Portland was to break his engagement with Cindy, he had been met, at that time, with cold anger. Although Henry was certain that, now, his son and Adela would be eagerly welcomed by his adoptive parents, who loved chil-

20

dren, he was less certain about their reaction to him. As a result, he made arrangements to pick up the baggage later, in the event that he would need to find separate accommodations for himself. Adela, Peter, and he boarded a ferry to cross the Columbia.

It was late afternoon on a windy, wintry day when the ferry began to move across the broad river. A lieutenant saluted when he saw Henry. "I don't believe we've met, sir. I'm John Forrester. Have you been transferred to Fort Vancouver?"

"I'm here on leave," Henry replied, returning the salute. "I'm Henry Blake."

"*The* Major Henry Blake, sir?" he blurted. His face flushed. "I've heard so much about you. And about the baroness, of course. . . . My condolences, sir."

"Thank you, Lieutenant Forrester. As far as what you heard, you may be sure it was improved upon with each retelling. This is my son, Peter, and his nurse, Miss Adela Ronsard."

As the lieutenant touched his cap, Adela curtsied.

"It was a very great pleasure indeed to meet you, sir," Forrester said, moving away. "I certainly hope to see you again while you're here."

A few minutes later, the ferry edged up to its slip along the waterfront of Vancouver, a tidy, thriving town. A row of neat, comfortable houses for married officers overlooked the river on the far side of the fort. As they walked in that direction, Henry, with Peter perched on his shoulders, helped Adela around muddy spots on the road.

The Blake residence, a larger house at the end of the row, looked cheerful and inviting. On the porch Henry put Peter down, straightened the boy's coat, and then knocked.

A moment later, Eulalia Blake opened the door. She remained as Henry remembered, attractive and immaculate in a lovely dress, her graying hair coiled at the back of her head. When she saw Henry, her eyes became hard.

"Hello, Mama," he ventured, steering the boy into the light from the foyer. "This is my son, Peter, and his nurse, Adela Ronsard."

The boy started to bow, but Eulalia, now smiling radiantly, pushed past Henry and picked up the child. Her eyes took in every detail of his face. She kissed and hugged him. "Come in, my dear, come in," she said, carrying Peter and leading Adela inside. Raising her voice, she called, "Lee, our grandson is here!"

Left standing on the porch, Henry stepped inside as the general emerged from the parlor. With snowy white hair and a ruddy complexion, Lee Blake had an athletic build and light step that belied his seventy-odd years. He hooted in delight, then kissed and hugged the boy before turning to Henry and smiling happily. His expression conveyed deep pride in Henry. They grasped hands and then hugged.

Eulalia, fussing over Peter, turned and addressed a point in the air a foot to one side of

Henry's head. "Where is the baggage? I must get young Peter and Adela settled."

"It's still at the terminal, Mama," Henry replied. "I wasn't sure what kind of arrangements would be made."

"My grandson and Miss Ronsard will stay here as long as they are in the area," she said, "and you may stay here as well, naturally. Lee, please have an orderly send a work detail to get the baggage. I'll take Peter and Adela to their rooms while you talk with your son."

Henry reflected that Eulalia's attitude was thawing, but only slightly. A few minutes later, Henry and Lee were seated in comfortable chairs in front of the fire in the parlor, exchanging news.

Since his wife had been killed, Henry had been assigned to the Seventh Cavalry Regiment, headquartered at Fort Lincoln, near the town of Bismarck in the Dakota Territory. He had taken leave and gone to Germany on three separate occasions to check on the progress of the lawyers and accountants who were organizing Gisela's complex business affairs.

"The various investments are now set up so they'll attend to themselves," Henry explained, "with a staff monitoring them. There were two large estates, Grevenhof in Germany and Fenton in England. I turned Grevenhof over to Richard Koehler, Gisela's nephew, and kept Fenton."

"I met Major Koehler when he visited here. I was highly impressed with him. Have the authorities come up with anything about the murder, Hank?"

Henry shook his head sadly. "No, but I'm sure it was done by an enemy of mine, a Josef Mueller. He escaped from prison a few months before Gisela was killed. He was associated with a government official named Hermann Bluecher. They planned it together."

"Did you inform the authorities?"

"No, sir. I don't have evidence. Besides, Bluecher and Mueller have long since fled Germany."

"Any idea where to look for them?"

"No. I'd like to find them, but my army duty is awaiting me."

"Yes, duty comes first. Are you stationed at Fort Lincoln?"

"No, sir. I've been given command of a cavalry battalion at Fort Harland, about forty miles north of Bismarck."

Lee marveled at the changes in his foster son. He had been a cheerful, boisterous young man only a few years before, occasionally gauche in speech and manner. Now he was an urbane, seasoned officer with a forceful, authoritative air. Not all of the changes were good, however, Henry now had a brooding aspect to his character, which was in sharp contrast to his earlier amiable disposition. But all in all, Lee glowed with pride.

A work detail arrived with the baggage, and Lee and Henry broke off talking as Eulalia stepped into the room. This time she looked directly at

24

Henry. "I'm not sure of what your plans are, so I don't know how much of Peter and Adela's baggage should be unpacked."

Henry relaxed; Eulalia's attitude was much warmer. Peter had captured her heart, and she wanted to keep him with her. "I don't want to take Peter and Adela to Fort Harland," he said. "I was hoping they could stay here indefinitely."

"It's more than possible," Lee stated firmly, smiling. "Eulalia and I insist upon it."

Tears of happiness shone in Eulalia's eyes. "Well, let's see if we can't let bygones be bygones, Henry."

Stepping to her quickly, Henry embraced her. "I'm more than ready to do just that, Mama," he said, kissing her cheek.

She patted his shoulder, then rejoined Peter and Adela. Deeply gratified by the easing of tensions, Henry and Lee sat back down and resumed talking. Henry had hoped to find Toby at home, but Lee explained about Toby's duties and told Henry his itinerary.

"I should be able to meet him in Kansas City before I leave for Fort Harland," Henry mused.

"We'll work out the details," Lee offered. "Then I'll telegraph Toby to let him know. Cindy is here, by the way."

The offhand remark took Henry by surprise.

"She's at the Holt ranch now, visiting with Toby's wife. You must meet Alexandra."

"Yes, I'll do that, sir."

Henry had to force himself to concentrate on

the conversation. Unbidden thoughts of Cindy pressed in on him. At last they would meet again. On more than one occasion, Gisela had remarked that she realized he still loved Cindy. Knowing him well, she had been correct, as she always had been on important issues. The two women had always been completely different—Cindy like a spring flower, and Gisela a hothouse orchid—and had created entirely different responses within him.

More than that, the intensity and rapture of a first love had kept his feelings for Cindy alive through the years. He had been married, and so had she, but now they were both free. The pathway for their love was open, but he was keenly aware that Cindy's feelings about him might be entirely different.

The next morning, Henry took the ferry to Portland. The town had expanded enormously, and the new Reed Kerr Memorial Hospital was a point of pride. Henry rode past, admiring it, then turned onto the road leading to the Holt ranch.

When the ranch came into view, he reined up for a moment. Lee had told him that a new house had been built, but nothing had prepared him for the huge, majestic Victorian mansion.

Henry rode to the house, tethered his horse, and knocked on the door. A young, heavyset woman in a maid's dress and mobcap answered.

"Good day. I'm Henry Blake," he said, touching his hat. "Is Mrs. Holt in?"

"Miss Alexandra and Miss Cindy are both out in the barnyard. They're refinishing a bureau. If you want to come inside, I'll let her know that you're here."

Henry glanced at his horse, which had turned its rump to the icy wind. "I need to put that horse in a barn, so I'll go around and find Mrs. Holt."

Henry led his horse around the house. The new barns were impressive, and the stock enclosures looked more like paddocks than corrals.

Inside the barn Henry whistled softly in awe. He had heard about Alexandra's horses, but the huge, powerful hunters in the stalls were the most magnificent animals he had ever seen. After he tethered his horse, he went back outside.

A strong, distinct paint odor blew across the barnyard from the direction of a smaller building. Henry straightened his coat and hat as he strode toward it, hoping that Cindy would at least agree to see him.

It had occurred to Cindy that Henry and she would meet again, and she had always hoped the circumstances of their reunion would find her looking at her very best.

As the workshop door opened and Henry stepped inside, however, she and Alexandra were wearing old smocks spattered with paint, and their hair was carelessly tied back out of their eyes. Cindy knew she looked like a laundry woman. To make matters worse, Henry looked as if he had just stepped out of a bandbox.

27

"How do you do, Major Blake," Cindy replied coldly as he greeted her. "This is Mrs. Toby Holt. Alexandra, Henry Blake."

As he bowed, Alexandra placidly returned his greeting. Cindy reflected that Alexandra's Bradford and Woodling bloodlines gave her a social calm and stability in even the most humiliating circumstances.

"I've committed a grave discourtesy," Henry apologized. "I should have waited at the house."

"It wasn't good form," Alexandra agreed amiably, "but no one has suffered mortal injury."

Henry smiled. "If you'll permit me, I'll go to the house and wait there. I'd like to talk with both of you."

"Please stay here while I finish cleaning the brushes. We can get better acquainted." Alexandra turned to Cindy. "If you'll go and tell Amy that we'll have a guest for lunch? . . ."

Her cheeks burning with anger and confusion, Cindy darted a grateful smile at Alexandra and fled toward the house.

From all she had heard, Gisela von Kirchberg had been strikingly beautiful and highly sophisticated, as well as powerful and wealthy. Cindy had concluded that Henry had broken their engagement simply because she had been outmatched by Gisela.

Cindy knew she had changed since then, becoming cosmopolitan and successful. She had no wish to compete with memories of Henry's deceased wife, but she had wanted him to know that she was no longer a naive girl. Unfortunately, her appearance in the workshop had dealt her a devastating setback.

At the house Cindy found Juanita Zuniga, Alexandra's personal maid, scolding Abby Givens for having sent Henry to the barnyard.

"Mr. Blake accepted full blame, Juanita," Cindy interrupted, "as well he should. Abby, please tell Amy to set a third place for lunch. Juanita, would you help me put myself in order?"

"Yes, Doña Cindy," Juanita replied, following her toward the stairs and giving Abby a final, withering glare.

In her guest room, Cindy chose a blue muslin dress trimmed with lace, and Juanita fastened the innumerable tiny buttons at the back. Then the maid helped her arrange her hair. A short time later, when Alexandra came upstairs to her room, Juanita went to assist her.

Cindy dawdled until Alexandra was ready. She wore a green taffeta dress with an empire waistline that concealed the slight thickening of her body. The two women went downstairs together, Cindy savoring the thought that Henry had been left cooling his heels in the parlor. But as the two women stepped into the room. Henry came through the front door and explained that he had been admiring Alexandra's horses.

Because nothing seemed to go wrong for the man, Cindy smoldered with renewed anger as they seated themselves in the large, lavishly furnished parlor, where a warm fire was blazing in the fireplace. Henry mentioned that he had met Clayton Hemmings, Alexandra's young groom, in the barn.

"I'm fortunate to have him," she responded. "I'm unable to keep my horses exercised because I'm in what is politely called 'a delicate condition.' "

"I'm very pleased for you and Toby. I'm sure that giving up riding for a time is small sacrifice for such a happy event."

"It is," Alexandra agreed, "but Janessa has put so many restrictions on me, I sometimes feel like a hibernating bear. They're practices she learned from her Indian mother or concluded on her own."

"You're very wise to follow her advice. Cindy, have you been doing any work here, or are you taking a vacation from art?"

"I've done only a few sketches and some pen-and-ink drawings since I arrived."

"Only?" Alexandra protested. "What you've done is marvelous, Cindy. Henry, I'll leave it to you to judge. Look at that drawing of Mrs. Blake and the general over there, and at those of my horses. Aren't they lovely?"

He looked at the framed drawings on the wall. "They certainly are," he said emphatically.

Throughout the conversation, Cindy spoke only in reply to direct questions. In a way she felt that her anger was childish, but she also realized that her resentment was a form of self-defense. She still loved Henry with all the intensity of years before.

Her emotional wounds, however, had never truly healed, and she could not let him think he could walk back into her life whenever he pleased. Also, Cindy had to become reacquainted with Henry; they both had changed.

When the subject of the new hospital came up, Henry commended Alexandra on how well she had managed the project. She gave credit to the architect and her adviser, Dr. Robert Martin.

"Dr. Martin and I are on the board of trustees," she continued. "One of our trustees recently withdrew because of other commitments, so we'll have to elect a replacement as soon as possible."

Alexandra was a consummate hostess, and she was obviously highly impressed by Henry.

When the maid announced lunch, the three adjourned to the dining room, where Cindy found herself drawn into the conversation. While in Germany, Henry had read Heinrich Schliemann's book on his archaeological expedition in Turkey, which featured etchings Cindy had made at the site. She spoke freely about her work there.

The conversation continued for an hour after lunch, and Cindy found it entertaining. When Henry left, she was emotionally exhausted, but Alexandra insisted on talking about him.

"Toby told me something you should know," Alexandra said, settling into a chair in the parlor.

31

"Henry was ordered to become acquainted with the baroness. She had access to valuable information and influential people."

"He wasn't ordered to marry her," Cindy said. "And he wasn't straightforward with me. Please don't try to play cupid, Alexandra."

"No, no," the other woman cut in affectionately. "Your life is your own, and I wouldn't meddle. But I *would* suggest that we at least have dinner at Fort Vancouver this evening."

Cindy shook her head. "I've had more than enough turmoil for one day."

"The result will be worth the effort, Cindy. I want your mother to suggest a formal dining-out to the general. It would be held at the fort officers' mess to welcome Henry home."

A gleam in Alexandra's eyes conveyed the mischievous purpose behind the idea. During Cindy's visit, the young officers at the fort had vied to be her escort at parties and dances. At a party in Henry's honor, what could be better than for Cindy to be surrounded by officers wanting to dance with her? It would clearly show him that she had never had a need to wait for him.

Cindy smiled. "I'll do it."

"I'll send Clayton with a note to your mother that we'd like to have dinner with her and the general this evening. Then, when I can speak to your mother privately, I'll suggest the dining-out evening."

Cindy regarded Alexandra. "Why," she asked

dryly, "do I continue to have this idea that you're playing cupid?"

Alexandra laughed but said nothing.

By the time Clayton returned with Eulalia's response, it was all arranged. After leaving instructions with the cook for Timmy and Janessa's dinner, Alexandra and Cindy set out. Dusk was falling when they reached the Blake home. Henry was in the parlor with his son, and when Henry introduced Peter to Alexandra and Cindy, the women were captivated by the boy.

As the others talked, Cindy drew the boy to the couch beside her. "Did you enjoy your trip here?" she asked him.

The boy talked about his father taking him to the bridge on the ship. It was obvious that the boy enjoyed her attention. Smiling happily, he leaned against her as she put her arm around him.

When the time came for Peter to go to bed, he was reluctant to leave Cindy. His unhappiness was assuaged, however, when she assured him that she would see him again soon.

Later, during dinner, Cindy supported Henry in a difference of opinion with her mother. Eulalia remarked that Peter must have some children's clothes, or he would think that he was different from other boys. Henry replied that Peter was, in fact, different from other boys.

"Indeed he is," Cindy put in quickly. "I've never seen such a precious, intelligent child. It would be a shame to group him with other boys, Mama."

"Well, so much for my advice," Eulalia remarked wryly.

"I know that Toby has always valued your advice regarding his children," Henry assured her tactfully, "and you may be sure that I'll do the same, Mama."

After the last course was finished, Alexandra and Cindy remained a short time longer before making their farewells.

During the ride back to the ferry, Alexandra reported that Eulalia was enthusiastic about the suggestion to have a formal dining-out at the fort. But Cindy's feelings were more confused than ever.

The searing hurt and bitter, angry feelings of rejection and wounded pride that had festered within her for years were a barrier between Henry Blake and her. She was unable to even think of him in a romantic sense. Yet she was completely won over by Peter, and she was unable to stop thinking that if she were his stepmother, the adorable boy would be with her all the time.

III

At the end of the road, Fort Vancouver was ablaze with light, the powerful carbide lamps on the walls illuminating the quadrangle.

The coach lamps on several other vehicles could

be seen as the Holt ranch carriage moved away from the ferry slip toward the fort.

"It appears that General Blake invited most of the notables of Portland as guests at the dining-out, along with the mayor and city councilmen," Alexandra commented to Cindy.

The lights and bustle of activity fueled Cindy's excitement. With Henry Blake only one of many asking her to dance, she knew she would enjoy herself. Wearing a Parisian gown of blue silk voile that brought out the color of her eyes, she felt good about herself.

Clayton Hemmings, driving the carriage, reined up at the fort gate and handed down the invitations. The guard saluted, and the carriage moved in line to the officers' mess, where passengers were helped down.

The officers' mess was one of the original fort buildings. Inside, Alexandra and Cindy walked across its gleaming hardwood floor to the cloak-room, then joined the gathering having cocktails in the salon.

A lighthearted atmosphere that matched Cindy's mood pervaded the salon. Alexandra, deeply involved in civic affairs, was a leading citizen of Portland, and she spoke with Mayor Edwards about a proposal to pave the main streets, while Cindy chatted with friends.

Just before dinner, Lee and Eulalia Blake entered, with Henry following. Cindy felt a warm glow suffuse her as she saw Henry, so tall and handsome in his formal uniform. He glanced around, looking for her. When he smiled, she fought to control the eagerness of her response.

A gong sounded to announce the end of the social hour, and Lee and Eulalia led the way into the dining room. Henry, Cindy, and Alexandra filed in with the mayor and his wife.

Silver and china sparkled on the white tablecloths in the light from the chandeliers. Cindy and Alexandra went to a long table for guests and dignitaries, where their name cards were on each side of Henry's. Lee and Eulalia took their places at the center of the table and stood behind their chairs, and the others followed suit.

Lee called the mess to order and began the traditional ceremony that Cindy knew by heart from the many formal events she had attended. The chaplain gave the benediction. There were toasts to the President, the chief of staff, and those fallen in battle. After the last toast everyone except Lee sat down.

"As you know," Lee began, "this event is in honor of Major Henry Blake, who is on leave from his command in the Dakota Territory. I have asked him to address the mess. Major Blake?"

"Thank you, General Blake," Henry said, standing as Lee sat down. "I'm grateful for this opportunity to talk about those among us whose dedication and loyalty remain unwavering, even though their efforts are rarely acknowledged. They steadfastly contribute to every success, but their labors are never mentioned in official reports. I refer to army wives."

A ripple of surprise passed through the room. The murmur faded as Henry continued, displaying public speaking skills that Cindy had never suspected. The room remained quiet, which was unusual. Regardless of the rank and authority of the speaker, after a time the younger officers always began shuffling their boots and coughing to indicate that they had heard enough and wanted their dinner.

Their silence, Cindy realized, was a measure of their genuine interest. The wives sat up straighter in their chairs as they listened; even the senior and field grade officers nodded musingly at points that Henry made.

"In conclusion, I believe we should make a concerted effort to recognize the contribution made by army wives. I propose that we drink a toast to them on this occasion." He lifted his glass. "To army wives."

The men rose and roared an echo and followed it with enthusiastic applause for Henry. When he and the others sat down, a gong announced the beginning of the meal, and waiters brought in the first course.

"That was very interesting, Henry," Cindy said as they ate; then she laughed. "And you won over every wife at the fort."

"Because of time constraints I had to forgo the mention of one outstanding woman," he said. "This young wife was enroute to Fort Peck on a supply train when it was attacked by comancheros. After attending to the wounded during the battle, she saw her husband killed. But she remains as courageous and spirited as ever, which is remarkable."

"Remarkable indeed," Alexandra agreed emphatically. "I feel proud to call that young woman my sister-in-law and friend."

Blushing, Cindy looked down at her plate. Throughout the dinner, Cindy saw and felt the special warmth in Henry's eyes and smile. But, unable to overcome the lingering pain she felt from what had happened before, she remained polite and friendly but no more.

After the meal was finished, everyone stood for another benediction, and then the women filed back into the cloakroom, chatting. While the men talked in the dining room, the waiters arranged the chairs against the walls and removed the tables. Minutes later the regimental band appeared with their instruments.

Eulalia led the other women back into the room as the band struck up a waltz. Lee met her, and they took a turn around the floor to a round of applause. The senior officers danced with their wives, and Cindy expected the young officers to gather around her.

Most of the young officers, however, were clustered around Henry. Cindy and the other women waited. She realized that Alexandra's plan had one flaw: The officers wanted to listen to any anecdotes the young major was willing to share.

Several of the young women began grumbling.

"I didn't come here to stand around," one woman remarked bitterly. "This is intolerable!"

Cindy shook her head. "No, merely annoying."

A moment later, Henry inclined his head toward the women and apparently reminded the officers of their obligations. A number of the young men moved toward Cindy, but they made way for Henry as he stepped to her and asked her to dance.

Dancing with him years before had always been an ordeal of having her toes trampled. Now they moved as one. They danced together again and again.

After the affair had ended, Alexandra and Cindy settled themselves comfortably in the carriage. Alexandra summed up the evening's events. "Well," she said ruefully, "we certainly showed him, didn't we?"

"Yes, we did indeed," Cindy agreed wryly, and she and Alexandra laughed heartily.

The following day, Henry's last in Portland, he rode to the Holt ranch during the afternoon and was talking with Cindy and Alexandra in the parlor when Timmy came home from school. Henry commented on how tall the boy had grown, a fact that had also struck Cindy when she first arrived.

At almost nine years of age, Timmy showed every sign of being as large as his father. He had suddenly shot up to almost five feet tall. Even more remarkable was how he had matured under Alexandra's strict but loving guidance. He had become much more responsible about his actions.

"I like to be called Tim, sir," he said, greeting Henry.

"Very well, Tim," Henry replied. "From what I've heard, you're spending part of your time working with the horses now."

The boy explained. The quarter horses raised on the ranch were ordinarily gentled instead of being broken to saddle, resulting in animals that were more obedient and high spirited. An occasional horse was so uncontrollable that it had to be broken, and Tim worked with White Elk, the Indian foreman's ward, in breaking them.

"I'd like to compete in the rodeo at Philadelphia during the celebration," he added, "but I don't know if I'll be good enough. White Elk sticks to a bucking horse like glue, but I bounce off."

"Don't judge yourself against White Elk, Tim," Alexandra advised. "He won the best all-around cowboy belt buckle at the county fair. You're doing quite well at bulldogging and calf roping."

He shrugged and questioned Henry about Europe. "I'd like to visit all of those places," Tim said longingly. "And I'd like to go to Asia and all over the South Pacific."

"That's quite an itinerary," Henry observed. "But if that's what you want, I'm sure you'll manage. Don't forget, though, that there's plenty to see here in the United States."

"Oh, I know, sir," Timmy replied quickly. "And I *want* to see my own country. Most of all, I want to do things for my country, like my dad does."

"Well," Henry commented, "you certainly could never find a better example to follow than your father."

Janessa came in, her afternoon at the hospital finished. Henry went to her quickly.

Reserved and quiet, the girl was unsmiling as they hugged. "I've been wanting to see you," she said. "Have you found out who did it?"

Henry knew the reference was to who had killed Gisela von Kirchberg. Having learned to love the woman, Janessa's most treasured possession was a fabulous ring the baroness had given her. "Yes, but I don't know where they are," he answered. "And until I find out, I can do nothing." He smiled, then bent and kissed the girl's cheek. "I've also been wanting to see you, simply for the pleasure of it."

Smiling, Janessa sat down as Henry returned to his chair. He was deeply fond of the girl. She looked so much like Cindy at fifteen years of age—tall and slender with strikingly pretty features and brown hair. The only difference, and it was great, was in their personalities.

Janessa was dividing her time among working at the hospital with Dr. Martin, studying, and finishing school. Henry remarked on her busy schedule, and she smiled in agreement as she lit a cigarette. "I'm also still trying to stop smoking."

"You're under considerable pressure now," Cindy consoled. "You'll be more successful later in the year."

"I hope so," Janessa mused. "I've been trying

to stop for a long time, and it doesn't seem to make much difference what I'm doing." She looked at Cindy. "Jake Higgins was admitted to the hospital today. You remember him?"

"Certainly," Cindy replied, turning to the others. "When Janessa first came here, old Mr. Higgins gave her tobacco and cigarette papers in exchange for herbs for his rheumatism."

"Yes, it was that vile-tasting tobacco he smokes in his pipe," Janessa reminisced. "When he lit that pipe in the hospital this afternoon, it smelled like old rags burning." She sighed. "But he has something much worse than rheumatism now."

"What is it?" Cindy asked, concerned.

"Dr. Martin doesn't know. We'll have to make tests to find out. It's something to do with his lungs, though, and he's lost so much weight, you wouldn't recognize him."

The maid announced dinner, and everyone went to the dining room. The first course was a thick, hearty vegetable soup, followed by a juicy, tender rib roast. Henry and Cindy debated the relative merits of French and German wines. After dinner, Janessa and Timmy went to their rooms to study, and Alexandra diplomatically left Henry and Cindy alone in the parlor.

They discussed their plans for the coming months, and then Henry broached the subject that had been a source of constant tension between them. "Cindy, I know that what I did to you was detestable," he said quietly. "I know we can't pick up where we left off, but will we be able to make a new start?"

"I don't know, Henry. My feelings are very confused."

"That's perfectly understandable. Perhaps within a few months—"

"I can't be sure of that. You mustn't feel obligated to me in any way."

"There'll never be anyone else for me," he vowed. He took out his watch and glanced at it. "I must go. I want to spend some time with Peter this evening. Will you express my thanks to Alexandra for her hospitality?"

"Certainly," Cindy said, standing and walking him to the front door. She helped him with his coat and started to bid him a polite farewell. Suddenly they were kissing, as though it were the most natural thing for them to do. When he left, Cindy leaned against the door with her eyes closed, overwhelmed by the torment of conflicting emotions seething within her.

The next morning, a dismal rain fell and turned into ice on the ground as Cindy went to the docks to see Henry off to Dakota. Having slept poorly the night before, her mood matched the weather. She joined the rest of the family, who were already there.

Peter, clinging to his father, began to cry. Adela gently pulled her young charge away and tried to soothe him. Henry shook hands with Lee, kissed Eulalia's cheek, then turned to Cindy. Their kiss seemed to last for an eternity and yet be over within an instant. Then he walked toward the gangplank.

Its horn blaring, the packet inched away from the dock. Cindy waved at Henry, who stood at the rail and waved back. As she watched the vessel fade into the misty rain, Cindy realized she had given him no word of encouragement, and she had offered no alternative. She was just as despondent as she had been when he broke their engagement.

As his train moved out of the terminal at St. Joseph, Missouri, Toby Holt sat in his Pullman compartment and read through telegrams that had been delivered to his hotel. After discarding informational notices sent to him as commissioner of the West, Toby smiled happily at the last telegram: Henry Blake would meet him in Kansas City, after his conference with the negotiators who were holding discussions with the Sioux chiefs.

Preferring to sit with other people, Toby rearranged his baggage in his compartment so the valise containing the great seal and articles of statehood for Colorado was safely hidden; then he tucked his newspaper under his arm as he left the compartment.

The next car was a passenger car. Toby found an empty seat facing a woman in her sixties and a boy about ten, perhaps her grandson. Toby smiled and asked if the seat was taken. The woman told him to feel free to sit down.

"We're going to Denver," the woman volunteered. "We've been visiting relatives in Saint Joe."

"I'm going to Denver as well, ma'am. My name is Toby Holt. If there's anything I can do for you, don't hesitate to call on me." He sat back, relaxed, and unfolded his newspaper. Suddenly he stiffened, staring in disbelief at a story on the front page. He slammed his fist on the arm of his seat in frustrated rage.

The woman jumped. "My word, young man! If reading newspapers upsets you that much, you should leave them be."

"Sorry, ma'am," Toby replied absently, folding the newspaper as he rose. "Please excuse me."

Striding along the aisle, Toby angrily wondered who had leaked the secret information. A reporter had found out the precise shipping information on the gold and currency being sent to the new federal reserve bank in Denver, and every detail, including the amount, was on the front page. Furthermore, the shipment was on this train.

Toby went from car to car, looking for the conductor. He finally caught up with him. "Excuse me. My name is Toby Holt," he said. "I'd like to speak with you."

"Yes, I know who you are, Mr. Holt," the man replied respectfully.

Because nearby passengers looked up with curiosity, Toby pointed to the vestibule at the end of the car. When they were alone between closed doors, he showed the conductor the newspaper.

"Have you seen this?" he shouted over the roar of the wheels.

The man nodded glumly.

"We have to take added precautions. Where is the money? Do the Pinkerton guards know about this article?"

"The money's in a special car between the mail car and the caboose. The guards know, as do many of the passengers. Some have been joking about it."

"They'll stop laughing if they end up in the middle of a train robbery. I need to talk with the guard in charge."

Toby followed the conductor from car to car. The mail car was locked, but a man opened the door when the conductor knocked on it. The conductor and Toby made their way through the cluttered car. Mail bags were piled on every side, and men braced themselves against the motion of the train as they sorted letters.

At the next vestibule, the conductor pounded on the door of the special freight car. A man inside shouted and asked who it was. "The conductor! The commissioner of the West is here and wants to talk with the captain!"

A steel bar and a chain clanked inside, and the door was cautiously opened. The conductor returned to his duties as Toby went inside.

The windowless car was illuminated by lamps swinging from the ceiling. At the far end were stacked bunks, and a half-dozen men were asleep on them. Four other men, cradling rifles and shotguns, sat on a bench beside the wooden crates of currency and coins, which were stacked against a wall. On the opposite wall was a large railroad map. The route to Denver was marked in red.

Toby introduced himself to a tall, broad-shouldered man with steely gray eyes and a short, neat beard who stepped forward.

"I'm Malcolm Mahar, the senior agent here. Pleased to meet you, Mr. Holt. Someone has talked his fool head off, but my men and I can deal with trouble."

"I'm sure you can, Malcolm, but if there's a robbery attempt, scores of passengers will be caught in the middle of it. Some of them are sure to be hurt or killed."

"That's true, Mr. Holt," Mahar agreed. "Do you have any suggestions?"

Toby examined the map. The railroad line from St. Joseph joined the one leading westward from Kansas City at a place called Hooten Station, then stretched across Kansas and Colorado. The train had a single stop at Salina and was due to arrive in Denver the following morning.

"Well, things could be worse," Toby decided. "The information was printed only this morning, and robbers need time to get organized."

Mahar looked at the map. "If anything happens, it'll be west of Salina."

Toby nodded. "I'll talk with the engineer when we get to Salina. Maybe he and I can come up with an idea how to prevent the attack."

"If there's anything my men and I can do, just let us know."

"I appreciate your cooperation. I'll get back to you."

The train slowed and swayed heavily from side to side as it crossed the switches at Hooten Station. Then it picked up speed again. Toby made his way forward and found the conductor in the dining car.

"We can't order the passengers off the train," Toby said, "but if you'd warn them of the danger, many will get off at Salina and wait for the next train to Denver."

"Good idea, Mr. Holt," the conductor said. "Anything else?"

"Please put a message in the next mail bag that's dropped off, to be sent to Salina by telegraph, warning people there not to board this train. If the engineer would lean on the throttle and get ahead of schedule, it might help. I'd much rather have an ambush set up behind us."

The conductor laughed as he turned away toward the engine. Toby returned to his compartment, and by the time he reached it, the train's speed had increased. Looking out at the landscape rushing past, he imagined the train hurtling toward the rendezvous with danger. He opened a large suitcase and took out his Colt and Winchester, making certain they were loaded.

During late afternoon, the train stopped at Salina, where passengers flooded off it. Only a handful of the several dozen passengers awaiting the train came out to board it. Malcolm Mahar stepped down to the platform with Toby, trying to dissuade them. "You've been warned that there might be trouble. I advise you to wait for the next train."

"And I advise you to get out of my path," a grizzled man in well-worn prospector's clothes retorted. "Because if you don't, there'll be trouble. I've bought my ticket, and I'm going to Denver."

When the others echoed these remarks, Mahar turned to Toby. "Well, I tried, Mr. Holt."

"That's all you can do," Toby replied, smiling wryly. "We can't order the passengers from the train. Americans do as they like. The fact is, I wouldn't have them any other way."

Mahar laughed. The last passenger boarded, the whistle hooted, and the train moved away to a coaling hopper and water tank on the siding.

While the fuel and boiler water were being replenished, Toby and Malcolm Mahar walked over to talk with the engineer. "If we're jumped, Mr. Holt, it'll happen at Beacon Ridge."

Toby and Malcolm exchanged glances.

"Why do you say that?" Mahar asked.

"Beacon Ridge is the only sharp rise 'twixt here and Denver. It's so steep that trains slow to a crawl getting over it, which would make it real easy for robbers to hop aboard. The rest of the track is mostly level."

Toby thought for a moment about his previous

trips to Denver. "It's about eighty miles east of Denver, isn't it?"

The engineer nodded. "And about forty miles west of Buffalo Springs. We should reach Beacon Ridge at dawn."

Toby pondered. "If we had another locomotive sent out from Denver to meet us at Buffalo Springs, two locomotives could haul the train across the ridge without slowing. That wouldn't eliminate all the danger, but it would take care of one problem."

"Sure would," the engineer agreed. "But the company might not want to spend the money to send the extra locomotive."

"The company doesn't want a train robbery, either. I'm sure they'll cooperate. I'll send the request."

Toby and Malcolm turned away. Walking back along the tracks, Toby took out his notebook and wrote a message to the Central Pacific office in Denver. Mahar gave the message to one of his men, who ran it to the station. When the man returned a few minutes later, the message was already on its way to Denver. Toby and Malcolm boarded the train, and it rumbled out of the yards, then turned onto the main tracks.

Malcolm Mahar had brightened. He considered the danger eliminated. Toby, however, foresaw another potential problem: Outlaws waiting in ambush might not depend upon the train slowing at Beacon Ridge; they might block or rip up the tracks to stop the train.

50

Sitting on a bench in the freight car, Toby and Malcolm speculated as to the length of time required for robbers to organize an attack. The Pinkerton captain maintained an optimistic attitude; Toby's sixth sense, however, warned of danger.

Later, half the guards left to have dinner. When all had returned, Toby and Malcolm went to the dining car through ice-cold vestibules as the train rushed through the night. The train was virtually empty. A few traveling salesmen and others had ignored the warning. Toby was surprised to see that the old woman and boy were still aboard, the youngster asleep and his grandmother knitting.

Toby tipped his hat to the woman. "Ma'am, weren't you told that there might be some danger?"

"I was, young man," she replied amiably. "But I've lived through tornadoes, floods, prairie fires, and Indian attacks, so no pack of rascally outlaws is going to keep me from doing what I want to."

"Very well, ma'am," Toby said warily. "But if trouble starts, get down on the floor with the boy."

While having dinner, Toby devised a strategy to counter an attempt by robbers to immobilize the train, then told Malcolm about it: Instead of coupling the extra locomotive to the train, Toby and a few guards would go ahead of the train in the locomotive to check the tracks. "If I find nothing, good. But if the tracks are blocked or pulled up from the ties, the train and passengers won't be exposed to danger."

"Yes, but how about you?" Malcolm countered. "There won't be four or five robbers—there'll be twenty or so."

"The locomotive will give us some protection. Once the train is safe, you can bring more men to assist us. In any event, it'll be much better than the alternative of risking the train."

Mahar agreed. "But *I'd* better go in the locomotive. You're the commissioner of the West, Mr. Holt."

Toby shook his head. "If I'm ever offered a position that would necessitate my shying away from a little trouble, I'll turn it down. I'll go in the locomotive, and you see to the train."

Malcolm reluctantly agreed. Before they returned to the freight car, Toby found the conductor and explained the plan.

Some thirty minutes from Buffalo Springs, the conductor pounded on the door to signal their location. The four guards chosen to go in the locomotive gathered up their weapons. Toby had his rifle and extra bullets. A short time later, the train slowed.

Buffalo Springs was a tiny, isolated station and community. The windows in the handful of houses set back from the tracks were dark during the early morning hours. Toby and the four men crossed the graveled yard to the short siding where the second locomotive was waiting, steam hissing softly from its valves and melting the small snowflakes flying in the icy wind.

The tall, rangy engineer climbed lithely from

52

the cab and listened as Toby explained what he wanted to do. "Because there's a potential for danger, you don't have to go. I know enough about locomotives to make one go forward."

"I go where my engine goes, and my fireman goes where I do, Mr. Holt," the man responded. "Let's be on our way."

Toby and the four Pinkertons followed the engineer into the cab. Sliding onto his seat, the engineer called instructions to the grimy fireman and opened the throttle. The locomotive snorted, the drive wheels spinning, then moved forward as the fireman opened the firebox to accept the coal.

As the locomotive chugged onto the main tracks, Toby looked out the window. The cab was frigidly cold, the howling wind dissipating the heat from the firebox. He hunkered down with the four guards while the locomotive roared along the tracks. When the first gleam of daylight lightened the sky, he rose to look out at tufts of prairie grass near the tracks and the rolling hills set back from the tracks. Ahead was Beacon Ridge, more of a mountain than a ridge, rising abruptly from the surrounding terrain.

As the engineer opened the throttle wider, the thundering locomotive picked up speed for the steep grade. Behind, thick smoke eddied back. When the locomotive started up the incline, the engineer glanced back and adjusted the throttle to stay no more than a mile ahead of the gold-carrying train, which followed.

The locomotive gradually slowed, laboring on

the incline. The tracks curved slowly right, then left. The engineer held a moderate speed. Toby saw nothing suspicious ahead, but the peak of the rise was still a few hundred yards away.

Minutes later, just before the locomotive went around another curve and blocked his view, Toby thought he glimpsed something on the tracks. Simultaneously the engineer straightened in his seat. "Logs are piled on the tracks ahead, Mr. Holt!"

"Warn the train!" Toby ordered. "Pull up to the logs and set the brake. Then you and the fireman stay down on the floor!"

The engineer pulled a cord; the whistle screamed in warning. When the tracks straightened, Toby could see the mound of debris at the peak of the ridge. Of greater concern was the movement he saw on the left side of the tracks, just above the barricade. He ran to the other side of the cab.

The cold wind stinging his eyes, he peered closely at the embankment and counted a dozen or more men on the left side and four more robbers on the right. He looked back at the gold-carrying train and saw it grind to a stop.

The Pinkerton guards were also counting the robbers on the embankments above the tracks. "There's about fifteen on the left side and three on the right, Mr. Holt," one said.

"Four on the right," Toby corrected him. "We'll take care of them for starters, so we won't get pinned in a crossfire. After I take the first shot, you can fire at will."

The men gathered behind Toby as he knelt at the side of the doorway, his rifle ready. As the train pulled closer to the debris, the robbers above the tracks stood in open view, apparently startled by the advance locomotive and unsure of what to do. Although they were within easy range, Toby waited for a hostile move, hoping the robbers would simply back away and leave.

He centered his sights on a man shouldering a rifle. Smoke puffed from the man's weapon, and the shot rang out as the bullet pinged off the side of the locomotive. Toby squeezed the trigger of his rifle. The bullet hit the man, and he tumbled backward.

The guards began firing rapidly now at the other three, who dived for cover. One sprawled over a rock; another, felled by a bullet, dragged himself behind a boulder; the third dropped out of sight and fired back. Then a blistering hail of gunfire erupted from the embankment on the left side, peppering the locomotive with bullets.

The fireman, lying prone, lifted his head for a moment then pressed it to the floor as steam spouted from bullet holes in the boiler. The locomotive continued toward the debris, the engineer crouching down and ready to apply the brakes.

When Toby peered up the embankment, he glimpsed the wounded man's foot sticking out from behind the boulder he was using for cover. Toby fired at it. The bullet found its mark, and the man jerked up, his face twisted in agony. Toby put a bullet through the man's chest. Just then, the locomotive came to a stop against the logs on the tracks. After the engineer set the brake, he laid down beside the quaking fireman.

The outlaws on the opposite embankment kept up a rapid rate of fire, and bullets drummed into the cab. Knowing that the guards and he had to get out of the locomotive, Toby tried to get his sights on the fourth and last man on the right embankment, but the man was too wary. Although he fired steadily, no more than his rifle and the crown of his hat came into view.

"Wave your coat in front of the door!" Toby shouted to a guard.

The guard shrugged out of his coat while Toby took careful aim just above the rocks where the fourth man was concealed. The guard flapped his coat in the doorway; the outlaw, seeing it, lifted himself higher to take better aim, placing his head in clear view. Toby fired. The bullet punched through the man's forehead and propelled him backward. The guard, putting on his coat, flashed Toby an appreciative grin.

After reloading, Toby leapt from the locomotive and shouted to the guards to follow. Crouching and shouldering his rifle, he ran behind the debris on the tracks. With only one man firing at them, the main group of outlaws had been careless about concealment. Toby got off four quick shots, bringing two men rolling down the embankment and wounding a third; then he ducked as bullets hit the logs around him.

As the guards joined Toby, the outlaws moved back from the edge of the embankment to take cover behind boulders. Four Pinkerton guards armed with rifles fired at them. Eddying steam from the locomotive helped to conceal Toby and the guards, but they remained pinned down behind the logs. Toby estimated the open distance to the foot of the embankment, where he would be out of the outlaws' line of fire. He decided he could make it.

"I'm going around to one side of them!" he shouted over the gunfire. "Get ready to cover me!"

"Don't try it, Mr. Holt!" a guard warned. "Mr. Mahar will bring some men up soon. Then we can break loose from here!"

"If we don't make a move now, some of the outlaws will sneak around behind us. Get ready!"

The guards drew their pistols. Toby moved to the end of the logs, braced himself, then nodded. As all four guards fired rapidly, he lunged into the open and raced toward the base of the embankment.

Again, steam concealed him for the first couple of strides. He took another three strides before the outlaws had time to react. Bullets exploded around him. One clipped his hat from his head; another ripped through his coat and grazed his shoulder, while others raised spouts of dirt and gravel as he ran a zigzag pattern. Leaping the last few feet, he made it to the foot of the embankment.

One outlaw crawled to the edge, thinking to shoot down at Toby, but bullets from the guards' rifles ripped into the man before he could fire. He tumbled down the embankment, landing at Toby's feet as he hugged the dirt wall and moved along the cut.

Keeping a watchful eye on the edge above, Toby crept around bulges in the hill. He had moved thirty yards away from the locomotive and was approaching the end of the cut. The embankment here was only twenty feet high, and he noticed dirt and rocks spilling down on the other side of a huge boulder in front of him. Holding his rifle ready, he peered around the boulder.

Two men were sliding down the embankment, intending to get behind the guards. Seeing Toby they raised their rifles. Toby shot the nearest one, ducking as he worked the lever on his Winchester. He fired after a bullet from the second man slammed into the boulder over his head. The man, jolted by the blast, rolled down the dirt wall.

Digging the toes of his boots into the dirt, Toby scaled the embankment. From its edge he saw Mahar and five more Pinkertons running up the tracks from the train. Keeping low, he crawled up onto a large boulder.

From its top, he could see into the draw, where a large number of horses were picketed. Along with the saddle horses, the outlaws had brought a dozen packhorses to haul the currency and gold. The outlaws were pulling back to the draw, hoping to escape.

At one end of the picket line was a roan tied to a large rock. Toby knew it would be a long shot, but he rested his rifle on the boulder, took careful aim, and squeezed the trigger. The bullet struck the rope, and the roan reared up in fright and broke free. The horses raced out of the draw, and bullets fired in rage peppered the other side of the boulder while Toby slid back down, grinning in satisfaction.

The outlaws pulled back from the cut as heavy gunfire exploded on the other side of them from Mahar and the men he was leading straight up the ridge. Toby moved back along the edge, rejoining the four guards from the locomotive as they, too, clambered up the embankment. The five men shot at the fleeing outlaws, working their way along the crest of the ridge to join Mahar and his reinforcements.

When the groups of Pinkertons met, the last outlaws were climbing into a large cluster of boulders, leaving scattered dead men behind. Bullets pinged off the rocks around Toby and the guards as they crawled closer to the boulders. The desperate outlaws fired rapidly. Mahar peeked around a rock at the boulders, then shook his head. "It's like a fortress. We're going to need dynamite to get them out of there, Mr. Holt."

"Let's see if we can talk to them," Toby suggested.

He and Mahar shouted to the guards to cease fire. The guards stopped, reloaded their weapons, and waited. Then the gunfire from the boulders gradually died out. "Throw out your guns and come out with your hands up!" Toby shouted. "I'll guarantee you a fair trial!"

"Says who?" a man shouted back.

Toby peered over a rock. "I'm Toby Holt, commissioner of the West," he called. "You have my word."

Seeing a movement in the boulders, Toby ducked just as two bullets struck the rock. He turned to Mahar. "Let's shoot between the boulders and make bullets bounce around inside there."

Mahar nodded his quick agreement, then shouted to his men as Toby took aim. The roar of gunfire was immediately joined by the shrill whine of bullets ricocheting inside the boulders. Dust and flying bits of rocks spewed up, and three panicked outlaws leapt into the open. They were immediately cut down. The gunfire stopped.

Cautiously walking forward with the guards, Toby took one look inside the boulders, then turned away; the dead men inside were like mincemeat. "Were any of our men wounded?" he asked Mahar.

"Just a couple of minor wounds, Mr. Holt. You took a bullet there yourself. Is it bad?"

Glancing at his shoulder, Toby shook his head. "No, it'll heal. My coat won't, though, so I guess I've ruined another suit."

"Looks that way," Mahar agreed, smiling. "Well, what'll we do about these bodies?"

"Let's take them to Denver. If you'll have a couple of your men round up those horses, we can make room for them in a freight car. Between selling the horses and all of the guns around here, there should be enough money to bury those men."

As Mahar nodded to his men to begin the grisly task, Toby tucked his rifle under his arm and trudged wearily back toward the locomotive.

IV

People standing about in the luxuriously furnished lobby of the Fortham Hotel in New York glanced curiously at the leather gun cases among Edward Blackstone's baggage because they were so incongruous to the sedate, sumptuous atmosphere of the hotel.

Placing his hat on the registration desk, Edward tucked his cane under his arm and took off his chamois gloves. "Edward Blackstone," he said crisply. "Do I have any messages?"

The desk clerk placed the registration book in front of Edward for his signature, then thumbed through a stack of mail and separated two telegrams, which Edward accepted. "Please have a bottle of Napoleon brandy sent up."

"Yes, sir," the clerk replied, bowing. "Immediately."

A few minutes later, Edward was settled in a comfortable chair in a well-appointed room, his luggage and brandy having been delivered by Fortham staff.

The first telegram was a reply from the port master at Portsmouth, New Hampshire, and stated that Isaiah Sterch, the sea captain who had helped Edward take Brahma cattle from India, was presently in Portsmouth at the Seaman's Hostel. The captain's ship, the *Mercury*, had been heavily damaged during its last voyage.

Frowning regretfully, Edward opened the second telegram, from Edgar Dooley. The wily, well-traveled Irishman wrote that he could provide plenty of advice and assistance to get rubber tree seeds out of Brazil, and he was eager to go. In fact, he was already on his way to meet Edward in New York.

The last sentence stated that Dooley was well-acquainted with an explorer he had met in India, who might be free of commitments and interested in Edward's project. Edward reflected that if the explorer were familiar with Brazil, as many were, he would be invaluable.

Edward considered the *Mercury* to be an old, outmoded sailing vessel. If a better ship, preferably a steamer, could be obtained, the skilled and reliable Captain Sterch would undoubtedly be willing to command it.

Edward's research had told him that rubber trees propagated by seeds. That was heartening, seeds being much easier to conceal and transport than plants. But he knew he needed the services of a naturalist such as Cecil Witherspoon, Ramedha's friend in India. In addition, he needed to confirm that the East India Company was willing to devote resources to his project. He knew his proposal would interest the company, which owned ten plantations and other investments. But what he intended to do was risky, and he wanted at least a tentative commitment from the company before proceeding.

Edward decided to contact his uncle Winslow by telegram to resolve those points. The message, transmitted over the international telegraph cables, had to be worded carefully; if it clearly stated his plans, the Brazilian authorities might be alerted.

The next morning Edward sent the obliquely worded request to his uncle, asking that the reply be sent to the Mayfair Hotel in Portsmouth. He then telegraphed the Mayfair for reservations and Captain Sterch at the hostel, to arrange their meeting.

When he returned to the Fortham lobby, Edward was greeted by a familiar voice: "Sure and it's none other than my good friend, Edward Blackstone!" Edgar Dooley exclaimed, a grin on his round, ruddy face.

Wearing his usual baggy, wrinkled wool suit, the portly Irishman was even more disheveled than usual, unshaven, and wearing a grimy, wilted collar.

"I'm delighted that you're here, Edgar," Edward said, smiling and shaking hands with Dooley as the desk clerk and others in the lobby cast disdainful glances at him. "But you're in a wretched state. Didn't you have funds for a sleeper car?"

"It's this thirst of mine, you see," Edgar explained. "To buy whiskey I had to make do with a freight car for accommodations during the last part of my journey."

Understanding, Edward turned toward the registration desk. "Do you have a room for my friend?" he asked.

The clerk nodded reluctantly.

Upstairs in Edward's room, as Edgar pounced on the bottle of brandy and poured himself a generous drink, Edward asked about the explorer.

"Teddy Montague," Edgar said, taking a gulp of brandy. "We've been the best of friends since we first met in India. What's more, Teddy has been to Brazil and knows it well."

"Excellent!" Edward responded. "Montague is the earl of Banbridge's family name. Is he related to the earl?"

A sly smile passed over Edgar's face but immediately disappeared as he shrugged. "That I couldn't say. Teddy has a high-faluting way of speech, like your own, but kin to an earl? If I knew anyone kin to a lord, it would be from the wrong side of the blanket."

"Well, what is his proper baptismal name? Theodore?"

As he poured more brandy into his glass, the smile flashed across Edgar's face again. "I couldn't say, Edward. Teddy is the only name I've heard mentioned."

Seeing the furtive smiles on Edgar's face and knowing the Irishman's love for practical jokes, Edward frowned suspiciously. "Very well. Where do you think this Teddy Montague might be at present?"

"In Egypt," Edgar replied. "You could send a telegram in care of the British consul in Cairo."

"Yes, I'd like to find out if your friend is free of commitments and interested in an adventure." He took out his notebook. "I'll send Mr. Montague a telegram tomorrow."

Edgar lifted his glass quickly, but not fast enough to hide completely his grin.

Edward glared back. "What is so damnably amusing? If you think this undertaking is an opportunity for pranks, let me assure you it is not. Now have you been entirely truthful with me about this explorer?"

"Why are you taking on so, Edward?" Dooley protested. "On my sainted mother's grave, every word I've told you has been the honest truth."

Something about Dooley's attitude still bothered Edward, but his vow of honesty was straightforward enough. Shrugging, Edward opened his notebook and drafted the telegram, addressing it to Mr. Montague, in care of the British consul, Cairo.

The following day Edward and Edgar—freshly groomed and wearing a new shirt—set out for Portsmouth. When they arrived, tiny, stinging snowflakes were flying ahead of a raging gale that turned the harbor into a mass of whitecaps.

Leaving Dooley at the Mayfair Hotel with a bottle of brandy, Edward took a carriage to the Seaman's Hostel. It turned out to be a spartan but spotless lodging house near the waterfront.

Several men were playing cards at a table in the parlor, while others lounged about and talked. The tall, angular man Edward had come to see, a taciturn New Englander with craggy, weathered features, was sitting alone and reading. Looking up, Sterch smiled. He put the newspaper aside and offered his hand to Edward.

"I've been looking forward to seeing you, Mr. Blackstone."

"And I, you, Captain Sterch," Edward replied sincerely. "I'm sorry to hear about the *Mercury;* I know what the vessel meant to you. But I have the means to obtain another ship."

Sterch nodded, extremely interested, then led Edward upstairs to a neat, modestly furnished room. He listened as Edward briefly outlined the project. "I can see why you want a captain you already know."

"Would you be willing to undertake the voyage, Captain Sterch?"

"More than willing. Also I know of a steamer in port, the *Galatea,* that you might be able to obtain—owned by the same men as the *Mercury.* In addition to the loss of the *Mercury,* they've suffered other financial losses recently, and the

Galatea has been seized by a bank. You might be able to work out some arrangement."

"That sounds promising. What condition is the *Galatea* in?"

"I've heard she's perfectly seaworthy. I'll take you to see the owners, if you like."

"Yes, I would appreciate that, Captain Sterch. I'd like to keep this project quiet, so please keep everything I've told you to yourself."

"Indeed, I will, Mr. Blackstone." Sterch took his overcoat and cap from a hook on the wall. "I'll leave all the talking to you."

Edward and the captain went out into the icy wind and walked a short distance to a large office building occupied by various firms connected with the maritime industry. On an upper floor were the offices of Markham and Harrison, shipping investors.

Thomas Markham, the middle-aged senior partner in the firm, seated Edward and Sterch in his cluttered, musty office. Edward broached the subject of the *Galatea*.

"You find us hard on the shoals of misfortune, Mr. Blackstone." Markham shook his head mournfully. "She's our most valuable asset but is gathering barnacles at a pier because of a pinchpenny banker. The *Galatea* is under a lien of two thousand dollars."

"That being the case," Edward said, "we could come to terms, and the *Galatea* could put to sea within the next few days."

Markham brightened. "You'll have to talk with

67

John Pendleton at the Seaman's and Merchant's Bank first. He isn't an easy man to deal with. If you can clear it with him, I'll scout around for a cargo. Where are you bound?"

"Calcutta." Edward rose. "I'll go to see Pendleton now."

Markham smiled doubtfully as he wished Edward well. Edward and Sterch left, after agreeing to meet Markham the next day. The captain pointed out the way to the bank, then went back toward his lodgings.

At the bank Edward met with a cold reception. John Pendleton, a small man with a sallow complexion, heard Edward out, then shrugged. "Markham and Harrison are indebted to the bank in excess of eight thousand dollars. That must be paid in full before I will lift the seizure on that vessel."

"But I have no interest in buying the firm, Mr. Pendleton. All I need is the temporary use of the vessel, and I have no intention of paying off all the debts of the firm in order to secure that."

"You have no alternative, Mr. Blackstone."

"I can contact the bank's major shareholders and inform them that I was turned down on a reasonable offer to retire an outstanding lien held by the bank."

"I won't listen to threats!" Pendleton snapped.

"That was, sir, a statement of intention. I assume that some of the shareholders are shippers, and I understand there is great need of vessels to transport cargoes. Your denial pits some of their

68

business interests against others. I should think you would want to extricate yourself from that uncomfortable predicament."

Pendleton's frown revealed that some of the shareholders were indeed shippers. "Well, perhaps we can work something out, Mr. Blackstone."

"Think it over, Mr. Pendleton," Edward agreed briskly. "We'll discuss the matter again."

From the bank Edward took a hired carriage to the pier and looked at the *Galatea*. Even in the fading light the large, well-maintained steamer looked impressive. Edward felt confident that the steamer would take him back to Ramedha.

The next morning, the desk clerk handed Edward two telegrams, both from India. The first was from his uncle; Witherspoon and officials of the East India Company were enthusiastic about participating in his project. The second telegram, extravagantly long, was from Ramedha, expressing delight that Edward was returning to India. Smiling as he read it, Edward could picture the beautiful young woman as she penned the lengthy, costly sentences that mirrored his feelings.

That morning, Edward concluded agreements with Pendleton and Markham for the use of the vessel. Many of the *Mercury*'s crew were still at loose ends, and Sterch began signing on hands and readying the vessel for a voyage.

A telegram from Egypt arrived two days later, while cargo and provisions were being loaded aboard the *Galatea*. Edward read it as he went upstairs to Dooley's room. The explorer had no commitments and was interested in Edward's project. The last sentence conveyed warm regards to Dooley, and it was signed Teddy Montague.

His eyes bleary from brandy, Dooley read the telegram, then handed it back to Edward. "Aye, there's welcome good news, isn't it? And I didn't mislead you in any respect, did I?"

"No, apparently not," Edward replied absently, looking at the telegram and pondering. "I'll send him a response and give him our estimated date of arrival at Port Said."

Edward detected a fleeting smirk on Dooley's face. Then the Irishman suddenly turned away. "Aye, you do that."

Frowning, Edward looked at the telegram again and wondered if Dooley had a confederate in Cairo who was collaborating with him in an elaborate practical joke. Why was Dooley so quietly amused each time the subject of the explorer came up?

Josef Mueller, sitting in the office of his Philadelphia restaurant, felt deeply dissatisfied. The restaurant was making a profit, and Salima, a young woman Mueller had met in Turkey, belly danced nightly to Turkish music—a strong attraction for customers.

But business had declined during the winter, and Mueller had, in the past, been accustomed to earning lavish amounts of money. More than that, however, he was simply bored; after years of living on the edge of danger, he found the life of a restaurant owner dull.

But it was, he reminded himself, also very safe. In 1874 he had barely escaped from Germany after killing Gisela von Kirchberg. When he had returned to Turkey, it was to find that his employer, Hermann Bluecher, planned to have him killed. He had fled and eventually ended up in the United States.

There, he had decided to buy a restaurant. He had met an immigrant Turk named Suleiman Bey, who had once managed a restaurant in Istanbul. Suleiman agreed to manage Mueller's restaurant. Because a lifetime of subterfuge had made Mueller desire anonymity, he had used Suleiman's name on the restaurant, and Salima was billed as Fatima. For the same reason, he had chosen Philadelphia over the mainstream of activity in New York.

Mueller turned as Suleiman uneasily stepped into the office doorway. "A man wishes to speak with you, sir. He has dined here several times and spends freely."

Mueller stepped into the restaurant dining room and immediately recognized the man who wanted to talk to him: Klaus Lukenbill.

"I'm here on business," Lukenbill plunged in. "I have a proposition that might interest you."

Mueller nodded toward a table, while calling to Suleiman to send cognac and cigars to the table. When the drinks were poured and the cigars lighted, Lukenbill leaned forward and spoke quietly in the almost empty room. "I need someone to bring something back from a foreign country. Would you be interested?"

The mention of a foreign country made Mueller wary. Under no circumstances would he go to Germany, where he was a wanted man. "Perhaps. Would this item be kept in a vault or under heavy guard?"

"No, no," Lukenbill assured Mueller. "It will be kept under lock and key, but nothing that would cause you much trouble. It is also small enough to carry easily. Meet me in my hotel in an hour, and I'll tell you all about it."

"First I have to know what country it is in and if I have to go there under my own name. Also, I want to know how much I'll be paid."

"The item is in Switzerland. I'd rather you didn't use your own name. I already have false identity papers that you can use. And you'll be paid eight thousand dollars."

The amount of money struck a false note to Mueller. The amount was uneven, and Lukenbill had just barely hesitated over the words. It was obvious that Lukenbill was trying to keep part of the money. "I'll do it for ten thousand," Mueller said.

Lukenbill flushed, ground out his cigar in the ashtray, and nodded. "Ten thousand," he agreed, standing. "I'm in room two-sixteen of the Burlington Hotel. Be there in an hour."

Lukenbill left the restaurant clearly annoyed, but Mueller smiled in satisfaction. Lukenbill was more greedy than cunning. Mueller finished his cognac and cigar, then went to the apartment over the restaurant to talk with Salima.

A slender, dark woman with large brown eyes and beautiful features, Salima was proud and independent, energetic and ambitious. Mueller had learned that it was futile to try to dominate her. They had been married in order to enter the United States as man and wife, and while their relationship was harmonious, it was based on need rather than affection.

She was poring over English language texts as he stepped into the parlor. "I'm going to be gone for a few weeks," he announced.

"Where are you going and for what purpose, Josef?"

"It's business. You and Suleiman can look after things while I'm gone."

Salima looked up, suspicious. "It isn't illegal, is it?"

"Of course not," he lied easily. "But it will pay well, so my time will be usefully spent."

Salima nodded and turned to her books as Mueller returned to his office. The deeply gratifying prospect of earning ten thousand dollars prompted Mueller to plot ways to get much more. If he could supplant Lukenbill, it might turn out to be extremely lucrative to work directly for the wealthy man behind Lukenbill.

Cyril Jenkins struggled to conceal his nervousness during the interview by the personnel officer of the United States Mint in Philadelphia. Mr. Hollings stroked his chin and read over the employment application that Jenkins had completed. "You have very good handwriting, Mr. Jenkins."

"Thank you, sir."

"And you wish to be employed as a clerk."

"Yes, sir."

The man continued reading the form as Jenkins twitched with anxiety. He had written several false statements on the application and had glossed over anything that might raise questions. The one thing that Lukenbill had emphasized was that Jenkins had to appear an average man and not create any suspicions.

The preparations for this day had been elaborate. Two weeks before in New York, Jenkins had, at Lukenbill's orders, found employment in a department store accounting office. He had worked industriously but resigned after a few days, citing an illness in his family. His disappointed employer had written him a glowing recommendation to take with him.

Now Hollings picked up that recommendation. "This is a very good testimony to your skill and dedication, Mr. Jenkins. Very good indeed."

"Thank you, sir. I always try to please my employers."

Hollings smiled apologetically. "Unfortunately we don't have any openings for clerks at present. I'll keep your application on file, however."

Having heard precisely what he had hoped for, Jenkins concealed his relief. "Thank you, sir. I appreciate that very much."

74

The guard who had escorted Jenkins to the office was waiting in the hall and started to lead him back toward the front of the mint. "Isn't there another door?" Jenkins asked, pointing in the opposite direction. "If I could go out that way, I wouldn't have as far to walk in the cold."

The guard shrugged, then went in the requested direction. Jenkins took in every detail as he followed. They turned into a wider hall that ended in a small foyer, where two guards were seated beside a door. One of them unlocked and opened the door. Jenkins nodded his thanks as he exited.

Outside was a loading dock, its steps leading to the street beside the huge stone building. Jenkins now knew the layout of the building and the number of guards—the information that Lukenbill wanted—and as far as he could tell, he had aroused no suspicions.

Hurrying toward the hotel, Jenkins reviewed what he had learned. The front section of the building was devoted to management and business offices, open to the public. The center section housed the storage vault and production offices; everyone except employees who entered it had to be escorted by a guard.

Currency was printed and coins were minted in the rear of the building. No more than eight guards were in the building. A police station directly across the street provided more than adequate security against any robbery attempts.

A few blocks from the mint, Jenkins passed yet another, even larger, police station.

At the hotel he stopped at Lukenbill's room, which was adjacent to his own. He knocked, and a moment later Lukenbill snatched it open and frowned impatiently. Jenkins got a momentary glimpse of a heavyset man inside.

"Go on to your room!" Lukenbill snapped. "I'll talk to you later!"

Jenkins went to his room, wondering if Lukenbill also headed anarchists in Philadelphia. Curious, he tiptoed to the connecting door and pressed his ear to it. Although Lukenbill and the other man spoke quietly, Jenkins was able to make out snatches of the conversation.

Lukenbill said, "Here you are, and now your name is Kramer."

Both men laughed as papers rustled. The heavyset man asked, "How do I contact you when I get back with the explosives?"

Lukenbill replied inaudibly, and the conversation ended a few minutes later. Jenkins quickly stepped away from the connecting door and hung up his coat just before Lukenbill knocked.

Jenkins detailed for Lukenbill what he had seen at the mint. Having already concluded that the man intended to rob the mint, Jenkins guessed that the explosives would be tossed into the smaller police station to eliminate any intervention.

"I saw another police station just a short distance from the mint," he continued. "The police from that other station could reach the building within minutes."

"I know that!" Lukenbill retorted irately. "I

know all about every police station in the city! Now shut up!"

They went downstairs to the hotel dining room, where Lukenbill ordered for both of them. Jenkins picked at his food, wishing he could disentangle himself from the anarchists. Lukenbill gulped down his meal, lighted a cigar, and unfolded a newspaper.

On the front page was a drawing of the torch of the Statue of Liberty, scheduled for display in Philadelphia. Jenkins commented on it. "There's a lot of interest in that. Many people will want to go inside it."

"Yes, plenty," Lukenbill agreed, grinning savagely. "But a lot of them are going to wish they never—" He stood abruptly. "When you finish eating, go to your room and stay there. I'll come for you when it's time to leave for the train."

Perplexed, Jenkins nodded. When he was in his room, the full implications of what Lukenbill had said finally dawned on Jenkins. He gasped in dismay, realizing why Lukenbill had been unconcerned about the police station a few blocks from the mint: All the police would rush to the scene of an explosion.

Lukenbill was brutally indifferent to the toll in human life and suffering. After the explosives in the torch detonated, the scene would be one of shattered bodies. It didn't matter how many people he killed, as long as he succeeded in robbing the mint.

Jenkins decided that he had to try to prevent

the explosion. While he was unsure of what to do, he knew he had to do something.

V

Standing in the milling crowd on the platform of the Kansas City train station, Toby saw Henry Blake stepping off the train. Henry saw Toby at the same time, and the two of them moved through the crowd toward each other.

They greeted each other with heartfelt warmth. "It's been far too long, Henry."

"Indeed it has," the younger man agreed.

"When do you have to leave?"

"Tomorrow morning. I checked my baggage on through, so I only have this bag here with me."

"Let's go, then. I reserved a room for you at my hotel."

In the carriage Henry talked about his visit to Portland. "I've never met anyone quite like Alexandra."

Toby grinned with pleasure. "A new life started for me when I met her. Peter and his nurse are settled in?"

"Yes, and Peter is particularly taken with Cindy. And I'm finally reconciled with Mama."

"That pleases me very much, Henry. How about you and Cindy?"

Henry fell silent for a moment. "We got on well enough, but I'd like it to be far more than that—

and so would she. But what I did to her stands between us like a wall."

"Give it time, Henry."

He brightened. "I wouldn't have known Tim, he's grown so tall, and Janessa is quite the young lady. And still trying to stop smoking."

"When she makes up her mind to stop, she will," Toby said, smiling fondly. "So you're commanding a cavalry battalion at Fort Harland now?"

Henry told Toby about the fort and the situation there. A few minutes later, after Henry checked in at the hotel, he joined Toby in his room and listened to an account of the attempted train robbery.

"That's where we differ," Henry said. "When a man threatens me, he won't have an opportunity to surrender. I'll kill him in his tracks."

"You've had to be that way, Henry, defending yourself against professional assassins. At least some of the men I've come up against can turn into decent citizens if guided onto the right path."

Seeing Henry's skeptical expression, Toby pressed the point. "From all accounts Luther Bingham was a worthless drunk, shot while trying to rob a store in Portland. Now he's a doctor in southern Illinois."

Henry nodded, but Toby could see that he was still unconvinced. While Henry remained a man with strong loyalty toward friends, over the years he had developed a cold, lethal attitude toward his enemies.

Toby changed the subject. The previous day he had met with negotiators from Washington who had held discussions with the Sioux chiefs. "It ended without any agreement, and the situation looks very bad. The Cheyenne have left their reservation and joined the Sioux. About four thousand warriors have disappeared into the Montana Territory, with a few scattered into the Dakota Territory."

"Then I may be seeing some of them," Henry mused grimly.

"The War Department is trying to head off trouble. They're moving additional forces into the region under Colonel Gibbon, General Terry, and General Crook."

"The Sioux and Cheyenne don't scare very easily. Still, we've had similar situations arise before. Many times, they've simmered for a while and settled back down."

Toby agreed quickly, although he left one vital point unmentioned: In a number of other instances, the situation had exploded into conflict and bloodshed.

Cindy Holt Kerr's preparations to leave Portland were under discussion in the parlor at the Holt ranch. Eulalia and Lee had come to visit, bringing Peter with them, in an effort to get Cindy to change her plans. Cindy, holding Peter on her lap, gently but firmly defended her decision.

"I'd like to stay, but I need to get back to work. My etchings of scenes in the West were the foundation of my art career, and I want to travel, to do some sketches in Nevada, for instance, that I can use to make etchings when I return to Paris."

"We're very proud of your success," Eulalia said. "I see that you've made up your mind, so I won't argue. I do wish that the freighter wasn't leaving at such an early hour, though. Lee and I would like to see you off."

"I'd like that too, but I'll see you both in Philadelphia this summer."

Eulalia asked Cindy about her travel plans. Cindy replied in vague terms, not having given them much thought. She only knew that ever since Henry had left, an unbearable restlessness had gripped her.

Eulalia and Lee put on their coats to leave, and Cindy helped Peter with his coat, then kissed him. She carried him to the front door for a final kiss and hug before giving him to her mother. Tears filled Cindy's eyes, and she regretted leaving, but she knew she had made the right decision.

The wisdom of what Cindy had done was a point of disagreement between Janessa and Alexandra, but they could amicably debate anything.

"She was becoming more uneasy every day, Janessa," Alexandra said, when they returned to the ranch after seeing Cindy off at the pier. "She had to do something."

"I see very little point in traveling about the West in the middle of winter without a destination."

Alexandra pursed her lips. "Well, she may find a destination," she mused. "Do you have time for a cup of coffee?"

"No, I'd better get to school. I have oral quizzes today. This afternoon I'm going to the hospital to check on Jake Higgins. I'm really worried about him. What are you doing today?"

"I have to organize my notes for the hospital trustee meeting the day after tomorrow. We'll be electing a new member."

Janessa nodded, lit a cigarette, then winced in distaste and looked at it. "I wonder what they put in these things. One of these days I'll stop smoking. I've tried and tried, like Dad asked, but I haven't been able to so far."

"He isn't the only one who wants you to quit, dear. But when you decide to stop smoking, you will."

Alexandra's gentle reproach made Janessa feel vaguely ashamed. She immediately extinguished the cigarette, but after she saddled her mare, she lighted another and smoked it as she rode off to school.

Few pupils from Portland went to college—and certainly no one as young as she—so Janessa was being tutored in preparation for her entrance examinations. She was grateful for the assistance, but being singled out by the teachers made her feel under intense pressure to succeed.

Her answers during the afternoon testing proved satisfactory, and after the teachers had assigned new material for her to study, Janessa went to the hospital. In the hallway outside Dr. Martin's office, she stopped an orderly.

"How's Mr. Higgins today?"

"Sinking fast," the orderly replied somberly. "He wouldn't eat any breakfast or lunch."

Janessa was worried. She went into the examination room adjacent to Dr. Martin's office, opened a cabinet to get cotton swabs and two microscope slides, then went upstairs to see Higgins, who was in a room by himself.

When Janessa had come to Portland five years before, Higgins had been a burly, hearty man with a garrulous disposition. Now he was deathly thin and frail, and the pallid skin on his face had collapsed into folds around his deep-set eyes. It was difficult for Janessa to hide her horror.

"The orderly said you haven't eaten today, Mr. Higgins. How do you expect to get well if you don't eat?"

"I just ain't hungry, Miss Janessa," he replied in a hoarse, breathless whisper.

"That's because you're sick. But you must force yourself to eat. Have you been coughing up blood?"

"Yes, but not much, Miss Janessa."

His black, odorous corncob pipe was on the table beside the bed. "You should try not to smoke for a while, Mr. Higgins. It makes your breathing more difficult."

"I've got to have my pipe, Miss Janessa. You understand that."

Janessa laughed and nodded. "Yes, better than many, I suppose. Stick out your tongue, please."

Janessa used the cotton swabs to smear saliva specimens on the microscope slides. Then she gave him an encouraging smile she did not feel and went downstairs to the examination room, where she stained the slides.

While she was examining the second slide, Dr. Martin walked in. Semiretired for years, the elderly physician was the girl's mentor and friend. His tall frame was shrunken with age, and age spots on his wrinkled face reached into his thin, white hair. "Jake Higgins?" he asked.

Janessa nodded, lighting a cigarette as she turned away from the microscope. "I still haven't found a sign of *Mycobacterium tuberculosis*, so it isn't consumption. He looks so much worse! I wish he would leave that pipe alone."

The doctor stared meaningfully at her cigarette. "As I've told you many times, smoking isn't a healthy practice."

"You smoke cigars, Dr. Martin."

"I have a cigar now and then. That isn't the same thing as smoking constantly. There's much that we don't know, Janessa." He shrugged. "Dr. Wizneuski wants us to look at a boy with a septic leg, upstairs, and we'd better do as the hospital director asks."

Janessa crushed out her cigarette and went with the doctor. Each patient was important, but Jake Higgins was a special case, a friend she was unable to help, which gave her a sense of frustration.

She found time to spend a few minutes with him during the late afternoon and looked in on him again before she went home. He was sleeping restlessly, his breathing hoarse and loud.

When she returned to the hospital the next day, Dr. Martin was waiting for her in his office to tell her that Higgins had died during the night. "At least we'll find out the exact nature of the disease. Anton wants us to help with the postmortem."

"I'd rather not, Dr. Martin. Mr. Higgins was my friend."

"That has nothing to do with it. Seeing a condition firsthand may teach you something that will save another patient's life."

Janessa reluctantly agreed, but she dreaded the ordeal.

During late afternoon, when their rounds were finished, she and the doctor went to the morgue with the hospital director. The orderlies had prepared everything for them.

Janessa avoided looking at the sheet-covered corpse on the long table. While she had a wide knowledge of medicine, she was still a young girl.

Wizneuski placed a bottle of smelling salts on the instrument table, and a bucket had been positioned nearby, in the event Janessa became nauseated. In consideration for her feelings, he left Higgins's head and shoulders covered during the procedure.

While the doctor was sawing upward through the sternum, Janessa kept her eyes on the far wall. Suddenly Wizneuski exclaimed: "Good Lord!

Well, there's no question now about the cause of death, Robert."

The old doctor adjusted his glasses and peered into the chest cavity, and Janessa leaned forward and looked: The entire left lung was a shapeless, swollen mass of tissue, engorged by cancerous growth that was a deep red. Angry red streaks of tumorous growth on the bronchial tubes led into the deadly cancer that had begun to absorb the right lung.

"It was that pipe of his, all right," Dr. Martin concluded. "I've seen this before in heavy smokers, but never this advanced."

"But many people smoke without getting lung cancer," Janessa objected. "Couldn't something else have caused it?"

"I've seen this too many times, Janessa," Wizneuski replied. "I've also had patients with carcinoma of the mouth, and each one either chewed tobacco or dipped snuff. Something in tobacco can cause cancer."

Later, Janessa and the doctors went upstairs to Dr. Wizneuski's office to discuss patients. The girl started to light a cigarette, but then a vision of what she had just seen rose in her mind. She tossed her cigarettes into a waste can, then went to the door. "I have a lot of studying to do, so I'd better get home. Good night."

Neither doctor made any reference to what she had done. The need for a cigarette tugging at her, Janessa rode home through the cold, wintry twilight. At the house, when she put away her schoolbooks, she looked at the bureau drawer where her cigarettes were stacked, then left her room.

After dinner Alexandra, who had noticed that Janessa had failed to light a cigarette, took the girl's hand as she left the table. "Let me know if there's any way I can help, dear," she sympathized.

"Just keep up the encouragement," Janessa affectionately replied.

Sitting down at her desk, Janessa studied the material she had been assigned that day in school. The cigarettes in the bureau became a nagging temptation, and she considered throwing them into the fireplace downstairs. But tobacco was readily available on every side, so she knew determination was the only solution.

The next day, feeling nervous and irritable from a sleepless night, she had difficulty answering questions about the homework she had studied, and one teacher criticized both the content of her essay and her shaky handwriting.

It was well into the afternoon when she reached the hospital. Although the door to Dr. Martin's office was closed, his loud voice, trembling with uncharacteristic fury, could be heard in the hallway. Janessa opened the door a crack and peeked inside.

A disgruntled Anton Wizneuski beckoned her to come in, then explained what had just transpired at the hospital trustees' meeting: Frank McDowell, a retired businessman who was active in civic affairs, had been elected to fill the board's vacancy. He had questioned the propriety of Janessa's working at the hospital.

Dr. Martin and Alexandra had stoutly affirmed Janessa's right to work there if she wished, pointing out that had it not been for her, the new facility would never have been built. Not contesting that issue, McDowell had firmly maintained that the hospital's reputation was being jeopardized by allowing a girl of fifteen to treat patients. The matter was certain to come up again at future board meetings.

Janessa felt far more concerned about Dr. Martin's reaction than the threat to her working in the hospital. The old man was beside himself with rage, his face pale and his hands trembling. He was obviously in a state that was perilous to his health.

"What does he know about medicine?" Dr. Martin demanded. "Or about running a hospital? He's on the board of trustees ten minutes and starts trying to tell us what do do!"

"Robert, calm down," Wizneuski warned. "You're not helping the situation or your health. We'll deal with this in good time. Now go home and rest."

"Certainly not!" the old doctor retorted. "He might try to run Janessa off, but he's not going to run *me* off!"

"I won't be able to work with you this afternoon, Dr. Martin," Janessa put in. "I did very poorly at school today, so I have to study."

Wizneuski glanced at Janessa gratefully as he

tried to convince the older man to go home. Finally persuaded, Dr. Martin sent an orderly to the stables to bring his buggy. Janessa accompanied him home and discreetly took the doctor's wife aside to explain what had happened. When his temper had subsided somewhat, Janessa left.

On her way home, she reflected that McDowell had merely voiced what many people, including her own grandmother, had thought all along. Moreover, she knew McDowell. He was a reasonable man, kindly and wise, well-liked and respected in Portland. The trustees would give careful consideration to what he had said.

At the dinner table, Timmy commented that he knew McDowell's grandson at school. "His name is Benny McDowell. He lives in California, but he and his mother are visiting here for several months."

"Yes, I've heard about them," Alexandra said. "Mr. McDowell's son is on an extended business trip, so his daughter-in-law and grandson are staying here. Well, concerning Benny and this dispute, you know what you must do, Tim."

"Yes, ma'am. He's not involved, so I won't be mean to him."

"That's correct. Janessa, I'll talk with the trustees and try to enlist their support if this issue comes to a vote—which it probably will. I can't promise anything, but I'll do my best."

Janessa thanked Alexandra, then went to her room and sat at her desk, holding her head in her hands. Her hospital work was vitally important, but Dr. Martin was a cornerstone in her life. She shrank from thinking about what might happen to him if the majority of trustees voted in favor of her dismissal.

Reaching for one of her books, Janessa glanced at the bureau drawer with her cigarettes. When she had done poorly at school that day, her nagging desire to smoke had grown into a hungry need. After what had happened at the hospital, smoking had become a raging necessity, and she tried to force it from her mind as she opened the book to the pages she had been assigned to study.

High in the Sierra Nevadas, on the eastern border of California, Cindy Kerr sat on a train that had been stalled by heavy snow on the tracks. Just inches outside the misted window was a wilderness scene of striking beauty. The boughs of giant pines sagged with snow as large, fluffy flakes settled in the drifts around them.

Inside the car the scene was no less interesting: The passengers—some disgruntled by the delay, others taking it in stride—interacted in a way that gave Cindy a constantly changing choice of scenes. She blocked them in rapidly, turning page after page of her sketchbook.

A few minutes later, the snow was cleared, and the train jerked forward. Several people cheered. When the train reached the crest of its route across the mountain range, it started downhill into Nevada. At Reno Cindy quickly finished a sketch and stepped off the train to look at the schedule board and pick her next stop. Her entire excursion had been based on spontaneity. Armed with a large stock of sketch pads and charcoal sticks, she had boarded trains as the spirit moved her, with no specific destination in mind. It was a wondrous experience; never before had she known such a sustained burst of artistic energy and inspiration. She begrudged the few hours she had to sleep at night and was at work virtually every other moment.

Upon reaching a Union Pacific branch line railhead at Medicine Bow in the Wyoming Territory, Cindy was forced to choose between doubling back or going on by stage. She chose the latter, even though sketching while being jolted along rough roads would be difficult.

The journey was uncomfortable in every way. The stages were icily cold, and the nightly accommodations scarcely deserved to be called inns. But these shortcomings were more than outweighed by the new, fresh source of scenes.

Three days later, when a stage left her at Cedar Springs, in the Dakota Territory, Cindy emerged from the world of her work and realized with a start what she had done: By unconscious choice or by somehow deceiving herself, her zigzag journey had brought her toward Henry Blake.

A handful of people looked curiously at Cindy as she stood beside the stage, waiting for the driver to hand down her baggage to the grizzled station manager. A heavyset woman came out of the station, shivering in the cold and wiping her hands on her apron.

"My word, ain't you pretty!" she exclaimed. "Is somebody supposed to meet you here, honey?"

"No, I'm traveling on. Do you have a room?"

"We sure do, honey. Bring them bags in, Gus." She led Cindy toward the door. "How long do you aim to stay with us, honey?"

"When is the next stage to Bismarck?"

"Tomorrow afternoon."

"I'll stay until then, if I may."

VI

Bismarck was a law-abiding, orderly boomtown. A Missouri River traffic terminus, it was a supply point for the gold miners and prospectors in the Black Hills to the west. Surveyors and advance working parties for the Northern Pacific Railroad were also based in the town, along with other commercial interests. The sheriff was vigilant, and Fort Lincoln, on the opposite riverbank, was a powerful resource for maintaining law and order.

Furthermore, Major Henry Blake, the legendary officer who had tamed the lawless town of Fargo, commanded an entire battalion of cavalry forty miles to the north, at Fort Harland.

When Cindy checked in at a hotel, the conversation in the lobby centered on the possibility of war with the Sioux and Cheyenne. She heard about roving Indian bands that were attacking solitary travelers and stealing livestock. As she walked around Bismarck, she also heard talk about Henry Blake, in terms that were anything but complimentary. Couriers were sent to Fort Harland every day or two, and all soldiers tried to avoid that duty because discipline at Harland was rigid. They were greeted with blistering reprimands over the condition of their uniforms, equipment, and horses.

During the afternoon, when she went to a general store, Cindy saw an attractive, well-dressed woman in her early thirties shopping, and the young officer who was escorting her addressed her as Mrs. Custer. Cindy walked up to the woman and introduced herself.

"The artist?" Elizabeth Custer exclaimed in delight. "It's such a pleasure to meet you, and so unexpected! Copies of your etchings of the battle at Sandstone Butte are among my most treasured possessions. Are you engaged this evening, Mrs. Kerr?"

"No, but I'm afraid that visiting upon such short notice would be an intrusion."

"Intrusion?" Elizabeth scoffed. "It will be a great pleasure. The general also admires your work very much. I'll send an escort to your hotel. Will six be satisfactory?"

That evening, when Cindy came into the lobby, a lieutenant from the fort was waiting with a buggy. The sky had cleared, causing the temperature to plummet, and the horse's hooves crunched through ice on the road leading to the married officers' quarters outside the sprawling fort.

In a kennel beside the Custers' small, neat house, a dozen dogs created a bedlam of barking as Cindy went up the path. Elizabeth opened the door. "In the event you didn't know, the general has a great fondness for animals," she explained merrily. "We always know when a visitor is arriving."

General Custer was sitting in front of the fire. He was a tall, slim man with tanned features, short blond hair, and blue eyes. His bearing reflected the leadership and steely, headstrong courage that had earned him the brevet rank of major general and command of a Civil War division while only in his twenties.

While he was presently at the permanent rank of lieutenant colonel, it was a courtesy to address an officer by the highest grade he had held. "I'm very pleased to meet you, General Custer," Cindy said, returning his greeting. "Needless to say, I've heard very much about you."

"It's an honor indeed to host a world-famous artist," Custer replied gallantly. "My wife tells me that you're gathering material to make more etchings."

Cindy told the Custers about her recent travels, while Elizabeth poured glasses of wine for her guest and herself and a glass of juice for her husband, who never drank alcohol. While they were talking, a pet raccoon scurried through the room, followed a moment later by a squirrel.

Elizabeth smiled tolerantly. "George enjoys having them about. But once, while we were stationed in Kansas, he brought home a porcupine that tried to sleep on the end of our bed. I drew the line at that."

During dinner, mention was made of Henry at Fort Harland, and Cindy let the subject pass without comment; she knew that if the Custers suspected a romance between Henry and her, the colonel would promptly send for him. Cindy knew that Henry would be delighted to hear that she was in Bismarck and would gladly come to see her, but the last thing she wanted was to make an issue of her presence. In the hope of helping resolve her feelings, however, she intended to see him.

When she made a passing reference to the possibility of going to Fort Harland, the Custers reacted strongly. "Only if you travel with an escort," Elizabeth advised.

Custer agreed. "A traveler anywhere in the West can always run into Indians. There's also the changeable weather to consider."

The next day Cindy went to a livery stable to ask about renting a horse. She had thought about the Custers' advice, but she considered a trip to Fort Harland to be safer than many other things she had done alone. A horse could cover the distance in a single day if the road was in good condition.

"I'd like a good horse," she said to the owner, "one that can hold a canter without becoming winded."

"All right, ma'am. I'll be here before first light, and I'll have a good horse saddled up and waiting for you."

Cindy spent the rest of the day walking and sketching along the riverfront. When she returned to the hotel, she paid for her room several days in advance so she could leave her baggage in it and asked the desk clerk to have a lunch made up for her to take with her the next day.

The following morning, she was up before daylight, packing a change of clothing in a small bag. Carrying that and her lunch, she walked through the quiet streets to the stable, the cold wind tugging at her coat. Dawn was breaking as she rode out of town, her bag and lunch tied behind the saddle. Moments later, as the last houses fell behind, the only sign of civilization was the road, which was no more than a narrow ribbon of bare ground leading across the rolling, sage-covered terrain. But she had no fear of becoming lost; the only road was the one that led north to Fort Harland.

As Cindy passed over a ridge, she noticed dark clouds on the northern horizon, but Cindy dismissed them since the rest of the sky was completely clear and the sun shone on crusted snow, making its surface sparkle.

The young, strong mare cantered easily as the miles passed. Cindy fell into a reverie, thinking about what she would say to Henry. Seeing him again was the only way she could resolve her feelings, but he might misinterpret her visit as something more than it was. She pondered, choosing just the right phrases to explain her visit.

A hunger pang reminded her that the hours had passed and it was near midday. She looked around and was startled to see that the dark, thick clouds on the northern horizon had spread across most of the sky, blocking the sunlight.

When the mare crested the next ridge, an icy north wind almost took Cindy's breath away. The sagebrush thrashed in frigid gusts that sent snowflakes to sting her face. She reined her horse to a walk and admonished herself: The Custers had warned of the changeable weather, but she had dismissed that as a ploy to discourage her from going out alone. Now she knew they had been telling her the truth.

Because she was approximately halfway between Bismark and Fort Harland, Cindy decided to try to make it to the fort and urged her horse to a fast canter. But within minutes, she was blinded by a blizzard. The thick snow forced her to slow her horse to a walk.

When her horse plodded through deep sage, Cindy reined up, realizing she had lost the road. Certainly, she thought, the stable owner would send word about her to Fort Lincoln, the nearest fort, and search parties would be sent out.

All she had to do was stay alive until they found her.

Fighting off the driving compulsion to race around in search of any sign of civilization, she turned her horse to the east. With the snow coming from one side, both she and the horse were able to see a short distance ahead. After several minutes, the horse stopped at the edge of an arroyo, and Cindy led the animal into the shelter of a deep gulch, which was a watercourse during flash floods.

At a sharp curve she came upon a tangle of driftwood that had been deposited by the last flood. She tethered the horse, picked out a sheltered spot at the deepest part of the curve, and gathered sticks from the driftwood.

The wind put out her first match, creating a stab of fear, but the next one ignited the carefully placed slivers. She fed sticks and then a large limb to the fire as it blazed up. Next she unsaddled the horse, then carried the saddle and her belongings to the small circle of heat. With the saddle blanket wrapped around her feet and legs, she leaned back against the saddle. The fire warmed the sheltered nook, but the hours seemed to drag past.

The temperature remained about the same, and the blizzard continued throughout the night causing snow to drift deeply in the arroyo. At daybreak, as the wind and snowfall died away, the temperature plummeted.

After Cindy ate a few mouthfuls of food, she climbed out of the arroyo and to the top of an adjacent hill. In all directions, she saw nothing but rolling, snow-covered terrain. She returned to the arroyo and put live brushwood on the fire to make it smoke.

The day passed. Cindy collected fodder for her horse and kept thick smoke billowing up from the fire. The temperature continued to drop. The night was frigid, but she slept for an hour or two at a time, until the penetrating cold awoke her to build up the fire.

At dawn she again built up the fire, put brushwood on it, and ate the last of her food. Pulling her coat more tightly around her, she went out to gather fodder.

At midmorning she heard approaching hoofbeats. Relieved, she climbed out of the arroyo just as fifteen Indians rode down a slope toward it. The surprise was mutual. As she turned to run for her horse, a half-dozen Indians scrambled off their mounts and seized her. Their leader, a tall, long-muscled man with hawkish features and three feathers hanging from the back of his headband, shouted orders and pointed. Three Indians leapt down into the arroyo, quickly saddled Cindy's horse, tied her bag behind the saddle, and led the horse to her. They lifted her onto the horse and scrambled back onto their own.

"Can you understand me?" she asked their leader. "If you'll take me to Fort Lincoln or Fort Harland, you'll be given much gold!"

The leader rode alongside Cindy, snatched out his knife, and put the long, sharp blade to her throat in warning. The Indians laughed as the leader smiled sardonically. He turned away, and another Indian grasped Cindy's reins as the band rode to the top of the rise overlooking the arroyo, where they paused and carefully scanned the wilderness in all directions.

The leader grunted, pointed, and kicked his horse to a gallop. The others closed in around Cindy and followed him. She was numb with despair, afraid to even contemplate her fate. Stories of women who had been ransomed after years of captivity rose unbidden from her memory.

An hour passed, but nothing distinguished one mile of rolling hills from the last. Suddenly one of the Indians shouted and pointed behind. The leader looked back and shouted a command. As the Indians whipped her horse and theirs, Cindy, bouncing wildly on the saddle, turned to look and felt a surge of joy and relief: A cavalry patrol was coming across the crest of a hill.

With their horses running hard, the Indians at first began pulling away from the patrol, but soon their thin, shaggy mounts slowed, while the sleek, well-fed cavalry horses maintained a hard, fast canter. When the patrol closed the distance to a quarter mile, Cindy counted ten men, an officer, and four Indian scouts. The Indian ponies were panting heavily and beginning to falter, forcing her captives to rein up. They surrounded Cindy, holding their weapons ready.

The patrol stopped a hundred yards away, the soldiers deploying in a line abreast, with their rifles ready to shoulder. Cindy's heart lurched when she realized that the officer was Henry. He rode forward at a slow walk, and the four Indian scouts followed. As he approached, Cindy's captors closed in around her. The scouts reined up, but Henry continued riding forward, his face expressionless. When his horse was about two feet from the Indians' horses, he jabbed with his spurs, and the animal leapt forward.

The large, heavy cavalry mount slammed into the smaller ponies, creating a melee of plunging animals and furious protests from the Indians. Cindy almost fell from her saddle. She clutched the horn tightly until the confusion settled. Then Henry was directly in front of her, gazing at her as the Indians surrounded them.

Concern softened his eyes as he scanned her. When he saw that she was unharmed, his handsome features abruptly hardened. For the first time, she saw the man his enemies faced: brutal, dangerous, and cold. Compared to him, the Indians appeared almost benign. Henry's furious but silent rebuke was too much for her to bear. She turned away, tears stinging her eyes as her lips and chin began trembling.

Henry shook his head in amused resignation. "Please forgive my aggravation, Cindy, but the past hours have been anxious ones for me. You are all right, then?"

Cindy cleared her throat. "Yes, Henry," she croaked.

The Indians surrounding them overcame their confusion, and the leader bellowed something and shook his fist at Henry. With the man's fist inches from his face, Henry calmly drew off his cavalry gloves.

Perplexed by his indifference, the Indians watched Henry as he tucked the gloves under his belt, found a cigar, and lit it. He examined the glowing tip, tossed the match away, and turned to his scouts. "Ask them what they want to release the lady."

The scouts moved closer and with hate-filled glares communicated in language punctuated by exclamations.

"My scouts are Crow," Henry explained conversationally. "Mortal enemies of these Cheyenne."

Cindy watched them worriedly. Eventually negotiations broke off, and one of the scouts spoke to Henry. "They say no let lady go, sir. They say you ride away, no fight. You take lady, you die."

Henry nodded slightly. Puffing on his cigar, he glanced at a bird soaring high above the snowy landscape. He slid his rifle out of the saddle scabbard while the Indians, frowning suspiciously, leveled their weapons toward him. They watched in astonishment as Henry shouldered the rifle, cocked it, and aimed at the bird, which was barely more than a speck.

As he fired the Indians jeered for the second or so that the bullet sped upward. When feathers exploded from the bird and it fell from the sky, the Cheyenne quieted. The bird hit the ground some two hundred feet away, the thump clearly audible.

Henry turned to the scouts as he replaced his rifle in the scabbard. "Tell them I'm a very poor shot, compared to my men. Then ask them again what they want to release the lady."

The negotiations were brief and successful. "Sixty dollar, sir," a scout said. "Sixty dollar, gold."

After tossing away his cigar, Henry took out his purse, counted out the money, and handed it to the Cheyenne leader. As he reined his horse around and cleared a path for Cindy, he gestured to her to ride ahead of him. She heaved a sigh of relief and rode toward the patrol. Henry followed, his scouts behind him exchanging insults with the Cheyenne as they rode away.

"Harris," Henry called, "ride to Fort Lincoln and inform General Custer that he can call in his patrols. Jones, circle to the east and see if you can pick up Lieutenant Thompson's trail. Tell him to bring his patrol back to the fort. Keep an eye open for hostiles."

The men saluted, then galloped away as the others formed a column of twos. The scouts fell in at the rear, with Henry and Cindy at the front.

"No words can truly express my gratitude, of course," she told him. "Naturally, I'll repay your sixty dollars."

"No, you won't," he replied, laughing. "I've bought you, and you're not about to buy yourself back. I'm delighted that you decided to visit."

"Thank you, Henry." She paused, then forced

herself to say, "But please don't construe my visit to mean that my feelings have changed."

"I construe your visit only to mean that you're here, Cindy. That in itself means the world to me."

She smiled, pleased that there was no misunderstanding, and described her zigzag journey and the creative energy that had possessed her. As they talked, her ordeal seemed as though it had happened months before. She felt happy and cheerful.

In a way Henry now seemed more the man she had known and loved. The dark side of his nature was only a part of him; she could accept that frightening aspect because it had enabled him to survive treachery and assassination attempts. But other obstacles between them—including her own ambivalent feelings—were not so easy to accept or dismiss.

Fort Harland, she found, was as neat and orderly as she had expected it to be with Henry in command. He dismissed the patrol and led her across the quadrangle to his quarters.

After kindling a fire in the sitting-room fireplace, he gathered up his shaving gear and a few items from the bedroom. "I'll move in with my adjutant. We'll have dinner later, but in the meantime"—he opened a cabinet and pointed—"in here are pâté, caviar, Vienna sausage, bread, and so forth. Please help yourself."

Cindy thanked him, and after he left, she looked around in bemusement. At the remote fort, his quarters were charming. While she knew that he had immense wealth, she was certain he had bought none of the furnishings. The rosewood liquor cabinet, Persian carpet, and inlaid mahogany table had been chosen with infinite care by a woman who had loved him. Cindy knew these items had been selected as a means of reaching out across the distance to him. They did that now . . . across the greatest distance of all.

Her purpose in coming to Fort Harland and seeing Henry was suddenly fulfilled: A moment of penetrating insight swept aside all of her confusion and mixed feelings, allowing her to see the situation with total clarity: A ghost hovered between Henry and her, and before she could adjust to what had happened and start anew with Henry, she first had to make peace with the specter of Gisela von Kirchberg.

The remote outpost was like a beehive. Work details were constantly coming and going, repairing the fort walls and buildings, and those platoons not busy hammering and sawing were at military drill and training.

Since every American man was presumed to know how to shoot a gun and ride a horse, many commanders expected recruits to learn what they needed to know from the more experienced soldiers. At Fort Harland, however, all the soldiers benefitted from an organized training program.

A spatter of gunfire sounded from the firing range throughout the day. In addition to one course with straw dummies for saber practice, there was another with low hurdles for training in horsemanship. Noncommissioned officers attended lectures on discipline and leadership, and illiterate soldiers learned to read and write at night.

The vibrant atmosphere at the fort inspired Cindy. She did some of the finest sketches she had ever done. The ones she liked the most were of Henry dealing with his men. He was a disciplinarian but not a martinet. His men were loyal, for he had instilled in them pride, both in themselves and in the regiment.

Although Henry's good-bye embrace in Portland had left her pleasantly breathless, they avoided any physical contact now as if through unspoken agreement. Both seemed to understand it would only confuse matters.

In the time Henry and Cindy spent alone, she asked about Gisela, and Henry answered freely.

"Her business affairs came first," he told her at breakfast one day. "She never avoided pain, and as far as I know, she had no physical fear whatsoever. Those would have been distractions from her enterprises."

"But she loved you."

"Yes, but more than once she told me that she hated me because I took her attention away from her business ventures. Toward the end, though, she became more affectionate to those around her. When Peter was first born, she was indifferent to him, but she grew to love him."

Cindy was left with an impression of a beautiful,

but aggressive woman with a complex, charismatic personality.

"When I get back to Europe," she said, hoping to sound casual, "I might find myself in the vicinity of Fenton and Grevenhof. Would it be possible for me to visit the baroness's estates?"

"Of course, Cindy. I'll write letters for you to take to the stewards."

Later that day, Henry handed her two letters in unsealed envelopes, one in English and the other in German. Feeling impatient to visit those places where Gisela had chosen to spend her life—places that could prove intimately revealing—Cindy told Henry that she wanted to leave as soon as it was convenient to provide an escort.

Henry was scheduled to attend a conference at Fort Lincoln the next day, so he offered to accompany her to Bismarck.

Before daylight they left the fort at the head of a patrol. Custer had summoned Henry to show him a war plan from Washington, to be implemented in event of hostilities with the Sioux and Cheyenne. Custer, impressed with Henry's training regimen, wanted to implement training programs at Fort Lincoln; if full-scale war with the Indians did begin, the Seventh Cavalry, with a huge proportion of raw recruits, would be the main force, at the forefront of the battle. After Henry took her to her hotel, that thought haunted Cindy.

The following morning, Henry returned to the hotel and took Cindy to the stage station. A boy was selling newspapers there, and the headline announced the likelihood of war with the Indians. Knowing that she might never see Henry again, Cindy found it difficult to leave him with no word of encouragement. But unless she was prepared to make a full commitment to him, she could not in fairness say anything.

While they were waiting, Henry asked if her visit had helped her sort out her feelings.

"Not really, but we've revived the very good friendship that we once had," she said fondly.

"Your friendship is far more than I deserve," he said.

"Anyone who has your friendship is fortunate, Henry. You're an admirable man and the very finest of army officers."

"I'm also impossible to embarrass, or I'd be flushed red now," he joked, beckoning the boy and buying a newspaper, which he handed to Cindy. "Here, this will give you something to read for a few miles."

Cindy noticed an article about Indian raids along the Mexican border in Arizona.

"Toby and I discussed that when we met in Kansas City," Henry said when she pointed it out to him. "It's a small band of renegade Pima. If there were more of them or if they had good weapons, they might pose a serious threat to settlers and travelers."

"Let's hope they don't become anything more than an annoyance," Cindy said.

"We have more than enough around here to keep us occupied," Henry agreed wryly.

After the baggage was loaded, the other passengers boarded the stagecoach. As she and Henry gently kissed good-bye, Cindy had to fight back tears. He helped her into the stagecoach, then closed the door. As it moved away, Cindy looked through the window and waved, and Henry waved to her.

On a narrow dirt road southeast of Tucson, near the Mexican border, seven men stood beside a stagecoach, holding their hands in the air and trembling in terror. Twenty renegades had arrows notched and trained on the men, waiting for the order to kill.

The renegades' leader, a half-breed Pima named Setanka, slowly lifted a hand, savoring his victory as the pale, quaking passengers watched in dread. Before, with only twelve followers, Setanka had been limited to stealing livestock. But more men had joined him recently, enabling him to ambush the stagecoach. Four of his renegades now lay dead, but the stagecoach, a rich prize, was his.

Setanka laughed as he dropped his hand. "Now!"

Arrows thudded into the passengers, some of whom screamed in agony as they fell. "They're yours!" Setanka shouted.

Waving tomahawks and knives, the bloodthirsty renegades rushed forward. Several began scalping and pulling the clothes off the passengers,

109

who still moaned and twitched. Other Pima scrambled onto the top of the stagecoach and tossed the baggage down. Suitcases burst open, spilling clothes into the dirt.

Intent upon more valuable loot, Setanka climbed up to the seat and removed the weapons from the bodies of the driver and guard. When he saw the mailbox under the seat, he dragged it out and hurled it to the ground.

His men hammered at the lock with stones and tomahawks, then flung the top back. Setanka leapt down, elbowed the renegades aside, and threw away bundles of letters from the box. Then, finding a bag of gold coins, he held it up and danced joyfully. Money for guns had been his goal from the first. Now he had the means to buy Winchesters and Colts, the best of weapons. The achievement sobered him.

"Unhitch those horses!" he commanded, pointing to the teams harnessed to the stagecoach. "Gather everything! Hurry!"

The men complied as Setanka mounted his horse, clutching the gold. A few minutes later, he and his men were galloping across a wide valley, watching for cavalry patrols from Fort Peck and Fort Yuma.

On the other side of the valley, he turned toward the familiar rocky hills whose narrow valleys offered concealment. Once they were south of the hills, he and his men would be safe in Mexico, where cavalry was forbidden to follow.

Some sixty miles south of the border was the

town of Caveta, his base of operations. He had a tacit understanding with the Mexican army: It offered him no trouble as long as his raids were limited to north of the border. The people of Caveta feared Setanka and his men but welcomed the loot they brought to the town. And in Caveta was a merchant who traded north of the border and could obtain Winchesters and Colts. Once armed with these modern weapons, Setanka's renegades would be unstoppable.

VII

A few miles from Bern, Switzerland, Colonel Andrew Brentwood stepped out of a hired carriage at a railway construction site. The military attaché at the American embassy in Bern, Andrew was a tall, well-built man in his late thirties. Strong, handsome features and a touch of premature gray in his dark-brown hair gave him a distinguished air.

A bise, the local name for a sharp northerly wind, sliced across the construction site, a roadbed for the new railroad. Ahead was a sheer wall of granite. Turning up the collar of his uniform overcoat, Andrew strode toward six supervisors huddled in discussion.

"It appears that everything is ready, Herr Kruger," Andrew said, touching his cap.

"Yes, we will proceed very shortly, Colonel Brentwood," the engineer replied, bowing. "I don't believe you've met Herr Bjorgstrom, from the Nobel laboratories in Stockholm. He will instruct us on the placement of the explosive gelatin."

Two kilograms of the new gelatin had incredible explosive force, and the men planned to blast away the granite in a single, large explosion. The new explosive could be detonated by a simple timing device, eliminating wires and fuses, and Andrew had come to observe the operations to see if the gelatin might prove useful as ordnance.

One of Kruger's assistants ran up, breathless and distraught. "The new explosive is gone! The lock on the dynamite shed has been broken. And the new workman, Kramer, is missing!"

"Summon the police!" Kruger ordered. "That explosive is very dangerous!"

The man rushed away, leaving Kruger, Bjorgstrom, and the others to rage in anger. The operation indefinitely delayed, Andrew returned to his carriage for the trip to Bern.

He dismissed what had happened. His personal life was in such turmoil, he could scarcely think of anything else: Two years before, he had met the Duke and Duchess von Hofstetten, relatives of the Hapsburgs, who lived in Bern. The duke was a frail, temperamental eccentric; the duchess was a beautiful young woman with whom Andrew had fallen in love. Their mutual feelings were so intense that Lydia and Andrew had been swept into a love affair.

The real head of the family was Count von

Lautzenberg, an aged, crafty man who was the duke's uncle and an official at the court in Vienna. Knowing everything about everybody, he had merely warned Lydia and Andrew to be discreet. Lautzenberg's tolerance had seemed strange—until Andrew realized that he was being used to sire an heir to the duke's title. The duke, whose health had always been poor, was now seriously ill.

Andrew and Lydia's son, now a year old, had been christened Franz Wilhelm von Hofstetten. The count had warned Andrew that if he demanded any rights to his son, he would be cashiered from the army, and Lydia would be divorced from the duke and sent back to her family in disgrace.

To complicate matters further, Andrew was about to be transferred to Washington. Using all his influence, he had temporarily delayed the transfer; but matters were approaching a climax that promised to be extremely painful.

It was late afternoon when the carriage reached the ancient, staid city on the Aare River and the huge von Hofstetten town house. A daily visitor for the past two years, with the freedom of the house, he went straight upstairs to the duke's bedroom, where four doctors conferred in whispers at the foot of the immense canopied bed. Emil Villach stood in a corner. Nominally the duke's private secretary, he was, in fact, an employee of the count, who insured that the erratic duke did nothing to embarrass the family.

Andrew exchanged bows with Villach and the

doctors, then sat next to the bed. The duke smiled wanly, moving a hand across the silk coverlet toward Andrew. "My friend . . ." he mouthed weakly.

Andrew took the duke's hand. "You look much better today, Your Grace," he lied comfortingly. "How do you feel?"

"Somewhat better, I believe. I ate lunch."

"Well, that's an improvement, isn't it? Soon you'll be able to look at the artwork your agents have been purchasing for you."

The duke smiled with hope as Andrew continued talking. While Andrew was unsure if von Hofstetten suspected his love affair with Lydia, he was certain the man would be completely indifferent about it. Fanatically devoted to his art collection, he had always considered Lydia an intrusion upon his time.

After a few minutes, the duke fell asleep. The doctors smiled. "That is the first time His Grace has slept today, Colonel Brentwood," one whispered. "He is always more content when you are near."

Andrew nodded. He sincerely liked the man.

The door opened, and Andrew and the other men bowed as Lydia stepped in. The large, dim bedchamber suddenly seemed brighter, her presence like a cool, sweet-smelling breeze. A member of Rumanian royalty, she was radiantly beautiful, with blond hair and large blue eyes. With her air of innocence, she was the kind of woman whom men always rushed to protect.

Lydia curtsied gracefully, then spoke softly and at length with the doctors. No one could pinpoint the duke's ailment, but Andrew thought the man would fare better if the doctors would stop bleeding him.

"Thank you, and let us pray that His Grace continues to improve," she said earnestly when the doctors finished. "I will look in again later. Colonel Brentwood, will you keep me company at dinner?"

"Yes, thank you, Your Grace."

The doctors and Villach bowed, and Andrew followed Lydia out. In the hall he pointed upstairs, silently indicating the nursery. Lydia smiled and nodded, then turned toward the stairs to the third floor.

The nurse, a stout, middle-aged Austrian, was a woman Count von Lautzenberg trusted to be discreet. She cared for the baby, who looked like Andrew. And his sunny disposition reminded Andrew very much of Samuel, his son in Independence.

Andrew loved the boy deeply, and because Franz was the result of his ardent love for Lydia, the boy was even more precious. Lydia was similarly devoted to the child. She and Andrew played with Franz for a time before going down toward the dining room.

Andrew took Lydia's arm at a corner of the stairs and pulled her to him. Holding her close, he kissed her. "I love you, Lydia," he murmured against her lips.

"And I you, Andy."

They kissed again. Although she had been his lover for almost two years, Lydia blushed furiously as she smiled up at him. She paused outside the dining room, pressing her hands to her cheeks and composing herself; then they went inside. The hours passed swiftly in their total enjoyment of each other's companionship.

When it was time for Andrew to leave, Lydia went to the front door with him. They kissed in a dark corner of the entry. "You have heard no more about your transfer, Andy?"

"No, nothing."

She smiled in relief, then lifted her lips to his again. He kissed her once more, and left.

In his apartment a few blocks away, the tormenting uncertainty and anxiety of their predicament besieged Andrew with renewed force. He tossed in bed for hours before finally falling asleep.

Just before dawn, a knock on his door awakened him. A footman in the von Hofstetten livery handed him a note from Lydia. It concerned her husband, but Andrew's thoughts immediately went to the child. Minutes before, the baby had become Duke Franz Wilhelm von Hofstetten.

At nine o'clock that morning, Andrew met with American Ambassador Howard Ely and explained that the duke had died.

"I'm grateful that you thought to tell me about this, Andrew. I'll make certain that the embassy is properly represented at the funeral, of course.

In the meantime, you must devote yourself entirely to the situation."

Andrew returned to the von Hofstetten town house and joined Lydia in a drawing room. Although she had never loved the duke, she was genuinely saddened by his death.

Andrew also felt the loss, but he felt more worried about Lydia, their child, and himself. The duke's death had set events in motion, and he was unsure of what they were or where they would lead.

During the afternoon, Emil Villach came into the drawing room and asked them to accompany him; Count von Lautzenberg had arrived and wanted to see them.

The small, wizened octogenarian sat in front of the fireplace with a blanket wrapped around him. While his body was aged, he had an air of dictatorial, unyielding authority.

He bowed to Lydia from his chair. "Please accept my most sincere condolences for the tragic and untimely death of your husband," he rasped.

Lydia, fearing the count and always nervous in his presence, was uncharacteristically stiff as she curtsied. "Thank you, sir."

"Are you familiar with the provisions of your late husband's will, Your Grace?"

"No, sir."

"Briefly, it designates me to dispose of his estate as I see fit. I will arrange for you to be maintained in a manner befitting your station. I have brought in a group of lawyers and accountants to inventory the estate. I trust that their presence will not inconvenience or disturb you, Your Grace."

"It will not, sir."

"We are indeed fortunate to have a devoted friend of the family with us in our time of grief," the count continued, turning his startlingly bright eyes to Andrew. "Colonel Brentwood, I trust that you will be free of other commitments so you can comfort Her Grace in her distress and take the place of a family member and escort Her Grace during the funeral and on other occasions?"

"That will be an honor, sir."

"Very good," the count said, pulling his blanket closer. "We will speak more later."

Andrew and Lydia withdrew to the privacy of her apartment. They sat on the couch in her sitting room, Lydia's anxiety having overcome her sorrow.

"The count is unnerving, but he is not omnipotent, Lydia."

Lydia sighed and nodded, unreassured but simply dropping the subject.

When they went downstairs for dinner, there was a quiet bustle of activity as the lawyers and accountants conducted their inventory. The task was immense; the duke's art collection alone contained tens of thousands of etchings, prints, paintings, and other treasures. In a drawing room, clerks responded to the messages of condolence pouring in from all parts of Europe.

The count used a drawing room as an office to continue his official duties as interior minister for the Austro-Hungarian Empire. Aides carried a stream of telegrams from his offices at the court in Vienna.

On the day of the funeral, the cathedral was filled to overflowing. When Andrew and Lydia returned to the house, Villach brought them to see the count.

He again bowed from his chair, then mentioned the inventory of the estate. "It will take a few more days, Your Grace, but in the meantime, what do you wish to do? Would you like to return to your family in Rumania?"

"No, sir," Lydia replied, surprised. "I wish to stay here, with my child."

"His Grace is to be taken to Vienna," the count announced, "to be raised and educated in appropriate surroundings. I suggest that you not attempt to follow him there. You will not be allowed to see him."

"You can't take a mother's child from her!" Andrew cut in angrily.

"This does not concern you!" the count retorted harshly. "Colonel Brentwood, you would be well-advised not to meddle in this."

"More than meddle, sir, I'll broadcast it. When people know about this, all of Europe will rise up against you."

The count's face momentarily darkened with anger; then he controlled his temper. Sighing, he sat back in his chair. "You are a sensible man, Colonel Brentwood. Surely you realize that I could easily discredit whatever you say."

"People could be made to know the truth, sir."

"Nothing is easier to manipulate than the truth," the count said patiently. "I do it daily. If you wish to be of assistance, help Her Grace to adjust. If she desires to remain in Bern, so be it. If she would like to marry a certain army officer and vacate her title, that is also up to her. But my decisions regarding the duke are irrevocable."

"I see." Andrew fell silent, as though he were considering what the count had recommended. Then he left with Lydia, who was in tears. He took her upstairs to her apartment, where he quietly explained the only course open to them.

"But he will find out," Lydia objected fearfully.

"It's the only thing we can do, Lydia," Andrew insisted.

She reluctantly agreed. Andrew talked with her a few minutes longer, then left for the American embassy, where he sent a telegram to the director of personnel at the War Department in Washington. He requested that his transfer be put into effect immediately and that he be granted a leave of absence before reporting for duty.

The anchorage at Port Said, Egypt, was crowded with vessels of all sizes and descriptions.

Captain Sterch nodded to Edward. "We're ready to go ashore, Mr. Blackstone. I'll make arrangements for our passage through the canal while you're interviewing that explorer fellow."

"Very well, Captain." Edward spotted Edgar

120

Dooley on the quarterdeck. "Come on, Edgar! We're ready to go."

"You go ahead," Dooley replied. "I'll be along later."

"Come with us, Edgar. What on earth is wrong with you?"

The Irishman shrugged and came down from the quarterdeck with slow, reluctant steps. Edward frowned suspiciously. Instead of being amused whenever the explorer had been mentioned, Dooley now acted guilty and apprehensive.

Dooley, Sterch, and Edward went down the rope ladder and into a boat that weaved among anchored vessels toward the docks.

At last the waterfront of Port Said was in clear view, and Edward scanned the piers, which teemed with activity. He saw only one European. He started to look at the other piers more closely, but the truth suddenly dawned on him.

He glared angrily at Edgar. Recalling the names of the earl of Banbridge's children, he thought of one that fit: The explorer was Lady Theodora Montague.

She was a tall, stocky, large-boned woman in her thirties. She was wearing sturdy hiking boots, an ankle-length, dark-brown skirt, a man's hickory shirt, and a hunting coat with bullet loops over the pockets. Her choice in headgear, which made her appear even taller, was an Indian army officer's pith helmet, with a high crown and long, low peaks to shade her face and the back of her neck.

Her clothing, obviously chosen for comfort and durability, was meticulously neat. Her boots gleamed and she wore a tie around her shirt collar. Spotting Edgar, she waved and called out in a powerful, contralto voice that boomed across the water, "Edgar, you old rascal, are you on your way to jail, or from it?"

Grinning lopsidedly and avoiding Edward's eyes, Dooley waved weakly. As the boat drew up to the pier, he scrambled for the ladder to get away from Edward. The woman reached down, gripping his hand, and effortlessly hauled the portly man up to the dock. She greeted him boisterously, hugging him and slapping his back as he grinned and wheezed.

Dealing with the situation as best as he could, Edward climbed up the ladder, smiled politely, and put out his hand. "Lady Theodora Montague, I believe. I'm Edward Blackstone."

"I'm very pleased to meet you, Mr. Blackstone," she replied, "but Lady Theodora is my grandmother. I'm Teddy Montague."

As her large, warm hand clasped his firmly, Edward had second thoughts; he had known both capable women and ineffective men. She had the total assurance of the upper class, plus a competent, resourceful air. She seemed filled with energy and enthusiasm, her blue eyes sparkling in her round, rosy face. An ebulliently outgoing woman, she instilled the impression of being utterly trustworthy.

Captain Sterch muttered and nodded uncomfortably as Edward introduced them. Immediately realizing from the captain's attitude that he had been expecting another man, Teddy gripped Edgar's collar and yanked him to her. "I say, I do believe we've been Dooleyed, Mr. Blackstone," she remarked. "Now I know why your telegrams were addressed to *Mr.* Montague. Shall I chuck him into the drink and teach him a lesson?"

"No, don't do that," Edward replied, laughing. "He did me a favor. It shames me to admit it, but I would have probably made an unwise decision if he'd told me you were a woman. Let's get acquainted while Edgar and the captain see about getting clearance for the *Galatea* through the Suez Canal. And call me Edward."

"Very well, Edward," Teddy said, releasing Dooley and giving him an affectionate slap on the back that staggered him. "I'm eager to hear about your project, so we'll go to my lodgings, if you like."

The captain and Dooley took their leave.

From remarks she made, he got the impression she was at loose ends in Egypt because of a shortage of funds. Knowing her family was wealthy, he concluded that they had become reluctant to finance her expensive and unusual adventures.

His conclusions were supported when discussing her trip from Cairo to Port Said to meet Edward. She shook her head after he remarked that she had traveled by boat. "I came across the desert on a caravan. That takes only a day or two longer than by steamer, and it costs pence instead of guineas."

"A more memorable journey, I'm sure," Edward added. "But uncomfortable, which would prompt some to forgo it."

"Those who want comforts should stay at home," she remarked.

They turned down another narrow, crowded street. Instead of a European hotel, Teddy had chosen the spartan and thriftier accommodations of an ancient, sun-baked stucco Egyptian hostel. The rickety stairs swayed and squeaked under Edward's and Teddy's weight.

After unlocking a large, strong padlock, Teddy led him inside. The small, austere room was spotless and neat. Teddy's gun cases drew Edward's interest, and she showed him her weapons: The carefully cleaned and oiled rifles and shotguns were among the best available, and Edward commented admiringly.

"This is my pride and joy," she said, wiggling her eyebrows and opening the last case. "Jennings and Franklin of London custom made it for me."

At first Edward thought it was a double-barreled shotgun, but then he saw that the gleaming barrels were rifled. "What caliber is it?"

"It's a sixty-five two-forty."

"My word!" he exclaimed. "It isn't a rifle, it's a hand held cannon! Sixty-five caliber is exceptionally large, even for an elephant gun."

"It'll stop one in his tracks, though," she explained, replacing the rifle in the case. "As well as a water buffalo or rhino, which can be even nastier than an elephant. Well, let's make ourselves comfortable."

She moved a small table and stools to the window and opened the shutters, while Edward hung his coat and hat on a hook. When she took off her coat and turned up her shirt cuffs, he noticed a scar on her sturdy forearm. "I got that in Tibet," she said, observing his glance, "from a Sherpa. For the most part, they're some of the most trustworthy people in the world. But when you find one who's a rogue, you have a really bad egg to deal with. This one sneaked into my tent to see what he could steal, then gave me that chop when I kicked up a fuss."

"I trust that you returned the favor, but sliced him under his chin rather than on an arm? . . ."

"No, I wouldn't have left Tibet alive. If you kill a Sherpa, his whole village will turn on you."

"What did you do?"

"I boxed his ears, held him down, and dumped a shovelful of hot coals in the seat of his breeches. The others laughed their heads off, watching him hop around and slap his bum. I made more friends in the village from that. . . ."

Edward laughed, enjoying the story. Teddy took a fire-blackened billycan from a canvas bag, went out on the balcony, and shouted to a vendor, then tossed the billy down to him. A moment later, the vendor came up to the room with the billy full of dark, steaming coffee. Edward gave him a coin.

"I see that you use ingenuity and knowledge of local customs in dealing with natives," Edward remarked. "I'm sure it takes that, to stay alive."

"And more," Teddy added, rummaging in a bag. She turned toward Edward, her hands empty. Then, as she gesticulated swiftly, two tin cups miraculously appeared in her hands. "Tricks such as that amaze primitive people, so I worked at them until I became quite proficient. On a few occasions, sleight of hand has enabled me to avoid being invited to dinner as the main course."

Laughing, Edward reflected that she was remarkable; instead of relying on modern weapons to intimidate natives, as many explorers did, she used her wits and careful preparation. Teddy sat at the table and filled the cups with thick, sweet coffee, flavored with cardamom seeds.

"So you're going to Brazil," Teddy remarked. "I was there about four years ago. I spent about six months inland from Rio de Janeiro, collecting botanical specimens for the Royal Gardens of Kew. I also learned to speak passable Portuguese."

"Did you get on well with the authorities?"

She shrugged. "No one can take a blade of grass out of Brazil without arousing suspicions. The authorities are afraid their monopoly on rubber will be broken if someone steals rubber—" Her eyes widened as her quick mind grasped his purpose.

Edward nodded slowly. "Yes, that's what I have in mind. There is a potential for huge profits—or for a very long term in a Brazilian prison. What do you think about it, Teddy?"

"I'd like to go with you," she replied with alacrity. Her blue eyes danced with excitement, and she started to say more, then stopped herself.

Edward could see that she was too proud to try to talk him into taking her, but she urgently wanted to go. He was already convinced that she could do anything required of her, and more. He had never met anyone he liked better.

"Very well," he said brightly. "I'll pay all your expenses, and you'll get ten percent of any net profit. How does that sound?"

A beaming smile on her round, ruddy face, Teddy nodded happily as she reached out and pumped Edward's hand.

The day after a majority of trustees of the Reed Kerr Memorial Hospital voted to curtail Janessa's work there, she was sitting at Dr. Martin's bedside.

"How I could have let McDowell get the better of me," he murmured in a hoarse, trembling voice.

"Dr. Martin," Janessa said patiently, "Alexandra's in the same position you are. The difference is, she's taking it as a setback instead of a defeat."

"Mrs. Holt is an intelligent, energetic young woman, but she hasn't spent the years here that I have, working all hours of the day and night."

127

"Dr. Martin, the trustees didn't vote against you because they don't know that; they voted against you because they disagreed with you."

The elderly man fell silent. The previous day at the trustee meeting, he had become so enraged that he had fainted. Janessa helped to bring him home and had been at his bedside every possible minute since then. He was very weak and still furiously angry. Janessa feared he would suffer a stroke or a heart attack.

Urgently wanting to smoke, she smothered a heavy sigh. Ever since the night she had thrown her cigarettes away, there had been periods when she would go for hours without even thinking about smoking. At other times it was impossible to think of anything else.

Hearing approaching footsteps and voices, Janessa looked up to see Dr. Wizneuski in the doorway, and behind him was Dr. Martin's wife, a sweet, white-haired woman.

"Now what is this, Robert?" Wizneuski demanded jovially. "What are you doing in bed when there are ill people who need you?"

"Go tell the trustees how many patients are around," Dr. Martin retorted weakly. "In their opinion, healing sick people is secondary to their idea of behaving appropriately."

"Well, we'll deal with that when the time comes, Robert. In the meantime, you have a very nice clinic right here in your house. Why don't you and Janessa work here?"

Janessa knew that Dr. Martin would be unyielding. As she looked at his pale, drawn face and trembling hands, she felt a shiver of fear.

As the ranch wagon moved along the road beside the river, Tim Holt turned to Calvin Rogers. "Mr. Gooch wasn't much help, was he?"

"No, but he's always been very secretive about his inventions. When we go to Philadelphia this summer, we'll probably see several kinds of ice-making machines." He shivered in the cold wind. "And July will be a better time to think about them, won't it?"

"Yep." Tim said and laughed. Wanting to do something nice for Alexandra, he had hit upon the idea of building an ice-making machine. She liked ice for her lemonade, but Janessa had warned that river ice was unsafe to use. Rufus Gooch, a reclusive inventor living near the river, had such an invention, but he had adamantly refused to let Tim and Calvin see it, much less offer advice on building one.

Pulling his coat closer, Tim looked out over the river, where scattered, thin sheets of ice floated downstream. The thick, solid ice that would be collected and stored in the Portland icehouse was far upstream, where it would remain until the spring thaw.

When he noticed a boat upriver, he pointed it out to Calvin. "Benny McDowell is in that boat."

The man frowned. "What in the world is the boy doing?"

"Something he shouldn't," Tim replied, "because he has no business being out on the river."

"Well, don't be *too* critical," Calvin advised. "It hasn't been all that long since you acted foolishly like that yourself."

"That's true," Tim acknowledged. His eyes narrowed. "He's not paddling. Do you think he's in trouble?"

Calvin stopped the wagon. "I was wondering that myself."

They watched as the boat floated downstream toward them, a hundred yards from the bank and low in the water. The boy held onto the side and looked back toward the docks. Then he saw Tim and Calvin. "Help! Help me! I lost the oars, and the boat is leaking!"

Tim leapt from the wagon, then tore off his coat and boots. "No, Tim, no!" Calvin barked. "You can't swim out there. We'll go for a boat and get help."

"We don't have time, Calvin. That boat will sink before we can get anywhere near the docks."

Calvin fell silent. The tall, muscular boy had suddenly displayed his father's self-possessed, resolute air.

Tim dived into the frigid water. Surfacing, he swam with long, hard strokes, looking at the boat each time he took a breath. The river current was carrying it rapidly downstream; he estimated the distance it would travel by the time he reached it and angled toward that point.

Thirty feet from the bank, he ran into a thin,

soft sheet of ice several feet across. He swam straight through it, but it slowed him. He compensated, adjusting his estimate and angling deeper downstream.

The numbing effect of the cold water began to take its toll. His arms and legs felt sluggish, but he forced himself to keep moving. He fought his way through another sheet of ice, breaking the ice with his forearms.

When he was a hundred feet from the boat, he saw it was very low in the water. Benny, a small, thin boy of eight, was in tears. "Hurry, Tim, hurry! It's about to sink!"

The gunwale tipped precariously close to the surface of the water as the boy stood and reached out. Tim sacrificed precious concentration and energy to shout, "Sit down, Benny! *Sit down!*"

The gunwale tipped under the surface, and the boat rolled, pitching Benny headlong into the water. Tim expended every effort to reach the boat. It turned completely over, its mossy bottom just above the surface of the water. Tim could see no sign of Benny.

Ten feet from the boat, Tim dived and groped in the icy water until his lungs burned for air. He surfaced, gulped in a deep breath, dived, and felt around in the water again. Still not finding Benny, Tim came up for air, then continued diving. Knowing the boy would float downstream at about the same speed as the boat, Tim stayed near it and searched the water.

The numbing cold penetrated his bones, and

he felt dizzy. When he surfaced, he heard Calvin screaming at him to give up. Trying one more time and then just once more, Tim kept diving around the boat. As he surfaced, his hand brushed something. He snatched at it, and gripping Benny's hair, he pulled the boy to the surface.

The boy was limp, and Tim used the last of his energy to pull the boy toward the bank. But his arms and legs felt like lead. He tried to concentrate on keeping Benny's head above water, but he himself was starting to sink.

The water seemed soft and inviting, making him want to slide down and rest. Everything seemed to be a dream, his struggle pointless. But something within him made him continue the effort to swim toward the dim, blurred bank that reeled in front of him.

Standing in the shallow water, Calvin pulled Tim and Benny up onto the bank. The air felt unbearably cold to Tim, and uncontrollable tremors rattled him. He gulped in deep breaths, his body demanding more air than he could inhale. Calvin rolled Benny onto his stomach and lifted him in the center of his body, trying to get the water out of his lungs and stomach.

"This isn't doing any good, and I'm not sure he's breathing, Tim. We'll have to get him to the hospital."

Tim, trying to get up on his hands and knees, fell flat. He shook his head, panting. "Dr. Martin's house," he gasped. "Janessa at Dr. Martin's house."

"Yes, but Dr. Wizneuski has all the—"

"Dr. Martin's house! Janessa knows more than ten doctors!"

Calvin hoisted Benny in his arms. "All right, Tim," he said, hurrying toward the wagon.

Gathering his strength, Tim managed to lift himself to his hands and knees by the time Calvin came back. The man helped him up to his feet and supported him. They staggered to the wagon, where Tim crawled into the back and lay beside Benny as Calvin scrambled to the seat and gathered up the reins.

The horses lunged into a headlong run as Calvin whistled shrilly and whipped the reins. The wagon bounced wildly along the road, and Tim was rolled along on the hard boards as the wagon slid around a corner and onto a main street. Calvin, standing in the front seat and snapping the reins, bellowed, "Make way, there! Make way!"

Others took up the cry, shouting at vehicles and riders to get out of the way as the wagon sped down the center of the street. Someone shouted a question, and Calvin replied, "It's Benny Mc-Dowell! Fetch his family to Dr. Martin's house!"

The wagon raced through the streets until it careened into the quieter avenue where the doctor lived. Heartsick, Tim looked at Benny. The boy was absolutely lifeless.

Gripping the edge of the seat, he lifted himself and saw the doctor's house ahead. "Janessa!" he shouted. "Janessa! *Janessa!*"

When Janessa heard the frantic note in Tim's distant shout, stark terror seized her. She burst from the bedroom, raced down the hall, and slammed out the front door at a headlong run as the wagon drew up at the house.

She leaped into the wagon and had her arms around Tim, her eyes searching his face before dread fear relaxed its grip. Seeing he was in no mortal danger, she pushed his damp hair back from his face and kissed him as he shook with cold. She turned to the McDowell boy as Calvin explained what had happened.

Wizneuski and Dr. Martin's wife, Tonie, had followed Janessa out, and now the stocky doctor carried the McDowell boy inside as Calvin, Tonie, and Janessa helped Tim along the path. The girl impatiently interrupted Calvin as he praised Tim's heroism. "It bordered on the insane. Mrs. Martin, please get him in front of a hot fire as soon as possible."

"Certainly," Tonie agreed. "I'll build up the parlor fire and make some hot cocoa for him."

Dr. Martin called from his bedroom and asked what had happened. Wizneuski, carrying the boy into the examination room, explained briefly. The crisis energized the aged doctor; he emerged from the bedroom in his slippers, tying the belt on his robe. As Calvin and Tonie half carried Tim into the parlor, Janessa followed Dr. Martin into the examination room and closed the door.

The doctors shook their heads somberly. The

boy had no pulse and was not breathing. They turned him onto his stomach and lifted him, hoping to drain water from his stomach and lungs, then went through other traditional procedures. Janessa heard the McDowells and the boy's mother arrive in a staccato of anxious, tearful voices.

Wizneuski finally shook his head and sighed heavily. "It's no use, Robert. The boy is gone."

"I'm afraid so," Dr. Martin agreed sadly. "The last words that McDowell and I exchanged were harsh ones, so it would be much better for you to be the one to tell the family."

"No doubt, Robert. The boy needs to be dried off and cleaned up some before the family sees him."

"All right, keep them out for a few minutes. You might need something to calm the mother and grandmother. If you do, there are opium pills and laudanum in the cabinet out there."

Wizneuski left, opening the door minimally and closing it behind him. The elderly doctor took a surgical towel and began wiping the boy's face. Janessa studied Benny, convinced that she was looking at a living human being. She felt a demanding compulsion to do something to revive him.

Years before, her mother had told her about a technique Indian healers employed to revive people who had drowned or been near where lightning struck. To restore breathing and heartbeat they blew tobacco smoke into the victim's mouth and pressed the chest over the heart to make it beat.

Janessa's mother, Mary White Owl, had expressed doubts about the tobacco smoke, telling her daughter that simply forcing air into the patient's lungs was better. In the light of what Janessa had learned since then, she knew her mother had been correct; although the smoke might cause irritation and make the patient cough up water, what was needed most of all was oxygen.

Going to the table, she drew in a deep breath, pinched the boy's nostrils closed, positioned her lips over his mouth, and forced her air into him. She felt his chest rise. Then, straightening, placing her left hand over her right, she put the heel of her palm on his chest and heaved her weight down, to compress his heart and make blood surge through his veins.

As she repeated the process, the old doctor watched her curiously. "What are you doing, Janessa?"

"Something I learned from my mother." Janessa panted, pushing on the boy's chest.

"Does it work?"

Janessa shrugged as she inhaled. She forced air into the boy's lungs, then pushed on his chest again. "Sometimes," she gasped. "It must depend on how long the patient has stopped breathing and other things."

After Dr. Martin watched her a moment longer, he opened the door a crack and called to Wizneuski, who came back into the room. Janessa heard grief-stricken weeping in the parlor, with Tonie Martin murmuring in consolation.

Dr. Martin quietly repeated what Janessa had told him.

"It seems reasonable," Wizneuski allowed. "Of course, nothing will revive the dead, and we certainly wouldn't want to raise the family's hopes."

"Certainly not. I'm not capable of relieving Janessa, but I thought you might want to. She looks like she's going to give out any minute."

"I'm willing to try anything. Here, let me take over for you, young lady."

Exhausted, she reeled back from the table as Wizneuski forced a deep breath into the boy's lungs. She stumbled to a chair and sat down heavily, bending over to get blood to her brain. After a moment she sat up to watch.

Wizneuski went through the steps of the technique over and over, his round, ruddy face becoming even more flushed. After a few minutes, his breathing became labored. Janessa returned to the table.

Knowing that Wizneuski had less confidence in the method than she did, she continued for as long as possible. Dizzy from lack of oxygen, she numbly kept going until her legs were weak. When Wizneuski took over again, she collapsed in the chair and put her head between her knees, then drew in deep, rapid breaths.

After they took several more turns each, Wizneuski was for giving up. Although she was barely

137

starting to recover, Janessa pushed herself to her feet and staggered back to the table.

"It's not doing any good, my dear," Dr. Martin advised her gently as she forced air into Benny's lungs. "Maybe it does work sometimes, but you've given it a good try, and it's just not—"

He broke off as Janessa started to push on the boy's chest and the boy suddenly gagged and vomited, the water from his lungs and stomach gushing out his mouth. "Good Lord in heaven!" the old doctor exclaimed. "It's working! A corpse can't cough!"

Wizneuski was elated. Janessa, feeling contractions in the boy's stomach, turned him onto his side. Water from his stomach spewed from his mouth as he continued coughing and choking up water from his lungs.

Wizneuski stepped back to the table and took Benny's wrist. "He has a pulse, Robert!" he whooped. "The boy has come back around!"

"He certainly has!" Dr. Martin agreed happily. "Here, let me see to him, Janessa. You're almost falling off your feet, my dear. Anton, I think it's safe for you to tell the family. Bring them in to see him in a moment or two."

Beaming, Wizneuski turned toward the door. Dr. Martin worked over the boy as Janessa returned to the chair, trembling in exhaustion.

Just after Wizneuski went out, jubilant exclamations erupted in the parlor. A few minutes later, he led the family into the examination room, warning them to be quiet. Both the middle-aged couple

138

and the younger woman wept with joy as they looked at the boy.

"This makes me very ashamed of what I did," McDowell confessed to Janessa and Dr. Martin. "I intend to go to each of the hospital trustees and explain how wrong I was and rectify what I did."

Dr. Martin, struggling to be gracious and forgiving, was fighting a losing battle. "Well," he muttered gruffly, "I told you that Janessa has much to offer. Anton and I have been doctors for a long time, but she taught us something new today."

"Yes, that's what Dr. Wizneuski told me," McDowell replied. He turned to Janessa. "Miss Holt, I'll be grateful to you for the rest of my life for saving my grandson's life."

"My brother was the one who saved his life, sir. I'd better settle him in bed at home so he doesn't become ill."

Janessa went into the parlor to find Tim sitting in front of the fireplace, talking animatedly with Calvin. The McDowells offered them heartfelt thanks. Janessa borrowed some of Rob Martin's clothes from Tonie to put around the boy, then left with Calvin and him.

At the ranch Tim rebelled against the suggestion that he go to bed. After changing into warm, dry clothes, he went out to join White Elk at a corral while Janessa told Alexandra about the afternoon's events.

"He's his father's son, and he did what he had

to," Alexandra said. "And, I might add, you're your father's daughter."

"I guess so," Janessa replied. "But I'd better get upstairs and do some studying, or Dad will disown me. I haven't been doing well on quizzes lately."

Janessa went to her room. As she started to sit down at her desk, her glance passed over her bureau. She stepped to it and took the packages of cigarettes downstairs to toss them into the fireplace. After surviving the turmoil of the past hours without a cigarette, she no longer needed one.

VIII

Moving quietly through the cold, late night darkness, Andrew Brentwood found the side door of the von Hofstetten town house more by feel than by sight. He tapped on it softly, and it immediately opened, the scent of Lydia's perfume wafting out.

"Andy? Is it you?" Her voice quavered with tension.

"Yes, darling. Everything is ready. Do you have a bag?"

"Yes, here. The nurse fell asleep only a few minutes ago, so I will go for the baby and return in a moment." Her hand found his in the dark to pass a carpetbag to him. The door closed soundlessly, leaving Andrew to wait. His telegraphed request for transfer and leave of absence having been immediately approved, he and Lydia had been preparing during the past days to flee the country with their child.

Acting as though they had accepted the count's demands, Lydia and Andrew made their secret preparations against a continuing background of activity in the house. Andrew had surreptitiously sent Lydia's most treasured possessions to the United States with his belongings. She had secretly collected one of the maid's plain dresses for the first stage of the journey, while he had set aside his own civilian clothing to wear.

Andrew was thankful for the darkness, but he longed to glance at his watch. His bag was in a hired carriage waiting down the street, and the train tickets were in his pocket. The train left in a matter of minutes; everything was timed so he and Lydia could avoid waiting at the station, where they might be recognized. Any delay would be disastrous.

The door opened again, and Lydia stepped out, carrying their child swathed in a heavy blanket. Andrew guided her to the waiting carriage.

As he helped her inside, Andrew said to the driver, "To the train station! And hurry, please!"

The carriage lurched forward, throwing Andrew down hard into his seat. He put an arm around Lydia and whispered reassuringly. The train station finally came into view—an island of bright light in the darkness. The carriage stopped, and Andrew climbed down and handed money to the driver.

Andrew heard a train whistle hoot. He ran

through the station, carrying the bags, and Lydia ran after him with their son in her arms. Reaching the platform just as the train was beginning to move, Andrew helped Lydia up the steps of a third-class car and breathed a sigh of relief. They settled themselves into the already moving car.

Lydia was wearing a deep bonnet—Andrew's suggestion, because her lovely face always drew attention. Dressed like a Swiss couple of modest means, they sat isolated near the center of the car, where they could avoid being drawn into conversation.

Although she had fulfilled her part of the arrangements, Lydia was still convinced that the count would find out about their plan.

"It's obvious that he hasn't found out," Andrew soothed. "We wouldn't be here with our son, would we?"

"We are still well within the reach of his authority."

"But Franz always sleeps until morning, so there's no reason why the nurse would check on him and raise an alarm. By then, we'll be in France. There's only one way out of Switzerland, but once we reach France, we can choose among many routes and means of travel."

"Andy, I have never known the count to be outwitted."

Andrew smiled, although he privately shared Lydia's fears.

The hours seemed to drag. The other passengers slept, but Andrew and Lydia remained awake and jumpy. Finally, during the early hours of the morning, the train slowed for the border crossing.

"They will check our papers here," Lydia said fearfully.

"It's only a formality," Andrew assured her.

The village on the Switzerland-France border was dark and quiet, but at the customs office adjacent to the train station, there was more activity than usual. Instead of a single sleepy guard boarding the train to glance at papers, a captain and two sergeants entered the car and ordered the conductor to turn up the lights.

For a moment Andrew was as anxious as Lydia; then, he relaxed—the guards were checking closely only the men traveling alone. "The authorities must still be searching for that man I mentioned, the one who stole the explosives."

Lydia forced a wan smile as the captain touched his cap to Lydia and walked on. The delay was long, but Andrew knew it had to end eventually, and safety was only a matter of a few yards away.

A fourth guard jogged through the car, carrying a telegram and obviously looking for the captain. Andrew momentarily considered fleeing with Lydia and their son, but he knew that they would be unable to get far on foot, and it would be dangerous to expose their child to the severe cold. He rationalized that the telegram could be notification that the man who had stolen the explosives had been apprehended. But that feeble hope withered as the guards came back into the car, eyes riveted on Andrew.

"Your papers, please." The captain was courteous but firm. He glanced at the papers. "You and the lady will please come with me."

"May I ask why?" Andrew said.

"I believe you know why, sir," the captain replied, handing Andrew the telegram. "But this should resolve any question."

It was as Andrew had feared. Returning the telegram, he took Lydia's arm. She clutched the baby and burst into tears. The captain, clearly discomfited by the situation, brusquely ordered his men to bring the bags, then led Andrew and Lydia to the customs building's spartan waiting rooms. Lydia, weeping, sat and rocked the year-old baby as the guards brought in the bags and kindled a fire in the fireplace. The captain disappeared for a moment and returned with a bottle of schnapps and glasses. "A drink may help the lady feel better," he suggested apologetically. "If you need anything else, knock on the door."

Andrew thanked the captain gratefully, knowing that kindness and consideration would soon be rare. By the law, Lydia and he were guilty of kidnapping. He could expect a long prison term and a dishonorable discharge from the army, while she would probably be deported to Rumania, penniless and in disgrace.

The captain closed the door, and the lock clicked firmly. "We are ruined, Andy," she murmured mournfully, looking up at the barred windows. "We are ruined, and all is lost."

"Yes, I'm afraid so. I'm very sorry I got you into this, Lydia."

"We had to do something, Andy. We had to make some effort to resist."

He held her close, dreading a separation from her—she meant more to him than life. She clung to him, wanting him to hold her during the few hours that they had together.

When dawn broke, it was a bleak, overcast day that matched the most depressed state Andrew had ever experienced. An hour later, a train arrived, consisting of only a lounge car, a passenger car, and a caboose behind the locomotive. The windows of the lounge car were steamed up from the heat being turned on high. Soon the waiting-room door opened, and the captain beckoned them. In the lounge car, the count was seated in a deep chair and wrapped in blankets. Villach stood behind him, flanked by several aides and four policemen. The nurse came from the rear of the car with outstretched hands. Lydia kissed the fretting child before reluctantly handing him over.

The policemen moved toward Andrew, but the count stopped them. "Wait in the other car," he rasped.

One of them protested. "This man is guilty of—"

"Do as you are told!" the count barked. "I will send for you if you are needed."

Andrew glanced at Lydia. She too had caught the implication and looked with hope at Andrew. The policemen left, the nurse following them with the baby, and the count turned to Andrew. "You did a very stupid thing, Colonel Brentwood."

"I did what I had to do, sir."

"I would gladly see the two of you suffer the most severe penalty, but that would be self-indulgent and could lead to publicity I would rather avoid. You can either be married immediately and leave Europe, or I will risk that publicity. I strongly suggest you choose marriage."

Exchanging a glance, Andrew and Lydia nodded in agreement. The count turned to Villach. "Fetch the village burgomaster, and tell him to bring his marriage registry."

Villach bowed and left. Andrew put an arm around Lydia, leading her to a seat as she struggled to maintain her composure. A few minutes later, Villach returned with a pudgy man who, eager to please the count, performed the ceremony quickly.

When the certificate was completed, the burgomaster handed it to Andrew, who numbly led Lydia to the small train station, where they waited, racked with sorrow, for the next train into France.

Edward Blackstone's reception in Calcutta left no doubt that the East India Company was genuinely interested in his project. When the *Galatea* anchored in the teeming harbor, a company boat came out to the ship and allowed them to bypass the customs inspection. Robert Toland, a company official, was present, along with several aides.

Brought to the port master's large, well-furnished reception room, Edward was greeted warmly by his uncle, a hearty, jovial man of fifty. Winslow's attractive wife, Mathilda, exchanged a hug and kiss with Edward. But the one who held the center of his attention was Ramedha Cochrane.

Slender and of medium stature, she had delicate, lovely features, along with thick, glossy black hair and large, expressive eyes an unusual shade of gold. Edward bowed over her hand, almost overwhelmed by her exquisite beauty. "This moment more than repays the journey, Ramedha," he said.

"As it does my wait," she replied in her soft, melodious voice. "Welcome back to India, Edward."

Edward introduced Teddy. Dooley, well-known to everyone, was regarded with friendliness mixed with caution because of the trouble he had created for the East India Company from time to time.

Toland handed Edward a folder. "This is a confidential agreement we've drawn up. We propose to establish a subsidiary company, with you as a principal shareholder. I'll be ready at any time to discuss whatever changes you wish to make. All your expenses will be paid, and we stand ready to render any other assistance. We've contacted Mr. Witherspoon, the naturalist, and agreed upon terms of employment. I'll have the *Galatea* unloaded, and we'll locate a cargo destined for Belém, Brazil."

The meeting ended. Toland escorted Teddy and Dooley to their hotel, and Edward went with his relatives. They now lived in Chandannagar, where Cochrane commanded a battalion of Bengal rifles at the garrison adjacent to the town. As their carriage moved through Calcutta and into the open countryside, there was a cool, fresh breeze.

"So your sons are in England now, attending school?" Edward asked his aunt and uncle.

He attempted to concentrate on their reply, but his gaze kept settling on Ramedha. She had matured but was essentially unchanged. Veering unpredictably between Christian and Hindu attitudes, she was a fascinating study in contrasts. Her aggressive pursuit of Edward was now more subtle, but no less determined. In the late afternoon, when Edward had been settled into the family's comfortable bungalow, Ramedha's fingers brushed his with a gentle pressure as she handed him his glass of gin, and her smoldering eyes lingered on his. He took a drink from the glass, collecting his thoughts with an effort.

During dinner Edward described the large, hardy strain of crossbreeds that he and his partner at the M Bar B, Rob Martin, had developed from the Brahma cattle he had spirited out of India. His uncle assured him that the authorities had never discovered his identity, and in the intervening time, the entire incident had been forgotten.

148

The meal, served at twilight, was delicious. Edward enjoyed the curried beef with spicy vegetables as much as the conversation. After dinner he and the Cochranes sat in the parlor and continued talking over brandy. Later, when his aunt and uncle retired for the night, Edward went out into the garden behind the house with Ramedha.

They sat in a wicker lounge, talking. When he took her in his arms and kissed her, she responded eagerly, her warm, soft lips opening under his, her fingertips caressing his face. She lay back, pulling him down to her. For a moment he wavered in indecision, fighting his passion. Firmly reminding himself that he was a guest in his uncle's home, he sat up, kissed her hand, and lifted her to her feet as he stood. "We'd better go back inside now."

"Very well, Edward dear."

In the hallway Edward kissed her once more, then went into his room as she stepped into hers. He took out the draft agreement but was unable to concentrate. After going to bed, he was sleepless for hours, thinking about Ramedha.

At the breakfast table the next morning, Ramedha asked, "Did you wish to visit with Mr. Witherspoon this morning, Edward dear?"

"Yes, to learn what preparations to make for transporting the rubber-tree seeds. After talking with him, I'd like to see if the *Galatea* has been brought to the Howrah docks to be unloaded."

"Then we'll make a day of it," Ramedha declared happily.

The naturalist lived several miles from Chandannagar on a farm where he conducted research on plants and animals. He was a man with fanatical interest in a subject and the money to pursue it; however, he was absentminded and eccentric.

Cecil Witherspoon, a tall, thin man, was working in his fields with his employees when Edward and Ramedha arrived. He greeted Ramedha warmly—they had been friends for years—but his interest faded as he shook hands with Edward. "You say we've met before?"

"Yes, we have," Edward replied, relating the circumstances of their previous meeting, but Witherspoon's mild blue eyes became vacant, and he stared blankly into the distance, lost in his thoughts. Ramedha plucked at his sleeve and suggested that they have tea.

At the house Ramedha and Witherspoon chatted for several minutes before Edward mentioned the journey to Brazil. "Brazil?" Witherspoon echoed, perplexed.

Edward frowned in concern. "Mr. Toland said that you had agreed to go and provide expert advice."

Witherspoon pondered for a moment. "Yes, that's correct. I even told my foreman what was to be done in the fields during my absence."

"You do want to go, don't you?" Edward persisted.

"Yes, indeed," Witherspoon replied. He drained the rest of the tea in his cup, then stood and reached for his hat. "Let's be on our way, then. Are you coming to Brazil with us, Ra-medha?"

"We're not leaving this moment," Edward said. "I've come to talk with you about the prepara-tions."

The man sighed in disappointment and sat down.

Ramedha turned to Edward. "I'd better have a word with his housekeeper," she whispered. "She can organize his packing for the journey."

"Excellent idea," Edward firmly agreed. As Ra-medha went into the house, Edward reflected that the long voyage to Brazil with Witherspoon would undoubtedly be a memorable one, as well as one he would rather forget.

At noon they turned the buggy onto a grassy, shaded verge, and while the horse grazed, Edward and Ramedha sat in the shade to enjoy a picnic lunch she had brought. Edward felt deeply con-tented, and Ramedha was the reason. He kissed her.

"When I return from Brazil," he said, "I'd like very much for us to marry, Ramedha. Will you marry me?"

Ramedha smiled radiantly and hurled herself into his arms, knocking him off balance. They laughed and kissed again and agreed to defer their formal engagement until his return. When they continued their journey, Ramedha sat close to Ed-ward and hugged his arm in happiness.

At the Howrah waterfront, Edward found the

Galatea berthed at a pier, its cargo being unloaded while Teddy watched. She told him that Dooley, having become embroiled in a tavern brawl the night before, was in a Calcutta jail.

"It's the best thing that could have happened," she added. "I can take him food and an occasional bottle, and we'll know where he is."

Edward agreed. "I'll reimburse you for whatever you spend on him, Teddy. I've talked with Cecil Witherspoon, and he said the rubber-tree seeds should be transported in metal cans that are tightly sealed. We should take about two or three hundred."

"I'll find them," Teddy volunteered. "I've been pricing trade goods that we'll need for dealing with natives, and a sufficient stock will cost about five hundred guineas."

Edward considered the amount excessive for a store of beads, mirrors, and other trinkets, but he wrote out a check for Teddy without complaint before setting out with Ramedha toward Chandannagar.

Over dinner Edward told his aunt and uncle that he had proposed to Ramedha. "With your permission and blessing, we'll be married when I return from Brazil."

"Of course, my boy!" Cochrane boomed jovially. "You have our most wholehearted permission and blessing, along with our best wishes. Nothing could please us more, could it, Mattie?"

"Absolutely not," Mathilda agreed. "And the

timing is perfect. Since the wedding will be a large one, I'll need time to make all the arrangements."

Cochrane sent the maid for a bottle of choice wine. Glasses were filled and lifted in toasts. It was late when the happy foursome finally retired.

Before going to bed, Edward studied the draft agreement and included Toby Holt's name as an investor. The next day after breakfast, he and Ramedha set out for Toland's Calcutta offices.

At the end of an hour-long meeting, Edward was pleased with final terms of the agreement; if his adventure was successful, he would be assured of great wealth.

Toland, proud of having been chosen to oversee a new major investment by the company, announced that he would host Edward, his family, and his travel party for dinner and dancing at the Empire Hotel in the city. "I'll invite all my assistants and their wives," he said. "It should be a very enjoyable evening. Traveling back to Chandannagar late in the evening will be inconvenient, so I'll make arrangements for you to stay at the hotel. We'll discuss it again when you return tomorrow to sign the agreement."

The final preparations for the expedition had begun when Edward and Ramedha went to Calcutta again the next day. After signing the agreement at Toland's office, Edward brought Ramedha to the ship, where the cargo going to Brazil and the crates of metal cans were being stowed, along with cartons of beads, hatchets, knives, and Teddy's other trade goods.

The following afternoon, Edward traveled to Calcutta in the carriage with the Cochranes. The dinner at the Empire Hotel was scheduled for that evening. At the hotel he found the rooms elegantly furnished. Ramedha's suite had Indian decor and furnishings, favored by rulers of independent states on their visits to Calcutta.

At six o'clock, wearing his formal suit, Edward went downstairs with the others. Cochrane was resplendent in his formal uniform, Mathilda and Ramedha dazzling in their gowns. A waiter showed them into a large private banquet room, where the others had assembled. Edward looked twice at Teddy. Wearing a stylish gown, she was very attractive.

No expense had been spared. The food was superb, the conversation witty, and Toland made a speech in which he extolled Edward's and Teddy's courage. A small orchestra provided music during dinner and for the dancing afterward. It was a festive evening, although the imminent sense of leavetaking added a poignant overtone to the festivities.

When a final dance ended the gathering broke up. When Edward returned to his room, it was quite late. He got ready for bed but was too restless to sleep. After putting on his robe and slippers, he looked over notes he had made on last-minute preparations.

A knock on his door startled him, and he opened it to find a staff servant standing there. "The memsahib in room three-twelve summoned me and asked me to bring you a message, sir. She wishes to talk with you."

The room was Ramedha's. Edward wondered why she had sent a servant instead of coming herself. Concerned that she might be feeling ill, he immediately went to her room and rapped on the door. She called to him to come in.

A single lamp dimly illuminated the voluptuously lavish suite. On a table sandalwood incense sent up a wisp of smoke from a brass plate. Instead of a bed, a thick, soft pallet draped with a silk canopy was at one end of the room. Ramedha, barefoot and wearing a diaphanous silk sari, was lying on the pallet.

"Is anything wrong, Ramedha?"

She shook her head. "I'm unable to sleep. Please keep me company."

"I couldn't sleep either," he confessed.

"Yes, I know. I could sense that you were awake."

He sat on the edge of the pallet, looking at a different woman from the one who had been his companion at the dinner-dance. She was wearing her caste mark, and her eyes were circled with kohl. The young Englishwoman had been replaced by a sultry, exotic creature of the Orient.

As she lay back on the pillows, gazing at him with her huge, golden eyes, the constraints of convention melted. His arms enfolded her, and their lips met in a kiss that unleashed an explosion of passion.

In a quiet corner of the train station in Philadelphia, concealed behind a baggage cart, Josef Mueller handed Klaus Lukenbill a small satchel. "Be careful with that," he advised. "If you bump it too hard, there'll be nothing left but a hole where you were standing."

Lukenbill winced apprehensively as he took out a heavy purse and handed it over. "Isn't it cushioned or anything?"

"It has some felt around it," Mueller replied indifferently as he opened the purse and fingered the coins. "You should be able to get it to where you're going." He closed the purse and pocketed it. "The timing device is also in there, so you have everything you need."

"If I have anything else for you to do, I'll contact you," Lukenbill said, his tone indicating that he considered the entire matter finished.

For Mueller it was far from finished. He had often thought about supplanting Lukenbill, but first he had to learn the identity of the man's employer.

Lukenbill went into the waiting room, and Mueller followed to the door and spied through the window. Because Lukenbill had made himself comfortable in a seat and unfolded a newspaper, Mueller knew he had the time to retrieve his small suitcase from the baggage counter and to go into a commode closet to change.

He emerged a few minutes later wearing nondescript clothes, spectacles, and a gray wig and beard. Walking with a slow, stooped shuffle that matched his aged appearance, Mueller carried the suitcase to the waiting room and sat on a bench a few feet from Lukenbill.

When the train drew into the station, Lukenbill folded his newspaper and stood up. Mueller scanned the schedule board and saw that the man's destination was either New York City or some intermediate point between Philadelphia and Manhattan. He followed Lukenbill onto the train, bought a ticket from the conductor, and took a seat at the end of the car in which Lukenbill was sitting.

During the journey Mueller pretended he was dozing, but he kept up his surveillance through slitted eyelids. When the train arrived in New York hours later, Mueller followed Lukenbill to the queue of carriages for hire outside the station. Mueller gave a driver a large tip in advance, telling him to follow Lukenbill's carriage.

It was a long trip. The carriages left the city and traveled along a wide avenue on Long Island. When Lukenbill's carriage turned onto a drive leading back to one of the mansions along the avenue, Mueller ordered his driver to stop. After paying the fare, he followed Lukenbill on foot.

Mueller quietly circled to the side of the magnificent home and peered through a window. He saw Lukenbill in a drawing room, talking to another man.

When the man turned, Mueller gasped, pivoted, and fled, forgetting all intentions of taking

157

Lukenbill's place. Why and when Hermann Bluecher had come to the United States was a mystery to Mueller, and irrelevant. His only thought was that Bluecher had tried to have him killed in Turkey.

The German was wealthy, powerful, and cunning, and very few had escaped his deadly wrath. Bluecher did not know specifically who had gone to Switzerland for the explosives, and Mueller planned to take advantage of that stroke of good fortune and stay completely away from the man.

IX

An early spring storm battered the coast of England as Cindy Kerr stepped out of the Bristol customs building. A porter followed with her baggage.

A hired carriage driver intercepted her. "May I be of assistance, mum?"

"I'd like to go to Fenton Hall. Do you know where it is?"

The driver hesitated in surprise. "Aye, everyone knows. But it's over thirty miles away, and the owner isn't in residence."

"Yes, I know."

"I'll have to charge fifteen shillings, mum."

Cindy opened her purse and handed the money to him. In trying to exorcise the ghost that stood between Henry and her, she was blindly following her instincts and trying to learn more about Henry's past with Gisela von Kirchberg.

Because her wounded pride might remain as a barrier, Cindy realized that her quest could prove futile; no effort was too great, however, if it set free the yearning love that ached within her.

The carriage jolted along narrow country roads for hours before turning into the broad cobblestone courtyard of an immense mansion. Lamps illuminated the wide front doors. Stone gargoyles at the entrance spewed rainwater into drains.

The driver helped Cindy out and waited as she climbed the steps. The heavy door knocker resounded loudly. A few minutes later, a tall, thin man opened the door, and Cindy handed him the letter that Henry had written.

He glanced over the letter, held the door for her to enter, then bowed deeply. "I'm Wilkerson, madame. Welcome to Fenton Hall. We have a limited staff but will do our best to make you comfortable."

"And I'll try to be as little trouble as possible. If it wouldn't be too inconvenient, I'd like the driver to have some warm food before he leaves."

"It won't be at all inconvenient if you wish it, madame. Please come this way, and I will have a room prepared for you."

He led Cindy into a drawing room, where he served her a warming cordial and had a boy in his early teens kindle a fire in the fireplace. A few minutes later, Wilkerson returned to show her to a large, luxurious guest room that had been quickly and expertly prepared. Her baggage had been unpacked. Cindy changed clothes and washed, and precisely one hour after her arrival, Wilkerson tapped on the door to announce dinner.

In a dining room the size of a ballroom, Cindy sat at one end of a gleaming table that could seat sixty. The delicious meal consisted of four courses, accompanied by superb wines. Weary and comfortably full, she returned to her room and immediately fell asleep.

The next morning, she woke momentarily, detecting a faint scent of perfume. Drowsily wondering if someone had come into the room, she dozed off again. A few minutes later, a stout, rosy-cheeked woman in a crisp uniform ventured in with a large tray, cheerfully bade Cindy good morning, and placed the tray across her lap. As the maid built up the fire, Cindy sipped her coffee and lifted the dishes' silver covers to find an enormous breakfast of ham, eggs, kippers, toast, and a variety of jellies and jams.

"This looks delicious, but I'm not sure I can eat all of it," she commented. "Did you peek in a few minutes ago to see if I was awake?"

The woman looked at Cindy in perplexity. "No, mum, I didn't come upstairs until just now."

The woman, adjusting the pillows behind Cindy, smelled of starch and laundry soap, not the perfume Cindy vaguely remembered.

After breakfast Cindy washed, dressed, put on her coat, and left the room, a sketch pad tucked under her arm. The mansion had a vacant, lonely feel.

At the mezzanine overlooking the magnificent entry, Cindy's eyes widened in admiration. Huge supporting stone piers soared four stories to a glass dome. Daylight spilled into the vast interior.

Wilkerson materialized and opened the door for Cindy. She set out along the road, which curved down a slope, through the woods, and onto the main street of the village. A mile past the village, she found a sheltered spot where she could sit and sketch.

Seen from a distance, Fenton towered over its surroundings, a symbol of raw power. It was probable that Gisela had liked the estate for its straight, unadorned lines, evocative of authority.

Cindy knew why Henry was fond of Fenton: The huge, ancient structure had a timeless, enduring air. Its bleak winter setting had a spartan appeal, and during summer, she thought, the countryside would be lovely.

Rain was starting to fall when Cindy returned to the mansion at noon. Lunch was another enormous, delicious meal, with a hearty soup, fillet of sole in a piquant sauce, chicken Kiev with sage dressing and vegetables, custard over fruit, and a choice wine.

She felt overly full and drowsy as she began exploring the mansion's interior. The cold, silent rooms revealed nothing until she reached the master bedroom, which felt occupied. Twice Cindy had a distinct impression that someone else was in the room, but when she looked around, no one was there.

In one of the dressing-table drawers, she found a hairbrush. As she picked it up, she detected a heavy, sultry fragrance—attar of jasmine. It was the perfume she had smelled early that morning.

Unnerved, Cindy searched for a logical explanation. Out of the corner of her eye, she glimpsed a face in the mirror over the dressing table. Spinning around, she saw no one. She looked closely at the mirror, found a discoloration, and told herself that that was what she had seen. But the mirror's flaw was unlike the beautiful, aristocratic face she thought she had viewed.

Cindy put the hairbrush back in the drawer, then went downstairs to find Wilkerson. She asked him to send to Bristol for a hired carriage and to have a maid pack her things to leave.

She felt acutely depressed. Before, she had the feeling that the ghost of Gisela von Kirchberg was keeping Henry and her apart. She had hoped to change that feeling by journeying to Fenton. Now, however, Gisela's presence seemed stronger than ever.

Cindy took one train to London, another to Dover, crossed the channel on a ferry, and set out across France. She was weary of traveling, but her love for Henry compelled her to go on.

The following afternoon, she was in Frankfurt, Germany, where she boarded the train to Mainz, which slowly made its way down the valley of the

Main River. From a distance on the gray, gloomy day, the vineyards on the slopes above the river looked like countless acres of graveyards, the pruned stumps of the vines supported by wooden frames made in the shape of crosses.

At Grevenburg, a village of some forty houses, she was the only one who stepped off the train. The stationmaster spoke only German. There were no carriages for hire or anyone else about, but Cindy saw what appeared to be her destination at the top of the hill overlooking the village.

"Grevenhof?" she asked, pointing.

The man smiled and nodded vigorously.

She managed to communicate through gestures that she wanted him to keep her baggage in the station. She set out down the cobblestone street. The misty Mainz river valley came into view when Cindy reached the top of the hill. The road turned into a wide avenue with fountains down its center. It led back in a long, straight sweep through acres of formal gardens to a palatial mansion.

Grevenhof had been built in an early Gothic style, with pointed arches and spires. Through the gathering dusk, lights gleamed in a few windows.

After the estate steward read Henry's letter, Cindy learned that his name was Becker and that he spoke French.

The warm welcome and the staff's efficiency were the same as at Fenton. Cindy's baggage was brought from the station and unpacked in a luxurious guest room. But she still felt depressed as she went to bed. The decor of Grevenhof, like

Fenton's, symbolized wealth, power, and prestige. Cindy found this very discouraging; she already had discovered a surfeit of evidence about that side of Gisela von Kirchberg's character.

In addition, she never felt alone. There always seemed to be someone just around a corner in the hallways or on the other side of the furniture from her—someone she might be able to see if she turned or moved quickly enough. When she looked, however, no one was there, but the feeling remained.

In the guest room, with the fire burning down and shadows flickering on the walls, Cindy had a distinct impression that someone was watching her. She looked around the room, trying in vain to dismiss the uncomfortable sensation.

When she began stirring from deep sleep the next morning, the air bore the fragrance of attar of jasmine, causing her to awaken suddenly and sit up. The scent was abruptly gone—if indeed it had been there at all—and Cindy was shaken by the eerie experience.

A short time later, after breakfast, Cindy dressed and went outside. In the gardens behind the mansion, she had her first insight into a different facet of Gisela's personality: At the rear of the gardens were large marble tombs where those who had lived at Grevenhof had been interred. All were in the same ornate architectural style as the manor—except Gisela's, which had plain lines.

Its simplicity raised the possibility that her lavish life-style had been like a uniform for her, announcing her station in life, while her personal preference was for the opposite.

Janessa had told Cindy that the woman, facing the fact that she might die, had designed her own tomb.

Cindy went back into the house. As she went from room to room, she again felt that someone was always near. Cindy knew that nothing had been changed since the day the baroness had been killed. What she had left behind when she died was on every side. Her powerful personality also seemed to linger, that invisible presence following Cindy.

It gave her the sense of close contact with the woman that she had wanted, but it was eerily uncomfortable—much more than she had wished for. It gradually became less disconcerting, however, because Cindy realized that instead of being hostile, the presence seemed merely to be benignly there.

In the master suite, Gisela's clothes hung in wardrobes, her other belongings in drawers and on shelves. The rooms were permeated with the fragrance of jasmine.

In the sitting room, Cindy noticed the companion to the chair she had seen in Henry's quarters at Fort Harland. As she sat down in it, she suddenly felt like a guest who had chosen the wrong chair. The feeling that she had violated propriety became so intense, she nearly leapt from the chair.

She did not want to take Gisela's place; she wanted to coexist peacefully.

By noon Cindy had explored everything but the business offices on the lower floor. After lunch she began going through that area. Dozens of desks with dust covers on them were lined in neat rows.

She came to a tiny room, where only two desks, larger than the others, occupied the space. The door giving access to the next office was locked. She left the wing and went looking for Becker. She found him in the entry hall.

"The last office downstairs is locked," she said. "May I have the key?"

The man hesitated, then bowed. "Certainly, madame. One moment, please."

He returned almost immediately with a large key. While she might have expected him to go with her and unlock the door, he merely bowed and handed her the key. Cindy accepted it, wondering why the steward preferred to avoid the office.

Unlocking the door, she understood Becker's behavior: The room had been Gisela von Kirchberg's office. Her presence was nearly palpable.

The immense room seemed even larger because it was virtually empty of furniture—only a desk and a chair with a bookshelf against the wall—with no pictures or other decorations. The hardwood floor gleamed.

Cindy's footsteps echoed hollowly through the room as she walked toward the desk. A thin film of dust was on its top; the room had evidently been closed off since the day Gisela was killed.

Prepared for feeling the invader, Cindy slowly eased into the chair behind the desk. She felt surprisingly comfortable, the atmosphere in the room more welcoming. Then she stood and walked over to the bookcase. She picked up a small, thick book and opened it.

It appeared to be a business diary, the days of the week and month at the top of the pages, with entries in small, neat writing on each page. The page for the first of each month was filled with numbered entries, listing things to be accomplished that month. For some months, that list ran into the hundreds. Beside each one was a date, apparently a deadline. The deadline beside many entries had been changed numerous times, always to earlier dates.

Recalling what Henry had said about Gisela's dedication to business, Cindy reflected that he had understated it. The diary presented a picture of a woman who had constantly flayed herself to do things ever faster. Instead of being despised for her harsh demands on others to keep up with her, she should have been pitied for being a helpless victim, driven by the demon that lived within her.

Cindy put the book back on the shelf, then returned to the desk, where she looked through the desk drawers. All except the bottom one contained business papers. In that were letters from Henry. She started to close the drawer but noticed something protruding from under the letters: It was a small, familiar-looking leather case.

Taking the case out of the drawer, Cindy looked at it in shock. It contained a daguerreotype of herself, which she had sent to Henry before he had met the baroness. The woman had kept it as a treasured possession, together with letters from Henry. But why? Why had she not tossed it out as a hated reminder of Henry's love for another woman? The only possible explanation was that the baroness had accepted her as part of Henry's past and bore her no malice. Cindy realized that it was incumbent upon her to reciprocate that favor.

The atmosphere in the room suddenly felt congenial to Cindy, as if there were a friendly hand on her shoulder. She had achieved her goal. No ghost stood between Henry and her; his past was put to rest in her mind. Any negative feelings she had experienced while visiting Gisela's estates had been of her own making. Her wounded pride from their broken engagement remained, but in time the deep love she had always felt for Henry might overcome it.

Cindy replaced the daguerreotype, left the room, and locked the door. She returned the key to Becker and thanked him. "Do you know when the next train will go to Frankfurt?"

The man looked at his watch. "In about two hours, madame. If you wish to leave on it, I will send a maid to pack your belongings and have the carriage prepared."

"Please. I would like to leave as soon as possible."

A short time later, Cindy was sitting in the carriage as it moved down the drive. She enjoyed a deep sense of well-being. She also had a strange sense of having made a new friend.

A cold, dark night was closing in when Cindy reached the Frankfurt train station. After buying her ticket to Paris and checking her baggage, she bought a French newspaper to read while she waited.

On its back page, a brief news item immediately caught her eye. The details were sketchy, but the article said that a force commanded by General George Crook had recently clashed with Cheyenne and Sioux warriors at the Powder River in the Wyoming Territory. Cindy knew that the war with the Sioux and Cheyenne that would involve Henry had begun.

The battle between the Indians and General Crook's command was a topic of discussion at a dinner party in Washington. Those present included Thomas Caldwell, secretary of the interior, and Arthur Curran, former governor of the Dakota Territory and now an undersecretary in Caldwell's department. They were talking with Charles Rollins, an undersecretary in the War Department.

"I don't want to be overly critical, Charlie," Caldwell said to Rollins, "but my department is responsible for the administration of organized territories. When things are in such an upheaval, we can't do our job without enough soldiers. The Indians won't return to their reservations without a show of strength from us."

"We don't have those soldiers, Tom," Rollins protested. "Our forces are spread so thin now that we're asking for trouble. Also, when some odd job arises, it's always given to the War Department. We got stuck with Alaska, when the Bureau of Customs should be responsible for it. We have a detachment of soldiers up there at Anchorage, and we could make much better use of them elsewhere."

The conversation turned to a problem much smaller in scope but far more difficult to resolve: Renegade Pima from Mexico had been harassing settlers in the Arizona Territory and were now a severe threat because they had obtained a large supply of firearms. Their success had drawn other renegades, so the band was growing larger week by week.

"Diplomatic protests to Mexico City have been useless," Caldwell growled. "But that's nothing new. The border will always be a problem for us."

"It needn't be," Curran remarked quietly. "One instance of retaliation across that border by cavalry would teach everyone that our patience isn't unlimited."

Caldwell and Rollins laughed. "Don't let anyone from the State Department hear you say that, Arthur," Caldwell warned. "It gets them very upset."

"And for good reason," Rollins added. "Retaliation would amount to an invasion of a sovereign country by an armed force. Although that border is a thorn in our side, we can't have our cavalry shooting up towns in Mexico. Civilized nations just don't do that sort of thing, and it would put us in a bad light all over the world."

"That's true," Curran conceded. "But when I was governor of the Dakota Territory, Fargo was completely lawless, overrun with riffraff. Did you hear what Major Henry Blake did there?"

"He cleaned it up," Rollins replied. "It was outside his authority, but the War Department turned a blind eye to it."

"Blake did more than clean it up, Charlie," Curran said emphatically. "A dozen saloons and brothels were demolished, what amounted to half the town was burned to the ground, and an unsavory mob was driven out of Fargo. The place was actually the scene of a major battle. But"—Curran lifted a finger for emphasis—"not one person was killed. No one was even shot."

"That was remarkable luck," Caldwell mused. "I hadn't thought about it in those terms, Arthur."

"Henry Blake makes his own luck," Rollins said. "He's as cold as ice, and he always controls the situation."

Curran nodded. "Few men impress me as much. If there's an officer alive who could lead a troop into Mexico and wipe out those renegades without killing innocent Mexicans, that officer is Henry Blake." He smiled wryly, shrugging. "But the State Department would demand his court-martial, and it wouldn't be right to sacrifice an officer like Blake."

"The State Department *would* be in an uproar," Rollins mused, "but for years they've been trying to get Major Blake permanently detached to them. I believe they would have taken the matter to the President but for the fact that Major Blake himself wanted a field assignment."

"If he could be transferred to Arizona, matters could take their course. He doesn't need orders or permission to take the situation in hand; knowing him, there's a very good chance of his catching those renegades north of the border."

"Then the problem would be solved without diplomatic hard feelings," Caldwell chimed in. "Charlie, if you could help us with this problem, we'd certainly appreciate it." He hesitated, thinking. "You mentioned Alaska, didn't you? If you were to bring that up at the next Cabinet meeting, my department would support yours in having that responsibility transferred to the Bureau of Customs. Together, I'm sure we could get that done."

"I'd be very grateful for that, Tom," Rollins replied. "All right. Tomorrow, I'll have a chat with Colonel Bolton, our director of personnel, and see about having Major Blake transferred to Arizona."

Two days later, Henry Blake rode into Fort Lincoln at the head of a cavalry platoon. During the past weeks, in preparation for a summer campaign against the Sioux and Cheyenne, he had been taking platoons with a high proportion of recruits from Fort Lincoln to Fort Harland for training.

The men with him had just completed training, which was confirmed by their appearance and horsemanship. In the quadrangle of the fort, they reined up and wheeled their horses into a double line facing Henry. After exchanging salutes, he turned the platoon over to the sergeant, then rode across the quadrangle, where Custer stood on the porch of the headquarters building.

"As usual, they look like good cavalrymen now," Custer commented, returning Henry's salute as he reined up.

"They'll do, General," Henry replied, dismounting and tethering his horse. "I'd like to spend more time with them, but we have more recruits than time. Do you have another platoon ready for me?"

"No, there won't be any more."

"What do you mean, sir?"

Custer beckoned, leading Henry into the headquarters building. In his office he silently handed a telegram to Henry, who read it and looked up in surprise.

"That makes a lot of sense, doesn't it?" Custer remarked sarcastically. "With a summer campaign coming up, the War Department decides to transfer one of my best officers to the Arizona Territory."

"Well, they know things we don't," Henry rationalized. "Even so, it's hard to find any logic in my being transferred to Fort Peck." He frowned.

"I believe there's a major already assigned there, a major Kelly."

"That's right, and he's no youngster. Patrick Kelly was an old trooper when I was a shavetail, but if they think he needs help, there are plenty of other officers they could send. They're worrying about a little band of Indians down there, when we have whole tribes up here that are going on the warpath."

Henry put the telegram on the desk. "It might be temporary, and I'll be transferred back within a few weeks. But an order is an order, and that says I'm to leave immediately."

Custer sighed in resignation. They exchanged a salute, then Henry left the office.

X

Everyone at the dinner table sat up expectantly as Toby finished saying grace. Alexandra nodded to Abby Givens. The maid, standing stiffly beside the sideboard in her crisp dress and cap, started to pick up a silver tray. "May I interrupt for a moment?" Lee Blake asked, lifting his wineglass. "I'd like to propose a toast to welcome Toby home and to hope that he'll be here for a while this time."

The sentiments were echoed around the table, and Eulalia, Janessa, and Tim lifted their glasses. Alexandra winked at Toby as she sipped the water in her glass.

Toby raised his glass. "I won't drink to myself, but I certainly will to the part about staying here for a while this time."

The others laughed and agreed, but the most emphatic concurrence was in Alexandra's loving expression.

While Toby's remark had been meant to be amusing, he had never been more sincere. His time at home had always been precious to him, but it had become even more enjoyable since his marriage. Alexandra had provided him with a genteel, well-ordered household, where he was proud to entertain his family and friends. But most of all, he had her love, which was more precious than life itself. While he remained as ready as ever to serve his country, he regretted that it took him away from Alexandra for months at a time.

The conversation turned to a subject that Lee had briefly mentioned to Toby the day before: At a recent Cabinet meeting, the decision had been made to transfer responsibility for Alaska from the army to the Bureau of Customs. As the senior officer on the West Coast, Lee had been ordered to officiate at the formal transfer in Alaska.

"While I'm gone," Lee said, "General Cummings at the Presidio in San Francisco will assume command, but my staff will attend to all of your correspondence and other matters as commissioner of the West."

"When do you plan to leave?" Toby asked.

"Well, that brings up a bit of news," Lee replied, grinning widely at Eulalia. "The Bureau of

Customs needs time to get organized for this responsibility. In view of that, I decided to wait until the weather turns warm, and I've asked Eulalia to go with me. We're going to make a vacation of it."

The announcement was greeted with exclamations of pleasure. "That's great news," Toby commented. "It's past time when the two of you should have had a vacation, and while you're gone, Peter and his nurse will be more than welcome to stay here."

"Thank you. We accept your offer."

Everyone at the table took a turn relating stories or information about Alaska. While it was popularly reputed to be a place of year-round ice and snow, often called "Seward's Icebox" in a reference to the secretary of state who had negotiated its purchase, more reliable sources described it as a beautiful land with valuable timber and fishing grounds.

"Well, we'll see when we get there," Lee said. "In any event, it should be a pleasant, interesting trip,"

"Our only regret," Eulalia added, "is that by waiting until summer to go, we'll miss the celebration in Philadelphia. We did so want to go to that, but one can't do everything."

After dinner everyone adjourned to the parlor. Lee filled his pipe, while Toby lit a cigar. The most welcomed news that had greeted Toby upon his homecoming was that Janessa had stopped smoking. Each time he had smoked a cigar since his arrival, however, she had stared in silent disapproval.

Noting the look now, Eulalia came to Toby's defense. "For a man to smoke isn't the same thing as for a young lady to smoke, is it, my dear?"

"I see no practical difference in it, ma'am," Janessa replied somberly. "Tobacco is as unhealthy for a man as it is for a woman."

"Are you ready for your college placement examinations, my dear?" Lee asked, quickly changing the subject.

"Yes, sir. Dad's going to take me to Chicago."

Toby added that he had been looking forward to escorting her and that they had been invited to stay with the Schumann family. Before Eulalia and Lee left for home, Janessa mentioned she had failed to receive a reply to her last letter to Luther Bingham, her friend who had gone to medical college in Chicago. While she was in the Midwest, she intended to visit him.

The next morning while looking at horses in the corral with Stalking Horse, the elderly Indian who managed the ranch, Toby saw a rider approaching the ranch.

"Mr. Toby Holt?" he asked, reining up.

"Yes, I'm Toby Holt." He felt a twinge of regret; the man looked like a courier from Washington whose message might interfere with the trip to Chicago.

The man opened his attaché case and took out a large envelope with an official seal. "I was ordered to hand deliver this to you from Washington, sir."

"Thank you." Toby accepted the envelope. "Would you like to have lunch with us?"

"I'd better get back to town, sir. I'm leaving by freighter this afternoon."

The courier rode away as Toby turned toward the house. The envelope was from Thomas Haines, the deputy director of the Secret Service and a good friend of Toby's. With a note from Haines was a letter forwarded from the attorney general's office. A staff of investigators had dismissed it as a prank, from some lunatic with a twisted sense of humor. Haines, however, had sent the unsigned letter to Toby for evaluation. If he thought it deserved serious attention and was free to pursue the matter, Haines would provide assistance.

The letter in question had been posted in New York a few weeks before. It stated that the writer had become involved with a group of anarchists planning to blow up the torch of the Statue of Liberty with explosives provided by a man who called himself Kramer. The last sentence, a warning to take heed and act quickly, was underlined several times and followed by exclamation marks.

Alexandra stood in the kitchen, taking down mugs from a shelf. "Would you like some coffee, Toby?"

"If you'll join me. I'd like you to read something." He handed her the envelope.

When she finished she said, "Cindy is traveling

from Paris with the torch. If this isn't a prank, her life could be in danger."

"You're right," Toby said. "As well as the lives of many others. Our national celebration could turn into a massacre." He stroked his chin and pondered. "The attorney general's investigators must have good reasons for dismissing it, but I believe I'd better go to Washington to discuss this with Tom Haines and them."

"Does this mean that you won't be taking Janessa to Chicago?" She set a mug of coffee on the table.

"I can take her part of the way. I'll ask Calvin to go with us and escort her for the last leg, then back home. I'm sure he'll be glad to do that." Toby smiled wryly. "If this letter is legitimate, it could keep me busy for several months, Alexandra. There goes the time we had planned to spend together."

"Then there it goes, Toby," she replied pragmatically. "Some things are more important than our time together, and this is one of them."

He reached out and squeezed her hand. "What did I do to deserve you?"

Alexandra patted his hand. "I say the same thing to myself every morning. I'll find Janessa for you."

As she went out, Toby reflected that he was a very fortunate man.

"I had to get rid of one of my men," Lukenbill reported.

179

"Why?" Herman Bluecher asked.

"I didn't like the way he was acting, sir. You said never to take chances, so I didn't." Lukenbill drew a finger across his throat. "I dumped him in an alley and emptied his pockets of identification. I also had some men collect all the papers in his apartment, so he can't be connected with the Zeno Bund."

As Bluecher shrugged indifferently, Lukenbill sighed, relieved. Cyril Jenkins had, in fact, been acting normally, but he had foreknowledge of the plan to rob the mint. With Jenkins eliminated, no one would know about the plan until it was time to put it into operation.

"What about the torch?" Bluecher asked.

"Maritain, our man in France, has a job now at the Bartholdi studio in Paris. He'll keep me posted. Because he can speak English, he'll probably be one of the workers to bring the torch to Philadelphia."

"Excellent. Now what about Henry Blake?"

"I'll check on his whereabouts again."

"I keep hoping he will be transferred to Washington or some post near here. If that happens . . ." He clenched his fist and slammed it down on the arm of his chair to finish the sentence.

Lukenbill stood. "I'll catch a train to Washington tonight and check on Blake tomorrow."

The next morning, after a leisurely breakfast, Klaus Lukenbill went to the personnel offices of the War Department, the administrative section, and stood by a corporal's desk. "I'd like to find out the whereabouts of a friend of mine, Major Henry Blake."

The corporal pursed his lips. "Haven't you been here before?"

"I have," Lukenbill replied smoothly, "but I haven't managed to make contact with him yet."

"Have a seat, sir, and I'll see about getting the information that you want."

The corporal hurried to the office of the director of personnel, Colonel Frank Bolton. A reserved, stolid soldier in his fifties, the colonel wore an impressive array of decorations on his uniform, and his left sleeve was empty and pinned. His aide, a sergeant, stood inside the doorway.

"He's been here several times before, sir," the corporal explained, "and I don't think he's really trying to contact Major Blake. Besides that, he looks shifty to me."

The colonel looked to his sergeant. "Let's get a plainclothes policeman here. I want that man followed."

"Yes, sir. Do you want the policeman to follow him and then arrest him?"

"No, certainly not. There's no law against coming here to ask the whereabouts of an officer, so he hasn't done anything that would warrant being arrested. I do want to know more about him, though."

The sergeant rushed out, and Bolton turned to the corporal. "Take your time getting back to your office, so we can get the policeman here. Then bring the man to me so I can talk to him."

Lukenbill, already suspicious about the delay, became even more wary when the corporal asked him to speak with the colonel. "Why?" Lukenbill demanded. "I've never had to do that before."

"That's what the colonel wants, sir, and he's in charge here. It'll only take a moment."

Lukenbill reluctantly agreed. He followed the corporal down the hall and into an anteroom, where a sergeant was sitting at a desk. "Please have a seat, sir," the sergeant invited, pointing to a chair. "The colonel will be free in just a moment."

Muttering impatiently, Lukenbill sat. The corporal left, and the sergeant pored over papers, glancing at the door occasionally. Presently, a heavyset man in civilian clothes strolled past the door, casting a meaningful glance at the sergeant, who flicked his eyes toward Lukenbill. The plainclothes officer surreptitiously took in the man's appearance as the sergeant escorted Lukenbill into the colonel's office. "I understand you want to know the whereabouts of Major Henry Blake, sir. May I ask who you are and why you want to know where the major is stationed?"

"We're friends, that's all," Lukenbill muttered, perspiring from the heat of the colonel's gaze.

"Friends, eh? Where did you meet him? And you haven't told me your name yet, sir."

Trying to devise a believable story, Lukenbill

became more flustered. Realizing that he had already aroused too much suspicion, he jumped up and fled, pushing past people and glancing over his shoulder to make certain no one was following him. Minutes later he was in his hotel room, throwing his clothing into his bag.

When he reached the train station, Lukenbill had decided to tell Bluecher only that Henry Blake's status was unchanged. Lukenbill brushed past a heavyset man, purchased his ticket, and noted that his train would leave in less than an hour.

By the time the train departed, the plain-clothes policeman was back at the State, War, and Navy Department Building. "The name in the hotel register is Klaus Lukenbill, sir," the policeman reported to Colonel Bolton. "He gave his address as Philadelphia, but his train's destination was New York City."

The colonel wanted to avoid making something out of nothing, but Lukenbill had acted very suspiciously. He decided to write a personal letter to the major and inform him that a man from Philadelphia named Klaus Lukenbill had been asking his whereabouts. If Blake wanted him to take any action, he would certainly do so.

During her travels as a photographist, Marjorie White had discovered that the bearded lady in sideshows was usually a man with a small frame and feminine features and that magic health elixirs were a mixture of whiskey, water, pungent spices, and food coloring. When she heard about the outstanding belly dancer at Suleiman Bey's Turkish Restaurant, she suspected that Fatima might actually be a Bertha Jones from Schenectady, but she decided to go and see for herself.

The Turkish manager seemed genuine enough, and the moderately large restaurant was a clean, attractive place, well-furnished in Eastern decor. It was also crowded. On the stage a quartet with twanging stringed instruments provided music.

Just as Marjorie finished eating shish kebab and pilaf, a young woman in a filmy costume entered from one side of the stage and was enthusiastically applauded. As she danced the tempo of the music gradually increased.

The stage show was risqué without being disgraceful. Marjorie was struck by the absolute authenticity of the woman's graceful movements.

The next day, during midmorning, Marjorie stopped by the restaurant on her way to photographing the centennial celebration's displays. She wanted to meet Fatima.

"You are Marjorie White the photographist?" the manager enthused. "I'm sure Fatima would like to meet you."

Marjorie followed him upstairs to a small, comfortable parlor. It was immediately obvious that the strikingly attractive woman was Turkish, for she spoke English with a strong accent.

"You must call me by my real name," she told Marjorie. "It is Salima Mueller."

"Very well," Marjorie replied, laughing. "But I must say that it is an unusual combination, Salima."

"Yes. My husband is German. I met him in Turkey."

While they were talking, Marjorie concluded that at least some of Salima's eager friendliness arose from the fact that she was lonely.

Presently, Salima confirmed that fact, pointing to textbooks and a dictionary on the table. "I have no close friends here. People have difficulty understanding me."

"You speak excellent English, and I have no trouble understanding you. You also have a friend now, Salima. I'll be here for a while because new exhibits are being put up every day. I intend to photograph all of them and stay for the main celebration in July. Would you like to come with me sometime?"

Her eyes sparkling, Salima quickly replied that she would. Then a man came into the parlor, whom Salima introduced as her husband, Josef.

In contrast to Salima's buoyant, outgoing personality, Mueller was quiet, his eyes watchful. He was cool but polite, with an air that suggested that he could be an extremely dangerous man. He took some cigars out of a cabinet, but it was obvious that he had come into the parlor solely to find out who was visiting his wife.

The following day, Salima went with Marjorie when she photographed several exhibits. Marjorie enjoyed the day immensely, but the mystery of Salima's marriage remained unresolved.

"Do you ever miss your homeland?" Marjorie asked in a veiled attempt to find out what had brought Salima and Mueller together.

Salima hesitated for a moment, then smiled. "America is my homeland now. If I ever had to leave it, I would miss it very much."

XI

Secretary of the Interior Thomas Caldwell had just informed Toby that Henry Blake had been transferred to Arizona. He was taken aback by Toby's strong reaction. "Why do you object, Mr. Holt?"

"Because if Henry doesn't have specific orders to the contrary, he might chase those Pima across the border. I know Henry well. He'll use extra-legal means to achieve his ends."

"You've experienced the difficulties the army faces in that region, Mr. Holt," Caldwell pointed out. "And you know how unresponsive the Mexican authorities have been to our protests."

"If the State Department would stop being so mealymouthed and stomp on some toes in Mexico City, they'd get more cooperation."

"Well, I understand there's a chance the matter may be settled in an ordinary fashion," Caldwell soothed. "Major Blake may catch those Pima north of the border."

"That's true," Toby conceded, shrugging. He handed Caldwell the letters he had received from Thomas Haines. "This is why I needed to see you so urgently."

The secretary, Toby's contact in Washington for his activities as commissioner of the West, studied the letters, frowned, then handed them back.

"I might spend some time looking into it," Toby said. "I believe this should take precedence over my duties as commissioner of the West."

Caldwell agreed. Before Toby went to see Thomas Haines in the Secret Service offices, Caldwell and he talked about the likelihood of full-scale hostilities with the Sioux and Cheyenne.

Haines took Toby to meet with the investigators at the attorney general's office who had examined the unsigned letter. The chief investigator, Richard Johnson, was one of a new breed of lawmen who used systematic, scientific means of solving crimes. Keen intelligence shone in his eyes. Toby and Haines sat in his office with the opened file and discussed why the unsigned letter had been deemed a hoax.

"Our records section keeps lists of all known anarchists. We have no record of a Kramer, who's mentioned in the letter."

"Not yet, maybe," Haines objected. "Not having his name isn't conclusive."

"No, but it is indicative," Johnson said, "because we would have a record if anyone named Kramer had ever been an active anarchist. Now let's consider the physical characteristics of the torch of the Statue of Liberty."

The man took scale drawings of the interior and exterior of the torch from the file, then spread them out on his desk. Toby had seen illustrations of the torch in newspapers, but these drawings were much more detailed. Included were the hand of the statue, as well as its base. An entrance in the base opened onto circular stairs leading up to a parapet around the flame of the torch.

The drawings revealed only a few small nooks where anything could be hidden. All were much too small to contain enough dynamite for a large explosion, and detonator wires for nitroglycerin could not be concealed.

"Hence, we concluded that the threat posed in the letter is impossible to carry out."

"Do you know of any anarchist groups in New York?" Toby asked.

"Yes, there are three or four at all times. Anarchists often get into arguments and dissolve a group, then form another. The only stable one is the Zeno Bund."

"How did you find out the name?" Haines asked.

"Through a police officer in New York who had a cousin in the group," Johnson explained. "But our source of information has disappeared without a word."

"Think he was murdered?" Haines asked.

Johnson shrugged. "It's possible—especially if

they found out he had a cousin who's a policeman. They're very violent people."

"That's why this bothers me so much," Toby admitted.

"Anarchists are forever concocting wild schemes that never amount to anything," Johnson said. "Again, you must consider their nature, Mr. Holt. They're malcontents, failures, who think they have a right to what others have earned. If talk was action, they would have this nation in a shambles."

"I can't disagree with anything you've said, Mr. Johnson, but I'd still like to look into this further. Would it be possible for me to have the cooperation of the New York police?"

"I'm very sorry, Mr. Holt," Johnson replied, "but to request the cooperation of a city police agency, I'd have to certify this as a valid threat."

"This is a fine state of affairs," Haines grumbled. "Well, Toby, it looks like I wasted your time."

"You certainly did not," Toby assured his friend. "Something more might surface."

"In that event," Johnson put in, "I'll reconsider my position."

It was midafternoon when Toby and Haines left the office building. Because Toby wanted to return home as soon as possible, Haines accompanied him to his hotel, where he checked out.

On the train heading west, Toby was still uneasy, but he knew it would be futile to go to New York and undertake an investigation without sanction from Washington; it was unlikely that he would learn anything of value but probable that he would accidentally interfere with police activities.

He briefly contemplated going to Chicago to rejoin Janessa, then dismissed it. By bringing his daughter with him when he had set out for Washington, she had arrived in Chicago well in advance of the college placement examination schedule. She was doing her final studying for the tests, and Toby knew that it was the wrong time to distract her.

Arriving in Independence, Missouri, with a wait of several hours, Toby had an opportunity to visit Claudia Brentwood, a Holt family friend.

As the maid opened the door of the large, well-maintained Victorian home and Toby went inside, Andrew stepped out of the parlor into the hall. "We require peddlers to go to the back door," he said sternly.

Having thought Andrew was still in Switzerland, Toby was stunned. "Andrew!" he exclaimed. "This is a wonderful surprise."

They went into the parlor, where Andrew introduced his new wife. Toby was struck by Lydia's refined beauty and charm. Then Andrew's mother came in and greeted Toby happily. In her late sixties, Claudia was a healthy, active woman with matronly beauty.

"Toby, you can't spend a couple of hours here and call it a visit," she admonished when he outlined his travel arrangements.

"Why don't you stay overnight?" Andrew asked. "We'll have a chance to visit, and you'll get a good night's sleep."

Toby hesitated, then agreed. Claudia happily gave his ticket and baggage stubs to her handyman, sending him to the train station.

It was an enjoyable afternoon and evening. When Andrew's son, Samuel, came home from school, Toby noticed that he was somewhat smaller than Tim, although he was a year older. He was a handsome bundle of energy, and the light of mischief shone in his eyes. Andrew wanted Samuel to follow in his footsteps by attending West Point; Toby figured that if Andrew could get the boy accepted, the discipline would do him good.

Lydia listened to the conversation but rarely joined in. Toby detected a sadness about her, which he interpreted as homesickness. Then he realized that while Andrew was as outgoing as ever, he shared his wife's subtle undertone of melancholy.

Later that evening, Claudia, Samuel, and Lydia withdrew, leaving Toby and Andrew to talk, over cigars and brandy. It was then that Toby found out the nature of their misfortune.

"Left him behind?" Toby exclaimed angrily. "It's an outrage for a mother to be separated from her child."

"It's a complicated situation, Toby," Andrew said, changing the subject. "So you're commissioner of the West now."

"Yes, but what I've been doing lately has nothing to do with my duties and turned out to be a wild goose chase."

After telling Andrew about the letters and his Washington visit, Toby shrugged. "I just can't believe that the letter is a hoax."

"Perhaps it isn't," Andrew mused. "In Switzerland I heard about an explosive that could be hidden in that torch, Toby. It's a recent invention, very powerful, and detonated by percussion. It doesn't need a fuse or detonator wire. I went to see it used, but the explosive had been stolen by a man named—" He pondered for a moment, then shook his head. "I've forgotten. A lot was going on then, and it's slipped my mind."

"Stealing explosives in Switzerland to be used in Philadelphia would be a complex, expensive plan," Toby responded. "Hearing about the explosive and locating it involves considerable inside information—all completely uncharacteristic of anarchists. Still, I'd better send a telegram to Johnson."

Andrew agreed, then glanced at his watch. "Well, Toby, it's about time for me to turn in."

Toby nodded as he stood. "Andy, if there's any way I can help in regard to Lydia's child—"

"I appreciate that, but as things stand, there's nothing anyone can do." He suddenly snapped his fingers. "Kramer! That's the name of the man who apparently stole the explosives."

The color drained from Toby's face. "Andy, I

need you to drive me to the train station immediately."

"At this time of night?"

"I must get back to Washington as soon as possible."

Two weeks after leaving the Dakota Territory,
Henry Blake arrived in Yuma, Arizona, by stage.
Situated on the Colorado River, Yuma had grown
up as a river port and supply point for travelers
to California during the gold rush but was now a
quiet town of clapboard and adobe buildings. The
fort there was headquarters for the Third Cavalry
Regiment. Infantry and other personnel were also
stationed at the fort, which was the supply depot
for Fort Peck, sixty miles east, in an arid, sparsely
settled region.

The gate sentries snapped to rigid attention as
Henry approached in his immaculately neat cavalry uniform, his knee boots gleaming and his
buttons and spurs sparkling in the spring sunshine. When he learned that Colonel John Hatfield, the regiment commander, was having
breakfast with Yuma's mayor and councilmen, he
crossed the quadrangle to the quartermaster's
warehouse, where he asked the supply officer for
the requisition files submitted from Fort Peck
during the past year. There was a flurry of activity
as the supply lieutenant and clerks cleared a table
and stacked folders on it.

Henry thumbed through the requisitions rapidly. The amounts of munitions, uniforms, re-

placement weapons, horse fodder, and other items gave him a grasp of the fort's activities, as well as the efficiency with which those activities were being carried out. Neither pleased him.

The lieutenant stepped to the table as Henry was finishing. "Colonel Hatfield just went into headquarters, sir. Ah—you wouldn't happen to know anyone on General Crook's or General Terry's staff would you, sir?"

Henry, realizing the lieutenant must want a transfer, glanced around. Through a doorway he saw crates that contained Gatling guns and other heavy weapons stacked neatly with other crates. The warehouse was as clean and orderly as the office. "I don't," he replied. "Normally, when I hear someone trying to get a transfer, I tell him to concentrate on doing a good job where he's assigned. But it appears you're doing that, Lieutenant."

"I'm doing my best, sir, but I'd like to be assigned to field duty."

"Perhaps you will be in time. Thank you for your help."

The lieutenant called the officers to attention as Henry left for the commander's office, where the colonel motioned him to a chair. He expressed perplexity over the transfer to Fort Peck, where a major was already assigned.

"I'm as puzzled as you are, sir," Henry admitted. "I didn't ask to be transferred from General Custer's command. It occurred to me that this

194

assignment may be temporary, so I left most of my belongings in storage."

"Washington might have decided that Pat Kelly needs help in dealing with the renegade Pima. He's due for retirement soon, and his arthritis is so bad, he can't ride for any length of time."

"How many officers does he have, sir?"

"Ten—two first lieutenants and eight second lieutenants. They're inexperienced and have had only minor clashes with the Pima. I talked with Pat about your transfer—he has a good attitude about it."

Henry nodded in satisfaction. The colonel readily acknowledged that Fort Peck bore the primary responsibility for dealing with the renegades because it was situated in the center of the area where the Indian raids were occurring.

When the colonel offered assistance, Henry promptly accepted. "In looking through the requisitions, I saw that no remounts have been sent there in the past year. Also, the horses have been fed only hay. We'll be asking for a draft of horses and a couple tons of corn."

"I'll see that you get the corn and the best horses we have, Major Blake. We've heard of you here. Will you have lunch with my wife and me?"

"I'm very grateful, sir, but I'm sure that you understand my wanting to go to Fort Peck immediately."

The colonel accompanied Henry to the fort stable, where he picked out a saddle horse and packhorse. With fodder and grain loaded on the packhorse, Henry set out on the narrow, rutted dirt road heading east.

A cold, clear spring night settled over the rugged terrain, and Henry continued along the road by moonlight. He passed Sandstone Butte, where his close friend, and Cindy's husband, Lieutenant Reed Kerr, had lost his life while attacking the comancheros. Henry raised his hand in salute.

At noon the next day, he turned off the road a few miles from Fort Peck. When he set out again, an hour later, his horses were curried, and he himself was as meticulously neat as the day before.

The fort was in good condition, but two sentries were not only disheveled but amused by Henry's immaculate appearance.

Inside the gate Henry received a very pleasant surprise: He bumped into Walter Stafford, who had worked for Henry in Connecticut several years before. Stafford was a good young officer from South Carolina, a graduate of the Citadel. He was adjutant here.

At the headquarters a letter from the director of personnel in Washington was waiting for Henry. It concerned Klaus Lukenbill. Annoyed, he put the letter in his pocket. He had no time to worry about that conniver. "Is the commander in, Walt?"

"Yes, sir. He's been looking forward to meeting you."

The remark proved to be an overstatement. Major Patrick Kelly was cordial enough, but there was an undercurrent of jealousy in his manner.

"My patrols haven't been as effective as they should be," Kelly admitted. "I can't ride patrol myself, which is probably the reason you were sent here."

"You have only junior officers," Henry pointed out. "That's quite a handicap, sir."

Kelly shrugged. "You'll be deputy commander, and I'm going to give you a free hand. But full responsibility goes with it."

"It always does, sir."

"I'm glad we understand each other, Major Blake. I don't want any trouble with Washington."

Henry exchanged salutes with Kelly again, then went back out to the adjutant's office, where Stafford told him that four patrols were expected to return at any moment.

"I'd like to have a meeting with all patrol commanders an hour after they return," he said. "But first I'd like to see the patrol reports for the past month, plus the barracks and stable inspection reports. I'll also need a map of the area. While you're getting those things together, I'll look around the fort. Is there a conference room?"

"It's right next door, sir. And your quarters are ready. Your room is next to the commander's quarters."

The fort, constructed of logs and stone from the local area, had been built in the standard pattern: Long, low buildings fronted by porches flanked the side walls of the fort. Against the rear wall were the stables and fodder stores, with the smithy at one end. Henry noted that discipline and order were moderate—not slack but not good.

By midafternoon he had finished reading the reports. Stafford came in to say that the patrol commanders were assembled. After gathering the reports and area map, Henry followed the lieutenant into the next room, where the other officers and fifteen sergeants snapped to attention when Henry came in. Three officers were smoking, and one of the second lieutenants was wearing a civilian shirt with his uniform. Each man was introduced, and Henry saw that all were either good soldiers or could be in time.

"This is a staff meeting, gentlemen, not a social gathering. Please put out the cigars. Lieutenant, that is not a regulation shirt you have on."

Cigars were quickly extinguished, and the lieutenant named Hoskins flushed. "I'm sorry, sir. I'll wear an issue shirt tomorrow."

"You'll wear one today, Mr. Hoskins. We'll wait for you to go to your quarters and get into uniform."

Hoskins bolted for the door while the others remained standing. One lieutenant who started to sit down straightened when Henry glared at him. Five long minutes passed in tense silence, the men at attention in front of their benches and Henry beside the table, until Hoskins ran back in and took his place.

"You may sit down," Henry said as he spread

198

the map on the table. The men took their seats, and Henry picked up one report. "Lieutenant Medford, I see on your patrol report of two weeks ago that you saw tracks near Coyote Ridge."

"Yes, sir."

"Please stand up when you speak to me, Mr. Medford."

Flushing, the lieutenant stood at attention. "Yes, sir."

"Your report doesn't say what kind of tracks they were, Mr. Medford. Were they rabbit tracks? Antelope tracks? Elephant tracks, perhaps?"

As a second lieutenant smothered a laugh, Henry turned to him. "Is there something amusing, Mr. Simpson? If so, you should share it with the settlers in the region who go to bed each night in terror of being massacred."

Simpson's face grew crimson with embarrassment, and Henry turned back to the other man. "Well, Mr. Medford? What sort of tracks were they, and in what direction were they headed?"

"Horse tracks, but I don't remember the direction, sir," he blurted.

"Sit down, Mr. Medford. Did a sergeant accompany that patrol?"

A lean, wiry sergeant named Sprague stood. "There were over fifty riders, headed about ten points west of south, sir. It was Setanka and his men, no doubt about that."

Henry drew an arrow on the map to reflect that information. Picking up each report that mentioned tracks, he questioned each patrol commander in turn, extracting more precise information. In accordance with what was said, he drew more arrows on the map. When he finished, the arrows formed a large triangle, converging at a long, low range of mountains on the border, called Mesquite Hills.

As he held the map for all to see, there was an outburst of exclamations; the men were flabbergasted that the Pima always crossed the border at the same place.

"North of the hills is open terrain," Stafford pointed out, "with no places to set up an ambush."

"I'll ride there for a good look around, Lieutenant Stafford," Henry qualified. "I hope you've learned the value of complete, detailed reports. This discovery should have been made long ago."

The men nodded sheepishly. "On another subject," Henry continued, "Company commanders will have personnel inspections beginning tomorrow. There are too many shabby uniforms and dirty boots at this fort, and the stables are a disgrace. All officers will join me in the stables each evening for dinner until they are in satisfactory condition. Thank you for your attention, gentlemen."

The men stood stiffly as Henry left. Returning to a worktable in the adjutant's office, he went over the patrol schedule.

After dinner—which did not have to be taken in the stables, due to the energetic labors of a work detail—Henry made a courtesy call on the Kellys to meet the commander's wife. The day's end found Henry in his quarters, where he worked until late in the night on instructions for patrol commanders.

At dawn he saddled a horse and set out for Mesquite Hills; the renegades, he found, always crossed the border at the mountains and consistently used the same trail: a narrow canyon that reached through the range.

At a glance Henry saw that the north end of the valley, just over a mile from the border, was a perfect place for an ambush. Satisfied, he rode back to the fort, thinking about his men. While they vastly outmatched Setanka's men, annihilating the renegades in a single battle would require a high state of training and iron discipline.

Tighter discipline had to filter down through the officers and sergeants to the men. That would take weeks, as would the training. In the meantime, Setanka might realize his fatal error and change the route he used to cross back over the border.

XII

On a level field behind the fort, Henry Blake was preparing a horsemanship training course when he noticed a soldier riding to the fort from the east at a full gallop. Mounting his own horse, Henry rode around the fort, through the gate, and reined up in front of headquarters. The weary soldier was talking with Stafford, who interrupted and pointed to Henry. "Give your report to the major."

The man saluted and started talking breathlessly. He had been in a patrol led by Lieutenant Medford, which had happened upon an isolated ranch raided by the renegades no more than an hour before. A herd had been stolen, and a dozen Pima were driving it toward Mexico, while the remainder rode on in search of more loot. Medford and his patrol had gone to recover the cattle, while this messenger galloped back to Fort Peck with his report.

"No one at the ranch was hurt?" Henry asked.

"No, sir. The house is like a fort, and everyone ran inside when the renegades showed up. They're mad about losing their cattle, but that'll pass when the patrol brings the herd back."

Henry nodded. "When did Lieutenant Medford expect to get back there?"

"By nightfall, sir."

"And the majority of renegades was still headed north?"

"Yes, sir. About seventy-five of them."

"You did a good job. Dismissed."

Henry agonized over a decision: With the renegades well north of the border, there was time to set up an ambush at Mesquite Hills. But the training at the fort had barely begun, and Henry lacked firm control over every man. If he delayed, however, a wary Setanka might start using a different route to cross the border.

Henry turned to Stafford. "Mount up the first

and second platoons of companies A and B—full canteens and hardtack rations for overnight. I want both company commanders mounted up."

The lieutenant saluted and hurried away, shouting for the bugler as Henry went in to talk with Major Kelly. With the bugle blaring Boots and Saddles, the fort was a pandemonium of hoofbeats and soldiers racing about.

"Do you think you can catch them, Major Blake?" Kelly asked doubtfully.

"No, sir. I intend to set up an ambush at Mesquite Hills."

"Mesquite Hills? That's closer than a mile to the border."

"Not at the point where I intend to ambush them, sir."

"Well, just make sure you don't get closer than a mile."

"Yes, sir."

Outside, Henry mounted his horse and buckled on his pistol and saber. The platoons were forming in the quadrangle, one hundred men in double ranks. Lieutenant Hoskins and the other company commander, a first lieutenant named Barnes, took their places in front of their platoons.

His misgivings uncomfortably strong, Henry led the long double column of cavalry from the fort at a fast canter, sabers clanking and the hoofbeats a drumming roar. At least, he rationalized, he was taking the offensive against a savage enemy.

Dusk was settling as Henry led the column well

away from the path Setanka usually took across the open terrain north of the mountains. When the cavalry reached the gorge that would conceal them while they waited, it was dark. The horses were picketed, and a squad was posted to guard them. When Henry assembled the company commanders, platoon commanders, and squad leaders, he described the battle strategy.

"Hoskins, lead your soldiers across the north end of the canyon. Have the last men sweep the ground with brush to erase footprints. I'll stay with Lieutenant Barnes and his platoons on the west side of the canyon."

"Yes, sir," the leaders and commanders replied as if with one voice.

"Caution your men to keep still and stay hidden. We'll have a long wait, but everyone must be alert. Most important, I'll fire the first shot. I want the renegades positioned in a full cross fire before we start shooting. I want to wipe them out to a man."

After Henry had given the leaders a few minutes to pass the instructions along to their men, he led the platoons on foot toward the ambush area.

Henry had decided to stay with Barnes and his men because Hoskins's company was the more disciplined. Barnes's men were surprisingly silent and motionless once the squad leaders had them in place along the edge of the canyon. Henry, pleased, sat behind a rock at the center of the line, his Winchester across his lap.

The night passed slowly. Henry watched the

canopy of glittering stars, estimating the time. Before dawn he scanned the open terrain with his binoculars, searching for any sign of the renegades.

A distant dust cloud caught his eye as the sky lightened. He watched it for a moment. "Lieutenant Barnes," he said quietly, "ready your men. The enemy is on the north side of the valley and will be here at sunrise or a little later."

Barnes spoke to the second lieutenants, who moved quietly to their platoons, then talked to the squad leaders. Through his binoculars Henry saw the small, dark forms of riders becoming visible.

By the time the renegades were halfway across the valley, full daylight had come. They were whipping their horses to a fast pace, uneasy about being in the open. Many were leading stolen horses and carrying bundles of loot. Henry looked for Setanka.

He spotted the leader, who had a disfiguring scar across his face. The half-breed outlaw held a woman in front of him on the saddle.

Putting his binoculars aside, Henry picked up his rifle. He knew he would have to open fire somewhat sooner than he had wanted and pick off Setanka with his first shot in order to keep the woman from being killed in the cross fire. Setanka was riding in a safe spot in the center of the renegades, and Henry began tracking the man in his rifle sights.

When the riders were approximately one hundred yards from the canyon, a soldier prematurely fired his rifle. Then another fired, supposing the signal had been given. Seething with rage, Henry began shooting at other renegades; the danger of hitting the woman was too great to fire at Setanka. A thick cloud of gunsmoke billowed up the walls of the canyon as rifles fired in a deafening roar.

Renegades peeled from horses, dropping their loot. Setanka reined his horse around, his back presenting a clear shot. Just as Henry aimed his rifle, the half-breed leader shot the woman through the head with a pistol. She tumbled from the saddle, and Henry squeezed the trigger. But another renegade suddenly swerved into the bullet's path and fell from his horse.

Leaning low over his saddle, Setanka disappeared in a cloud of dust along with the other survivors. Henry fired the last two rounds in his rifle, then turned. "Lieutenant Barnes!" he roared. "Front and center!"

The lieutenant, his face pale, stepped up to Henry and stood stiffly at attention. "Yes, sir!"

"Within two hours of returning to the fort, I want a full written report from you that lists the reasons why your company failed to obey orders, plus the action you intend to take to prevent a recurrence."

"Yes, sir!"

"The leader of the squad to which that man is assigned is reduced to private. The soldier who disobeyed orders will be confined to the stockade for two weeks on bread and water. As a prisoner he will be escorted back to the fort under guard."

"Yes, sir!"

Fuming, Henry stomped down the slope to where the renegades had met the hail of lead. The soldiers filing down from the other side of the canyon were congratulating each other until Hoskins saw Henry's livid face and ordered them to silence. Henry counted twenty-six corpses. The knowledge that there could have been three times that many stoked his already boiling rage.

He turned to Hoskins. "Have the men collect these belongings and horses, to be returned to their owners. Appoint a detail to take the woman's body to the fort and build a coffin. An officer will accompany the escort that takes the body to her relatives."

"Yes, sir. What about these renegades' bodies, sir?"

"Leave them for the buzzards." Henry turned on his heel and stalked away.

In his office at the fort, Major Kelly was astonished by Henry's assessment. "Failure?" he exclaimed. "You got twenty-six of them, Major!"

"If I exercised adequate control over my men, the renegades would have been wiped out."

"And if a frog had wings, he wouldn't whack his backside every time he hops," Kelly joked, shrugging. "You're being much too hard on yourself, Major Blake. That ambush really hurt them."

"Not for long, I'm afraid. Setanka can probably

replace his losses within a few weeks. We won't have another chance like that for an ambush, but we can try some other tactics to see if they work. I think we can keep him from recruiting any more Pima."

"What do you have in mind, Major?"

Henry explained plans that he had devised on the ride back to Fort Peck. Kelly nodded thoughtfully in agreement.

The next morning, routine patrols resumed. Since the renegades would probably be licking their wounds, Henry felt free to leave the fort for a time, to implement his ideas. He and Lieutenant Medford, with two packhorses loaded with trade goods and supplies, set out for the Pima reservation on the Colorado River.

Three days after leaving the fort, Henry and the lieutenant stopped to shave and clean up, then rode onto the reservation. The Indian agent, wary of having his prerogatives challenged, greeted Henry and the lieutenant cautiously, then firmly refused Henry's request. "I won't allow it. If you want to talk to the chiefs and hire some scouts, you'll have to get authorization from Washington."

"I can get that," Henry coldly assured the man. "It will be brought here by the man who replaces you as Indian agent. If you want to keep your job, you'd better get those chiefs here—now."

A sickly smile spread over the man's face. "Well, I like to cooperate with the army, no question about that."

"I'll wait for the chiefs outside," Henry said.

He and Medford sat on a tree-shaded bench in front of the agent's office. Minutes later, the four elderly Pima chiefs arrived.

Henry greeted them courteously, then spoke with them about the renegade Pima.

The proud and dignified chiefs agreed that the renegades created trouble for the entire tribe. "You want to hire warriors from our tribe to track them down?" one chief asked.

"In part," Henry answered. "If some of your warriors join me, that will make others reluctant to join Setanka, and some who are with Setanka now may be persuaded to return to the tribe. It will be more clear to them that they're in the wrong. And brothers do not enjoy fighting brothers."

The chiefs quietly conferred. "You are a young man, but a wise one," one chief said. "We will choose six young men to go with you."

After the chiefs left, Henry set aside a portion of the supplies. "When the warriors get here," he instructed Medford, "tell them that these trade goods are for their families. Then settle the scouts in at the fort and get them tunics so the men can recognize them easily. I'm going to Yuma."

On his arrival at the fort, Colonel Hatfield congratulated him on his success.

Henry explained the reason he had come to Fort Yuma, causing the colonel to purse his lips doubtfully. "My quartermaster? That's Lieutenant

Howard, the best supply officer we've ever had here. I'm not sure he could do what you want."

"He's eager and intelligent, sir, so I think he could manage it."

"And sixty infantrymen?" the colonel continued. "That's a good portion of our total infantry strength. And I'm not sure they have heliographs."

"They should have; heliographs are standard equipment for infantry. In any event, it would be a temporary arrangement, sir."

"That's true," the colonel conceded. "All right, I'll let the infantry commander know I've authorized it. You tell Lieutenant Howard what you want him to do."

Henry exchanged a salute with the colonel, then crossed the quadrangle to the quartermaster's office. Howard was delighted with his new assignment. "I want ten or twelve heliograph posts on peaks east and north of Fort Peck," he told the young lieutenant. "The posts will have to be armed with Gatling guns because it won't take Setanka long to find out what we're doing. Do you see any difficulty in training the men to use heliographs?"

"No, sir," Howard replied happily. "Several are already qualified operators. For the others it's only a matter of learning the signals for numbers and the alphabet."

"The messages they'll need to send will be simple: If they spot a group of riders, I only need to know the riders' location and direction of travel.

The men will have to stay alert, though, because they'll be in danger of attack."

"They'll realize that, sir. In addition, I'll visit all the posts at frequent intervals to keep the men on their toes."

"Good. When you get organized, load your men and equipment into wagons and come to Fort Peck."

The lieutenant assured Henry he would be there as soon as possible. Feeling less impotent, Henry set out for Fort Peck. Heliograph posts spread far across the Arizona Territory could notify him within minutes of anything suspicious in that vast area, so his chances of catching the renegades would be increased manyfold. The indifference of the Mexican authorities galled him, making the thought of a swift, crushing attack against the renegades in their refuge very tempting.

Henry reached Fort Peck the following evening. After his first night of sleep in a bed for several days, he set about checking the activities at the fort. Alert men moved about in clean uniforms and shiny boots. Scouts were out with patrols, and the crackle of gunfire sounded from the range behind the fort, where the armory sergeant was conducting marksmanship class. At the saber training course, a platoon was charging past the straw targets, stabbing and slashing. Henry found that the horsemanship course had been completed, so he sent for Sergeant Sprague, one of the best riders in the battalion, and put the man in charge of the training.

Henry demonstrated the skills he wanted mastered. Using a single rein to control his horse, he rode through the series of low hurdles set at uneven intervals. Next, with his hands clasped behind his back, he held the reins in his teeth. After that he rode bareback around the course with a single rein and then with his reins in his teeth.

"It's easy to lose a rein or have one severed in combat," Henry pointed out. "Saddle girths can break at the wrong time, and there are many times when a cavalryman needs to have weapons in both hands. He still has to control his horse in those emergencies."

The sergeant smiled wryly. "I don't think very many of the troopers here can do that."

"If they could, it would be a waste of time to have the training, wouldn't it?" Henry pointed out, laughing. "I'm sure *you* can do that, can't you?"

"Yes, sir," the sergeant replied.

Returning to the headquarters, Henry pored over a map of the area, selecting tentative locations for the heliograph posts, then looked through the patrol schedule. He worked into the night. As he went to his room, lamps were glowing in the barracks across the quadrangle, where men were shining boots and readying uniforms for the next day and soldiers who could read and write were teaching those who were illiterate. In the conference room beside the adjutant's office, Stafford was lecturing sergeants and corporals on leadership. Lanterns were glowing in the stables, for some of the men were spending extra time grooming their horses. For the first time, Henry felt satisfied with the fort, although he was still unhappy with the situation. The battalion was turning into an efficient combat force, but it would be chasing around the territory when a single, deadly strike deep into Mexico would settle the problem for all time.

Edward Blackstone mopped the sweat from his face and neck with his handkerchief. With the sun beating down on the rusty iron roof and walls, the customs building at Belém, Brazil, was like an oven, and the humidity was so high, moisture trickled down the walls.

Teddy replied calmly in Portuguese as the suspicious customs officer barked surly questions and Edgar Dooley swayed on his feet and stared into the distance in a blissful alcoholic daze. Cecil Witherspoon gazed in fascination at a large insect with wicked-looking pincers as it crawled up the wall; then he looked out the window.

"I see two fine specimens of rubber trees out there," he commented. "But because the pods are still green, the seeds are far from ready to gather."

Edgar snapped out of his reverie. "You aren't supposed to mention rubber trees or seeds, Mr. Witherspoon," he warned in a loud, slurred voice. "If the authorities overhear you, we could end up in prison, remember?"

The customs officer, apparently understanding some English, pointed at Witherspoon and Dooley as he snarled a question. Teddy replied placatingly, beckoned Edward, and surreptitiously rubbed her thumb against the tips of her fingers.

Edward separated a bill from the roll in his pocket and pulled it out far enough for her to see the denomination. She glanced at it and continued talking with the official. Putting a hand behind her back, she held up two fingers. Edward slipped two bills from his pocket and pressed them into her palm.

Still talking, Teddy offered to shake hands with the officer. He glowered at her, reluctantly putting out his hand, but his expression brightened when he glanced at the money. He pocketed it and slammed an official stamp down on the expedition's papers.

The ordeal finished, Edward and the others left the building. "I told you not to mention rubber trees or their seeds," he hissed to Edgar angrily. "In fact, I repeated it many times over."

"Aye, I know, Edward," the Irishman replied in befuddled surprise, his bleary eyes wide and innocent. "But instead of telling me, you'd best speak to Mr. Witherspoon before he gets us into trouble."

Edward turned to Teddy. "Do you think that man is suspicious?"

"No question," she said quietly. "He cleared us to enter the country, but I'm sure he'll notify the authorities to watch for us when we leave. We'd better get out of Belém as soon as possible."

"I agree," Edward said. "If they figure out that the *Galatea* is our private transportation, they'll check her closely, and if they find those seed cans, we're on our way to prison. Do you want to try to arrange our transportation upriver?"

"Yes, I'll do that now. I'll meet you at the ship." The tall woman strode away.

Dooley and Witherspoon followed Edward to a a pier where a boat from the *Galatea* was awaiting them.

An international port and trading center for the cities scattered up the immense length of the Amazon River, Belém's appearance was that of a vastly overgrown tropical village. Indian women crouched before fruit and handicrafts for sale, while vendors peddling live fowl, fish, and vegetables trundled carts among the carriages. Stone buildings and sprawling warehouses of corrugated iron abutted thatched bamboo structures.

The pier, lined with large riverboats, was crowded with sweating laborers hauling off-loaded cargo to warehouses. A blend of odors emanated from bags of coffee beans and raw sugar, bales of tobacco, cotton, and hides, and crates of fruit. Edward grasped Cecil Witherspoon's elbow and steered him past crates filled with dark, round balls a foot in diameter—raw rubber—and to their boat.

The *Galatea* looked conspicuously neat and clean among the ships in the harbor. This worried Edward; he wanted to avoid attention. Worse, he noticed that two Brazilian gunboats prowled the harbor.

Dooley weaved on his feet as he stood and

grabbed the rope ladder hanging down from the rail of the ship. He sang a bawdy ditty as he climbed.

Edward smiled and shook his head at the man. Dooley often consumed a prodigious amount of liquor, but somehow he always managed to do what had to be done, and even when in his cups he had a sly, native cunning. Teddy had quietly suggested that they leave him behind because he was troublesome; more than enough uncertainties faced them. But Edward had firmly refused because while Dooley did create problems, he could also prove unexpectedly helpful.

On the ship Edward told Captain Sterch what had transpired.

"I'll get those seed cans unloaded without drawing attention," Sterch promised. "While you're gone I'll watch what happens here and let you know if the authorities seem prepared to arrest you when you come back downriver."

"How will you let us know?"

Spreading a map on the table, the captain pointed to Porto de Moz, a city at the junction of the Amazon with the Xingu, the first major tributary upriver. "I'll station some men there and keep them advised on what's happening here. When you come back downriver, look for their longboat."

"But we could be gone several weeks. Won't you attract suspicion by loitering here that long?"

"No, this is one of the slowest ports in the world to get cargo off-loaded. I'll kill more time by looking for a cargo going to Cairo or Port Said. If you still aren't back by then, I'll report engine trouble."

Edward noticed a shabby hulk of a steam launch moving up alongside the ship. His first reaction was disdain. Then he saw Teddy on the foredeck.

Forty feet long and fifteen in the beam, it apparently had never been painted since it had been built, which had been many, many years before. Edward could just barely make out the name on the bow, the *Amazonia,* and it was powered by a wheezing, knocking engine. It had a distinct list to port that was balanced somewhat by the fact that its smokestack leaned sharply to starboard.

Eyeing the launch dubiously, the *Galatea*'s sailors turned their boat toward it.

"Well, here it is, Edward," Teddy said cheerfully, reaching down to help Edward step up to the deck. "Our transportation up the Amazon and back. This is the owner and master, Captain Santos."

The man who stepped out of the wheelhouse as Teddy beckoned matched the lopsided appearance of his vessel, for his right ear was missing. He displayed blackened teeth in a larcenous grin as he gave Edward a limp handshake with a filthy hand. The crew consisted of several ragged, surly Indians with knife scars on their faces and bare chests.

When Santos returned to the wheelhouse, Edward quietly expressed his misgivings to Teddy.

"I saw much better vessels," she admitted, "but

each captain asked why I was going up the Amazon. Any would have reported us immediately to the authorities."

"And Santos wasn't interested in why we want to go up the Amazon?"

"He couldn't care less. The only thing that interests this man is money."

"Do you trust him?"

"As long as I have a pistol within reach. But we knew we were going to be in a dicey situation when we set out, didn't we?"

Edward sighed and glanced around. "Yes, but I didn't expect it to get this bad this soon. How much does he want?"

"The equivalent of fifty guineas, and we have to furnish provisions."

"That seems reasonable," Edward declared. "Very well, let's hire him."

"All right. We'll give him half the money now, and the other half when we return. I'll also need the money for the provisions." She moved closer, so the captain and crew could not see the money that Edward counted out and shoved into her hunting jacket pocket. "I'll get the provisions now and be back at sunset. Late tonight we can transfer the trade goods and the seed cans from the *Galatea*."

When Edward went back aboard the *Galatea*, Sterch and several crewmen stood at the rail, to watch the launch steam away, wheezing and belching. The captain shook his head meaningfully.

The launch returned during the late afternoon,

its deck littered with baskets of fruit and vegetables, crates of fowl, and tethered pigs. It tied up at the bow anchor chain of the *Galatea,* and as darkness settled, Santos dozed in the wheelhouse while his Indian crewmen sat around a brazier, sipped coffee, and glared up at the hands on the ship. At midnight the harbor was quiet, so Edward, Witherspoon, Dooley, and Teddy carried their belongings to the rail. The sailors rigged out a boom and cargo net and lowered the bundles and seed cans to the launch.

There were only two small, cockroach-infested passenger cabins on the launch. Teddy took the smaller, and Edward moved into the other with Witherspoon and Dooley.

Worried that the authorities would notice the activity and become suspicious, Edward rushed the process as much as possible, but the crates of cans seemed never-ending. Finally, just before dawn, they were done.

Edward had a last word with Captain Sterch, and then the *Amazonia* moved across the harbor and set out on its voyage up the Amazon. The prospect of steaming jungles, unknown dangers of the upper Amazon, and the rickety launch made the thought of a Brazilian prison less threatening to Edward than it would have been under other circumstances.

The air over the vast, turgid river was muggy. The squealing pigs and cackling chickens on the deck almost drowned Dooley's voice as he sang between swigs of whiskey. A pistol at her waist and crossed ammunition belts on her chest, Teddy chatted in Portuguese with the grimy, one-eared captain. Two crewmen were boiling leafy vegetables into a foul-smelling soup for breakfast, while Witherspoon peered through a magnifying glass at insects on those same vegetables.

Edward looked around glumly. Only through a concentrated effort could he relate his present situation to a conversation with Toby Holt in a comfortable, fashionable Chicago restaurant.

Two days after completing the college-readiness examinations, Janessa Holt stood in the college's administration building lobby with Calvin Rogers. The lobby was crowded with anxious prospective but underage students waiting for the results to be posted.

A murmur rose as a man emerged from an office with a sheaf of papers and made his way through the gathering to the bulletin board. He posted the first sheet of paper, and the young and precocious surged forward, craning their necks. The administrator glared around angrily at the people jostling him. "That is the list of examinees who achieved a score of ninety percent or better," he snapped. "How many of you believe your name is on it?"

The crowd receded. Calvin winked confidently at Janessa as they moved toward the bulletin board. The young people made a path for Calvin because he was leaning on a cane and limping, so he reached the bulletin board first and whooped as he pointed; Janessa's name was on the list.

After several people congratulated her, she and Calvin walked to the Schumann buggy, which was parked on the street.

"I certainly appreciate that last-minute coaching you gave me in math, Calvin. That was what got me into the top ten percent."

"No, your intelligence and hard work did it." His smile faded. "I'm glad you didn't receive that letter from Dr. Hendersen while you were taking the examinations. The worry would have distracted you."

"Yes, it would have," Janessa said soberly. Luther Bingham had been an assistant for Dr. Hendersen in Careyville, Illinois, near the Kentucky border. Wondering why Luther had failed to answer her last letter, Janessa had written to the doctor.

The hastily scribbled reply had explained that Luther had gone to Cedar Flats, Kentucky, on personal business and had intended to be gone only a few days. A month had passed however, and Hendersen had received no word from him.

Janessa and Calvin decided to go to Careyville. When she explained their intentions to the Schumanns, Dieter supported the decision.

"Men don't just disappear," he had said. "If there's anything I can do, just let me know."

Janessa wanted to believe that a simple explanation would account for Luther's disappearance, but something told her that much more serious circumstances were involved.

XIII

Janessa wondered why Dr. Hendersen had failed to check on Luther himself; when Calvin and she arrived at the doctor's clinic, she saw the reason. Hendersen was extremely busy. Tethered horses and wagons lined the street in front of his modest house, and the parlor was crowded with patients.

Hendersen was a spare, tall, affable man with white hair, beard, and mustache. "So I get to meet you at last, Miss Holt. Luther has told me much about you."

After warmly shaking hands with Calvin, the doctor gestured toward the parlor. "It's like this every day, so I miss Luther's help. He's an excellent doctor. I wish I knew someone in Cedar Flats to contact, to look into Luther's disappearance. It's a remote little backwater town, not on a railway line or major road."

"Do you know if he received my last letter?"

"Over a month ago," the doctor confirmed. "He said that he was going to wait a few days to answer it because he thought he would have something important to tell you."

"Was it connected with his trip to Cedar Flats?"

"I don't know, Miss Holt," the doctor said, stroking his beard. "But I have a hunch a lady was involved. Luther had that look about him that

222

young men get when they're thinking about a lady."

Janessa looked at Calvin. "We'll have to go to Cedar Flats. It's probably too late to set out for there today, though."

Both the doctor and Calvin agreed, so Janessa and Calvin rented hotel rooms for the night. But Janessa was too worried to sleep.

Years before Luther had moved to Portland, she remembered he had been a schoolteacher in Kentucky with a bright future until something horrendous had happened. Janessa only knew that a woman had been involved.

After breakfast the next morning, Calvin and Janessa, in a rented buggy, crossed the expensive toll bridge across the broad Ohio River, to arrive in Paducah, Kentucky, on the opposite bank.

Calvin stopped to ask directions. A wide road led toward Lexington, Louisville, and Frankfort; a similarly well-traveled road led southwest to Memphis and intermediate points. A narrow byway to the southeast led into the country and eventually to Cedar Flats.

Cedar Flats was as large as Careyville, but obviously few strangers visited the town, because people stared at Janessa and Calvin as their buggy passed. The town had a vaguely somber atmosphere.

"Let's ask the authorities if they've seen or heard of Luther," Calvin suggested.

223

"Let's find a hotel first," Janessa replied. "We'll certainly have to stay overnight, at least."

Calvin drove for several minutes before finding a tiny inn, the only lodgings in town. After they rented rooms, they set out on foot to find the sheriff. By this time it was after sunset.

Janessa pointed to an alley. "That should come out right beside the sheriff's office."

"I think you're right," Calvin agreed. "Let's try it."

Janessa stopped abruptly halfway past the jail. Luther Bingham was looking out one of the barred windows.

"Luther!" she gasped, running forward. "What are you doing in jail?"

Luther frantically motioned the young woman to be quiet as Calvin caught up. "Seeing you is a great relief. The sheriff is dishonest. If he finds you talking with me, you'll end up in here, too."

"Why are you in jail?" Janessa whispered. "What's going on, Luther?"

He glanced over his shoulder apprehensively. "There isn't time to explain. Talk with Melissa Lawson. She lives in a yellow house on a farm six miles west of town. You can't miss it. She'll explain everything, and then you can decide what to do."

"Nonsense, Luther," Calvin said firmly, without lowering his voice. "If you've broken the law, we'll hire a lawyer. Now tell us why you're in jail."

"Quiet, Calvin!" Luther pleaded. "I haven't

done anything wrong, but the sheriff runs this town. On top of that, he's not very bright and won't listen to reason."

"That's absurd, Luther!" Calvin snapped. "Law enforcement officials are public servants, not dictators."

"Calvin," Luther whispered patiently, "please accept my word for it that you can't—" He broke off with a groan of despair as two large men wearing badges came up behind Janessa and Calvin.

With her first look at the sheriff, Janessa knew Luther was not exaggerating.

"What are you doing?" he roared.

"Talking to my friend!" Calvin retorted heatedly. "I demand to know the charge on which he is being held!"

"You *demand?*" the sheriff erupted. "You gimpy little runt, you ain't in no position to demand nothing. You're under arrest!"

The sheriff charged forward and seized Calvin's arm. He tried to resist but was no match for his adversary. The sheriff dragged Calvin down the alley and motioned the deputy to bring Janessa.

Janessa offered no resistance. While she agreed with Calvin in principle, she realized that his attitude was misplaced in Cedar Flats. Her friends and she needed outside intervention, and she had to remain free in order to summon help.

As the sheriff hauled Calvin onto the boardwalk in front of the office to take him inside, the two of them were arguing fiercely. Janessa followed, deliberately hooking her toe under the edge of the walkway and stumbling. The deputy jerked on her arm to hold her up, and as if to keep her balance, Janessa clutched his elbow with her free hand, locating the olecranon and the internal condyle, the bones at the back of the elbow. Stabbing her thumb between the bones, she caught the sensitive tendon that rested between them and pulled it almost up to the crest of the condyle before it snapped back. The man bellowed in agony and released her.

The sheriff stopped as Janessa sprinted away. "Catch her! Don't stand there squealing!"

The deputy lunged after the girl and almost caught her; after the first few paces, however, she pulled away from him, her dress and coat gathered up to her knees, her legs churning. Her bonnet flew off her head and trailed down her back as she ran.

"Somebody catch that girl!" the deputy shouted as he chased her down the street.

"Catch her yourself!" a man called back. "I ain't risking my life catching somebody as dangerous as a girl!"

Another citizen whooped with laughter. "We'll help you when you catch her! We don't want our precious officer beaten up!"

The deputy snarled at them as the laughter swelled. The townspeople, obviously holding the sheriff and deputy in low esteem, cheered for Janessa.

Farther down the street, she passed a church. Several women stood on its lawn, and one shouted,

"Come here, my dear! We'll take you into the church and protect you!"

The other women beckoned and shouted, but Janessa just waved and ran on, unwilling to accept the women's assurances. A moment later, she glanced over her shoulder and saw that the deputy, winded, had stopped and was shaking his fist at her. He turned back.

She continued running as the street turned into a road, the last houses falling behind. Open countryside surrounded her. She staggered into a grove and sank down behind a tree, catching her breath and watching the road for any sign of pursuit.

Dieter Schumann, she recalled, was acquainted with high-ranking officials in Kentucky and Illinois and could help Luther. She had to contact Schumann, but he was in Chicago. Returning to the inn to get the rented horse was out of the question; the place would be watched. She thought about the woman Luther had mentioned, who lived in a yellow farmhouse. Janessa knew she had to find her.

"Melissa Lawson? I'm Janessa Holt, a friend of Luther Bingham's."

"Miss Holt!" the beautiful young woman exclaimed. "Come in."

"Is anyone else here? I apologize for being suspicious, but some men in town are after me, and I'm not sure whom I can trust."

"The sheriff and his deputy, I'll bet," Melissa

227

seethed. "You'll be safe here. I'm alone except for my two children."

Janessa followed Melissa into a large, spotlessly clean kitchen and accepted an offer of freshly baked bread and cheese.

"Please tell me why Luther is in jail."

Sighing heavily, Melissa sat across from Janessa and explained that the situation's genesis could be traced to when Luther had been a schoolteacher in Cedar Flats. "I was sixteen at the time," she continued, "but I knew my own mind. Luther and I were very much in love, but my father wanted me to marry Lawson, who owned this farm. He was a widower and almost as old as my father." She blushed and looked away. "Well, my father caught Luther and me in a barn. We weren't doing much improper, you understand, except being alone and kissing. That was enough for my father to have Luther arrested. To prevent that, I told my father that I would go ahead and marry Lawson, like he wanted."

"It was shameful of your father to put you through that," Janessa sympathized.

"Life seemed almost too hard to bear," Melissa confided. "Then my husband became ill and died a few weeks ago. When Luther read the newspaper obituary, he came to Cedar Flats, and we made plans to marry after a decent mourning period. But my father came between us again."

"How?" Janessa exclaimed. "Why?"

"He's always had his eye on this farm," Melissa explained. "I wanted to sell it so I could contribute the proceeds to my marriage with Luther. But my father made a deal with the sheriff that would force me to turn the farm over to him. The sheriff arrested Luther and won't release him until I relinquish the farm. Then my father and he will divide it."

"So that's what all this is about."

Tears filled Melissa's eyes. "Luther doesn't care about the money," she concluded, "but he wants me to do what I think is right. My father warned that if I went to the federal marshal in Frankfort, Luther would be shot while 'trying to escape.'"

Janessa leaned forward in her chair. "You and Luther are the victims of a criminal conspiracy. I have friends who can put a quick end to it; but first, I must get to where I can contact them. Do you have a saddle horse?"

"Yes, but he's young and feisty."

Janessa grinned. "That's the kind I need. I must get to Careyville as soon as possible. I'm worried about what the sheriff might do to Luther and my friend Calvin."

"I'm worried about what he'll do to you if he catches you, Miss Holt," Melissa admitted. She took a lantern from a shelf. "Keep a sharp lookout at the Paducah bridge. The sheriff might have concocted some story to get the authorities there to arrest you."

"I'll be careful. But if he does anything to me, my dad will tear this town apart."

Melissa lit the lantern and led her guest to the barn. Inside, Melissa helped Janessa saddle a young, spirited gelding, then gave her directions on how to circle around Cedar Flats.

Janessa took off. On the other side of town, the lively horse finally settled down. It maintained a rapid canter, covering the miles quickly as the hours passed. When the first houses on the outskirts of Paducah finally came into view, Janessa reined the horse into a trot as she rode toward the bridge.

Janessa saw a man standing in a circle of lantern light at the toll booth, talking with the bridge keeper. As he gestured, she saw a badge glint on his coat. She slowed the horse to a walk.

The men remained motionless until the gelding was a few feet away. Then the deputy sprang forward, grasping for the bridle. The young, skittish horse shied back, and Janessa tugged the reins to the side and kicked hard with her heels. The horse raced away from the bridge as the men shouted at her to come back.

When Calvin had needled the toll collector at the other end of the bridge about its high cost, the man had mentioned a ferry as an alternative. Janessa rode to the downriver edge of the town and searched for a road leading to the riverbank. If she couldn't find the ferry, she thought ruefully, she'd have to swim across the Ohio. After a few false starts, she found one that followed the contours of the bank. She came to a dock illuminated by lanterns, where a small steam ferry was tied.

Janessa dismounted, led the horse to a shed on the dock, and peered inside, where a middle-aged, heavyset man was curled up on a cot. "Excuse me, sir," she called out. "Would it be possible to cross the river tonight?"

The man woke, sat up, and looked at Janessa in surprise. "You're out mighty late, young lady."

"I need to get to Careyville, sir."

The man stood and stretched. "Well, I've got some folks sleeping on the ferry who would prefer to cross in the morning, but I usually start my day on the other side of the river. I'll take you over. That'll be a quarter, young lady."

Janessa paid him, then led the horse onto the ferry while he went to the small wheelhouse. The boiler worked up a head of steam. Two men sleeping in a wagon on the ferry sat up, looked around drowsily, and laid back down. Janessa watched the road, fearful that the deputy might pursue her.

The ferryman finally cast off the lines. When they were a few yards away from the bank, the deputy sheriff did ride onto the dock shouting and waving, but his voice was lost in the sound of the engine. The owner, in the wheelhouse, was looking in the opposite direction for traffic on the river.

Illuminated by a lantern, Janessa cheerfully waved at the deputy, who gestured in disgust before disappearing into the darkness.

His leg still throbbing with pain from his struggle with the sheriff hours before, Calvin sulked on a bunk beside Luther. Through the bars of their cell, they had a full view of the sheriff, sitting with

231

his feet propped on his desk and talking with two of his deputies.

"The sheriff's challenged the wrong family," Calvin grumbled. "His small-time empire will be crushed by the Holts."

Luther nodded. "No question about that. Janessa undoubtedly got a horse from Melissa."

"If she's on her way to Careyville, nothing will stop her. Luther, I can't understand how this sheriff had remained in office."

"I was told that he won his election through intimidation and graft. The people here are about ready to tar and feather his deputies and him and drive them from town. It's a bad situation."

"It'll end soon. I don't think we'll be here any longer than a day or two."

A vein in Luther's temple throbbed as he shook his head somberly. "This sheriff is stupid and unpredictable. He may try to keep the situation quiet by killing us and hiding our bodies."

The two men fell silent.

A few minutes later, a delivery boy entered the office and handed a telegram to the sheriff. He tore open the envelope, read the message, then angrily wadded it and hurled it to the floor. "The girl got away in Paducah," he announced in disgust. "She took a ferry across the river."

The deputies exchanged uneasy glances. "Maybe we'd better clear out of here, Sheriff," one suggested.

"Cut and run?" the sheriff jeered. "That's coward talk. What can a girl do to us?"

"She's probably got relatives in Illinois," a deputy speculated. "She'll talk to them, and we'll end up with a federal marshal riding in here. And when he talks to them two in the cell there . . ."

"You're right," the sheriff agreed. He fixed his gaze on Calvin and Luther. "We need to get rid of some witnesses."

Calvin felt a wave of nausea. "That wasn't just any girl," he called to the sheriff. "She's Janessa Holt, and she has very influential friends. If you kill us, you'll be making the situation worse for yourself."

"You sure have a big mouth." The sheriff sneered. "I'm going to enjoy closing it for good."

"Excuse me, sir," Janessa said to the man sleeping on a cot in the Careyville telegraph office. The man rose stiffly, holding his back, but gave Janessa a puffy, red-eyed smile as he turned up the lamp on the counter and put a form in front of her. A boy slept on another cot, but he did not stir. "It's the middle of the night, my dear. Are you all right?"

"Yes, I am now, sir," Janessa replied.

Addressing the telegram to Dieter, she described what had happened and requested help. The man put on his spectacles to read the telegram and count the words. He grimaced in disgust at the content. "That will cost seventy-five cents."

She put the money on the counter, and the man took the form to his desk, turned up the lamp, and tapped on his hand key. A moment later, the receiver clicked, and he transmitted the message. When he finished, the receiver clicked in acknowledgment.

"Sir," Janessa said, "I need to take my horse to a livery stable but have to come back here to wait for a reply."

"The boy here can put your horse in my stable, my dear. I'll send a note to my wife. She'll be over directly with something warm for you to drink."

"I don't want to be any trouble. . . ."

"It's no trouble to help a young lady who's by herself and who's suffered what your telegram describes. Boy, get moving."

Shortly after the boy returned, the old man's wife came in, carrying a basket with sandwiches and hot cocoa. After Janessa's travails, the couple's genuine concern was a healing balm.

When the receiver on the desk clicked, the man copied down the message and handed it to Janessa.

Dieter demanded she reply immediately and inform him if she was presently in danger. She wrote out a reply, which was transmitted to Chicago. A moment later, another telegram from Dieter came in, informing Janessa that he would arrive in Careyville at eight o'clock in the morning.

Overruling Janessa's reluctance, the kindly woman brought her a short distance to a small, neat house. A few minutes later, the girl was deep in a dreamless sleep in a soft, warm bed.

That morning, after a hearty breakfast, Janessa went to the Careyville station. She watched Dieter step down from his train, followed by a half-dozen burly lumberyard workers, all wearing pistols and toting rifles or shotguns. The dark concern on Dieter's face melted into relief when he saw Janessa. And seeing Dieter caused Janessa to weep a bit from the tension she'd been under.

"I have a bad feeling about this business," he said, hugging her fondly and drawing out a handkerchief. "That sheriff has Calvin now, as well as Luther?"

Janessa blew her nose and took a ragged breath. "Yes, and I'm very worried about them."

"We'll be on our way, then. I've sent a telegram to the federal marshal in Frankfort, and he'll arrive in Cedar Flats by this evening. Until then, my men and I'll take the situation in hand. You can fill me in on the details on the way."

They walked quickly to a livery stable, where the man who was a driver at the lumberyard chose young horses in good condition. The other men helped to harness them to a carriage.

The unquestionably skilled driver was also fearless. Wedged between two of the muscular men in the crowded carriage, Janessa was squeezed tightly in one direction, then another as the carriage careened around curves at breakneck speed on two wheels. On the rutted road to Cedar Flats, it became even worse. The young, powerful horses hit their full stride, and as they charged along the rutted road, the carriage lurched into the air and slammed back down with bone-jarring impact. Janessa held on as best she could.

The carriage roared into the town, skidding to a stop in a cloud of dust in front of the sheriff's office. Dieter threw the door open, and he and his men spilled out, Janessa after them.

On the boardwalk in front of the office was the same group of women Janessa had seen in front of the church the day before. Now, armed with rolling pins and iron skillets, shotguns and pitchforks, they looked just as resolute as the men who were poised to charge into the sheriff's office.

The men and women looked at each other in mutual bemusement. Dieter lifted his hat as he moved toward the door. "Excuse me, ladies. My men and I have business in there."

The leader of the women had a frustrated set to her chin and mouth. "I presume you're also looking for the sheriff and his deputies. They aren't in there." She turned to Janessa. "I'm very relieved to see that you're all right, my dear." Turning back to Dieter, she said, "We were fed up with waiting for our men to do something about that sheriff, so we decided to take matters into our own hands. We had hoped to free the two men being unlawfully detained, but we got here too late."

Dieter's eyes took on a dangerous light. "Do you have any idea where the sheriff or those two men might be?"

"The sheriff and one deputy apparently took the men somewhere on the road west of town."

"They must have gone to the Lawson farm, Mr.

236

Schumann!" Janessa shouted. "I'll show you where it is!"

"Let's go, men!" Dieter roared, pushing them toward the carriage. "Move! Move!"

Janessa sprang back into the carriage, where she was almost crushed by the stocky laborers climbing in after her. The horses lunged into a headlong run with the doors swinging wildly and men still on the steps clambering in. The doors slammed as the carriage skidded around a corner onto the street leading west of town.

A short time later, the Lawson farm came into view. Several horses were tethered by the barn. Dieter called to the driver to stop on the road. The men would approach the barn quietly, on foot. The carriage pulled up, and the men jumped out. Janessa followed them. "You stay back, Janessa," Dieter cautioned.

"I will," she said. She climbed over a fence behind the men and followed them across a field. As they approached the barn, she heard a furious argument inside. She recognized one voice as the sheriff's and assumed the other was Melissa's father's.

"You can't get away with hanging those men!" Thompson barked. "I won't be an accomplice to murder!"

"You'll be a party to whatever it takes!" the sheriff shouted. "You promised me half this farm, and I'm going to get it!"

Dieter motioned his men into position as he edged toward the barn door. When his men and he had their weapons at the ready, he threw open the door. "Put up your hands!" Dieter shouted.

Everyone in the barn froze in surprise. Luther and Calvin were standing to one side, their hands tied, and a deputy was beside them. Melissa stood trembling and white-faced beside her father. The sheriff seized her, pulling her in front of him, and put his pistol against her head. "No, *you* put up your hands, or you'll see her brains blasted all over this barn!"

No one moved. Thompson, standing at one side of the sheriff, and Melissa turned pale. Janessa watched him, realizing that the threat had unhinged him. Snarling, he leaped forward and pulled the pistol away from Melissa's head. She wrenched free.

Dieter and his men barreled into the barn. The deputy dropped his pistol and raised his hands. As the sheriff and Thompson struggled, the sheriff's pistol fired with a loud report. Thompson reeled back, clutching his chest. He fell as Dieter yanked the pistol from the sheriff's hand and overpowered him. Shot through the heart, Thompson was dead when he fell.

Sobbing, Melissa ran to Luther. She untied his hands while Janessa untied Calvin's, and then the four of them followed Dieter and his men as they shoved the sheriff and deputy toward the door. Just then, a wagon careened up in front of the barn. The townswomen, still grasping skillets, pitchforks, shotguns, and other weapons, surveyed the scene.

One woman looked at Dieter. "It appears there's nothing left for us to do."

"Yes, there is," Dieter replied, ripping the badge from the sheriff's lapel and handing it to her. "A federal marshal will be here by this evening. Until then, you ladies may take over law enforcement. My men and I will assist you with these two prisoners, Madam Sheriff."

XIV

The New York police commissioner crossed his office to greet Toby Holt. "Sorry I was out of town when you arrived. I understand the chief of police has been assisting you."

"He's been most helpful indeed," Toby assured the commissioner. "He's assigned Detective Lester Elliot to work with me full-time, and we call upon the chief when we need additional officers."

"Good, good. Have a seat, Mr. Holt, and please bring me up to date."

"I'd better begin with my conversations with the officials in Washington."

Toby had met again with Thomas Haines and the attorney general's investigators. Everyone agreed that in light of Andrew Brentwood's information, the anonymous letter should be taken seriously. This was obviously a well-laid plan, the explosive having been stolen in Switzerland to be used in Philadelphia. Logically, the plotters would have infiltrated the group working on the Statue of Liberty in Paris, so he had sent a telegram to Cindy, requesting full particulars on all workers in the sculptor's studio.

Toby then proceeded to New York, where the warning had originated. Assuming that the letter had been mailed from a postal substation in the vicinity of the writer's residence, Lester Elliot and Toby had obtained sample cancellation marks from every substation in the city, then compared them with the one on the letter. They had found one that matched perfectly.

"We've been canvassing all apartment houses in the vicinity of the substation," Toby continued. "The letter was beautifully written, so we know we're looking for an accountant, a clerk, or a man in some other trade requiring good penmanship."

"Any prospects?" the commissioner asked.

"Not so far. Lester is talking with more apartment building managers this morning."

"Let's hope something turns up soon."

Toby nodded. "The investigators at the attorney general's office suspect that the group involved is the Zeno Bund. More important than their name is the fact that an extremely dangerous explosive is hidden somewhere." Toby paused for a moment, thinking. "They must have an ulterior motive; these anarchists are going to too much trouble simply to kill people. More must be involved."

Before Toby left, the police commissioner and he speculated about hidden purposes but came to no conclusions. As he walked to the restaurant where Detective Elliot and he had agreed to meet for lunch, Toby turned his face to the sun. It was the first balmy spring day in New York, which made him uncomfortably aware that time was slipping away. He had to track down the plot to its source and locate the deadly explosive before the first week in July.

At the restaurant Elliot said that he had talked with the managers of four apartment buildings, two of which had an accountant and two clerks living in them.

"One is an accountant at a bank," Elliot said, reading from his notebook. "He's in his forties, with a wife and three children—doesn't fit your criteria for a suspect. The second clerk works at a hardware store, is married, but has no children. The third one is a very close match to your criteria."

"Tell me about him."

"He's a clerk, but his landlord said that he's had only one job for a short time during the past months. He had been slow paying his rent, but recently he's paid it on time or in advance. It's paid up now, but the landlord hasn't seen him for weeks."

"That's the one, Lester. What's the man's name?"

"Jenkins, Cyril Jenkins."

At the apartment building, the landlord reiterated what he had told Elliot. "He's a good tenant," the man added, "but it's been weeks since I've seen him."

"Maybe we can find out why he's gone," Toby suggested. "We'd like to take a look inside the apartment."

The landlord led Toby and Elliot upstairs, unlocked the door, and exclaimed in surprise as the door swung open. The apartment was a shambles: Furniture was tipped over, drawers were hanging open, and clothing was scattered over the floor.

At first Elliot speculated that Jenkins might have left town, but then he found suitcases in the bedroom. Toby noticed an oddity in the apartment that had started a somber train of speculation. Standing at a window, he gazed down at the street, lost in thought as Elliot finished searching through the rooms.

"There's no blood," Elliot reported, returning to the room where Toby was standing at the window.

"If you intended to dispose of a member of your anarchist group, what's the first thing you'd do?"

"Eliminate all traces of a connection between him and the group."

"Right. Now what's missing here? Look at the desk, Lester."

"Letters and other papers," Elliot answered grimly, looking at the open, empty drawers. "There's not a scrap of writing in this apartment. If he's the one who wrote the anonymous warning, perhaps they did get rid of him."

Toby nodded. "Now, assuming that's true, the

killers probably removed all identification from his body. What's the police procedure here if a body is found with no identification?"

"I'll show you at headquarters. We'll have to review all the recent, unsolved murder cases. And we'll need a police detail to go over this apartment with a fine-toothed comb."

Toby told the manager to lock the apartment and let no one else in it until the police arrived. Elliot and he went to police headquarters, where they dispatched a squad to search the apartment and spoke with the captain in charge of homicide investigations.

The captain explained to Toby that if a body without identification was found, a tintype was made of the face before burial. The captain had a clerk bring in the files on all unsolved murders, which Toby and Elliot reviewed. When they had finished, only one involved a relatively young man with no identification.

They returned to the apartment house, and Toby showed the tintype from the file to the landlord. "Yes, that's Mr. Jenkins, all right," he said sadly. "And he's dead? He was such a nice fellow!"

"Do you know where he worked when he had that job?"

"Yes, sir. The Broadway Department Store."

The next morning, Toby sent a telegram to Herbert Johnson in Washington, asking if Cyril Jenkins was on the list of known anarchists. When he returned to his hotel, the desk clerk handed him a letter from Cindy, consisting of the information on the workers at Bartholdi's studio. It listed each individual, giving all the background information she knew and her assessment of the person's character. The information on one man, a French Canadian named Maritain, was scanty because he had worked at the studio only a short time and was reclusive. Because he spoke English as well as French, he would be among the group escorting the torch to Philadelphia.

When Elliot saw the letter, he agreed with Toby that Maritain was most likely the anarchist infiltrator.

"I'd like you to interview the other residents in Jenkins's apartment building today. Someone may know something that will prove useful."

"I'll do my best, Mr. Holt."

"I'll go to the Broadway Department Store, then see what I can do with this information Cindy provided. Let's meet at the hotel restaurant for dinner."

They went their separate ways. Toby took a hired carriage to the department store, where the personnel supervisor found a business letter Jenkins had written. Toby took it with him to police headquarters. A handwriting expert provided the first piece of conclusive evidence; Cyril Jenkins had written the anonymous warning.

During the afternoon Toby went to talk with the postmaster at the city's central post office, where all incoming and outgoing mail was processed.

"You're asking me to do the impossible, Mr. Holt. You don't realize the volume of mail we process here and how much work would be involved. There must be some other way you can obtain the information."

"If there is, I don't know about it. Certainly it's within the bounds of possibility for your people to review all incoming mail."

"Then let's say impractical rather than impossible. It would take hundreds of hours, and our personnel are overworked as it is."

"I can get a court order to require you to do it, but that shouldn't be necessary. There are plans to slaughter innocent men, women, and children. Now I honestly believe that you should be willing to make any effort necessary to prevent that."

The man hesitated, embarrassed. "All right. I'll find a way to do it. You're interested only in letters with a Paris postmark?"

"Yes, and only those to be picked up at the post office. The people involved in this wouldn't use a street address."

Toby thanked the man and told him how to stay in contact. It was late in the day when he met Elliot for dinner.

The detective had interviewed over a score of people at the apartment building, spending hours to uncover only one significant fact: A man in the building had seen Jenkins leave with a suitcase a few weeks before.

"He saw Jenkins again two nights later," Elliot went on. "So wherever he went, it was a short trip."

"Possibly just overnight. Well, I'd certainly like to know where he went, Lester, and who went with him."

The detective nodded.

Toby told Elliot the outcome of his day.

"Now that you have the full cooperation of the post office," Elliot remarked, "we have a good chance of identifying the leader of the group."

"Assuming Maritain is a member of it and they communicate by post."

Darkness had fallen by the time the men left the restaurant for the busy street. A mixed district of businesses and apartment buildings, people were still arriving home from work and doing last-minute shopping. Toby, who was always instinctively aware of his surroundings, noticed that, amid the bustle of the street, two men were lurking in the shadows beside a building directly across from the restaurant.

Realizing that Elliot and he were silhouetted against the restaurant window, Toby ducked, reached for the pistol in his shoulder holster, and shouted to Elliot in warning. At that instant the deafening roar of gunfire rang out, and Elliot crashed backward into the restaurant window, sending shards of glass to the sidewalk. Pedestrians screamed, running in all directions. Toby took careful aim as bullets struck around him.

People ran between the gunmen and him, but

Toby finally had a clear shot. He squeezed the trigger and took one man out of the fight. The other one dashed toward an apartment-house entrance while Toby tracked the fleeing form in his pistol sights. Just as he was about to pull the trigger, a woman ran past in front of the gunman.

Toby eased the hammer down, and his opponent disappeared. Toby sadly stepped through the broken window, to see his friend sprawled on his back on the restaurant floor, sparkling glass fragments scattered over him and the front of his shirt soaked with blood.

Seeing there was nothing he could do, Toby dashed across the street in pursuit of Elliot's murderer. Suddenly a carriage appeared out of nowhere, the galloping horses almost running him down. One horse bumped him with its shoulder, spinning him to one side, but he regained his balance and charged into the apartment building.

The stairs and landings were full of people commenting excitedly about the gunfire. Shouting at the people to go to their apartments, Toby started up the stairs. Leaning over the railing, he looked up the stairwell. He quickly jumped back as a shot rang out and a bullet slammed into the rail, sending chips of wood exploding.

He was almost trampled in the mad dash of shrieking people fleeing to their apartments. Then the stairwell was deserted except for Toby taking the stairs three at a time after the gunman. As he ran he listened for the gunman's footsteps to make certain he was not waiting in ambush at a landing.

It was obvious that the man was headed for the roof, intending to escape across the top of neighboring buildings. Toby closed the distance between them, occasionally leaning out and catching a glimpse of the gunman. Once his opponent paused, aiming, but his pistol clicked on an empty chamber. Toby fired twice, and the man howled as splinters from the rail struck him. Then he ran on up the stairs.

The gunman reloaded, then tossed empty shells on the floor. By the time Toby passed the spent casings on the stairs, he had replaced the fired bullets in his own pistol. He reached the top flight and saw the door to the roof standing slightly ajar. He ran up the stairs with intentionally heavy footsteps, then kicked the door hard.

A bullet slammed into the door as it flew wide open, but Toby hurled himself out, staying low and rolling as he hit. Two bullets struck the roof behind him, tracking him as he rolled. The gunman, standing near the roof's edge, was clearly silhouetted by the city lights. Toby snapped off a shot at the man's legs to wound him.

The man yelped in pain, and his legs folded. He reeled toward the edge of the roof, trying to stop himself, then screamed hoarsely as he plunged over. Toby cursed as he stood and walked to the edge, to look down at the body on the sidewalk. Then he reloaded his pistol and put it back in his shoulder holster.

By the time Toby reached the street, it was swarming with policemen. He identified himself

248

to the sergeant in charge, who nodded and touched his cap. "I guess you know that Detective Elliot and both gunmen are dead, sir."

"Yes. Have you had a look at the gunmen?"

"Yes, sir. There's nothing in their pockets but extra bullets, Mr. Holt. Not a scrap of identification."

"It's what I expected." Toby scratched his head, disgusted. "Just take them to the morgue."

The policeman nodded, touching his cap again as Toby went to Elliot's body. He hunkered down, looking at the dead man in remorse and burning rage. The investigation had been vitally important to him from the very beginning, but now it had taken on an additional purpose: to find the killer of his friend.

The following day, Hermann Bluecher sat at his desk in his study and listened as Klaus Lukenbill made excuses for his men's failure. Sweat trickled down Lukenbill's pale face as he talked rapidly, anticipating an explosion of rage from his employer.

Remaining perfectly calm, Bluecher tossed out a casual question. "If the other man isn't a policeman, who is he?"

"I'm not sure, sir," Lukenbill admitted. "Whoever he is, though, he's a mean one. Those were my two best men with pistols, and he killed both of them."

"But they both died before they could be questioned?"

"Yes, sir."

"You say the policeman and this other man were only investigating Jenkins's death and have been asking no questions about the Zeno Bund?"

"That's right, sir. I sent a couple of men to a saloon down the street from the apartment building, and they heard all about the questions that the policeman had asked everyone. Nothing was said about any kind of organization."

Bluecher nodded. At other times he had been enraged when his underlings had failed, but now he was indifferent. A few days before, he had read a long newspaper article that had deeply affected him. It explained something about the United States that had always puzzled him. It seemed to Bluecher the nation should be a confused mass of warring individualists, yet some force bound the factions together. Bluecher had been unable to identify that force until reading the newspaper article.

It explained how the nation was united by bonds of patriotism and respect for the Constitution. In many other countries, leaders were replaced only through uprisings, but in the United States it was accomplished by the ballot box. The leaders, patriotic and respectful of the Constitution, bowed to the will of the people.

That patriotism and respect for the Constitution, invisible forces more powerful than regiments of dragoons crushing protests in the street, overcame the divisiveness of individualism. It could overcome any stress, create compromises

250

between opposed interests, and provide resilience that could endure any conflict.

Being keenly intelligent, Bluecher had realized after reading the article that using the anarchist group in an attempt to undermine the government in Washington was like using a toothpick in an attempt to move a mountain.

Because the plot had been set in motion, Bluecher intended to continue with it, but now it served only as a test for the anarchist group, for which he might someday have further use—in another country. Having dismissed the overall plan of which it was a part, he was even contemplating a move to South America, where such plans would be more successful.

He shook his head as Lukenbill outlined other means to kill the man who had been with the police investigator. "No, leave him alone. It is extremely unlikely that he'll find out anything about our plan before it is put into action. Another attempt to kill him would merely create an unnecessary risk of exposing our plot. For now, concentrate on keeping your men under control and attracting no suspicions."

"Yes, sir."

"It has been some time since you have checked on Henry Blake. Go to Washington and see if he has been transferred yet."

"All right, sir," Lukenbill replied, standing up and moving toward the door. "As soon as I get back, I'll let you know what I found out."

Leaving the house, Lukenbill wiped the cold

sweat off his brow. He was intensely relieved. In addition to expecting a blistering reprimand from Bluecher, he had feared questions that might reveal his plans to rob the Philadelphia mint.

Having no intention of going near Washington, he planned to wait a couple of days, then visit Bluecher and lie to him, saying that Blake was still at the same post. After he robbed the mint, he would forget all about Bluecher and the Zeno Bund.

As the *Amazonia* moved slowly up a wide, turgid tributary of the Amazon, Edward Blackstone stood in a patch of shade beside the wheelhouse and fanned his face with a large leaf. Stirring the torridly hot air did little to cool his face, but the motion of the leaf drove away at least some of the voracious, oversize mosquitoes that whined around his head.

Witherspoon stood at the rail, using binoculars to scan the occasional clusters of rubber trees on the riverbanks. Many rubber trees had been sighted, but the seeds were not yet ready to gather. For the seeds not to rot in the cans, they had to be dry and ready to break out of their pods.

At a bend in the river a hundred yards ahead, a canoe with a half-dozen Indians in it came into view. Feeling listless in the breathless heat, Edward gazed at the canoe indifferently. Natives had been sighted occasionally. They were curious about the launch and wanted to sell fruit and vegetables.

Teddy, standing beside Witherspoon, squinted intently at the canoe. Noticing her interest, Edward shook off his lethargy and looked more closely. The Indians lifted long, slender poles and put the ends of them to their mouths.

Teddy and Captain Santos shouted in Portuguese while Teddy seized Witherspoon's arm and dragged him down with her as she fell prone to the deck. The Indian crewmen scrambled for cover. Not understanding what was happening, Edward leaped to Dooley and threw him to the deck as he himself fell flat. Then he saw what the Indians were blowing—poisoned darts four inches long—into the wheelhouse and rails.

One of the darts found a human target. An Indian crewman screamed in terror as he stood frozen, looking wild eyed at the dart in his shoulder. Teddy rolled across the deck and kicked his feet from under him, then plucked the dart from his shoulder as he sprawled beside her. Panic-stricken, he struggled to scramble to his feet, but she gripped his long hair and rapped the back of his head solidly and repeatedly against the deck until he subsided, dazed. She took out a knife and opened the puncture the dart had made in his shoulder.

Crawling along the deck to the bow, Edward took out his pistol. Having thrown the engine into reverse, Santos was trying to back the launch in a straight line, but the rudder was worn and loose, so the vessel fishtailed violently, causing the sights on Edward's pistol to pass back and forth across the canoe as he tried to take aim.

With the advantage of the current, the canoe was pacing the launch as darts continued thudding into the woodwork. Edward turned to Teddy, who was sucking blood and poison from the cut on the crewman's shoulder. "Teddy, tell Santos to throttle down! I can't hit anything with the vessel veering about!"

Teddy spat blood on the deck, then wiped her mouth with the back of her hand as she turned and crawled toward the cabins. "I will in just a moment, Edward! I'll get a gun and join you!"

Seeing her pistol in a holster at her waist, Edward wondered what she was talking about. He snapped off shots at the canoe in frustration, but the bullets went wild. He started to reload as Teddy, a dart sticking in the tall crown of her pith helmet, crawled up beside him with her elephant gun. Opening the breech of the gun, she seated two bullets the size of cigars in the double barrels, closed the breech, and shouted to Santos.

The wild hammering of the engine subsided to a murmur when Santos closed the throttle. The vessel stabilized, and Teddy shouldered the heavy rifle and fired both barrels simultaneously. There was a shattering clap, and a huge cloud of smoke belched from the muzzle. Edward, peering under the smoke, saw the bow of the canoe explode into splinters.

The canoe sank, and the Indians dropped their blowguns and swam toward the bank.

"You see, that's far more effective than killing them," Teddy explained as she and Edward stood. "They think more of their canoes than they do of themselves, and that lot will soon spread the word far and wide of what happened. We won't have that trouble again."

Edward nodded, then turned as Dooley exclaimed in despair. Thinking the Irishman had been hit by a dart, Edward rushed over to him. "What is it, Edgar?"

"I broke my bottle, and all and all," Dooley wailed in distress, looking at shards of glass in his coat pocket. The side of the coat was soaked with brandy. "My sainted father would disown me!"

"It's only a bottle, Edgar," Edward said impatiently. "You have plenty more in the cabin."

"Not that much more," Dooley moaned, "and it's a dreadfully sinful thing to break a bottle, isn't it?"

He continued lamenting, stumbling off toward the cabin as the launch started forward again. Santos was shouting his thanks to Teddy in Portuguese as Witherspoon climbed to his feet, apparently mystified as to what had happened. The crewman who had been hit by the dart, surprised to find himself still alive, tearfully expressed his gratitude to Teddy.

Shrugging off the thanks, she grasped a boat hook and stepped to the rail to fish the blowguns out of the river as they floated past the launch. "The curator at the Ethnological Museum in Lon-

255

don will be very pleased to have a few of these," she explained to Edward.

As he went to help her, Edward reflected that she had been the life of the expedition. When they had taken four blowguns out of the water, Edward and Teddy began pulling darts from the rails and wheelhouse. Laughing, he commented about Edgar's despair over having broken his bottle. Teddy laughed, then grimaced. "I'll be glad to have a drink myself presently. Taking care of that crewman has left a horrid taste in my mouth."

"I'm sure it has. We're all very fortunate to have you as one of the party, Teddy, because you deal with situations very handily. That crewman in particular is fortunate that you're here."

Teddy laughed heartily and shook her head. "No, he's fortunate that he got that dart in his shoulder. If it had hit his grubby rump, I'm afraid he would have had it."

XV

Weary after the long, hard ride to Fort Peck, Colonel John Hatfield sank into a chair with a sigh of relief. He took out two telegrams, which he handed to Patrick Kelly. One was from the territorial governor and the other from the secretary of the interior in Washington. After he read them, Kelly passed them to Henry. Addressed to Hatfield at Fort Yuma, both demanded that the regiment take immediate action to prevent further

256

outrages by the renegade Pima, who had massacred nine men, women, and children four days before.

"Although nine people have lost their lives," Hatfield said, "this wouldn't have seemed such a shock a few months ago. But now we have those renegades on the run."

"Through Major Blake's efforts," Kelly pointed out generously. "But I have to agree, Colonel Hatfield. It is all the more surprising because Major Blake has the situation largely under control. Over sixty of the renegades have been killed in several engagements, and it's almost impossible for them to move about without being spotted by a heliograph post."

"We're going to have to tighten the screw on them some more," Hatfield said. "I can send another company of cavalry from Yuma, which you can position as a striking force west of here. We can requisition more heliographs, and I can bring your infantry strength up to a full company so you can set up additional heliograph posts."

Henry shook his head. "Let's assess what Setanka did: This is the first time he's slaughtered people simply for the sake of killing."

"What about those people on the stagecoach?" the colonel pointed out.

"The stagecoach was his target. The people happened to be there. This time, he came out of Mexico with murder on his mind. He only stole horses, which were remounts."

"What are the implications?" Hatfield asked.

257

"Revenge. It's hard for him to move around during the day without being spotted. He certainly can't move a herd. The only thing he can do is seek vengeance at night. This sort of thing will happen again."

Hatfield and Kelly nodded. "I hadn't thought of it in those terms," the colonel admitted. "How does it affect our handling the situation?"

"Dealing with a killer isn't the same as dealing with a thief. He'll come in with fewer men, and only at night. More importantly, he won't be burdened with loot when he leaves, so it'll be more difficult to catch him."

The colonel rubbed his eyes with the heels of his hands. "Would additional forces enable you to defend the territory against him?"

"No, sir. The territory is simply too large and rugged. I know of only one way to end this problem."

"What's that?"

"If Major Kelly will go on leave and take Mrs. Kelly to visit her relatives in California, placing me in command here, Setanka and his men will be annihilated within two days."

It took a moment for the two officers to realize his meaning. Kelly spoke first. "You can't invade Mexico, Major Blake. It's out of the question."

The colonel agreed. "We'd have a hornet's nest on our hands, and your army career would be on the compost pile."

"Without boasting, I believe I could incur some official disfavor without seriously damaging my career, sir. Beyond that, the lives of people here are more important than my career. We must serve notice that Mexico is not a safe refuge."

Stroking his chin, the colonel thought for a moment, then turned to Kelly. "Why don't you take a leave, Pat? I'm sure Martha would enjoy seeing her folks."

"Very well, sir," Kelly replied in resignation. "Major Blake, I wish you luck. But for the record, Colonel Hatfield, I have to state that I object to taking cavalry across the Mexican border."

"Your objection is noted, Pat," the colonel acknowledged. "When would you like to begin your leave?"

"Tomorrow morning, sir." Kelly stood and moved toward the door. "If you'll excuse me, I'll tell Martha to start getting ready."

The following morning, Henry exchanged salutes with Major Kelly as the fort carriage moved away. Henry turned to Walter Stafford. "Have the bugler sound Officers' Call."

Moments later, there was a pounding of boots to the conference room. Henry went in, and the officers were standing at attention.

"Sit down, gentlemen," Henry said. "We're going into Mexico for Setanka and his men." He lifted a hand, frowning at the outburst of joyful exclamations. "This won't be a pleasure trip. The renegades are probably located in a town, and any officer or trooper who kills a noncombatant will be court-martialed for murder."

The officers nodded.

"The first two platoons of both companies will go, along with an additional platoon made up from the rest of the battalion. Both company commanders will go, and there will be two officers for each platoon. Are there any volunteers for platoon officers?" When all of the second lieutenants immediately stood, Henry turned to Stafford. "Have them draw straws."

A few minutes later, the winners were grinning with excited anticipation. Henry gave them instructions on choosing horses and briefing their men, then came to the final topic: "This is a diplomatically questionable undertaking. Therefore, I will sign written orders to be issued to all officers. You will thus be released from any personal responsibility that might adversely affect your career. You will present these orders to any authority who questions why you went into Mexico as a part of an armed force."

During early afternoon, Henry led the long column from the fort, with the Pima scouts riding ahead. At the rear were thirty horses, to replace those that might be killed or wounded in battle. It was a bright, warm day, the blossoming sage making the air fragrant. Henry's mood matched the weather. Prepared to accept all repercussions, he was eager to go into Mexico after the renegades.

As soon as he led the column across the border, the scouts picked up the many trails that Setanka and his men had made. By nightfall they had converged into an easy-to-follow path.

Stopping to rest the horses, Henry conferred with the guides, who had concluded where the trail was leading. "Setanka at Caveta," the head guide assured Henry.

Knowing where the town was located, Henry nodded. "Very well, you can go back to the fort now."

"We stay. We fight," the head guide offered.

"No, I don't want you fighting your tribesmen." Henry called the officers to the head of the column. "With the moonlight illuminating the trail, we can reach Caveta before dawn. We'll alternate between a canter and a trot, and stop for a few minutes every hour to rest the mounts."

The officers got back in position, and Henry resumed the lead. He watched the stars as the hours passed. Finally, when the road went over a rise, he saw the town a mile ahead.

Henry led the column in a wide circle off the road and left the spare horses with a squad to guard them in a narrow ravine far from any houses. The column advanced toward a low, long rise east of the town, where he again summoned the officers. It was almost an hour before sunrise.

"I have time to reconnoiter the town and surrounding area with Lieutenant Stafford. The rest of you keep the men quiet and in platoon formation."

The north side of the town, where the road entered it, consisted of several streets of adobe buildings. A few lights glowed in stores or cantinas. Separated from the town by a hundred feet was a mass of darkened huts, obviously where the renegades lived.

A dog among the adobe buildings began barking. Henry turned south, riding around the end of the town, where corrals held over a hundred horses and forty cattle.

"Not a lot of sentries," Stafford remarked quietly, amused. "Do you intend to spread the men around these shacks with their carbines?"

"No, it would take too long to root them all out by sniping at them. Using the shock force of a charge, it'll all be over within a few minutes. I've seen enough. Let's get back to the men."

Henry walked his horse slowly along his expedition's column and in a quiet, clear voice described the town and told the men what to expect.

"There may be women in those huts, so don't shoot at everything that moves. Take your time and pick your targets. When we get among the huts, change to pistols and sabers."

The first light of the dawn was beginning to glow; it was time to cross the hill before the men would be silhouetted against the eastern sky and be spotted by the townspeople. Henry, at the front of the column, led his men down the foot of the hill.

As the officers quietly called Henry's orders, the men, assembled into long lines, wheeled their horses around to face the town. Having led his men into a foreign country, Henry had brought a full set of battle flags, including the American flag, the Third Cavalry Regiment pennant with battle honors, and company guidons.

"Colors, post!" Henry ordered. "Color guard, post! Uncase the colors!"

The men with the flags assembled in a short rank behind him, removed the canvas covers from the flags, and seated the staffs in sockets on their stirrups. The twelve men of the color guard assembled around the flags. Silence settled, broken by an occasional jangle of a bit as a horse shook its head.

"Carbines, lock and load!" Henry called. The officers repeated the order, and there was a metallic clatter as the men drew their carbines from the saddle scabbards and loaded the chambers. Just at full daylight, Henry lifted his reins. "Forward at a trot, ho!"

The long line of cavalry swept into motion in a rumble of hoofbeats and clatter of sabers, wind-whipped flags, and rising dust. On the north side of the town, people ran out of the adobe buildings and peered into the sunrise. When the company was halfway across the field, the renegades started to stir. Henry drew his saber and pointed it toward the huts. "Charge!"

The penetrating notes of the bugle rang out as the horses broke into a headlong run. The hoofbeats became a drumming roar, and the dust billowed up behind, thickening into a dense cloud. Henry put his reins in his teeth and took out his pistol as renegades ran from their huts. He took aim at a man and shot him between the eyes.

Carbines boomed, and other men fell. A few renegades shot back, firing blindly against the glare of the sunrise. Others tried to flee. The loud reports of the carbines blended into a steady, thunderous pounding of gunfire, and renegades jerked and dropped as bullets ripped into them.

The cavalry's horses reached the huts. Henry's mount veered between two hovels, while others plunged straight into the structures, causing the flimsy walls to buckle and roofs to collapse. Naked women screamed and clutched at clothes while men struggling out of blankets and reaching for weapons were cut down by pistol fire and gleaming sabers. Corpses sprawled in the wreckage.

One large structure still stood at the center of the huts. Henry guided his horse toward it, through a pandemonium of smoke and gunfire, charging horses, bellowing voices, and disintegrating huts.

A man leapt out of a doorway, leveling a shotgun. Henry chopped his saber across the man's neck, while another man ran out of a hut, firing a rifle wildly. Henry felt the bullet pluck at his shoulder as his horse reared from the blast of the rifle beside its muzzle. He leaned forward in the saddle, extending his arm and shooting the man in the face at point-blank range with his pistol.

Controlling his horse and riding toward the largest building, Henry saw a man crawling out a window at its rear. With long, ragged hair and a deep scar reaching diagonally across his face, Henry realized he was Setanka. He looked at

264

Henry and snapped off a pistol shot as he climbed out the window. The bullet clipped Henry's hat as he tried to aim his pistol, but Setanka had darted out of sight among the huts.

Henry spurred his horse, chasing the renegade half-breed between the huts. Running toward the corrals, Setanka fired again over his shoulder. The bullet grazed Henry's shoulder, and another creased his mount's flank, the horse flinching in midstride. Henry was unable to fire as Setanka nimbly leapt over the corral fence and hid among the horses.

Crouching low in the saddle, Henry spurred his horse into a dead run toward the corral. The horses, already frightened by the gunfire, buffeted nervously as Setanka crept through them. At the fence Henry's horse bunched its flanks and vaulted over. He fired his pistol over the horses' heads as his mount plunged down among them.

The mass of horses wheeled as one, lurching away. The fence on the other side of the corral collapsed from the tons of horseflesh surging against it, stampeding from the corral. Over the roar of the hoofbeats, Henry heard a thin wail of panic. As the last of the horses fled, he rode slowly forward through the cloud of dust. Setanka's crumpled, bloody form was sprawled in the dirt, trampled to death by the very horses he had stolen.

The battle had drawn to an end. Only fifteen minutes had passed since the attack began. The cavalrymen were milling about among the remains of the huts. "Lieutenant Barnes," Henry called, "have a squad count the enemy dead, then torch this place. Bugler, sound Assembly."

At a creek east of the town, Henry sent for the spare horses and had the men make a temporary camp. Two soldiers were in serious condition, each of them with a bullet in the shoulder, but they could ride. All the horses were weary. Henry walked among the animals and examined them, pondering how long to rest them before starting back. Several had bullet wounds and skinned legs from crashing through the huts, but none was injured seriously.

Ninety-six renegades, including Setanka, had died. Townspeople, furious over the attack on the renegades, began collecting at a distance. A few fired pistols and rifles. The gunfire was inaccurate, but it was nonetheless dangerous.

Stafford walked up to Henry. "You'd think they'd be glad to get rid of those renegades, sir."

"I'm sure many are, but others were making money from the loot that was brought here. Have a squad of sharpshooters disperse them. Make them dance; I don't want any of them hit."

A few minutes later, a dozen men with carbines fired a volley that raised dust in front of the people, who immediately fled toward the town.

The warning shots proved ineffective against a few Mexicans, however, who took cover and fired occasionally from a distance. Although Henry wanted to give the horses and the wounded more

266

time to rest, he decided it would be best to get well away from the town.

After the men had saddled their horses and assembled into a column, he led them away from the creek at a walk—the only pace the weary horses could maintain. Setting out to the north, he found that word had spread rapidly, arousing the entire countryside. People from ranches and mobs from nearby towns were scattered along the road, bellowing in rage, heaving rocks, and shooting at the column. Henry designated sharpshooters along the length of the column to fire warning shots, which were of limited success.

One man, apparently realizing that the shots were meant to miss him, stood his ground. He fired at the column repeatedly, and one bullet grazed a horse's rump, making it scream. Enraged, Henry began firing his Winchester. With rocks exploding into dust within inches of him, the man fled as the soldiers cheered.

The colonel was standing on the porch in front of headquarters as the column filed briskly through the gate into Fort Peck's quadrangle, late in the afternoon of the next day.

"Encase the colors," Henry ordered. "Men, the way you performed on this mission makes me proud. Company commanders, assume command and dismiss the men."

Having received the company commanders' salute, Henry turned his horse and rode across the quadrangle to headquarters. Dismounting, he exchanged a salute with Colonel Hatfield, who nodded toward the column with a grimace. "Major Blake, did you *have* to take the Stars and Stripes down there with you?"

"If I'm going to lead men into battle on foreign soil, they'll fight under their own flag," Henry replied firmly.

"I suppose," the colonel acknowledged reluctantly. When Henry informed him of the outcome of the battle, the colonel's eyes widened in astonishment.

"That's remarkable," the colonel marveled, turning to the door. "Well, come on in. The telegraph lines have been burning up with messages from Washington, as you might expect."

Wondering if his army career was over, Henry followed the colonel inside. There were a number of outraged protests in stiff diplomatic terms from Mexico City. The replies were profuse apologies, with assurances that the responsible officer would be relieved of command.

"That's the State Department talking," Hatfield advised. "We won't know how much official disapproval we're going to run into until we hear from the War Department. This is all we've received from them thus far."

He handed Henry a terse order to send an immediate report on the battle to the War Department. Henry wrote the report, adding that there were no civilian casualties.

In little more than an hour, the telegraph clattered a brief message requesting that Henry confirm the casualty report and state any special circumstances contributing to the wide imbalance of casualties between the renegades and Americans.

Hatfield laughed. "They can't believe it. Well, the special circumstances consisted of the company being led by a cavalry officer who is second to none. The tone of this message suggests that official disapproval, if any, isn't very strong."

Henry, feeling more optimistic, wrote out a reply, explaining his tactics. An hour later, the telegraph rattled again.

The message was an order for Henry to report to Washington for a staff position, pending a later field assignment.

"Well, that's it," Hatfield said happily. "They're removing you from command to satisfy the diplomatic fracas, but that's all."

"Yes, sir," Henry replied, regretful that he would be unable to return immediately to the Seventh Cavalry. It would, however, give him the opportunity and pleasure to confront Klaus Lukenbill. "I believe I'll ask for leave before reporting to Washington. I have some business in Philadelphia."

That evening, freshly shaved and wearing an immaculately neat uniform with gleaming boots, Henry went to the officers' mess for dinner, where the battle was the topic of loud, lively conversation. As he stepped in, a spontaneous burst of applause greeted him. The lieutenants stood at their tables, clapping and cheering heartily, while Hatfield sat at a table in a corner, smiling widely.

Henry lifted a hand as he moved toward the colonel's table. "This is very rowdy conduct for the mess, gentlemen," he remarked, laughing. "Where's your decorum?"

The lieutenants laughed and took their seats, and Henry joined Hatfield. When they had almost finished eating, a telegraph technician brought Henry a message just arrived from Washington. It approved his leave but ordered him first to report to the chief of staff.

"I'm not going to argue with an order," Henry remarked, puzzled, "but if they wanted more information on the battle, I could have done that in writing."

"No, I don't believe they want that," Hatfield ventured. "Unless I'm mistaken, Major Blake, you're going to be very quietly promoted to lieutenant colonel."

XVI

"Those rubber trees look the same to me as all the others," Edward Blackstone commented, peering through the binoculars. "What's different about them?"

"The petioles—the leaf stalks—are darker," Witherspoon replied. "That's an indication that the plants are near the end of their propagation cycle, with seed pods that are fully formed."

The trees were located on a low rise, about a mile back into the dense jungle from the tributary of the Amazon River. Edward shook his head doubtfully, turning to Teddy. "What do you think? I only see a few trees, and they're a long way back into the jungle."

"It's up to you, Edward," she responded. "We might find more when we get up there, and it's only a matter of our chopping our way through the jungle."

"Well, we're here to get rubber-tree seeds," he said. "Let's go—but only if there are no natives about."

Teddy shouted to Captain Santos, who called to the crewmen as she peered through the binoculars at the edge of the foliage.

"How can you possibly spot natives in that?" Edward asked, squinting at the impenetrable foliage on the bank.

"You have to look for a foot, an arm, an eye—not a person," Teddy replied. "I didn't see anything. Let's get ready to go."

The crewmen dragged a boat to the rail and put it over the side while Edward helped Teddy carry out axes, machetes, weapons, and other paraphernalia. The amount of equipment seemed substantial to Edward, and they still lacked the seed cans.

"Don't you think we should take some seed cans?" he asked her.

"I recommend against it. Once we get a path cut to the trees, carrying cans back and forth will

271

be easy to do. It'll only be a matter of keeping an eye open for snakes and so forth."

Edward sighed, nodded, and beckoned to Dooley. The Irishman took a swig from his bottle and climbed unsteadily down into the boat as Witherspoon and Teddy followed. Edward handed the equipment down to them and got into the boat. Teddy gestured to the crewman to row.

For some reason she had chosen a specific but reluctant crewman. When he backed away, she seized him by the nape of the neck, propelled him across the deck, and shoved him into the boat.

As they made their way toward the bank, she explained. "All four of us are off the *Amazonia* now. I want it to be there when we get back."

"You mean Santos would leave without us?"

"He has twenty-five guineas—an enormous amount of money in this part of the world."

"But why would bringing that particular crewman make Santos stay?"

"There are three brothers among the crewmen, and people here have strong family loyalties. I brought one of the brothers with us. If Santos tried to leave, that man's brothers would cut off his other ear."

Edward reflected, as he had many times before, that he was extremely fortunate to have Teddy along on the expedition. Then his attention was drawn to the riverbank, where crocodiles slithered into the water as the boat approached. The crocodiles glided away as the boat was grounded, and everyone climbed out. The bank was a narrow ribbon of slippery mud bordered by a wall of lianas and brush under the dense tree trunks. The crewman unloaded the boat, and Teddy walked along the bank, choosing a point to enter the jungle.

Edward, meanwhile, tucked his Winchester under his arm and eyed Witherspoon. His attention had been drawn to a species of brush, which he was examining closely.

Dooley had wandered away, and Edward glanced around for him. Then he rapidly worked the lever on the Winchester to load the firing chamber because the Irishman was about to sit down on an enormous crocodile, half-sunk in the mud on the bank. Edward fired the rifle just as the crocodile started to lash at Dooley with its tail, its mouth opening and revealing rows of long, sharp teeth. Startled by the loud report of the rifle and the sudden movement of what he had thought was a log, the Irishman sprang away from it. Shot through the head, the crocodile thrashed furiously in its death throes as Dooley regarded it with belated alarm.

"I don't have time to keep a constant eye on you," Edward warned him.

"Aye, I know, and I'm grateful for that, Edward," Dooley replied.

"Good shot, Edward," Teddy remarked. "There's dinner. Crocodile tail makes a very tasty dish."

Teddy, Edward, and the Indian took turns with the machetes, chopping a path Teddy had selected into the jungle. It was laborious work, but fifty yards from the river there were only occasional patches of impenetrable growth, and Teddy picked a path around the worst of them.

They filed through the trees in the steaming heat and eerie green twilight under the solid canopy of foliage, the jungle noisy with the chatter of monkeys and strange bird calls. In his eagerness to investigate everything, Witherspoon tried to push ahead of Teddy or wander off to one side. Both liking and understanding the man, she patiently restrained him.

Where the jungle opened out at the edge of the swampy creek, Witherspoon saw a lizard and started toward it. Teddy pulled him back suddenly by the collar while slashing upward with her machete. An anaconda that had been draped on an overhanging limb crashed to the ground, its head severed. Forgetting the lizard, Witherspoon knelt and peered at the snake.

"Eunectes murinus," he marveled. "Fascinating, and very beautiful."

"I see nothing beautiful about that poisonous, slimy thing!" Dooley exclaimed.

"They're not poisonous," Teddy corrected Dooley. "They crush their prey and swallow it whole. It wouldn't have been able to swallow Mr. Witherspoon, but they're greedy things, and it might have injured him by trying." Teddy gathered up the snake and heaved it into the creek. The muddy water immediately exploded into boiling foam as scores of small fish ripped the flesh from the snake.

"*Serrasalmo scapularis,*" Witherspoon murmured in wonder.

"The local name for them is piranha," Teddy added. "They're interesting enough, but going wading when they're about is a good way to ruin a pair of boots." She looked around. "We'll need a fairly long tree to bridge this creek, and a long tree means a thick one. We may as well get started on that one there."

After taking off her hunting coat, she rolled up her sleeves, hefted an ax, and began chopping. Edward took an ax and joined her. Presently the tree crashed down across the creek.

Teddy guided Witherspoon along the tree trunk, and Edward and the others followed. The piranhas leapt from the water, snapping as the people crossed the creek. On the other side, the terrain climbed toward the rise with the rubber trees.

At their destination Teddy smiled as she looked around. "This grove is much larger than it appeared from the river."

"Yes," Witherspoon agreed. "These are fine specimen of *Hevea brasiliensis* and would make good parent stock. It's unfortunate that the seeds aren't ready to gather. These trees are near the end of their propagation cycle, with pods that are fully formed. But look at the color of the petioles. The pods haven't dried out enough to gather."

His voice trailed off as a colorful moth caught his eye. Mopping sweat from his face and neck with his handkerchief, Edward sighed heavily, relieving his anger with a fantasy of slowly throttling Witherspoon.

Witherspoon had taught Edward that the jungle was a checkerboard of microclimates: Prevailing winds, humidity, and other factors affected the trees. The rubber trees on higher ground than those they had just seen were certain to have seeds ready to gather.

During midmorning on the third day after the trek through the jungle, the launch was brought to a halt. Directly ahead were terraced falls where the river flowed out of foothills, but the higher slopes of the mountains were still many miles away.

The crewmen anchored the vessel in midstream while Teddy studied the riverbank through the binoculars and discovered another problem. "There must be a dozen Indians over there, Edward, but they're definitely more curious than hostile. We're within range of their blowguns, but they aren't trying to pick us off."

"That's very reassuring indeed," Edward remarked dryly. "Let's hope we're interesting enough to keep them from losing their curiosity."

"I think we might be," Teddy replied, "because this is a very remote area. The natives here might never have seen anyone from the outside. I'd say they're a hunting or fishing party from a village in the mountains." She lowered the binoculars then turned to Edward. "And in that case, we have two alternatives."

"What, Teddy?"

"We can't go any farther up this tributary, so the first option is to go back downstream and find another tributary, which will take a week or two. The second is to make friends with these natives and get them to take us back into those mountains to see if we can find rubber trees."

"What are the chances of making friends?"

"A first contact with natives is always dicey, but I've done it a few times. It requires a slow, easy approach, along with a confident attitude. But as curious as this lot is about us, I think some trade goods might get us off on the right foot."

"I don't want to waste time looking for another tributary," Edward decided, "particularly if Cecil is right and we're near where we can get seeds."

Teddy looked again through the binoculars. "If we can get the natives to take us to their village and win the confidence of the chiefs, we'll have all the workers we need to fill cans with seeds and carry them to the launch. It will only be a matter of explaining what we want."

"Very well, let's try it, then."

Teddy spoke to Santos in Portuguese. The crewmen immediately objected in alarm to what she said. Sighing in resignation, Teddy turned to Edward. "Will you row me to the bank? Cecil and Edgar will stay here to keep Santos from stranding us. If the crewmen see us go to the bank and come back safely, it might stiffen their backbones."

Not at all certain the crewmen's apprehension was inappropriate, Edward agreed. He climbed down into the boat, and Teddy joined him, bringing a half-dozen clackers from her cabin.

The clackers—toys used as noisemakers on holidays—had short wooden handles set into metal drums that made a loud clatter. Teddy stood in the bow of the boat and spun a clacker in each hand, the loud rattle echoing across the water, while Edward rowed to the bank.

Edward started to climb onto the shore. "No, stay there," Teddy advised softly. "They're only a few feet away, and we must avoid alarming them. Don't look straight into their eyes; that's almost always a sign of aggression among natives. But you mustn't look away, because that's a sign of fear."

Not entirely sure of how to avoid looking at someone without looking away, Edward nodded. Teddy stepped out of the boat, then slowly and deliberately crossed the muddy bank to the edge of the foliage, where she hung the clackers on branches. Through an opening in the wall of growth, two dark eyes peered at Edward malevolently. He fixed his gaze on a leaf beside the aperture in the foliage. Teddy returned to the boat, pushing it away from the bank and climbing in as Edward picked up the oars.

"I was within three feet of one little fellow," she reported, laughing. "When I smelled him, it occurred to me that they might have come to the river to bathe."

When they were on the launch, they stood at the rail and watched. The foliage moved, and one clacker furtively disappeared. It made a faltering sound, then presently the sound grew louder. The foliage shook vigorously as hands snatched the rest. A moment later, there was a bedlam of spinning clackers, punctuated with whoops of delight.

"We've got them now." Teddy grinned. "I'll get a small selection of trade goods. We'll take a crewman to translate Tupi for us."

She returned from the cabin with more clackers, as well as small mirrors, beads, and other baubles.

The noise from the clackers ceased when the boat neared the bank. The crewman huddled in the stern and shivered with terror as Edward rowed and Teddy displayed a mirror and a string of beads. When the boat reached the bank, she climbed out, and the crewman, pale and trembling, joined her.

It took several minutes to lure the natives out. They emerged cautiously, poised to dart back into hiding. Edward was amazed by their wariness, for they looked formidable.

Small, wiry men with dark brown skin, they had long, shaggy black hair and painted designs on their faces that made them appear extremely fierce. Wearing only skin loincloths and necklaces and bracelets made of animal teeth, they were armed with blowguns, crude knives, stone axes, and spears. Most of all, they appeared just as feral and unpredictable as any large carnivore of the jungle.

Edward was acutely aware of the dire peril and could see the tension on Teddy's face. Still, she maintained an attitude of supreme confidence. There were ten natives, six with clackers. Teddy held out a clacker to one of the others.

The man inched forward, then grabbed it from her. Beckoning another native, Teddy pulled out a string of beads. As the man stepped forward and took it, the atmosphere relaxed. Teddy towered over them as she handed out trinkets.

While she was handing something to a man, another leapt forward to snatch a string of beads from her. Jerking the beads away, she cuffed the native solidly on the side of his head. All of them recoiled and lifted their weapons, several edging back into the foliage.

Teddy took out her pistol and looked up at the trees. She fired, and the natives, flinching from the loud noise, were on the point of darting back into the foliage until a snake flopped onto the jungle floor. Teddy holstered her pistol as she glared at the native who had tried to take the beads.

In the moment that everyone's attention was on the pistol and the snake, all the trinkets had disappeared from Teddy's hands. That startled the natives more than anything—as well as disappointed them. Now smiling, Teddy moved a hand in a circular motion, and the beads the man had tried to snatch suddenly reappeared. She held the string out to him.

The man was almost afraid to touch it. The natives murmured in awe as Teddy waved her hands and caused other trinkets to appear. As they gathered around her once more, there was no crowding or shoving, and no one tried to snatch anything. Teddy smiled at Edward and cast her eyes upward in relief.

After the trade goods were passed out, Teddy and the natives sat at the edge of the foliage. She conferred with them through the crewman.

"As I thought, they're from a mountain village," she said to Edward. "They're willing to introduce us to their chiefs. No one is ever entirely safe among natives, of course, but these seem harmless enough."

"Well, we knew we were going to be taking risks when we came here. Let's go."

The next conversation lasted longer. The natives would be waiting for them the following morning, Teddy told Edward.

They stepped back into the boat with the crewman, then returned to the launch, where immediate preparations began for the trek to the village. While choosing an assortment of trade goods to pack into bags, Teddy took out a can of birdlime, which she spread on the deck, then scattered bread crumbs. Birds hovered constantly in search of tidbits, and a few minutes later, she had captured a tiny one. Teddy joined Edward in the hold, where he was bagging the trade goods. "I don't want to hurt this little fellow," she said, cleaning the birdlime from its feet and then placing it in a small cage.

"You need him for a trick?"

"Possibly," she replied, then changed the subject. "I don't like to keep bringing this up, but

Edgar will probably be a handicap, and possibly even a danger at the village. I like the man just as much as you do, but there are other considerations involved."

"Yes, that's true. But I feel much more secure in having a fellow of his sneaky cunning along."

Nodding amiably, Teddy dropped the subject. "I have a friend who disappeared somewhere along the Amazon, and while I was talking with those natives, I asked them if they had ever seen or heard of Ian MacInnes."

"What did they say?"

"They were noncommittal. Natives don't want to disappoint people. It could be that they realized I was very interested in Ian MacInnes, and they didn't want to tell me they had never heard of him. Or there's another explanation."

"What's that?"

"MacInnes could have met his end in this area, and they didn't want to frighten us off. Their lives are very monotonous, so our arrival is a great event. They'll be relating stories about us many generations from now."

Less interested in becoming a legend than he was in staying alive, Edward grimaced. "Let's hope that your friend is merely lost. By the way, these natives aren't cannibals, are they?"

"No, no," Teddy replied, laughing heartily. "No, they certainly aren't cannibals, Edward." Opening a carton, she began filling another bag with trade goods. "But they *are* headhunters, you know."

The trek to the village took several hours, with thorny brush snatching at Edward's clothing and roots catching his feet. The natives, immensely strong for their size, effortlessly carried the heavy bags of trade goods along the dim trail.

At last the trees opened out ahead into the first sunshine Edward had seen since leaving the river. In the center of the mountain valley was a clearing of several hundred acres, where crop fields surrounded a large village of thatched huts. The party filed out of the forest into a clearing and were greeted by a deafening roar of wonder and excitement from the villagers. The natives crowded in on all sides, reaching to touch Edward and the others. As he trudged along through the crush, the alien smells and atmosphere surrounding him, it seemed to Edward that his head was drawing a lot of attention.

The guides led the way to the large village meeting house. Inside, four older men, obviously chiefs, sat against one wall. Although the bedlam was left behind, the somber silence of the meeting house seemed ominous. The guides piled the bags of trade goods on the floor beside a smoldering fire, then pointed for Edward and the others to sit.

Villagers silently entered until the place was filled. Edward noticed that the two crewmen from the launch were looking up in terror. His eyes slowly adjusting to the light, he squinted at the dim, peaked ceiling around a smoke hole and saw that the rafters were festooned with scores of shrunken heads.

Teddy stood to speak, beckoning one of the crewmen closer to translate. She hesitated, then leaned over one of the chiefs. Pushing the man's long hair aside, she used her perfected sleight of hand to "remove" a large, colorful costume-jewelry brooch from his ear. Looking at it in wonder and delight, he probed a finger in his ear and felt for others, while the chief beside him leaned over and looked for one for himself.

The crewman translating, Teddy talked, showing the chiefs a small ball of raw rubber. As she continued, she occasionally waved her hands dramatically, and colorful handkerchiefs, beads, small mirrors, and other trinkets materialized in her fingers. She passed them out among the chiefs, who watched in joyful wonder.

Teddy presented each chief with an assortment of trade goods, including a kettle and a bolt of cloth. Then she performed her last trick. Pressing her palms together, she lifted them over her head. As she opened her hands, the small bird she had captured on the launch fluttered from between them and flew toward the smoke hole in the peak of the roof.

The building was crowded, but a silence gripped the thunderstruck gathering, and the flapping of the bird's wings seemed loud in the quiet as all eyes followed it. When it reached the smoke hole, Teddy tossed a string of firecrackers onto the fire. In the chaos that erupted when the firecrackers exploded, tossing embers through the air, she stood calmly with her arms folded and gazed at the chiefs.

The four chiefs were clearly awed by the demonstration and elated by the trade goods. Edward was sure the others and he would be welcomed to the village.

"They've placed the entire resources of the village at our disposal," Teddy told him after the meeting. "Huts are being provided for us, along with a cook. We'll have all the workers we need, as well as anything else we want."

"Excellent, Teddy! You're a marvel. Let's hope we can find rubber trees with seeds ready to gather."

"As soon as we're situated, our friends from the river will take us to rubber trees."

Within the hour, the natives from the river, radiating pride from having brought important, entertaining visitors to the village, led the way to a slope covered with rubber trees—thousands of acres of them.

Witherspoon plucked a seed pod and examined it. The pod was dry and brittle. It cracked open in his hand and seeds spilled out. "They're perfect," he announced. "These are precisely at the best time for the seeds to be gathered. Some trees here are better specimens than others, so it will be necessary to select seeds from the very best parent stock."

It was late in the day, and they went back toward the village, planning to make an early start the next morning. Teddy said she would take a large party of workers from the village to bring all of the seed cans from the *Amazonia*, together with another supply of trade goods.

"You supervise workers gathering seeds, Edward. They can put the seeds in baskets until I get back with the cans, which should be the day after tomorrow. You can make them understand what you want by gesturing, but I'll leave both crewmen here."

"Why both?"

"If I don't have anyone to translate for me, I'll learn Tupi that much sooner. I'd like to be able to speak it well enough to question the villagers about Ian MacInnes."

At the huts the cook prepared dinner, a dish of black beans and some kind of meat in a piquant sauce, but Edward avoided making comments to Teddy that might bring up the subject of the origin of the meat. The cook brought in a large earthenware jug of strong, flavorful manioc beer, which Dooley made short work of.

Early the next morning, Teddy set out for the launch, a long queue of men, women, and children chanting happily as they followed her. Edward left for the rubber trees with Witherspoon and twenty natives.

Witherspoon's absent, eccentric mannerisms were completely gone. The scientist filled test tubes with soil samples, marked trees from which he wanted the seeds gathered, then culled the seeds in the baskets to take only the choicest.

Edward supervised the workers, killing several large snakes during the day with his pistol.

At dusk when Edward and Witherspoon returned to the village, it was alive with the rattle of clackers. Other trade goods were in evidence, the familiar items only making Edward more aware that he was in alien surroundings.

Edgar A. Dooley, however, had made himself right at home. Having bored a hole in the lid of one of the iron kettles, he had used it and bamboo for tubing to fashion a still. He was blearily watching a thin trickle drip from the end of the bamboo into a gourd cup. The crewmen, apparently having freely sampled the product, were snoring beside one of the huts.

"That beer they make here is very bland," he remarked to Edward. "But when I run the mash through this, it stiffens up into a tolerable drink."

"And a poisonous one," Edward pointed out. "The iron kettle you're using will contaminate it."

Dooley picked up the gourd cup and took a swig. He wheezed and coughed, then replaced the cup under the spout. "No, that only gives it character, Edward."

The next morning the crewmen held their heads in nauseated agony, but Dooley was as perky as always. Before noon, Teddy returned with her crew of villagers, bringing all of the seed cans and additional trade goods.

Santos and the other crewmen, she said, were nervous, frightened of all the natives they had seen. "I'm certainly glad we have that one brother

287

here. Otherwise, I'm sure Santos would have left."

"I can understand his point. I've seen shrunken heads in many of these huts. But I don't think we'll be here any longer than a few days."

When she saw the baskets of gathered seeds, Teddy agreed that the work would soon be finished. She gave villagers directions in her broken Tupi, and they began to fill cans with seeds.

The following day, Edward took charge of transporting the seeds to the launch. The cans were heavy now, and because each man was limited by the weight, several trips were needed. Each round trip required just under two days. Teddy supervised the filling of the cans while still searching for information about her friend.

One afternoon Edward returned from the launch to find that the gathering of rubber-tree seeds had stopped. The village was in an uproar. Six men danced about, holding aloft about a dozen decapitated heads, while the others cheered wildly.

The natives with Edward joined in, whooping jubilantly. Edward hurried to the huts, where Teddy informed him that a war party had just returned from a successful foray against another village.

"The chiefs summoned me," she added. "They expect the other village to make a retaliatory raid, but the chiefs plan to ambush them at a pass in the mountains. They want you and me to go along, to give them the advantage of our firearms."

"What?" Edward exclaimed. "Teddy, we can't get mixed up in a war between tribes of head-hunters. Who'll look after Witherspoon? And that brother among the crewmen will go back to the *Amazonia* like a shot if we aren't here to watch him."

"I discussed all that with the chiefs, Edward. They said they'll appoint people to look after Cecil. As far as that crewman is concerned, they offered to kill him. I told them I didn't want that, of course, so they said they would keep him here in the village."

Edward sighed heavily. "If we refuse, our heads will end up hanging in that village meeting house."

Teddy nodded glumly.

"Then like it or not, we're mixed up in a war. Let's just hope our side wins."

XVII

Edward and twenty small, fierce natives had crept into the thicket before daylight. It was now late afternoon, and his back and legs throbbed with pain from sitting in one position for hours. Each time he moved slightly to relieve the muscle cramps, forty black, penetrating eyes glared at him.

Like statues watching the trail below, not one of them had moved a muscle during the long hours.

The thicket was on a bluff, a matching steep slope across from it, which also overlooked the trail. Teddy was on that other side, also hidden in the foliage with a group of villagers. Edward wondered if she was bearing the long wait any better than he was.

Suddenly he felt a change. Slowly turning his head, he saw a long line of natives coming around a shoulder in the mountain, headed toward the notch. He felt uneasy; his allies were substantially outnumbered by the approaching war party.

Without any signal or command, the blowguns that had been resting across his neighbors' thighs were abruptly at their lips, the angle tracking the natives.

Then the battle began in eerie quiet. Soft puffs of breath sent the deadly darts on their way; with no outcry from below, the enemy took cover in a whispering rustle of foliage, then lifted their own blowguns. Darts shot through the foliage, one thumping into a tree beside Edward. Friend and foe rapidly shot volley after volley, filling the air with deadly projectiles.

Edward felt almost relieved when a chorus of whoops from the other slope broke the savage quiet. Darts supply exhausted, the natives with Teddy came piling down the slope for hand-to-hand battle. Those around Edward dropped their blowguns and shrieking wildly, seized their clubs and spears. Edward leaped up, almost falling flat as his cramped legs started to buckle, then ran down the hill after them.

The darts had taken a toll on the enemy war party, but a formidably large group of angry, determined natives remained, flailing clubs and jabbing spears. Teddy and Edward, hoping to frighten the enemy rather than kill them, began firing over their heads.

The gunfire startled them, but they continued fighting. Edward dodged clubs and spears, firing the rifle and clipping hair from the heads of natives. They flinched and reeled back, shaking their heads from the loud report, then charged back in.

The battle raged back and forth, a blur of painted faces and a bedlam of blood-curdling howls and clattering weapons. Then Edward realized that the natives with Teddy were starting to fall back under the onslaught. He slung his rifle over his shoulder, then took out his pistol and drew his sword. Pushing forward, he fired high and slashed at weapons. The gleaming blade clipped the stone points off two spears and lopped a club in half. The enemy warriors fell back, more intimidated by the sword than by the gunshots, and the natives beside Edward shouted triumphantly as they advanced with him.

Moments later, Edward's group had joined up with Teddy's to form a solid front. "Do you have any firecrackers?" he shouted to her. "If you have, get behind me and light them."

She nodded and began rummaging in her hunting coat. She lit the fuses on two strings of firecrackers, then flung them into the midst of the enemy war party. The natives shrieked and leaped about, trying to escape. When Teddy heaved more firecrackers, the enemy war party disintegrated.

The battle ended as the villagers chased after the enemy to cut down stragglers. Edward sheathed his sword. "Are you all right, Teddy?"

"Thanks to you." She smiled gratefully.

"Those firecrackers saved the day. The chief should be more than content."

The leader of the ambush party, the youngest of the four village chiefs, was grinning as he and his men divested the enemy dead of their necklaces and bracelets. Before long, a few dozen heads dangled by their hair on a long pole that two men hoisted to their shoulders; the warriors chanted happily as the chief led the way back toward the village.

Edward helped Teddy gather up an assortment of the most lavishly carved and decorated spears and clubs for the curator of London's Ethnological Museum.

Early the next day they arrived at the village. When the people saw the heads on the pole, they cheered wildly. Edward and Teddy retired to their huts, pleased that the war was over.

Their relief quickly changed to consternation, however. Dooley was in one hut, sleeping beside a large jug of the liquor he had made, but there was no sign of the two *Amazonia* crewmen.

"When this uproar started," Edward suggested, "they probably took advantage of it and ran. They might be less than a mile down the trail."

"I'll go and talk with the chiefs," Teddy offered hopefully. "If the crewmen did leave only a short time ago, the villagers can catch them within the hour."

"Witherspoon is probably at the rubber trees. I'll see if he knows anything about the crewmen."

Edward hurried along the trail leading to the trees. A few minutes later, he spotted Witherspoon. The scientist nodded absently when Edward asked about the two crewmen.

"They left yesterday. Isn't this a marvelous specimen, Mr. Blackstone? It's one of the best I've found, and it has a fine yield of seeds."

Edward turned and somberly trudged back to the village. Certain that Santos had left as soon as the crewmen reached the launch, Edward knew that he and the others were stranded deep in the Brazilian jungle.

Edward and Teddy sat in the hut where Dooley was resting. With much of their remaining trade goods on the launch, the continued cooperation of the villagers was open to question. The best idea they could come up with was to build a boat.

Dooley listened blearily. "Why build a boat?" he asked in a slurred voice. "It would be easier to go back the way we came, wouldn't it?"

Edward impatiently explained the predicament.

"The boat's still there," Dooley assured Edward, pouring liquor into the gourd cup. "Santos won't leave."

"You can't trust him, Edgar!" Teddy exclaimed in disbelief.

Edgar took a gulp from the cup and shook his head. "No, I don't trust him, Teddy." He rummaged in a bag and turned back, holding up a metal box with gauges on the front and pipe fittings on the ends. "I took the pressure regulator off the engine."

Teddy cheered in delight, and Edward echoed her joyful relief. "Edgar Dooley, you've probably saved our lives, and you've certainly saved us from failure! When did you do it?"

"While you and Edward were getting ready to leave," Dooley replied. "Santos and the crewmen were watching you, not me, and I thought I'd best take precautions. My sainted mother didn't raise any fools."

Teddy smiled apologetically and put a hand on Dooley's arm. "I have a confession: I recommended to Edward that we leave you behind. I thought you'd be in the way. Will you forgive me?"

"Of course, Teddy," Edgar replied. "Here, we'll drink on it."

Taking the cup, Teddy eyed the oily liquor warily. "I don't suppose you could just accept my apology? . . ."

Laughing, Edgar shook his head firmly. Teddy took a cautious sip, then wheezed and coughed as she swallowed. Dooley offered a drink to Edward, who quickly declined, then the Irishman smacked his lips as he took a hefty swig from the cup.

The crisis averted, Edward and Teddy discussed plans for ending their sojourn in the village. A few dozen cans remained to be filled with seeds, which could be accomplished within a day if a substantial number of workers could be obtained. Teddy speculated that the village might settle back down enough by the next day so that there would be workers available.

Teddy's prediction proved correct. Edward spent a long, hard day supervising the workers at the rubber trees. At dusk the workers carried the crates of cans back to the village, all filled and ready to take to the launch.

Edward found Teddy seated beside the fire, in a subdued mood. She showed him a cloth bag, a pipe, match case, wallet, and a few other personal items. Edward sympathized; the creased, crumbling papers in the wallet bore the name of Ian MacInnes, and the same name was engraved on the silver match case.

"What happened, Teddy?"

"Ian was my friend, Edward, but he was thrifty to a fault. It seems that his miserly streak brought about his untimely end; he evidently showed up here without any trade goods."

Edward put a hand on her shoulder. "I deeply regret your loss of a friend, as well as his family's loss of a husband and father."

"He forced them to subsist on a meager allowance during his expeditions. Proof of his death will be more of a boon to his family than a cause to mourn. He was quite wealthy, and they'll come into a very good inheritance."

"In that event, what you have there might not be sufficient proof of death. Lawyers are undoubtedly looking after his estate. You can be sure they'll put considerable effort into fighting anything that would stop their fee."

In reply, Teddy silently untied the string at the top of the bag among the things and opened it. The features on the shrunken head with thick sidewhiskers would be clearly recognizable to anyone who had known the man.

The next morning, most of the village went to the launch with Edward and the others. Wearing bright beads and bangles, and loincloths and skirts made of colorful cottons from India, the natives carried seed cans along the trail in an uproar of chanting and din of clackers that sent birds and animals fleeing.

The *Amazonia* was several yards downstream from where it had been, Santos having tried to leave until he found that his boiler was unable to hold pressure. He grinned sheepishly as Teddy handed him the regulator. She shook her fist under his nose and shouted at him angrily in Portuguese. While the engine was getting up a head of steam, Edward and Teddy distributed the rest of the trade goods to the natives on the bank. Then the launch set out downstream, making good speed with the current.

"When I've been at a place for a time and grown to know the people," Teddy mused sadly, "it seems that I leave something of myself behind when I go." She shrugged off her reflective mood and smiled. "But one must always look ahead."

"Yes," Edward commented wryly. "There can be no doubt that the authorities are keeping a sharp lookout for us, and evading them will be extremely difficult."

The Sitka, Alaska, harbor was busy with whalers, trading ships, and other vessels riding at anchor. While it was the center of salmon, lumber, and other important industries, its surroundings set it apart from other places. The harbor was an emerald bowl surrounded by wooded slopes and snowcapped peaks. The early June day was warm and sunny, a few fleecy clouds drifting across the rich blue sky, which made the view even more splendid.

"One could never find a lovelier prospect," Eulalia Blake said to Lee, who had joined her at the rail of the steamer. "Just looking at it takes my breath away."

"It *is* very beautiful," Lee agreed. "I believe anyone could search the world over without finding a more pleasant place."

"You'll get no argument over that from me," a well-built man of about fifty standing nearby remarked. He lifted his hat and bowed. "Robinson is the name, Samuel Robinson. I own a fishing fleet and make my home here."

Robinson talked about the thriving port, admitting that the pace of life allowed him to spend much of his time sport fishing and hunting. As the vessel anchored, he expressed the hope that he would see Lee and Eulalia again.

A detachment of soldiers came aboard. The officer in charge exchanged salutes with Lee and introduced himself as Captain Latham. He escorted the Blakes to a small boat that ferried them ashore. At the docks a carriage took them to the hotel.

"The officials from the Customs Bureau should be here within the next two or three days, sir," Latham told Lee. "Until then, perhaps you'd like to inspect the facilities and equipment that we'll be turning over to them."

"Good idea," Lee agreed. "I'd also like an opportunity to meet the local community leaders."

"I've made arrangements for a dinner at the hotel this evening for you and Mrs. Blake. The guests include the mayor of Sitka and other civic leaders, plus a number of scientists."

Latham explained that weather-service employees under the Signal Corps were collecting data on the climate, ocean currents, and tides. The local scientific community also included biologists studying the plant and animal life in Alaska.

A few minutes later, the Blakes were ensconced in a comfortable hotel suite. While unpacking, Eulalia was surprised that it was almost time to get ready for Latham's dinner. The sun at the northerly latitude was still shining brightly at seven o'clock.

Downstairs, the private dining room was decorated with totem poles standing against the paneled walls. The long dining table and chairs were hand-hewn but comfortable.

Thirty people were present. After introductions were completed, the meal was served. Eulalia enjoyed the mussel and tomato soup, salmon, and moose roasted with vegetables.

Planning to spend her time sightseeing while Lee was busy, she asked two scientists seated near her about local points of interest.

"You'll find roads and trails all over the place," William Sutton, head of the weather-service personnel, said. "They lead around the shoreline and back into the mountains. Small Indian villages in the area have interesting totem poles. For longer trips you'll need a horse."

"Are the wild animals dangerous?" Eulalia asked.

"Not if you exercise care. Moose are very common, and if you see a cow with a calf, don't get between them. Black bears can get aggressive if you have something to eat or if they have cubs, but for the most part they'll run from you. While you're walking around the shoreline, however, you should avoid the mud flats. Tidal currents sometimes scour out potholes in them, which, filled with silt from glaciers, make pools of quicksand."

"We have mud flats in some areas of the coast where I live," Eulalia said. "But as far as I know, there is no quicksand."

"It all depends upon the existence of glacier silt.

299

You see, Mrs. Blake, glacier action grinds up stone to a texture finer than face powder. That's why it's exceptionally dangerous."

"I've heard about the quicksand potholes, Bill," biologist Alfred Burnett put in, "and I've often seen duck hunters out on the mud flats during autumn. To my knowledge, none has come to harm."

"A couple years before you arrived here, Fred, a duck hunter sank right out of sight as his friend watched. Before that, a fellow got into a fairly shallow pothole, and the tide got him. He wasn't found until the following day."

"How terrible." Eulalia cringed. "I take it, Mr. Sutton, that these quicksand potholes aren't very common."

"They're very rare, Mrs. Blake. I'm sure you'll enjoy your visit. It's worth a trip here just to see our vegetables."

"It certainly is," Burnett agreed. "When the Russians were here, Mrs. Blake, they were often on the point of starvation because all they did was harvest furs. We've had farmers settle in Alaska, and you'll be amazed at the size of the vegetables produced by the fertile soil, abundant rainfall, and long hours of sunshine."

The men continued, telling Eulalia about cabbages the size of bushel baskets and potatoes that weighed several pounds each. When she expressed incredulity, Burnett gave her directions on how to locate the farms and see for herself. He and Sutton then told her about other interesting places to visit, all of which she could reach within a few hours. By the time the meal ended, Eulalia knew her visit to Alaska would be memorable.

The next morning, Lee accompanied Latham, and Eulalia set out for a walk. It was another bright, warm day. Feeling energetic after the days on the ship, Eulalia decided to go for a long walk. She set out down the waterfront street, which turned into a road leading around one side of the harbor.

When the city and the harbor were out of view behind her, she found herself surrounded by misty hollows and small Indian villages. At many, intricate totem poles had been carved from huge cedars. A heavy crashing through the foliage a short distance ahead made her pause, and she glimpsed a moose running through the trees.

A mile from the city, the water receded at the edge of a sun-dried mud flat studded with clumps of tough, hardy saltwater sedge two and three feet apart. She passed an abandoned logging camp across the road from old, decaying piers that reached far across the flat, where boats had brought supplies to the camp during high tides.

Glimpsing a distant movement on the flat, Eulalia shaded her eyes to look. A short distance beyond the edge of the clumps of grass, where the mud was still damp, a gull was caught in a fishing net washed in by the tide. She watched, hoping it would free itself, but after a moment she saw that it was too hopelessly entangled and exhausted. When the tide came in, the poor creature would be doomed. But for what Sutton had told her, she would have rushed to help the bird.

She saw no one who might be able to help and was forced to conclude that the gull was condemned to a slow, terrifying death. Reluctantly, she started to walk away, but it was impossible for her to abandon the bird.

Thinking again about what Sutton had said, she regarded the flat. It looked the same as the many mud flats she had seen near the mouth of the Columbia River. Often, at the cost of a muddy dress and shoes, she had walked about to see things washed in by the tide. Sutton had admitted that quicksand potholes in the mud flats here were very rare, and abandoning the bird on the basis of that slight risk suggested a degree of cowardice to Eulalia.

The gull was only about two hundred yards from the road. Eulalia carefully stepped out onto a clump of grass, checking the footing. The mud underneath the grass proved as stable as the road. She stepped onto the next clump, then the next. The farther she got from the road, the farther apart were the clumps of grass, some separated by as much as four feet. Eulalia took long strides to cross the distance, taking a zigzag route to avoid wide stretches of bare mud.

Presently, she came to an expanse, ten feet wide, that she was unable to avoid. She cautiously stepped down to it. It was slick but firm. She crossed the gap, leaving deep footprints in the mud.

When she was halfway between the road and the gull, Eulalia heard a shout behind her. Balancing on a clump of grass, she stopped and turned. Two hunters with shotguns under their arms were on the road, and one was Samuel Robinson, whom she and Lee had met on the steamer.

"What are you doing, Mrs. Blake?"

"There's a gull caught in a net out there," she replied, pointing. "I'm going to free it."

The men shaded their eyes with their hands, looking, then Robinson stepped off the road. "I'll free it for you, Mrs. Blake. Walking around on the mud flats can be dangerous."

"Thank you, but I'm almost there."

The man nodded as Eulalia continued toward the bird. She reached the far edge of the grass; the gull was fifty feet farther, across damp, gleaming mud.

Eulalia hesitated, uncertain. Behind her, Robinson called out again, telling her he would free the bird. Shaking her head and replying, she stepped onto the mud. It was less firm underfoot than the other areas, but it supported her weight. Holding up her hem, Eulalia left deep tracks as she moved toward the bird. The gull flapped and squealed in terror as she approached.

Eulalia held its wings against its body, then lifted it and the rotting net. She freed the bird, and it flew away. Eulalia wadded the net so no other bird would get caught in it and tossed it aside. Her attention no longer occupied, she realized her feet had sunk into the mud up to her ankles.

She lifted her right foot, her weight on her left. The surface seemed to give way, turning into a quaking morass. As her left foot suddenly sank into the mud up to her knee, she windmilled her arms to keep her balance.

Instinctively, she tried to free her left foot, but her right leg also sank into the mud to her knee. Fear gripped her as she felt herself sinking deeper.

Robinson bounded across the clumps of grass toward Eulalia as soon as she began sinking and shouted to his companion to go for help. The man ran down the road toward Sitka while Robinson, slinging his shotgun over his shoulder, picked up the end of a long board the tide had washed in. Dragging the board, he leapt from clump to clump.

He crossed the bare mud cautiously, by using Eulalia's deep footprints. A few feet from her, he stopped and slid the board across the mud to her. "Hold onto this, Mrs. Blake," he said. "Rest your weight on it, and it should keep you from sinking deeper."

"Thank you very much, Mr. Robinson. It appears that I'm in one of the quicksand potholes, doesn't it?"

"Yes, but don't worry. My friend will have some assistance here in a few minutes."

His tone was confident, but he glanced worriedly out at the Pacific Ocean, and Eulalia turned to look. The tide was coming in. "I'm very grateful for your help," she told him, feeling oddly removed from the situation and marveling at her calm, good manners. "And I regret causing trouble."

"People in Alaska always stand ready to help one another." He turned and looked down the road toward Sitka. "Good! My friend has sent some men already. I'll bet he's gone on into town to find your husband."

Craning her neck, Eulalia saw a score of men wrenching boards loose from the old pier to lay a pathway across the flat.

Other men came from town, joining those who were pulling down additional boards. A few minutes later, the pathway of timbers was past the edge of the grass. Eulalia was in the mud up to her waist but sinking no deeper.

"That's good," Robinson observed. "Maybe you're in a shallow pothole, Mrs. Blake. In that case, we should be able to pull you out easily."

Looking between the men who were dragging timbers to lay on top of the quicksand, Eulalia saw Lee, Captain Latham, and Robinson's friend gallop up on army horses. Right behind them was Sutton. The men leaped from the horses and ran down the path of boards toward her. Then the men laying timbers encircled her, covering the quicksand with boards.

Lee pushed through them and knelt beside Eulalia in consternation. He and others took her arms and shoulders in a vain attempt to lift her. Her instant of relief faded; even though they tugged so hard she almost cried out in pain, they were able to lift her barely an inch.

"You can't free her that way, General," Sutton said. "Glacial silt quicksand is very viscous, and the vacuum formed behind anything being lifted is much more powerful than the lifting force. Your wife's arms would be torn from her body before you could exert enough force to pull her up twelve inches."

"Then what can we do?" Lee demanded.

"First let's see how deep that pothole is," Sutton suggested. "Men, sink a timber right beside her."

Scores of muddy men were standing about, eager to do something, so Sutton's words galvanized them into action. A thick support timber pushed into the mud beside Eulalia bottomed, reaching no deeper than her feet.

"Good! A shallow pothole," Sutton concluded. "Let's try to get the quicksand away from her so we can lift her out."

"Shovels!" a man shouted. "There should be shovels at the Indian villages! Let's go!"

Sutton watched a dozen men race away along the path of boards. "I don't think shovels will suffice. I think we need to use the high-pressure hose on a fire engine to blast the quicksand away."

"I'll get the fire engine from town," Latham volunteered. "I'll be back just as soon as I can, General Blake."

Lee looked out at the incoming tide worriedly, and Eulalia turned her head in the same direction.

The edge of the water was a hundred feet away. The milling men discussed and dismissed other means of freeing her. One man, eyeing the edge of the tide, suggested getting boats. He and several others quietly left.

The men who had gone for shovels returned and began scooping up the quicksand around Eulalia, but the effort was futile; as rapidly as they could dig it away, it flowed back in. The edge of the water finally reached the timbers covering the quicksand, slowly deepening. Those who had gone after boats returned in four large ones, which they had rowed around from the town. They edged closer to the potholes as the water became deeper.

Accepting the consequences of the situation, whatever they might turn out to be, Eulalia maintained firm self-control. The men standing on the timbers around her were in ankle-deep water. She smiled up at Sutton. "I should have taken your advice. In freeing that bird, I got myself into the same fix."

"Well, no matter, Mrs. Blake," he replied, trying to smile in return. "We'll get you out directly."

"The water isn't nearly as cold as I thought it would be."

"No, ma'am, not this time of year. Warm currents pass through here, and the sun has warmed the water. Also, we're in a phase of relatively low tides of short duration, with high tide lasting no longer than an hour. That makes the water warmer."

"But it will definitely get deep enough to cover me, won't it?"

The man nodded sadly and turned away. A moment later, however, he and the others began cheering wildly, pointing and shouting that the fire engine was coming. Eulalia glimpsed it between the men moving about in front of her. Its three teams of horses were pounding along the road, with Latham and firemen clinging to the heavy vehicle as it jolted over ruts, smoke boiling from its stack.

The cheering faded when Latham and the fire chief joined the others surrounding Eulalia.

"I don't have enough hose to reach out here, sir," the fire chief said. "And the fire engine is much too heavy to bring out here. I'll send to Killisnoo for more hose, but it'll take about an hour for the man to get here with it."

A somber silence fell in the wake of the man's words, for the last hope was exhausted. Deep remorse and fear tugged at Eulalia, but she forced them back with her strength of will. Having confronted life with courage for almost sixty years, she was determined to face death in the same way. She also knew she had to be brave for Lee, since he was almost beside himself.

The water lapping around the men's boots as they stood on the timbers was nearly up to Eulalia's shoulders. The boats had drawn up to the edge of the boards. She cleared her throat and took charge.

"Gentlemen, I'm deeply grateful for everything you've done. I've seen for myself that Alaskans stand ready to help. You've worked hard and bravely, but fate is against us. Is there a minister present?"

A man took off his cap and stepped forward. "I'm a lay preacher, ma'am, Cletis Underwood."

"Mr. Underwood, please say a prayer for me and commit my soul to God. Then I'd like to be alone with my husband."

The men around Eulalia removed their caps and hats. Lee knelt beside her and held her hand as he took off his cap. He and the others bowed their heads as Underwood prayed. Eulalia bowed her head and looked down at the water lapping toward her chin.

Toby Holt, at police headquarters in New York City, watched a laboratory technician steam open an envelope, one of a dozen that had been singled out for bearing a Paris postmark. This one was addressed to a Klaus Lukenbill.

The chief of police and Detective David Eubank, the officer who had taken Elliot's place, stood beside Toby as the technician finished. Toby slid the letter from its envelope and held it so the others could read it simultaneously. He smiled. The signature at the bottom was Maritain's.

It stated in ungrammatical English that the

torch of the Statue of Liberty would be on the ship due to arrive in Philadelphia in late June. That information was of little consequence to Toby, but the addressee of the letter was priceless knowledge.

The police chief grinned. "I'll have Lukenbill arrested at the post office the minute he picks up that letter."

"We can't do that, Chief," Toby warned. "Lukenbill might not talk, and we must find out the whereabouts of that explosive. I'm certain that something more is involved than simply blowing up the torch, and we have to learn what that is. The only way we can determine those things is by keeping Lukenbill under close and constant surveillance."

"Very well. You're in charge of this investigation, Mr. Holt," the police chief agreed reluctantly. "But many lives are at stake, and something could go wrong. I don't envy you that responsibility."

"It's one I accepted when I took on this task," Toby replied. "We'll proceed the way I said."

Toby handed the letter back to the technician and told the man to reseal it in the envelope, then return it to the postal authorities.

XVIII

"Lee, all the letters I ever received from Toby and Cindy's father are in my cedar chest, together with the Holt family bible and other family documents. I'd like you to turn those over to Alexandra. Tell Henry I completely forgive him and regard him with nothing but love. Concerning my jewelry . . ."

Eulalia spoke in a perfectly steady voice. Lee listened while his thoughts raced, searching for a way to save her. It seemed inconceivable to him that he could be at her side, yet unable to keep her from slipping away.

The boats were skimming away, and the other men sloshed through the water flowing over the walkway of timbers on their way to the road. Tears blurred his vision, as Robinson, almost dropping his shotgun into the water, fixed the strap more securely over his shoulder. Lee stared at the gun.

"Wait!" he shouted, releasing Eulalia's hand and standing. "Mr. Sutton, how deep will the water be right here?"

"About four feet deep, General Blake."

"Damn it, man!" Lee shouted angrily. "I don't want to know 'about.' I want to know precisely how deep it'll be. You've been studying the tides here."

Sutton glanced around, surveying the gradient of the mud flat. "Four feet and six inches, General Blake," he finally replied. "It may be an inch or two less, but certainly no more."

Looking at Eulalia, Lee estimated that the water would be no more than two feet over her head. He turned back to the men. "Mr. Robinson, I need to borrow your shotgun. Eulalia can breathe

311

through the barrel. The rest of you men, get back here and drive this post beside her in deep so I can tie the barrel to it. I need it positioned so she'll have easy access to the gun barrel. Let's move! Hurry! Hurry!"

The men raised a whoop of triumph as they churned through the water and raced back. In their rush they created waves that threatened to wash over Eulalia's head, so Lee bent in front of her and pushed at the water to break the waves' momentum.

The boats returned, and the men crowded around Eulalia. Lee positioned the post beside Eulalia's shoulder, so she could reach the gun barrel without straining. Then the men frantically pounded on the top of the post with other pieces of wood to drive it in until it was firmly entrenched. Robinson disassembled his shotgun and gave the barrel to Lee, then took the strap off his game bag and handed it over, too, so Lee could use it to tie the barrel to the post.

"Some of these boards are starting to float!" Sutton shouted, pointing to the timbers covering the quicksand. "Let's get some waterlogged beams on them so they won't bump into Mrs. Blake!"

Men splashed around, carrying heavy, barnacle-encrusted beams to the boards as Lee tied the gun barrel to the beam beside Eulalia, then set it with the end of the barrel touching her mouth. With seconds to spare, he finished tying the barrel to the post with the game-bag strap. Eulalia stretched and tilted her head back to keep her mouth and nose above the water.

Kneeling beside her, Lee took out the money clip she had given him the Christmas before and smiled thinly. Touching her face with his fingertips, he said, "Don't you lose my money clip, my dear."

His muddy fingers left streaks on her face, and she smiled weakly and chided her husband. "Stop getting mud on me, Lee."

He positioned the money clip to pinch her nostrils closed, squeezed her hand encouragingly, then moved away as she put her lips to the end of the shotgun barrel. The other men climbed into the boats as the water deepened. Eulalia smiled at Lee bravely once more before she closed her eyes and the tidewater covered her face. Then he could see only her hair floating on the surface.

He stepped into one of the four crowded boats as the men at the oars kept the boats near the beam. After he settled himself, he looked again. He watched in horror as the water became too deep for him even to see Eulalia's hair. Time dragged for him, each minute seeming an hour.

At first the men spoke words of encouragement to him but fell silent when he made no reply. He stared at the gun barrel in torment. Accustomed to being in control of every situation, he could only wait for events to run their course in this, the most terrifying crisis of his life.

The water continued rising. The waves lapped perilously close to the top of the shotgun barrel, before the depth finally stabilized. Even then, Lee feared that Eulalia might become numb and weak from the stress. If she did, a surge in the current could pull her away from the end of the gun barrel. Moment by moment, her life hung by a thread.

Moment by moment, his life also hung by a thread. After his first wife had died, he found satisfaction only in his duty. Into that drab, monotonous existence, Eulalia had brought sparkling color and her own vibrant joy in life. He had never fully lived until she had been at his side as his wife, and now that could be wrested from him.

On the road a wagon arrived with the fire hose from Killisnoo. Lee fervently prayed that there would be a need for it. At the same time, he felt an irrational flash of anger that it had arrived only now, when it would have made so much difference earlier.

The inactivity suddenly became unbearable to him, with Eulalia perhaps drowning only a few feet from him. Urgently needing to do something—anything—he bowed his head, laced his fingers, and fervently prayed for her life. The other men removed their caps as they joined him in silent supplication.

The long wait was the most grueling ordeal that Lee had ever endured. At last, a man touched Lee's arm and pointed to the beam. There was a dark, damp margin above the end of the gun barrel; the water level was finally starting to fall.

All eyes remained riveted on the gun barrel and the water that enveloped Eulalia Blake. Time seemed to pass even more slowly than before. Her hair finally became visible, then her forehead. Lee, filled with apprehension, and the other men climbed out of the boats.

At last her face, covered with mud, was visible. Her eyes were tightly closed, and her lips were still pressed to the shotgun barrel. The men gathered around anxiously, and as soon as the water level was below her mouth, she drew in deep, gasping breaths, shivering and sobbing from the cessation of tension. Lee knelt beside her, afraid his voice would break with a cry of relief and joy if he tried to speak. Gently he wiped the mud from her eyes and face with his handkerchief.

Opening her eyes, Eulalia smiled at him. "I've never liked the smell of gun oil," she remarked through her tears, "but for some reason, I believe I'll really like it from now on."

A roar of laughter rose among the men, mixed with shouts of triumph that echoed off the mountains set back from the shore. Still not trusting himself to speak, Lee simply bent lower and kissed Eulalia. Splashing through the water, the men ran to get the high-pressure hose.

Smoke billowed from the stack of the fire engine as it chuffed, building up pressure. The men dragged the hose close to Eulalia. The fire chief, holding onto the end, lifted an arm and signaled to the men at the engine. One of them pulled a lever, the hose jerked and grew taut, and water rushed through it.

Geysers of mud inundated everyone as the fire

chief expertly played the blast of water around Eulalia, splashing the quicksand away from her. It flowed back, diluted to thick, muddy water. Other men helped Lee as he held Eulalia's arms and shoulders.

Presently the quicksand became too fluid to hold her. The men applauded wildly as Lee and the other men hauled her up to the boards. Both soaked to the skin with muddy water, Lee hugged and kissed her. Then he lifted her and carried her toward the road, the men cheering and slapping each other on the back as they followed.

Eulalia suffered no ill effects from the incident. With a concerted effort, she also shrugged off the horror she had felt while submerged.

She continued her sight-seeing when Lee was busy with officials from the Bureau of Customs. She was now a celebrity in the city, and people stopped her on the street to congratulate her. Whenever she recognized a man from among those who had labored to save her, she always went to grasp his hand in heartfelt thanks.

Borrowing a horse from the army detachment stable, Eulalia visited the farms Sutton and Burnett had told her about. The huge garden vegetables fascinated her. Then she rode beyond the farms, following narrow trails into the mountains.

At dinner one evening, Lee discussed the arrangements for their journey home. "I've hesitated to mention it because I know how much you're enjoying yourself. There will be a six o'clock dinner tomorrow in our honor, then our hosts will see us to the steamer, which leaves at a quarter past eight."

"Would it be all right if I sent the baggage to the steamer tomorrow morning and go for one more ride?"

"Of course, my dear. I'll see to the baggage myself in the morning to give you a couple more hours."

Eulalia nodded happily and assured Lee that she would keep close track of the time.

The next morning, she set out early, intending to make the most of her last day. Far back in the mountains, she found one of the loveliest waterfalls she had ever seen. The water spilled over a high ledge and cascaded some fifty feet before splashing onto rocks. Mist wafted all around the fall, and the sun made brilliant rainbows in it. Eulalia sat, fascinated by the beauty. Then, looking at her watch, she realized that she had loitered longer than she meant to and that she would have to hurry to return to Sitka in time for the dinner.

Riding back toward the city, Eulalia stopped at a mountain stream to let her horse drink. She dismounted, looking for a colorful pebble to keep as a memento of Alaska. Something gleamed in the swirling sand that eddied about. Eulalia reached into the water, feeling around. Touching something solid, she picked it up and looked at it. Then she gasped in amazement. Resting on her palm was a large gold nugget that was the size of a robin's egg.

317

She stood and rolled it over on her hand, scarcely able to believe her eyes. Then she put the nugget in her dress pocket, scrambled into the saddle, and rode down the trail toward the city.

When the path allowed, she urged the horse into a canter, ignoring the brush and tree limbs flicking past and tugging at her dress. As soon as she reached the army detachment stable and turned the horse over to a soldier, Eulalia looked at her watch. She had returned in barely enough time to get ready for the dinner.

While leaving the stable, she reached into her pocket for her gold nugget. But she had evidently snagged her pocket on a limb, tearing it open and losing the nugget. She pushed her disappointment firmly aside, knowing that she had memories of Alaska more valuable than any gold nugget.

The other people at the farewell dinner were mainly those who had attended the dinner on the day Eulalia and Lee arrived.

"You gathered enough pleasant memories of Alaska to outweigh your mishap, didn't you, Mrs. Blake?" asked William Sutton, who was seated to Eulalia's left.

"Oh, yes," she answered. "I've certainly enjoyed exploring the city and my sight-seeing trips into the mountains. I found something today I intended as a keepsake, but unfortunately I lost it during the ride back. I found a large gold nugget."

An instant of silence fell, and the people at the

long table looked at Eulalia in astonishment; then they chuckled. "You couldn't have found a gold nugget, Mrs. Blake," the mayor assured her, vastly amused. "There isn't any gold in Alaska."

"But I'm positive it was a gold nugget," Eulalia insisted.

"No, it must have been a form of pyrite, Mrs. Blake," Sutton told her, smiling kindly. "That's very similar to gold."

Knowing the difference between pyrites and gold, Eulalia was certain what she had found had been gold. She politely dropped the subject, but during the remainder of the meal, the others mentioned it occasionally as a joke. When dinner was finished and the hosts escorted Eulalia and Lee to the dock, they laughed once more as they made their farewells. They invited Eulalia to come back again and find some more gold.

It was all in good fun, but Eulalia's smile was starting to wear thin. "I know gold when I see it," she said to Lee as they exchanged waves with the people on the dock. "I'm sure that was a gold nugget I found."

Lee nodded. "If you say you found a gold nugget, my dear, then you found a gold nugget," he assured her staunchly. "Regardless of what anyone says, by sheer dint of its size there must be some gold in Alaska."

The fear that swelled within Josef Mueller was so intense that his instincts and experience as an assassin deserted him. Instead of melting into the

Philadelphia crowd, he made himself obvious by standing paralyzed in terror.

Then he came to his senses and hurried around the corner of the building. Out of view from the street, he wiped cold sweat from his face and steeled himself to peek around the corner. It appeared that Henry Blake had not noticed him, but Mueller knew that the man was a master of deception.

Wearing the silver leaves of a colonel on the epaulettes of his army uniform, Henry Blake climbed into a carriage for hire in front of the train station. It moved toward him away from the curb, and Mueller backed well around the corner and turned away until it had passed.

He had no doubt that Blake had tracked him from where he had killed Gisela von Kirchberg, in Germany, to Turkey, then to the United States. Blake was the one man he feared more than Hermann Bluecher. Mueller pondered that thought. Bluecher, who hated Blake savagely, was just as indomitable as Blake. Making a decision, Mueller hurried into the train station, bought a ticket, and boarded the next train to New York.

It was late at night when Mueller's train arrived. Hiring a carriage, he directed the driver to the Long Island mansion where he had once followed Lukenbill.

In the darkest hours of night, Mueller stood facing a butler in Bluecher's doorway. "I wish to speak with the master of the house," Mueller said, unsure of what name Bluecher was using. "Announce me as a former employee from Germany and Turkey."

The butler soon returned to lead Mueller upstairs. In a dimly lit study, Bluecher sat at a desk, his hand in a desk drawer.

"Come in, Mueller, come in," he said with great affability, his eyes slits. "What a pleasure to see you again."

Mueller bowed. "It is a pleasure to see you again, sir."

"You left Turkey very precipitately, Mueller. Were you weary of Turkey or of my employment?"

"I was *not* weary of life, sir."

"What do you mean, Mueller?" Bluecher scoffed. "You must have misunderstood something I did or said."

"There was no misunderstanding, sir," Mueller said flatly. "You had made arrangements to kill me."

Bluecher's face settled into grim lines. "Surely you haven't come to return the favor."

"No, sir. I have come to tell you that Henry Blake is in Philadelphia to avenge Baroness—"

"Henry Blake?" Bluecher exclaimed, his face lighting up. "In Philadelphia?"

As Mueller explained, Bluecher took his hand from the drawer and invited Mueller to sit down. He poured drinks for both of them, then made an announcement: "I have decided that instead of having Henry Blake killed, I would derive far greater pleasure by killing the man myself." He took a sip of his drink, then asked, "How would you like to work for me once again, Mueller?"

"I believe you already have an agent working for you, sir."

"Lukenbill?" Bluecher sneered, dismissing the man with a wave. "He is incompetent. But you —you will be rich if you work for me, Mueller."

"What do you want me to do, sir?"

"Go back to Philadelphia. Leave a clear trail for Blake that leads to this house. You and I will be alone when Blake arrives. Together we will lure him to his death."

Knowing the man to be deceitful and cunning, Mueller wondered if his own future held any better prospects than a grave. But it was a risk he had to take; he was unable to face Henry Blake alone. He agreed to do as Bluecher had said.

Henry, unaware that Mueller was even within thousands of miles, commenced his search for Klaus Lukenbill in Philadelphia. Not wanting to trouble the police with a personal matter, he went to the central post office in the city to see if they had any record of Lukenbill.

The postmaster was cooperative but curious. "Does it pertain to some official military matter, sir?"

"No, I was informed by Washington that the man was asking about my whereabouts. He didn't get in touch with me, so I decided to contact him and see what he wants."

Satisfied, the postmaster sent a clerk to the directory files for information on Lukenbill. In a few minutes the clerk returned to report that no Klaus Lukenbill was listed in the files.

Henry thanked the postmaster and left. It appeared that finding Lukenbill would take time, but he had plenty of that, for he intended to remain in Philadelphia at least until Cindy arrived with the group escorting the torch of the Statue of Liberty.

The city was crowded with people participating in the celebration and admiring the exhibits. This also interested Henry; his nation's one-hundredth year touched a deep chord within him, which responded to the patriotic excitement that pervaded the city.

While passing Machinery Hall, an immense building devoted to displays of scientific developments, Henry spotted a woman toting a photographic case. She was accompanied by an exotic, strikingly attractive woman. Henry maneuvered himself through the crowd until he could read the name boldly printed on the side of her case; she was indeed Marjorie White.

Although he had never met the famous photographist, Henry knew that she was a friend of the Holt family, and Cindy in particular. He started toward her, but she and the other woman were moving out of the hall with a determination that expressed a pressing engagement and no time to talk. Certain that Marjorie would be photographing the celebration and exhibits, Henry knew he would happen upon her again.

As the *Amazonia* made its way into the harbor at Porto de Moz, Edward Blackstone spotted the longboat from the *Galatea* riding at anchor among other smaller vessels. He pointed it out to Teddy, who instructed Santos to turn the launch toward it. As the *Amazonia* drew up alongside the boat, Edward was surprised to see Gillis, the first officer of the *Galatea*, aboard.

Gillis climbed into the launch, pleased and relieved to see Edward's group.

"We have a full cargo of rubber-tree seeds," Edward responded to the sailor's question, "which I estimate to be some ten thousand seeds. That should be enough for several large plantations."

"That's good news, Mr. Blackstone," Gillis said. "But I'm afraid I have bad news for you." He took off his cap and rubbed his bald pate. "The Brazilians have apparently deduced your purpose. They have you bottled up in this river, and extra gunboats are waiting for you to show up."

"Are they watching specifically for this launch?"

"Yes, but in the event you've changed to another vessel, they're searching every small boat that arrives from upriver and asking if anyone has seen your party."

Edward frowned. He had feared for days that it might be necessary to make a fast run for the mouth of the river. Risky in any vessel, it approached being suicidal in the *Amazonia*.

He asked Teddy to get from Santos a chart of

the mouth of the river. The captain produced a creased, smudged map, which Edward spread on the deck in the shade of the wheelhouse. At the river's mouth was the sizable Marajo Island, with numerous bays surrounding it. Edward pointed to an isolated bay on the seaward side.

"Would that provide a safe anchorage for the *Galatea*, Mr. Gillis?"

The first officer peered at the depth markings and reef warnings, then nodded. "It would, Mr. Blackstone. That bay is miles from Belém, and the gunboats are patrolling upriver from Marajo Island."

"Is the *Galatea* ready to put to sea?"

"Yes, sir, within an hour."

"Very well. Teddy, please ask the captain if he'll make a run at full speed for that bay at night, with his lights off."

Teddy explained in Portuguese, and a greedy gleam illuminated the captain's dark eyes. He replied at length. "He'll do it for an extra twenty-five guineas, Edward," Teddy translated.

"Tell him I'll give him an extra fifty guineas, but I want the throttle wide open and this launch running at every knot it can manage every foot of the way there. And if we run into gunboats, he's not to heave to. He's to evade them, even at the risk of cannon fire."

Teddy translated, and the captain's eyes glittered when she mentioned the money. He replied emphatically, then bared his blackened teeth in a wide grin. Teddy turned back to Edward. "He said he'll get us there, regardless of what happens, Edward."

Although assured Santos would do his best, Edward remained uncertain about the capabilities of the rickety, old launch. He sighed. "It's settled, then. We'll meet the *Galatea* there sometime after midnight tonight, Mr. Gillis."

"Tonight?" the man exclaimed. "That doesn't give me much time to get to Belém, Mr. Blackstone. I would be much more certain of reaching the ship and having it at the rendezvous if you'd make that tomorrow night."

"True, but the *Amazonia* might not be at the rendezvous. Boats are leaving here hourly with people who've seen us. Police and other officials are stationed here. If we tarry until tomorrow morning, a gunboat might arrest us."

"Very well," Gillis agreed dubiously.

The first officer returned to the longboat and shouted orders. The sailors scrambled about, and the longboat moved out of the harbor and disappeared downstream.

In the stifling heat of the following hours, Santos made his own preparations: He sent two crewmen for bundles of seasoned wood—to use in place of the wet driftwood, flinty coal, and other cheap fuel he usually burned. The rest of the crew cleaned out the furnace and flue for more efficiency, while Santos inspected steam lines and attended to other long-deferred maintenance.

By sunset the launch was as ready as it would ever be. It moved out of the harbor and started downriver, slowly picking up speed. The channel was congested with traffic, and the *Amazonia* weaved among the vessels, even violating maritime law by cutting in front of sailing boats.

The deck hatch over the engine room was left open to vent the searing heat from the firebox, its sides red from the raging flames inside it. The shouting crewmen raced about the engine room, tying rags around steam lines that sprang leaks and contriving other hasty, makeshift repairs to keep the old launch running at full throttle. When darkness settled, all illumination on the vessel was provided by the ruddy glow from the engine-room hatch and the showers of sparks flying from the smokestack.

Darkness also changed the risky weaving through traffic to a nightmare of narrow escapes. "Does Santos have good eyesight?" Edward asked Teddy.

"Now that you mention it, I've noticed that he doesn't seem to be able to see things nearly as well as I do."

"I wish I hadn't mentioned it," Edward said, wincing as the launch sped past a small steamboat. "He almost took the paint off that one."

"A miss is as good as a mile," Dooley reminded Edward cheerfully. "Would you like a drink, Edward?"

"No, thank you, Edgar." He craned his neck. "A cluster of vessels is ahead, and Santos may have to slow to stay in the ship channel."

A short distance downriver, Edward and Teddy could see the navigation lights on a large sailing ship near the right side of the channel, with smaller vessels even farther to the right. Ahead and slightly to the left was a large cargo steamer, with other smaller boats filling the rest of the channel to the left.

A moment passed, and the *Amazonia* bore down with unabated speed on the congestion. "I believe," Teddy said in a soft, tense voice, "that Santos intends to try to run up behind that steamer and then cut to the right in front of the sailing ship."

"He can't!" Edward cried out. "There isn't enough room!" Clenching his teeth and waiting for the collision, he watched as the launch bore down on the steamer. Its stern looked like a black cliff looming high above as the launch tossed in its wake and veered to the right. A foghorn on the sailing ship blasted angrily almost overhead. The launch came within four feet of colliding with it. Then the *Amazonia* was in the clear, pulling in ahead of the steamer. Edward silently reached for Dooley's bottle. He took a deep drink and passed it to Teddy, who also took a generous swig.

The run continued to be a gauntlet of near misses. The *Amazonia* finally reached the stretch of river just above the harbor at Belém, where the danger of collision lessened because the channel was wider. It was, however, also the patrol area of the gunboats.

As the lights of Belém slowly passed to the right,

Edward entertained the hope that the launch would slip by the gunboats without detection. But when the launch sped between the two large steamers with almost no room to spare, the steam whistles on both shrieked deafeningly in warning.

An instant later, a carbide searchlight flared in the harbor and swept the water. Santos angled away from it, but another light joined the first. Then a third opened wide on the left, closing in on that side. Santos zigzagged, heading toward the mouth of the river as he dodged the bright beams.

Anxious minutes passed as the launch raced toward the mouth of the river and the searchlights combed the water around it. Then a red flash exploded beside the beam, the dull thud of a cannon carried across the water, and the whine of a cannonball passed overhead.

Edward, standing, beckoned Teddy. "We'd better keep an eye on Santos. He might not be up to facing cannon fire."

She followed Edward to the wheelhouse door. He braced himself in the doorway against the motion of the launch, watching Santos, whose grimy, sweat-streaked face was twisted with fright.

Several miles ahead, the enormous mass of Marajo Island and its companion, smaller, islands were dark shadows in the moonlight. Four gunboats gave chase, making it more difficult to evade the searchlights. Cannon boomed, but most of the balls missed the launch by a wide margin. When a light found it again, a cannon fired accurately, and a ball slammed into the smokestack with a deafening crash, bringing down a shower of soot and rusty metal shards. Santos screamed and reached for the throttle to close it.

Edward knocked the man's hand away, then drew his pistol, putting it to the man's temple. "Order him to run for the north of Marajo Island, Teddy!"

She translated Santos's reply. "He says that there are shallows and rocks among the small islands there."

"Tell him those gunboats draw more water than this launch! And tell him he has a choice between that and having his brains decorating the windshield!"

When Teddy translated, Santos whimpered in fright and complied. He zigzagged toward the island mass, flinching when the cannonballs exploded in the water around them and the searchlights passed near.

The launch was close to the island before the gunboat captains figured out the strategy. The pursuers rushed in, but the *Amazonia* was already close enough to a cluster of islets to speed into them, where the authorities were unable to follow. Thirty minutes of heart-stopping cat and mouse followed as the gunboats prowled around the islets and the launch eased through them at slow speed, passing within feet of jagged rocks.

When all of the pursuers were on one side of the islets, the launch raced out the other, at full throttle again. Ducking into another group of small islands before the gunboats could catch it, the launch went through a narrow lead, emerging on the other side of a larger island. The authorities were still searching, far behind. The launch then circled around the main island, hours away from the rendezvous.

Dawn was approaching when the *Amazonia* reached her destination. As she moved into the dark bay, Edward held his breath while Santos flicked the navigation lights on and back off. When there came an answering wink from the huge array of navigation lights on the *Galatea*, Edward heaved a sigh of relief.

The launch edged up to the side of the dark ship, and Sterch called down to Edward, "We were getting concerned, Mr. Blackstone!"

"We had to get away from some gunboats!" Edward replied. "They'll be searching all around the island, so we'd better get a move on."

Sterch and Gillis shouted orders to the sailors, and Santos did the same to his crewmen. Witherspoon, who had slept soundly in the cabin through the turmoil of the run from Porto de Moz, sleepily climbed the rope ladder to the *Galatea* as Edward and Teddy carried out the baggage. Dooley roamed about, singing.

When the cargo net was lowered, several sailors were riding it, to help transfer the crates of cans. The launch crewmen passed the cans out of the hold, then the sailors stacked them in the net. Load after load was lifted to the ship as the minutes fled.

Dawn was breaking as the last load was hauled aboard the ship. Edward paid Santos his bonus for the fast downriver run. The man chuckled and shook hands with Edward and Teddy. They climbed the rope ladder to the ship, and the launch moved toward the mouth of the bay.

The activity on the *Galatea* was frantic as the crew made an effort to get underway as quickly as possible. Smoke billowed from the ship's stack as the boilers worked up to full pressure. The ship edged toward the mouth of the bay under the minimum head of steam needed to turn its shafts.

Edward and Teddy stood at the rail and congratulated each other. Dooley, standing nearby, took a drink from his bottle and faced them. "Ahoy, Edward, me matey," he said with a laugh. "Shiver me timbers if I don't see jolly rogers bearing down on us here."

Turning to look, Edward saw the four gunboats coming around a point of land three miles away. Bells on the bridge clanged in a signal for flank speed, for Sterch had also sighted the boats. They put on a burst of speed, the smoke from their stacks thickening.

It was touch and go as the pursuers closed rapidly and fired cannonballs. But the *Galatea* finally worked up a full head of steam and drew away from the gunboats. When their pursuers turned back, Edward and Teddy joined in the rousing cheers of the sailors.

Witherspoon, having observed all that had transpired with his usual lack of understanding, failed to cheer. "The flora and fauna of Brazil are very fascinating. I wish we could have stayed longer."

"We might have remained for a very long time indeed, Mr. Witherspoon," Edward replied. "Specifically, we might have been in a Brazilian prison."

Witherspoon shrugged in perplexity as he turned away. Edward looked out over the waves, feeling very full of himself. The undertaking had been a complete success, and great wealth was in his future. But most important of all was that at the end of the voyage he would find Ramedha waiting for him.

XIX

"I understood that you were a major," Marjorie White commented. "Congratulations are in order, Colonel Blake."

"Thank you, Miss White. You're here to photograph the celebration and the exhibits?"

"Yes, I've been here for some months now."

Marjorie was barely cordial to Henry. She regarded him with a level stare, her attractive face unsmiling. He realized her reserve was in reaction to his broken engagement with Cindy, of whom she was very fond.

They stood at the edge of a busy sidewalk in the exhibit area, and other people crowded past them. Marjorie asked if he was on official business.

"No, I'm looking for a man who was asking about me in Washington. Also, I'm waiting until Cindy gets here from Paris."

"Indeed?" Marjorie cocked an eyebrow in surprise. "Have you seen Cindy recently?"

"I saw her in Portland, not long ago, and then she visited me at Fort Harland." He pointed to a concessions area. "Would you care for coffee?"

Having thawed after what he had told her about Cindy, she agreed and picked up her photographic equipment case. Henry offered to carry it for her, but she politely declined.

They found an empty table inside a coffee shop. After the waiter brought their order, Marjorie pursued the subject of Cindy. "She's immensely talented. Her work is in great demand in Europe, as well as here. In time, she'll be a very famous etcher."

"Yes, she does have a rare talent. You do as well, Miss White. You certainly deserve your fame."

"Thank you, Colonel. It's my life, so I give it all I have."

"I wish you every success. I happened to see you a couple of days ago with another woman. From her appearance, I judged her to be from the Eastern Mediterranean."

"Yes, Salima. She's from Turkey. A very interesting and entertaining companion. In fact, she's a dancer. She's married to a man named Josef Mueller—a real international mismatch."

The name immediately drew Henry's keen interest, which he concealed. "A German married to a woman from Turkey?" he observed casually, probing for more information.

"Yes, they're an unusual couple. Salima is charming and outgoing, while her husband is a very cold, secretive sort. If I didn't know he owns a restaurant, I'd say he was involved in something underhanded."

"The young woman is extremely attractive. If he's older than she, perhaps he's jealous."

"It goes beyond that, although he is older than Salima. He's about forty or so, a stolid, heavyset man. Salima isn't the sort of woman to be unfaithful, but even if she were, no man would want Mueller as an enemy."

Henry concealed his reaction, having just heard a perfect description of Josef Mueller. "You say they own a restaurant?"

"Yes, it's Suleiman Bey's Turkish Restaurant. The food is excellent. You should try it and see Salima dance."

"Yes, I must do that," Henry said casually, containing his sense of urgency. Presently, Marjorie's attitude toward him relaxed further. When they parted ways, Henry returned to his hotel, changed into civilian clothes, and checked his service revolver. After concealing it under his coat, he took a hired carriage to the restaurant.

As he entered the establishment, he unbuttoned his coat, and his hand remained poised to reach for his weapon. He scanned the dining room quickly: Mueller was not present. A small, slender Turk stepped up to Henry and bowed.

"I don't want a table," Henry told him. "I believe the owner is an acquaintance of mine. If he's in, I'd prefer to announce myself."

"I'm sorry, Mr. Mueller is in New York, visiting a friend—a former official of the German government. Would you like to have the address?"

"Why would you think I might want the address?"

"Mr. Mueller told me to say that, sir," the man answered. "He told me to give the address to anyone who asked for him."

"Yes, I see . . . I would like the address, please."

The man went to an office at the far end of the dining room and came back a moment later with a piece of paper, which he handed to Henry.

Returning to his hotel, Henry prepared to leave on the first train to New York. The situation was clear: Mueller had seen him in Philadelphia, and Bluecher had somehow ended up in New York. Mueller had gone there, leaving a message at the restaurant that was a challenge—a challenge Henry was more than pleased to accept.

Toby Holt arrived in Philadelphia late that evening and went straight to police headquarters. The police chief was waiting for him with Albert Kirby, a plain-clothes detective.

"Your telegram indicated you'd need an assistant and a liaison with the department," the chief said, "so Kirby will work with you. Now, could you tell us what this is all about?"

When Toby finished, both policemen were aghast. "Why blow up the torch of the Statue of Liberty?" the chief demanded.

"I haven't any idea," Toby admitted. "But time is running out, and we're going to have to learn that before we can deal with this situation effectively."

"You'll have complete cooperation," the police chief promised. "An office is already set up for you right down the hall, and we'll maintain close contact every step of the way. What can we do right now to help?"

"Lukenbill has been under close surveillance in New York. He's preparing to come here, so we need to have plain-clothes policemen at the train station to follow him. He could arrive at any time."

"Go to the squad room and get four plain-clothes detectives," the police chief said to Kirby. "Take them to Mr. Holt's office." He turned back to Toby as Kirby left. "Naturally, they'll need a full description of Lukenbill."

"We managed to get a good photograph of him while he was walking along a street, and I brought along tintype copies."

"Good, good. What else can we do, Mr. Holt?"

"The names I have of people connected with this plot are Klaus Lukenbill, André Maritain, and Cyril Jenkins. I'd like your records staff to search their files for any mention of those names."

The police chief wrote down the names. Toby and he were both concerned that the time available to foil the plot was short, since the torch was due to arrive by ship three days hence.

The chief led Toby to the comfortably large office prepared for him. A few minutes later, Kirby came in with four plain-clothes policemen, to whom Toby gave the tintypes and instructions. The four left for the train station, and Toby briefed Kirby. Satisfied that Kirby was an experienced, dedicated policeman, Toby left for his hotel. Because his family and friends were due to arrive from Portland two days later, he verified their reservations when he checked in.

The next morning, Toby was just sitting down in his office at police headquarters when Kirby came in and reported that Lukenbill had arrived. "The men followed him to a boardinghouse. They're waiting for us at a dry-goods store across the street from the place."

Toby and Kirby went outside to a waiting police carriage. Thirty minutes later it drew up at a corner, where a man was standing beside a building and looking at a newspaper. He folded the newspaper, tucked it under his arm, and walked away.

Toby and Kirby followed him into a dry-goods store, through aisles crowded with shoppers, to the rear of the store and through a door opening onto stairs leading up to the business's storage rooms.

Another policeman, sitting at a window, moved aside for the newcomers. The large, three-story boardinghouse directly opposite had at least ten rooms on each floor. One of the policemen quietly made his report on Lukenbill's movements. He ended by telling Toby that the man was still inside.

"Al," Toby said, "we may be watching that place for a while. Ask the owner of this store if we can use the alley door so we won't arouse suspicion. And have a man go across the street to ask about renting a room while he takes a look around."

Kirby and another policeman left to do his bidding. Kirby returned with the owner's permission to use the alley door. A few minutes later, the policeman returned from the boardinghouse.

"Lukenbill apparently went to his room and stayed there, sir. The landlady said she didn't have any vacancies. She was happy, of course, and bragged that she had just rented her last ten rooms."

"Lukenbill rented ten rooms?" Toby questioned.

"She didn't say that, sir," the policeman qualified, "but no one else has gone in there since his arrival. And many of her rooms could accommodate three or four men."

New York surveillance had revealed that Lukenbill was the leader of the Zeno Bund, which had some twenty members. He was apparently preparing for their arrival in Philadelphia.

Toby talked with Kirby. "Lukenbill wouldn't need that many men to set an explosive charge.

In fact, they would be a liability, drawing attention."

"And getting in each other's way," Kirby
added.

Toby sighed worriedly. "Does anyone know
what time the next train from New York arrives?"

"Eleven o'clock, sir," one policeman volunteered.

"All right, let's keep the boardinghouse under
surveillance around the clock. Al, make arrangements for the men to work eight-hour shifts."

The detective pointed to two of the policemen
and told them to remain; then he left with the
others for the train station.

At midmorning Lukenbill came out of the boardinghouse, and two of the policemen quickly left
to trail him. They were gone over an hour. They
came back upstairs a moment after Toby, looking
out the window, saw Lukenbill on the street with
six men with suitcases, who followed him at a
distance of a few yards. They all entered the
boardinghouse.

The policemen said that these newcomers were
passengers from New York, whom Lukenbill had
meet at the train station.

"His men are coming in a few at a time to avoid
arousing suspicion," Toby said. "Al, I'm expecting a telegram from my family, so I'll go to my
hotel and see if it's arrived. I'll have lunch, then
meet you at headquarters."

Riding toward the hotel, Toby reflected ruefully

that he might receive a telegram from Alexandra, informing him of the en-route birth of their child.

When he arrived, a telegram was waiting for him. He quickly tore it open, feeling relieved as he scanned it: Alexandra had sent it from Indianapolis. All the connections to Philadelphia had been confirmed, and they would arrive the next afternoon. She felt well, she said, but that satisfied Toby only to an extent—she still had to get from Indianapolis to Philadelphia.

Toby went into the hotel dining room, where he bumped into Marjorie White, who exclaimed in surprise and pleasure. She exchanged a hug with him. "Is your family already here?"

"Tomorrow, Marjorie. Cindy should be here the day after tomorrow. I plan to meet the ship."

"Henry Blake is here in Philadelphia, Toby. Did you know that?"

"I didn't. When did you see him?"

"A couple of days ago. I got the impression that he and Cindy might get back together."

Toby smiled wistfully. "I'd like nothing better. I thought about talking with Cindy and seeing if I could help the reconciliation along, then decided not to. They have to work things out for themselves."

"I agree. If I see her before she and Henry meet, I won't mention that I saw him."

"That would be best. As far as she knows, he's with the Seventh Cavalry. French newspapers wouldn't have covered his actions in Arizona. I hope his being here will be a pleasant surprise for her."

"What did he do in—" Marjorie broke off. "Was he the one who took cavalry into Mexico? Well, it mustn't have made anyone in Washington angry, because he's a lieutenant colonel now."

"He is?" Toby grinned with pleasure. "Do you know where he's staying?"

"At the Kennison, I believe."

Toby made a mental note of the name of the hotel. When they finished lunch, he left for the police station, and Marjorie went to her room for her photographic case.

A short time later, in his office, Toby was talking with Kirby when the police chief came in with all the information on Lukenbill that had been found in the records: The list included arrests for possession of counterfeit money, conspiracy to commit extortion, and involvement in a confidence scheme. The total picture was of a petty criminal.

"Nothing much here," Toby commented.

"I agree," the chief admitted. "We've nothing at all on Maritain, but there's a puzzling file on Jenkins."

"Why puzzling?"

"We have an arrangement with the United States Mint here to investigate all their employment applicants. In the records we came across an employment application on Jenkins they sent us a few months ago. Our investigation turned up all sorts of problems, so we notified them."

342

Toby slammed a fist down on his desk and sat back, hooting triumphantly. "Lukenbill made a mistake! A mistake that reveals everything!"

Exchanging a glance with Kirby, the police chief asked, "What are you talking about, Mr. Holt?"

"Lukenbill didn't know you investigate applicants for employment at the mint," Toby explained. "That was his mistake. Jenkins went there because Lukenbill sent him to learn the layout! Lukenbill intends to rob the mint!"

"He can't get away with that," the chief protested. "There's a police station right across the street from—" His eyes widened as he added the facts.

"That's right," Toby said grimly. "The explosion of the torch will draw every policeman in the city, leaving the mint unprotected."

"Shall we arrest him?" Kirby asked.

Toby shook his head. "We still don't know where that explosive is located. And thus far, we have only the flimsiest circumstantial evidence against Lukenbill."

The police chief nodded regretfully. "But it'll be very risky to let him proceed in the hope of catching him red-handed."

"I think we can deal with those risks," Toby said. "We can take the initiative. It'll simply be a matter of setting up a good counterplan to throw him off balance."

"You're in charge, Mr. Holt," the police chief

replied, going out the door. "When your plan is organized, let me know."

Telling Kirby to pull his chair closer, Toby reached for paper and pencil and made notes on possible ways to counter Lukenbill's plot. Toby knew that the personnel at the mint, plus those in charge of the centennial celebration and the group escorting the torch from France, would be involved. The hours of the afternoon passed as he devised a simple, effective plan.

Then, looking forward to seeing Henry, Toby went to the Kennison Hotel. The desk clerk reported that Henry had checked out. Disappointed, Toby left, wondering where Henry had gone and what he was doing.

Henry Blake was hunkered down in a copse of trees on the spacious grounds around Hermann Bluecher's Long Island mansion. He had left his baggage at the New York City train station and come straight to the house and watched all the servants leave. Instead of attacking, he had waited, knowing that Mueller would be suffering a torment of suspense, while Bluecher would be seething with impatience. He enjoyed the thought of their discomfiture, but dusk had settled and it was time to act. Lights had come on in a few windows, and Henry moved quietly across the grounds toward the lights. At the linen-room window, he slid his penknife under the sash, nudging the lock open, and lifted the window an inch. Next he went around the rear of the house and moved a lawn bench, potted plants, and other obstacles that he might bump into on his way back to the linen room. When he was at the other side of the house, he tapped his pistol against a window-pane and broke it as a diversion for his enemies. The glass fell with a loud clatter, and he raced around the house to the linen-room window.

Quickly and quietly opening the window, Henry slipped into the linen room, closed the window, then went to the door. The well-oiled knob made no sound as he tested it for squeaks. He opened the door a fraction of an inch and could hear Mueller's light footsteps as he passed the linen room on his way to investigate the sound of the falling glass.

When the footsteps were gone, Henry stepped out, closed the door, then silently hurried along the hall toward the front of the house. The door of one of the drawing rooms off the entry was ajar. Henry pushed the door open with his pistol and crouched low as he quickly slipped inside. No one was in the room.

Leaving the door ajar, Henry opened a window, crossed the room to a dark corner, and took a coin from his pocket. The evening breeze rattled the window and made the draperies billow. Henry watched the doorway, which darkened as Mueller approached. The man stopped, then edged closer.

Henry waited, knowing that Mueller was chagrined over having been drawn to one side of the house by a trick. Now he was listening to the rattle of the window, a loud, mocking noise. He was being treated like a child.

Mueller leapt through the doorway, ducking to one side to keep from silhouetting himself. The instant he appeared in the doorway, Henry tossed the coin toward the window. When Mueller landed inside the room, he fired twice at the motion and sound.

Henry laughed softly. Mueller and Henry both fired, the shots almost blending, but one was a fraction sooner. Mueller dropped to the floor, dead.

Listening to the gunfire downstairs, Hermann Bluecher noted the slight separation between the two shots. He knew that Henry Blake would win because Mueller was outmatched. That was how Bluecher had planned it, to kill Blake himself. He waited patiently in his study, shotgun ready, watching the door. The American's death had been a consuming part of his life. Now he would finally reach that goal.

As the echoes of the gunfire died away, Bluecher heard Blake searching for him, opening and closing doors. When the doors of the rooms adjacent to the study began slamming, Bluecher lifted his shotgun, cocking the hammers and aiming toward the door.

He was tense with anticipation. The door was suddenly jerked open, a man silhouetted in it. Laughing savagely Bluecher pulled both triggers.

Even as the shotgun roared, bucking against his

shoulder, Bluecher's laughter died. The buckshot ripped into Mueller's corpse, which was tossed aside. Then Henry Blake was standing in the doorway, his pistol leveled at Bluecher.

Setting the shotgun down, Bluecher shrugged. "You have won," he said in German. "Kill me."

"I intend to," Henry replied crisply in the same language. "But I will choose the time and method."

"Let us speak in English," he requested. "I find your Prussian accent to be very harsh."

Henry shrugged, changing to English. "Gladly, because your Pomeranian accent sounds effete to me."

Bluecher controlled his resentment. "Shall we have a drink?" He pointed to the cabinet. "I have a wide choice of liquors, and you appear to be in no particular hurry."

"No, I'm not. I'll have Steinhager."

Hope welled within Bluecher. As he poured drinks, he believed it would prove easy to turn the tables on the American, who was so self-confident that it was almost unbelievable. Blake actually put his pistol down on a table beside a chair, then sat down and lit a cigar.

Thinking about the double-barrel derringer in the top right-hand drawer of his desk, Bluecher wondered if Blake would tell him where to sit. But the man merely puffed on his cigar and said nothing as Bluecher put the glass of Steinhager on the table beside the pistol, then stepped toward the desk. Concealing his optimism, he sat behind the desk.

His elbows casually resting on the arms of his chair, Bluecher slowly and silently tugged at the handle on the right-hand drawer.

"You and I have battled for years, but always at long range," Bluecher remarked. "This is the first time we have faced each other. When I first heard of you, I sent two agents to kill you. You killed Weiditz in the train station at Bremerhaven, but Schneider simply disappeared. What happened to him?"

Henry took a drink from his glass and puffed on his cigar, pondering. "He was traveling under the identity of a Swiss merchant named Otto Brunfels?"

"Yes."

"He took passage on the *Loewengau* at the same time I did, but he . . . left the ship before it reached its destination."

"I see. Schneider was probably the best agent I ever employed."

"He was very good."

"Regarding the young king Alphonse of Spain," Bluecher said. "How did you manage to thwart the assassination attempts against him?"

"There were fundamental errors in the plans. One assassin who is willing to die can often succeed. A group will fail just as often, because there is a weakest member, attempting to stay alive."

The drawer almost open, Bluecher reflected that Blake epitomized the qualities he had always sought in agents: As cold as ice and consummately skilled, his only fault seemed to be his boundless self-confidence. "It is unfortunate that we didn't work together. We could have changed history."

"Our objectives are diametrically opposed."

"Come, come," Bluecher scoffed. "That is merely a matter of opinion, and our methods in reaching our objectives are certainly the same."

"I disagree. Worthy objectives are moral choices based on universal and unchanging principles. Our methods are similar, but that misses the point. There is a difference between shoving a child in front of a wagon and *from* in front of a wagon, even if it is shoving a child in both cases."

Bluecher's hand crept toward the derringer in the open drawer. "Each time we have matched wits, you have bested me. Why is that?"

"You have always been too confident. That has kept you from anticipating dangers and made you vulnerable to misdirection."

"Too confident?" Bluecher exclaimed, laughing. "Perhaps sometimes, but not this time, my young friend." His hand closed around the derringer, and his voice rose. "This time *you* were too confident!"

Henry's cigar flew through the air like a dart, straight toward Bluecher's face. He instinctively dodged the hot, glowing projectile. Henry was right behind the cigar, lunging out of his chair with blinding speed.

As his powerful hand gripped Bluecher's wrist and held it immobile, the German realized he had lost yet once more. "You were too confident again," Henry hissed softly. "You should have been watching me instead of my pistol."

Bluecher dropped the derringer. "Very well. Kill me."

"No," Henry replied grimly, replacing the derringer in Bluecher's grasp and closing his own hand around the German's fingers. "You're going to kill yourself."

Bluecher recoiled, struggling frantically, and tried to shake the derringer out of his hand so Henry Blake would have to pick it up and kill him.

But his enemy's grip was like steel; he was unable to drop the weapon. The American lifted Bluecher's hand and forced it around until the barrels pointed toward the German's temple. Bluecher could feel his finger being pressed back against the trigger. He screamed shrilly in a final, agonizing instant of terror, hearing the loud crack as the derringer fired.

Stepping back from the desk where Bluecher was slumped, Henry was aware that the final page in a long chapter of his life had been turned. He went out the front door, putting the past behind him and looking forward to the future. Cindy would be in Philadelphia in a couple of days, perhaps ready to begin life anew with him.

XX

As the train drew into the Philadelphia station, Toby looked over the heads of the crowd. Then he spotted Janessa hopping down to the platform and turning to assist Alexandra.

Everyone made room for the pregnant woman. Toby appreciated their consideration, but it made the crowd more compact and difficult to move through as he hurried toward his wife. Standing with a hand at the small of her back, she saw him and grinned.

His gnawing anxiety melted into joy as he tenderly kissed her. "I'm very relieved to see that you're all right," he said. "I haven't had a moment's peace since you set out from Portland."

"I'm only pregnant, Toby," Alexandra protested, laughing merrily. "It's a perfectly normal condition, you know."

"She's fine, Dad," Janessa confirmed. "In spite of Dr. Martin's concerns, I think the journey proved less tiring for Alexandra than for any of us."

Toby kissed Alexandra again, then greeted Janessa, Tim, the Schumanns—who had decided to come, after all—and the others. Dr. Martin was the last one off the train, accompanied by his wife, Tonie. Toby helped the doctor down the step, then beckoned porters to carry the baggage to the two hired carriages waiting near the entrance. He carefully helped Alexandra into the first carriage, and the others found seats.

"We're in no hurry," he warned the driver. "Take it slow and easy." Toby settled himself beside Alexandra and took her hand.

"Have you had any word about Cindy's arrival time?" she asked.

"The ship entered the Delaware Bay this afternoon, and it'll dock here on schedule tomorrow. Dear, while you get settled, there's a meeting I must attend."

"Isn't that matter settled yet?"

"No, but we've made considerable progress."

Tim asked his father about the rodeo.

"I didn't forget," Toby assured him. "I obtained forms for you to enter the bronco-and bull-riding events. You need parental permission, so I've signed the forms, but I want you to follow what White Elk taught you."

"I will, Dad. I know the difference between a lively animal and a killer, and if I draw a bad mount, I'll jump off as soon as I come out of the chute."

Toby felt proud of his young, handsome son. Not only was Tim taller and heavier than most boys his age, his judgment was that of someone older.

At the hotel, after Toby had checked everyone in, the group trooped to the steam-powered elevator.

As soon as Alexandra's baggage was in the room, Toby kissed her and left for the meeting at police headquarters. Janessa, waiting in the hall, accompanied him downstairs. "Alexandra is in perfect health," she assured him, "but the baby could come at any time."

The last remark, made in her usual matter-of-fact manner, electrified Toby. "What? It isn't due until August, and that would be very bad for the baby."

"Not necessarily, Dad. Perfectly normal and healthy babies can arrive a few weeks early. Dr. Martin knows a Dr. Hicks, who has a private clinic. He will assist with the birthing if the baby does come early. When Dr. Martin couldn't convince Alexandra to cancel her plans, he sent instructions to Dr. Hicks so the clinic can be thoroughly disinfected with phenol."

"Should we have Dr. Hicks come to the hotel instead, to deliver the baby in the suite?"

"No, he should have all his equipment at hand." She smiled. "Besides, if Alexandra goes into labor at night, the management might demand she be quiet so the guests could sleep."

Toby hugged and kissed her. "I love you very much, you know."

The tall, solemn girl—almost a young woman now—flushed with pleasure as Toby turned to the door and she went back toward the elevator.

Waiting for Toby were Kirby, the police chief, Chairman Hamilton of the centennial celebration committee, and Captain Keeler, of the police station across the street from the mint.

"The first purpose of the plan," he explained, "is to force Lukenbill to bring the explosive out into the open so we can seize it. The second purpose is to organize a schedule that will throw him off but coordinate all our efforts. Lukenbill thinks the torch will go on display the Fourth of July, but we'll make him think that it'll go on display in a couple of days."

"How will you feed him that information, Mr. Holt?" Keeler asked.

"Through his man Maritain. The man in charge of transporting the torch from France will tell that to his people, then Maritain will take it straight to Lukenbill."

Hamilton stroked his chin. "What's the advantage in making him believe the torch will be displayed earlier?"

"He has to put the explosives in the torch before it goes on display. If we set the time when his men will show up with the explosives, we can be there waiting for them."

"That makes sense," the celebration chairman said.

"Once we have his explosive secured," Toby continued, "we'll set off a dynamite charge in an open field. Lukenbill will hear that and go into action with his men."

"That will also be my signal," Keeler put in.

"Exactly. You and your men will rush out of the police station, as Lukenbill would expect. You'll assemble behind the livery station on Vine and Twenty-Second Street, where the chief will meet you with another battalion of officers. I'll join you, also, and we'll head for the mint. The chief will cover the front entrance, and you and I will take the side entrance, Captain Keeler."

The captain jotted the instructions in his notebook. Toby continued, explaining the measures that had to be taken to eliminate any possibility of damage to the torch. Hamilton assured him that the necessary men and equipment would be made available.

"Also," Toby added, "I'd like to have drays on hand at the port tomorrow. We'll need to unload that torch as quickly as possible to get everything done on time."

"The drays will be there," Hamilton promised. "As you know, the display area for the torch is surrounded by a high board fence. You want that left in place?"

"By all means," Toby replied. "In fact, it's crucial. The fence is tall enough so that no one can see whether or not the torch is there until they're inside. That makes it perfect for our purposes."

A few more points were discussed, and the meeting ended.

"It's easy to see why you have the reputation you do, Mr. Holt," the police chief commended.

The others agreed emphatically as Toby and they left the office. Toby knew that the plan was a good one, but he was also aware that the best plans could go wrong. And with the equivalent of a ton of dynamite still at large, any mishap could have disastrous consequences.

Toby strode up the gangplank of the cargo steamer *Orleanais*, and exchanged a hug and kiss with Cindy. Then she introduced him to Pierre Charcot, Bartholdi's principal assistant.

"Cindy informed me there might be some problem, Mr. Holt. Is that why you're here?"

"Yes, we have a very serious problem, Mr. Charcot," Toby replied. "I'd like to talk with you and Cindy in private. In the meantime, please keep all your employees on the ship."

"Of course," Charcot immediately agreed and called out orders in French.

Inside the Frenchman's cabin, the door closed, Toby told Charcot and Cindy about the plot.

"I'll certainly cooperate," Charcot assured Toby. "It makes me very ashamed to have Maritain in my employ."

"There's no way you could have known about him. Besides, he's going to prove very useful to us. We need to prevent him from contacting Lukenbill until we're ready, and we must avoid making him suspicious. Can you manage that?"

"I can give him work that will keep him busy. He must also avoid making us suspicious, so that will help, won't it?"

Toby grinned. "It will. And I've set up a schedule that will help to keep him occupied. I've arranged accommodations for you and your people. I'd like to send your baggage there, then have you take your employees to the display site and immediately assemble the torch. How long will that require?"

"Seven or eight hours."

"Good. When the torch is completed, take your people to the boardinghouse to get ready for a party that the centennial commission is hosting. After the party let them go their separate ways. By that time we'll be ready for Maritain to contact Lukenbill and tell him that the torch will go on display tomorrow."

The Frenchman voiced his concern that the torch might be damaged. Toby explained the precautions he had taken to avoid that.

The foreman and employees assembled on deck, where Charcot announced the change in the display schedule. As they gathered, Cindy surreptitiously pointed out Maritain to Toby. He was a small, handsome man with the grace of a dancer. The announcement about the party was greeted with loud cheers by everyone except Maritain.

The unloading of the torch sections began immediately; as promised, Hamilton had six drays in position while the group's baggage was transported to the boardinghouse. Toby helped Cindy into a carriage, and she warned him to be careful.

"Worry about Alexandra instead," he said wryly. "She's out seeing the sights. I'm worried that the excitement and a lot of moving might induce premature labor."

"She's probably trying to keep her mind off

what you're doing." Cindy laughed thinly and waved as the carriage moved off.

When the unloading of the torch was finished, Toby, Charcot, and his men climbed into a dray, which brought them to the main display area for the centennial celebration, in Fairmount Park. One of the largest parks in the world, it was the location of numerous historical monuments and shrines, botanical gardens, zoological exhibits, and many other attractions. The site that had been reserved for the torch was an open, grassy expanse at one end of the park. Curious onlookers gathered to watch as the drays lined up to be unloaded at the wide gates in the tall wooden fence. Toby recognized two as Lukenbill's men.

He called Charcot aside and quietly pointed out the anarchists. "We don't want Maritain to talk with them. Let's give him something to do inside the fence."

After a moment the Frenchman summoned Maritain and sent him into the fenced enclosure to work on the wooden platform that would serve as the torch's base.

When the unloading was finished and the gates closed, the onlookers dispersed. Lukenbill's men left also, to avoid being conspicuous by their loitering.

The men inside the fence bolted the torch's sections into position. When it began taking final shape, Toby had to force himself to concentrate on his purpose for being there. Consisting of the right hand and the torch, the monument was the most magnificent piece of statuary he had ever seen, perfectly proportioned and molded with consummate skill. But more than its being merely a beautiful example of sculptor's art, it conveyed the meaning it had been intended to symbolize. It was liberty in physical, concrete form, evoking a strong emotional response from the ardently patriotic Toby Holt.

When the work was finished and the gate locked, a guard arrived as Charcot and his men left for their boardinghouse. Toby accompanied them; he had arranged for Maritain's bags to be put in the wrong room to delay the man. Charcot changed clothes and joined Toby in the sitting room just as Maritain came downstairs and tried to slip out of the boardinghouse.

Charcot called jovially to Maritain, intercepting him at the door. The man had no choice but to sit down, and he tried to look calm. Presently all the workers gathered in the sitting room, eagerly anticipating the party.

Darkness had fallen when Toby accompanied Charcot and his group to Suleiman Bey's Turkish Restaurant, where a room had been set aside for the party. After it began, Toby quietly slipped away and returned to Fairmount Park.

Inside the fence centennial commission employees were working frantically under lantern light, disassembling the torch. Hamilton and Kirby were there to oversee the work. Toby told Kirby that the surveillance at the anarchists' boardinghouse could be ended.

"Bring three detectives back here," Toby added. "Make sure they're experienced and steady. Leave the carriage in an alley three blocks from the park and tell the driver to stay alert, even though he may be there a long while."

As the policemen left, drays arrived, and Hamilton's workmen carried the statue's sections from the fenced enclosure to the wagons, which rumbled away toward the warehouse where the torch would be temporarily stored.

When Kirby returned with three policemen, Toby asked the centennial-exhibit guard to lock the special police detachment—and Toby himself —inside the fenced enclosure and go home.

Once the five of them were locked inside, Toby explained what had been done. "Maritain is at a party, which will end in about an hour. Then he'll contact Lukenbill and tell him that the torch will go on display tomorrow. Lukenbill will realize that he must get the explosive into the torch tonight."

"We'll be ready for them," one of the men assured Toby.

"Fine. But gunplay is a last resort. I'd rather arrest people than kill them. Also, that explosive detonates by percussion. If a gunfight does develop, watch where you're shooting."

Toby led the men behind the wooden platform, where they sat down to wait.

As the early morning hours passed, Toby worried about Alexandra and wished he could be with her. The policemen whispered among themselves, beginning to doubt that the anarchists would show up. At dawn they were even more skeptical.

"Perhaps Lukenbill has the explosive stored somewhere outside the city," Kirby whispered to Toby.

"I don't think he'd do that," Toby replied quietly. "He's impatient to get things done. It's more likely that he—" He lifted a hand for silence as he heard footsteps of several men approaching the gate.

The men stopped outside. When Toby heard someone picking the lock, he motioned the policemen to stay down while he peered over the edge of the platform.

Maritain slid through one side of the gate with three other men, one carrying a satchel. The four stopped and looked around in astonishment, having expected to see the huge torch. Toby aimed his pistol. "Put up your hands! You can't get away, so don't make it worse for yourselves by doing something stupid."

Maritain spat an oath, snatched a pistol from his jacket, and fired. The bullet went wild. "This is your last chance!" Toby warned. "Surrender, or you'll be gunned down!"

Two conspirators dropped to the ground and drew their pistols as Maritain crouched and fired again. Splinters exploded from the platform in front of Toby, who cocked his pistol and called to the policemen, "Let them have it! But watch that satchel!"

The man holding the satchel was aware of the

peril, and he bellowed in alarm as the blistering exchange of gunfire erupted. He cautiously put the satchel down and ran for the gate, but Toby aimed at his legs and squeezed the trigger. The man screamed in pain and clutched one of his legs as he fell.

Maritain scrambled for the satchel and raised it, to hurl at Toby and the policemen. As the officers fired at Maritain, Toby also leveled his pistol and shouted another warning to aim carefully. But one of them fired too hastily, or Maritain moved, for the satchel took a direct hit from a bullet.

Toby saw a huge ball of blinding white flame and smoke swirl upward as if in slow motion, then the gate and the entire front section of the fence exploded outward into a cloud of splinters. The wooden platform, weighing tons, tilted up at its forward edge and broke apart. Then Toby, dazed, was vaguely conscious of being hurled through the air, back toward the rear of the fence as it disintegrated. He slammed down among broken boards, rolling as pieces of wood rained down on him.

A long moment passed. The world spun. Then Toby pushed away sharp pieces of wood and sat up slowly. The policemen were also stirring, choking in the dense smoke and eddying dust. "Are you all right, Al?" Toby croaked to the detective.

The policeman shoved boards away and climbed to his feet, blinking as he looked around in shock. "I guess I am, Mr. Holt." He sounded surprised to find himself still alive. He pointed to the platform. "Look at that, would you?" he exclaimed in awe. "That thing is made of solid oak, but it flipped right over and broke apart."

"It also saved our lives," Toby put in, listening to the loud ringing in his ears and hoping it would soon abate. "If we hadn't had that platform in front of us, the concussion from the explosion would have ripped us apart. Well, let's get a move on, Al. Everyone in the city heard that explosion, and it's the signal for things to happen."

"Lukenbill didn't expect it this early, Mr. Holt."

"I know, but he's been waiting for this moment for months and will still depend upon the explosion to draw the police. Send someone for the carriage, and let's find our guns."

The detective turned to the other policemen, who were numbly climbing to their feet and dusting themselves off. Kirby snapped orders, and one of the policemen ran to get the carriage. Toby found his pistol among the rubble and reloaded it as he looked around.

The explosion had made a deep hole in the ground, and all that remained of the four anarchists were shreds of bloody flesh and cloth.

When Toby and the policemen arrived at the livery stable where the various law-enforcement detachments were to congregate, the police chief, Captain Keeler, and forty officers had already gathered. When they were sure Toby and the others were all right, the police chief and captain had a belly laugh at their appearance. Toby looked down at his torn, filthy clothing and chuckled; then they were all back to business. Two plainclothes officers were watching the mint from a distance, the chief told him, as instructed.

Toby looked at his watch. "Lukenbill should show up there any minute."

Keeler put a hand on Toby's shoulder and pointed down the street. "There come the plainclothesmen. Something must be going on."

The two men breathlessly reported that Lukenbill was at the mint with twenty men and a wagon. His men had forced open the side entrance.

"Let's go," Toby said, grinning. "Chief, you and your men cover the front. Captain Keeler and I will take the side door with his men."

The forty policemen and their supervisors took off toward the mint. Toby and Keeler approached the side of the building through alleys, and minutes later, the roof came into view.

As he ran to the side of the mint, Toby saw men hurrying out the door, throwing gold bars into a waiting wagon. The robbers' lookout raised his gun and fired when Toby shouted at them to surrender.

A policeman behind him pitched to the ground, dead, as Toby leveled his pistol and squeezed the trigger. The pistol bounced in his hand, and the lookout reeled back and fell. The other robbers drew pistols and fired, crowding back through the side door. Toby and the policemen fired back, eliminating one conspirator.

The anarchists, kicking their dead comrade aside, tried to get the door closed and bolted; but Toby and his men, swarming up onto the loading dock, reached the door before it shut. Toby shot one of the men in the face as he lifted a pistol to fire through the doorway. He fell back, while the other robbers pounded down a hall.

The mint guards were bound and gagged in the small entry inside the door. Seeing they were unharmed, Toby raced down the hall in front of Keeler and the other policemen. The anarchists skidded around a corner into the main hall, then two paused to fire at their pursuers. The hall rang with the deafening blast of shots as Toby and the policemen fired at the two men, cutting them down.

Toby stopped, pressed himself against the wall at the corner, and peered around it, then ducked back as a hail of lead came from the anarchists, all of them fleeing down the main hall. It led to the front of the building, where a roar of gunfire met them from the police chief and his men. The desperate anarchists retreated toward the large, open doors of the vaults, with Toby and the policemen shooting around the corner at them.

Caught in a deadly cross fire, several anarchists fell. Only a dozen reached the vault doors; the remainder sprawled unnaturally in death on the marble floor. But as those twelve were streaming into the vault, Lukenbill darted from their midst and into a stairwell on the other side of the door. Toby snapped off a shot at him, but the bullet only clipped splinters from the doorjamb.

As the last anarchist took refuge inside the vault, Toby jumped up and ran down the hallway, Keeler shouting to him in warning. Ahead, the vault doorway he had to pass was like the jaws of death; there were a dozen men inside poised to fire. Gaining momentum as he ran toward it, Toby catapulted himself through the air past the vault, to land skidding on his belly, arms outstretched.

Pistols roared, two bullets plucking at his coat as he sprang to his feet on the other side of the vault and charged into the stairwell. Precious seconds had been lost since Lukenbill fled up the stairs, and Toby knew he could already have escaped over the roof.

Snapping open the cylinder on his pistol, Toby reloaded as he ran upstairs. At the next landing, he paused to listen for footsteps, doubting that he would hear anything. But he did. Listening to the labored breathing and slowed footsteps, Toby smiled knowingly. Lukenbill was obviously carrying several heavy gold bars as he made his escape.

A door slammed in the upstairs hall. Toby acknowledged that the sly man was hiding, intending to escape after the battle. He might have succeeded had he not been seen going into the stairwell. Toby finished reloading his pistol and stepped into the hall.

Downstairs, the hall reverberated with gunfire

as the police chief and Keeler closed in on the anarchists in the vault. Toby tiptoed along the hall, putting an ear to each door and listening. Hearing a movement on the other side of a door, he stopped. After a moment, he heard another sound. Lukenbill was in that office.

Standing to one side of the door, Toby yelled, "Come on out with your hands up, Lukenbill—"

Bullets punched a line of holes in the door from the office. Toby waited. A moment later Lukenbill opened the door, his pistol pointed at the floor, where he had expected to see Toby lying.

"Drop the gun, Lukenbill," Toby ordered quietly.

The man's head snapped around, his eyes wide with astonishment, his pistol still pointed toward the floor. Toby thumbed the hammer back on his weapon. The metallic click made Lukenbill's sharp, ugly features twitch as he hesitated in indecision. Toby's pistol was also pointed at the floor.

"Don't try it, Lukenbill," Toby warned softly. "At point-blank range, I can't risk just wounding you. I'll have to shoot to kill. I'm faster than you are. Just drop the gun."

Sweat rolled down the man's face, his eyes were glassy. Then his arm flashed upward, and Toby was forced to raise his own pistol, blasting Lukenbill between the eyes.

"Please sit down and rest, Alexandra."

"No, Cindy, I'm all right," Alexandra replied lightly. "Aren't I, Janessa?"

367

The girl, sitting in a chair on the other side of their suite's sitting room, shook her head indulgently. "You are on the go all the time, Alexandra. I told you that you shouldn't go to that horse show yesterday."

"I had to see it, dear," Alexandra explained placatingly, standing with her hands crossed and resting atop her extended belly. At last she lowered herself into a chair next to Abigail Schumann's. The explosion that rattled the windows in the hotel had awakened everyone an hour before. After hurriedly dressing, Cindy—and everyone else in the Portland group—had come to Alexandra's suite to sit with her. The Schumanns had done the same. No one knew if the explosion had taken Toby's life or if he would be mowed down by a conspirator's bullet before the danger was ended.

Except for a pallor on her face and an occasional tremor in her voice, Alexandra was as composed as always.

Cindy, unable to keep her own apprehensions from showing, envied her sister-in-law's iron self-control. She loved and revered her brother. While many men had courage and high principles, Toby also possessed an inner strength that lifted him above other people, prompting them to look to him for guidance. Cindy had met only one other man who had that quality, and that was Henry Blake.

The others helped to keep the discussion flowing. Janessa had no skill or interest in polite conversation, and Dr. Martin had dozed off. Dieter Schumann mentioned the trip that Edward Blackstone was making. No one had heard from him for months.

The door suddenly opened, and Toby walked in. He was dusty and smelled of gunpowder, and his clothes were ripped. But his strong, handsome face was set in his usual amiable, lazy smile. "Does anyone know where I can get a cup of coffee?"

As everyone expressed joyful relief, Toby kneeled in front of Alexandra, who had tried in vain to stand up, and gently kissed the palm of her hand. Then he shook his head at the questions from all sides.

"It was a nasty business—not worth talking about. Instead, let's enjoy the cheerful conversation of family and friends. Now I want to get cleaned up and have breakfast. Who'll join me in the dining room in thirty minutes?"

There was a chorus of replies as the others filed toward the door, but Cindy remained silent. Because she loved her family deeply, she had been keeping to herself, knowing she was poor company. She also wanted to be alone. She decided to have a light breakfast in her room.

The hotel was luxurious. Maids brought coffee and the newspaper to each room every morning. A silver coffee service was on the table in Cindy's room when she returned to it, the newspaper beside the tray. She poured herself a cup of coffee, then picked up the newspaper.

Most of the stories centered on the centennial

celebrations in various cities, focusing mainly on Philadelphia, and preparations for the gala celebration on the Fourth of July. On an inside page, something entirely different caught her eye: Several days before, General Crook had clashed with a war party of Sioux and Cheyenne.

The details from the remote reaches of the Montana Territory were few. Nine soldiers had been killed, and forty Indians had died. General Crook had returned to his base camp in the Wyoming Territory to resupply his men.

Tormented by conflicting emotions, Cindy put on her cape and hat and left the hotel. Loving and admiring Henry Blake, she was worried about him. At the same time, she had yet to overcome her wounded pride. The newspaper article had heightened her awareness that the Seventh Cavalry Regiment was in the field in Montana.

Cindy now had a clear understanding of Gisela von Kirchberg and the woman's relationship with Henry. She knew how one thing had led to another, resulting in Henry's breaking their engagement. But knowing those facts had failed to put to rest her negative emotional reaction to them. She had only made a partial commitment to her first marriage, and when she married again, she wanted it to be a full, wholehearted commitment. As long as wounded pride remained festering within her, that complete relationship would be impossible.

All day Cindy walked the streets of Philadelphia, past many centennial exhibits, tiring herself so she would be able to sleep that night. When sunset came, she was fatigued but anxious.

At dinner with her family and friends, someone mentioned little Peter Blake. Cindy felt a stab of regret that the boy had remained in Portland with his nurse; she had been looking forward to seeing him again.

She tossed sleeplessly that night, as she had since arriving in Philadelphia. When she finally got out of bed at dawn, she was emotionally weary and physically fatigued. She dressed, grimly contemplating the prospect of another day of inner conflict.

A maid brought in a coffee service and the morning newspaper, placing them on the table, and left. Cindy poured a cup of coffee, then sat down with the newspaper. Her eyes widened with horror as she read the headline.

She burst into tears as she dropped her coffee cup to the floor. The pride she had fought for so long abruptly shriveled in the face of her agonizing sorrow and deep, enduring love for Henry. She had always believed that they would be together eventually and that she had all the time in the world to work things out. But now her chance for happiness had been crushed, the one love of her life lost to her.

Through a blur of tears, Cindy tried to read the newspaper. Little was known of the massacre that had occurred in the far expanses of Montana a few days before, but she needed no further news from the distant, blood-stained battlefield to know that her life had turned into ashes. She knew Henry Blake, and if there had ever been anything of which she was certain, it was that he would have been at Custer's side until the very end, fighting and dying beside him. A deep moan escaped her lips as utter despair enveloped her.

A knock sounded at the door, but Cindy ignored it. She was sure it was Toby—he had probably read the newspaper and wanted to console her. But there was no consolation. She wanted to be alone. There was no point in waiting for casualty lists—she knew Henry Blake.

The knock sounded again and again, more insistently. Cindy stumbled to the door, blinded by tears, fierce words on her tongue to demand to be left alone. She angrily threw open the door. Henry stood in the hallway.

She was paralyzed by shock. A numbness seized her. Her knees buckled, and the world gave way beneath her. Henry stepped forward, taking her arms and holding her as she swayed on her feet.

As he touched her, her strength returned. She cried out in joy, wrapping her arms around his neck and pulling his lips down to hers.

XXI

Toby glowed with pride and love for his son, who was down in the center of the rodeo arena. The winning competitors were lined up to receive their awards from the chairman of the judges, and an announcer called out their names and prizes through a megaphone.

Tim, the youngest competitor to last through the preliminary events, had won a ribbon, second place in bull-riding. But to Toby's way of thinking, a far greater achievement was in how Tim conducted himself. Victorious, his bruised face was as red as a beet, but he was composed instead of looking at his feet and squirming like a child. Toby knew that innate dignity had been within Tim all along, but Alexandra had brought it to the fore.

The chairman shook Tim's hand and pinned the ribbon on his torn, dusty shirt. The announcer raised his megaphone: "Tim Holt!" the man bellowed. "Second place in bull-riding! At nine years old, Tim is seven years younger than our next youngest competitor to win a prize! Let's give Tim a real big hand, folks!"

Toby beat his hands together until they stung, and Alexandra, beside her husband in the spectators' stands, applauded just as enthusiastically. Their friends and relatives, sitting around them, applauded and cheered, adding to the roar from the audience. Tim's face turned even redder, but he remained composed as he lifted his battered hat to the crowd.

As the applause died away, Henry reached over and put a hand on Toby's shoulder. "A real chip off the old block, Toby."

"Yes, he's that," Toby agreed. "And he's going to be a lot bigger block on his own."

"No, no," Henry disagreed. "Almost as big, perhaps, but never more than that. Tim's a human being, Toby."

Alexandra and Cindy smiled at Henry and agreed, while Toby chuckled and shook his head.

A few minutes later, the last awards presented, the people stood and filed toward the aisles. Toby took his wife's elbow as she started to rise. "Let's wait until the crowd thins out, Alexandra."

"But I want to congratulate Tim, Toby," she protested.

"I do too, but we'll wait for a few minutes," Toby insisted. "I don't want you to get jostled around."

Alexandra smiled in good-natured resignation. The others remained seated out of deference to Toby and Alexandra, and Cindy chatted with her. Finally Toby took Alexandra's arm and helped her down the aisle to the arena, where Tim was talking with competitors with whom he had made friends. For the first time, Toby shook hands with Tim instead of hugging him. "Congratulations, Son."

"Thank you, Dad." Noticing the change in behavior, Tim stood a little taller.

Tim introduced Toby to the other participants, who were eager to meet him. Fame had always been a nuisance to Toby, but he was pleased by the pride on Tim's face and in his voice as the boy introduced him around, each time announcing that this was his father.

With the adept manners that Alexandra had fostered, the boy introduced all his family and friends to the competitors, who were interested in Henry in his cavalry uniform. Two young cowboys from Arizona shook hands warmly with him and expressed deep gratitude over his foray into Mexico.

Toby wanted to get Alexandra back to the hotel, where she could rest. He maneuvered the conversation to an end. By the time he left in a hired carriage with his family and friends, the sun was beginning to set.

The carriage moved slowly through the teeming streets of the city, where there was an expectant atmosphere for the gala celebration the following day, the Fourth of July. Toby also felt deeply content.

The breach between Henry and Cindy was now healed. Now that they were reunited, everyone expected a wedding to be scheduled soon. The prospect pleased Toby immensely.

Even the weather had been perfect while Toby had been taking Janessa and Tim to see the historical sights and centennial exhibits. The displays had been fascinating—particularly Machinery Hall. In it, a massive twenty-five hundred horsepower Corliss engine powered a variety of machines, and numerous inventions were on display, including the improved typewriting machine, the telephone, and the mimeograph machine.

When they reached the hotel, the clerk gave Dieter Schumann a telegram. After Dieter read it, he handed it to Toby.

Sent by Edward Blackstone from Gibraltar to

the office in Chicago, it had been forwarded by telegraph by the office manager. It consisted of a single word: *Success!*

"Good news indeed," Toby said, pleased and relieved, passing the telegram to Alexandra. "I knew Edward could do it."

"He's extremely resourceful," Dieter responded. "I'm very glad he got out of Brazil safely—for his sake and for mine. I wasn't looking forward to going to Brazil and hiring lawyers to get him released."

"Well, that worry is past, and Edward is on his way to being a wealthy man once again." Toby smiled happily. "Let's celebrate for him. Get changed and freshened up, everyone, then meet in the dining room to have a steak dinner with all the trimmings."

Everyone was in high spirits as they separated in the hallway.

In their suite, Alexandra went to change her dress as Toby put on a clean shirt, but the steak dinner was not to be.

Alexandra called to Toby, and when he came into the bedroom, she was sitting on the edge of the bed, a hand pressed to her stomach. "Would you get Janessa for me, please?"

He ran to his daughter's room down the hall. She immediately accompanied him to the suite.

"When did the pains stop?" she asked Alexandra.

"No more than a minute ago."

Looking at her watch, Janessa sat down.

"Abigail is such a pleasant, charming woman," Alexandra observed.

"Yes, she is," Janessa agreed nonchalantly. "I enjoyed staying at her home."

The two conversed as if nothing were happening. Toby, exasperated, interrupted. "Aren't you going to get Dr. Martin?"

"No, not right now, Dad. It's going to be a long night, and he isn't a young man. But we should ask the hotel to send a messenger to Dr. Hicks's clinic, so he can get everything sterilized."

Toby did as he was told. When he came back to the suite, he went to Alexandra and took her hand. "Can I get something for you? Would you like a sandwich?"

"If Alexandra tried to eat anything," Janessa said, "she would vomit."

Toby shifted from foot to foot as his wife and daughter continued talking. A few minutes later, Alexandra broke off and winced, prompting Janessa to check her watch.

"Isn't somebody going to do something?" Toby demanded in alarm.

Janessa turned to him. "Would you like a spoonful of laudanum, Dad?"

"No, I don't want a spoonful of laudanum. I want somebody to do something. Shouldn't I get a carriage? When are we going to that clinic?"

"In an hour or so," Janessa replied. "Why don't you go talk with Colonel Blake? Since we won't be having dinner together, you could let everyone know and ask Cindy to come in here."

Fuming, Toby left. After sending Cindy, Abigail Schumann, and Tonie Martin to the suite, Toby met Marjorie White in the hall and sent her there, also. Dieter accompanied Toby to Henry's room, where Toby paced the floor and puffed on a cigar.

After what seemed to be an endlessly long time, Cindy knocked on the door and said it was time to leave for the clinic. Deeming the elevator too slow for him, Toby went down the stairs to summon two carriages. Alexandra came out, walking between Janessa and Dr. Martin, with the others trooping out behind them.

The clinic was in a large Victorian house on landscaped grounds overlooking the Schuylkill River. Catering to a wealthy clientele, it was luxuriously furnished and well staffed. Dr. Hicks led Janessa and Dr. Martin upstairs with Alexandra, while a maid showed Toby and the others into a drawing room, then brought refreshments.

The strong smell of phenol was strangely comforting to Toby. Still very nervous, of course, he controlled himself and sat down for the long wait that he knew was ahead. The others took seats, talked, drank coffee, and ate sandwiches. After a time, Cindy mentioned to Henry a letter, forwarded to her, from Elizabeth Custer, written before the tragedy at Little Bighorn River.

"I suppose she'll go to her family in Michigan for a time."

Henry nodded. "Plans are being made to inter the general at West Point, which would be very appropriate. I hope Elizabeth will contact us if we can do anything for her."

The others took up the subject about Custer and the battle at the Little Bighorn River. Although the casualties had been disastrous, the initial reports that the Seventh Cavalry Regiment had been virtually annihilated had been proven untrue. A battalion had been lost—two hundred and sixty-six soldiers—out of a total regimental strength of nearly eight hundred.

Further details emerged daily: Custer had not been scalped, which was extraordinary and appeared to support the story that Indians had been in awe of him. The only survivor of the battalion that Custer had led into the battle had been Comanche, Captain Myles Keogh's horse. Wounded but recovering, he had become the regimental mascot.

Dieter mentioned something he had read in a newspaper: "Just before the battle, the general supposedly sent a message to Captain Benteen, who was with another battalion. When the general saw the Indians, he reportedly said to his men, 'Hurrah, boys, we've got them now.' Colonel Blake, considering that he was looking at several thousand Indians, could he have actually said something like that?"

"Well, no one could ever say General Custer was short of self-confidence," Henry replied reflectively. "On the other hand, that report came from an Italian immigrant named Martini. To be generous about it, he doesn't speak English very well. It's possible he was mistaken."

"But I simply don't understand why he chose to fight at all," Marjorie pressed. "Under the circumstances, if he had simply led his men away, no one could have accused him of cowardice. The odds were hopeless."

"He might not have known how many Indians were there," Henry suggested. "The terrain there is broken, so he probably didn't see the entire encampment. I'm sure he realized he was vastly outnumbered, but a cavalry charge is like a battering ram. It can break the line of a much larger force and overcome a great difference in numbers."

"That's true," Toby confirmed. "Any number of times during the Civil War, I saw a charge by a company of cavalry make an entire regiment of infantry take to its heels. It's like standing in front of a train."

"There's one other point," Henry added. "General Custer used a charge against much larger forces of Indians before, with good results. One example was a few years ago, on the Washita River. He attacked a force of Cheyenne led by Black Kettle and completely routed them. So it's possible he was intending to do the same at the Little Bighorn, but he didn't realize he had come upon the main body of the Sioux and Cheyenne."

As the others conversed, Toby wished Janessa would come out with a progress report. The maid brought in more coffee and sandwiches, and the hours dragged past. Then the quiet of the night was broken by fireworks, rockets shrieking aloft and exploding as firecrackers popped. Cannon at the armory, firing salvo after salvo, joined in with deep, booming thuds that made the windows rattle.

Toby took out his watch and looked at it. "Well, ladies and gentlemen, it's just after midnight. Our nation is now one hundred years old."

Just as he finished speaking, the maid came back in, pushing a serving cart with glasses and a bottle of champagne in an ice bucket. "With Dr. Hicks's compliments," she announced.

Toby thanked her and stood up to do the honors. The cork popped out, everyone cheered, and the champagne foamed up as Toby filled the glasses and passed them around. The atmosphere of gaiety took on a serious undertone as they lifted their glasses.

"God bless this great nation," Toby toasted.

"God bless America," the others chimed in.

As Toby sat down, Janessa appeared in the doorway. "Alexandra is fine, Dad. You have a new son, and Tim and I have a new brother. He's a few weeks early, of course, but he's perfectly healthy. Everyone can come up to see Alexandra and the baby for a moment."

Toby led the rush from the room, following Janessa up the wide staircase and into a room down the hall. Alexandra was propped up against the pillows, looking weary but more beautiful than ever, with the baby nestled beside her. Toby kissed her tenderly, then carefully gathered up the baby as the others looked at him, commenting in delight.

Someone asked what the baby's name would be. "Michael Bradford Holt," Toby answered, "after my father and Alexandra's mother's family."

Everyone agreed it was a wonderful name and congratulated Toby and Alexandra. The fireworks still exploded outside, punctuating the remark that the baby's birthday would be the Fourth of July—an appropriate date for a Holt. The room a hubbub of conversation, Toby studied the baby's features. Although he was only minutes old, his face was that of a Holt.

Tim took Alexandra's hand and bent over to kiss her. Toby looked at him and then at Janessa, thinking about the maternal origins of his three children. Tim's mother had been a traveler on a wagon train from Missouri to Washington. Janessa, every inch a Holt, had a heritage from the land itself, for her mother had been a Cherokee. The baby he held in his arms had maternal ancestors among the *Mayflower* settlers at Plymouth Colony.

While the mothers of his children were very different, there was a common factor among them. All three had bloodlines closely connected with building the nation from the wilderness. The combination of those backgrounds with his own gave his children a proud lineage.

His children having that heritage, Toby realized he had done something he had not consciously set out to do, but that made his life complete and meaningful in every respect: He had founded an American dynasty.